Praise for Laurie

LOOKING FOR MR. GOODFROG

"Navigating the cyber pond with Karrie Kline while *Looking for Mr. Goodfrog* leaves one laughing on the outside while your heart is breaking on the inside! I found it ribbiting."
—actress Jami Gertz

Praise for Laurie Graff's

YOU HAVE TO KISS A LOT OF FROGS

"A provocative and intelligent look at the ways people search for a meaningful life."
—*Publishers Weekly*

"More than just a catalogue of loser guys and bad relationships, Graff's smart and funny novel shows just how hard finding the right man can be and how easy it is for a relationship to fail."
—*Booklist*

"We're rooting for her to find everything she's been missing—which turns out to be less than she imagines."
—*New York Daily News*

"…a jaunty trek through the dating minefield in search of Mr. Right. Karrie handles the frogs with heart, humor and hubris. Look for the sequel."
—*Family Circle*

"The vivid vignettes that populate this meaty book will have you laughing and crying out loud at the same time."
—*Arabella*

"…this book ventures out of the frog pond in search of a deeper meaning of self worth and completion."
—*Fit*

For my friend Stew Zuckerbrod

Looking for Mr. Goodfrog

Laurie Graff

**RED
DRESS
INK**
™

LOOKING FOR MR. GOODFROG

A Red Dress Ink novel

ISBN 0-373-89573-9

www.RedDressInk.com

Printed in U.S.A.

Acknowledgments

You may write alone but you don't do it alone. Much gratitude to Margaret Marbury, Selina McLemore and *everyone* at Red Dress Ink/ Harlequin for all their work and enthusiasm. Special thanks and appreciation to my editor, Melissa Jeglinski, who dove head-first back into Karrie's dating pond and guided me with a keen eye. I am fortunate for the support of my lawyer, Danielle Forte, my agent Irene Goodman, so many friends, all of my family and, of course, my mother and brother.

For specific ideas, sounding boards, generosity and helping me through, I thank Jamie Callan, Steve Keyes, Marlene Kaplan, Jerry Graff, Tova Ronni Moss, Estare Weiser, Normie Graff, Deborah Schloss, Todd Graff, Donna Rosenstein, Sandy Eisenberg, Dorothy Graff, David Rigano, Ruth Kreitzman, Ellen Byron and Jill Cohen.

And finally, a big thanks to Jeanene Garro for her ingenious gift.

A Fact About Frogging

Frogs are members of a group of vertebrates called amphibia, meaning dual life. The exact number of frog types is unknown as new species are discovered every day.

This makes it hard to find a rule to catch a good frog, except to say that when it comes to frogs there are no rules at all.

One

With such a wide variety of frogs, it's safe to assume that out there, somewhere, is a frog with just about any pattern you could imagine.

June

It's not that I'm a killjoy. I'm really not. Or that I can't be happy for other people. I can. In fact, I am. I'm nice. Warm. And I truly understand that if you're one of the other people, not me, but if you are another person, the one everyone is supposed to be happy for because you're celebrating that *thing;* if you are that person, then you want to make sure that everyone you want to invite to celebrate that *thing* with you knows about it way, way in advance, so everyone is available to come and be happy and help celebrate your *thing.*

I understand this. What's more, if I had a *thing* to celebrate, I would want this, too. But I don't. I don't ever have any of those *things,* so when I open my mail and the faces of a smiling couple slip out of the envelope on the front side of a magnet I'm to stick on my fridge, so every time I reach for the milk I remember to Save The Date for their *thing,* I have to admit that I don't feel happy. I don't feel excited. I don't think, wow, I can't wait to go this *thing.* What a blast it'll be. I'll dance the night away in a brand-new spaghetti-strapped Betsey Johnson. No. I just feel worried. Very, very worried that I have now been given a whole year to Save The Date, and when it finally arrives I don't know if I will even have one to take me to the *thing.*

I wish I could say that did not happen. That last summer when the envelope arrived, and the picture of my friend Brooke and her then fiancé Mitch came tumbling out of the lavender lace-lined envelope, all I felt was sheer joy for their love. Sheer anticipation to celebrate their union. Complete happiness for my friends, without giving a second thought to myself. But I'm not one to lie.

Instead, I ran to the phone and called Brooke, because even though I don't have any*thing* to celebrate with my friends, they are my friends and I can tell them anything.

"It's gorgeous!" I said, fingering the gauzy white lace that outlined the perimeter of the envelope. "This is probably the most beautiful and classiest Save-The-Date card I ever got."

"Thanks," said Brooke. "I think that's what they're showing now." Brooke has really good taste, but she always undercuts it by saying that she's only following a trend. As this is America and when I last looked we still had freedom of choice, at least in stationery, I think she should take more credit for her tasteful selection. Let's face it, a group e-mail might also be a trend but Brooke chose not to go that way.

"So…" I began.

"Of course," she answered, reading my mind.

"And what if I don't?"

"Oh, Karrie. You'll be fine, even if you don't have a date. You know my family, we have people in common. I invited Jane and William. Fred, too, if he can fly in from L.A."

How many more years will I have to go through this?

"Okay. That's good. Hey—are you sure Mitch doesn't have any friends?"

"No," she said apologetically. "I'm sorry. Wait." She paused. "Well, there is one, maybe, but we don't really think he's actually—"

"Thanks, Brooke. Never mind. *I'm* sorry. I don't want to rain on your parade or anything. It's just—"

"Just forget it. It's a gorgeous day. Get outside. The wedding's a year away. An entire year. You can call me the day before and bring someone. But I'm sure you'll be with somebody next year at this time. Someone really great. A prince! God, Kar, you could be engaged by then."

Theoretically, I could have been. Theoretically, some day I still could. Theoretically, anything is possible. It's just that I am out of theories how I have reached this point in my life without it ever happening. People my age are going around for the second time, while I have yet to sign off on the first.

It was all I could think about when I woke up the day of Brooke and Mitch's wedding. The thought pressed up hard against my temples. The invitation had arrived two months ago addressed to Ms. Karrie Kline and Guest. Guest. A nice word. Inviting. It conjured up images of hospitality, good food and good cheer. Karrie Kline and Guest was only meant to be kind. Optimistic and inclusive. It was not meant to throw me into a tailspin where I had to spend the months before the wedding reexamining my already dissected dating life.

But that's what I did while I marked the days off the calendar and it came closer and closer to the wedding, and I still had no date. I still had no Guest. It doesn't matter, said everyone to whom it really *didn't*. Bring anyone. Bring a gay friend. For God's sake, bring a girl! Don't laugh. I once did.

Last spring I was invited to a Bat Mitzvah. In Connecticut. With Guest. Sounds lovely, but that was a particularly tricky situation. For this occasion I didn't just need a Guest. A simple escort would not do. I needed someone who was willing to travel to Connecticut, spend two hours attending the service at the synagogue and an hour eating at the *kiddush* after. Someone who would then travel on to the restaurant and spend four hours at the party seated at a table of strangers with whom they'd be able to socialize, and willing to converse. I needed someone who would make a ten-hour commitment, and someone who had a car.

I wound up taking my friend Anne because a) she wanted to go, and b) she could borrow her sort-of-ex's car. Her sort-of-ex was Jewish and Anne was not, which had never been a problem between them, until one morning Carl woke up and decided to become *religious.* That decision was unlucky for Anne because it created a wedge in their relationship, but lucky for me because as a Sabbath observer, Chaim, as he now preferred to be called, no longer drove on the Sabbath making both Anne, and his car, available to me.

To be quite honest, Anne turned out to be a pretty fun date. Chaim had interested her in the culture and she knew how to dance the *Hora,* and since she is a social worker, Anne knew how to bring out the best in people. After the stilted "How do *you* know the Goldmans?" chat over the French onion soup and the arugula salad, the men cliqued off and talked sports. The four other women, originally suspicious of Anne and me, the un-married, un-mom singles from the city, suddenly found themselves swept up in what turned into a woman's study group at Table Ten. Anne spurred the women into raising their glass and their consciousness. By the end of the day, we were all fast friends, the other women only wishing they could lead cosmopolitan and cultured lives like Anne and me.

Okay. I confess. There *is* something to that. I did not envy their suburban carpools and soccer games. But wait until the first day one of them comes home to a mailbox filled with an invitation to traipse off alone to a Bat Mitzvah in Connecticut via the subway, Metro-North train, and local taxi cabs, knowing the travel time would be spent praying you wouldn't feel awkward standing alone with no one to talk to during all the awkward moments you'd be standing alone with no one to talk to because that's what happened when you went to one of those *things* dateless and alone.

Well, I bet in that moment they'd happily trade their MetroCard for Metro-North knowing all they had to do was look across the dining room table and say, "Honey, we have a *thing* on the twentieth, so don't make any plans." At any rate, despite the success of the Connecticut Bat Mitzvah, Anne was unavailable to come with me to the wedding. Believe me, I asked.

So here it is. Already June. An entire year has passed since the arrival of the Save-The-Date card. Today's the day. Brooke and Mitch's wedding. Sadly, this gray, drizzly Sunday matches my mood. I lay in bed looking out the window and hoped everything would clear up. Soon.

Having locked myself in the bathroom stall just ten minutes into my arrival at the wedding, it became evident that while my location had changed my mood most definitely had not. I peered down the toilet as if I were Alice examining the rabbit hole before taking the plunge. That would not have been so bad, I thought, watching it automatically flush and wishing it could have taken me along.

The ceremony would not begin for at least twenty-five more minutes. Then cocktails, dinner, dancing and dessert. I didn't know a soul. The bride, groom, and their families never socialize when they're the guests of honor; they're too busy running around.

Fred couldn't fly in from L.A., and my cell phone rang on the M23 bus with terrible news from Jane telling me that she and William had to cancel last minute because little Eve had come down with croup. I knew the terrible part of the news was that this sweet little two-year-old girl was coughing her head off, achy and miserable, but I, too, was achy and miserable from my subway ride downtown and my fifteen-minute wait in the drizzly rain for the crosstown bus that would take me to the Lighthouse at Chelsea Piers.

Perhaps as a young girl I was overly influenced by reruns of Doris Day movies, but I could not imagine any circumstance in which Doris would don a strapless dress, dab a drop of perfume at her neck and exit her boudoir to be greeted only by her dog before she dashed out on the town with just the MTA to whisk her away.

I made my way down the steps of the bus, closing my phone, opening my umbrella, and buttoning my pink trench coat as the rain uncooperatively came down harder. It had taken my entire wherewithal not to beg Jane to make William stay home alone with Eve, so she could come in from New Jersey and be for me at this *thing* what Anne had been at that other one.

I did not feel good about me in those moments. I did not feel gracious and kind and caring. But then again, so what. Had I wailed into the phone, "Jane! No! You *have* to come. I don't care if Eve is sick, I don't care about William. Who's going to sit with *me* at the table when everyone else gets up to dance?"

Well, that might have been slightly inappropriate and maybe rendered me slightly insane. But, instead, I showed my concern, which in fact was genuine, and promised to go out to Ridgewood the following day. As an official grown-up I only get to act that stuff out onstage or in my imagi-nation, which thankfully remained highly overactive.

I crossed the parking lot and watched the valets usher couples out of their cars and into the Lighthouse. Mitch was my age, but Brooke was younger. Brooke had felt she was marrying late and Mitch was surprised he was marrying at all. To me, Brooke at thirty-nine, got in just under the wire. She'd turn forty next year and would not have to deal with the syndrome of being Forty and Still Single.

The people emerging from cars ranged in ages, but my eyes gravitated to a handful of couples in their late thirties to midforties that must have been cousins and college friends of both Brooke and Mitch. Well dressed and well-groomed, they stepped out of taxis, SUV's and BMW's. The women tucked their right hands into their men's while their left hands casually swung, showing off diamond rings that spar-kled as they caught the light of the day.

I observed the couples walking and noticed they did not speak, assuming it to be a silent ease between them. I as-sumed they were each privately replaying the happy mem-ories of their happy day. But as my mother Millie always says, "You don't know what goes on behind closed doors." In my all-consuming fear of entering solo, I found myself slightly comforted by the possibility that my happily-ever-after fantasy of them may really be more hoppily-ever-after.

That miniscule moment of comfort was instantly dis-pelled the second the front doors flung open. Before me stood more than a hundred people divided into clusters. Animated clusters. Tanned, well-dressed clusters dotted the entire front hall; laughing and *kibbutzing,* sipping champagne and smiling. The lights shone bright like the mood, violinists fiddled out cheerful, stringy tunes, and every variation on the white flower perched inside tall crystal vases that lined the small tables in and about the clusters.

"Can I take your coat?"

I removed last year's GAP creation of the raincoat, and handed it over with my wet umbrella and my library copy of the *The Between Boyfriends Book* that I read on the way down.

"You look very beautiful," said the young man at the coat check. I smiled back at him while I stuck the coat-check number inside my pink-and-white beaded purse. Knowing that two seats at my table would now be empty I was tempted to ask him to be my date.

The mirror in the coat-check room was angled so that I caught a glimpse of my hair. The newly blond highlights were woven just right into my natural brown head, and the slight humidity of the day had given an interesting little bounce to my shoulder length do. I ran my hands down to smooth out my dress; the pale pink strapless cinched at the waist with a big white faux flower, and puffed out to my knee where two inches of a white, lacey crinoline peeked out.

As I stepped away from the coat check and into the huge hall, I felt the breeze of a waiter rushing past me on my left. I took a champagne flute off his tray, lifted it and sipped a silent "Cheers."

I stood holding the champagne flute while the clusters of people surrounded and encircled me like a Fellini movie. Men in tuxes, women in basic black, they were the black-and-white out-of-focus characters that went 'round and around me. Me. In the center, alone, pretty in pink. I got paler and pinker while they got bright and brighter, happy and happier. The noise level growing loud and louder, as the laughter grew bigger and bigger. Their faces swirled by in a blur, ever so vaguely familiar.

I had seen them before; the shower, the engagement party, the housewarming in Brooklyn Heights. So I stayed in the hall, in the room, in the middle of the room, holding the champagne flute like a prop with a purpose, trying to make some eye contact. Hoping one of the clusters would make a space, open up and invite me in. But no one did.

I didn't know how I would make it through the day. The day stretched out ahead of me. It came up close and spun around me, making me feel dizzy. Off balance. Alone with no one to catch me. So I did what I always do when I'm going to fall. I went into the ladies' room, steadying myself when I saw that it was still my face that stared back in the mirror. Locking myself in the bathroom stall, I sat down atop the toilet seat and contemplated.

"Who's side? The bride or the groom?" I heard the sound of an elderly woman's voice. I didn't know how much time had elapsed when I heard the chatter from the sink outside the bathroom stall. I heard the water turn on and turn off. The delicate noises of lipsticks, combs and compacts clattered against the marble countertop.

"Groom," answered another voice in a flat New York accent. "Me and my husband know him from junior high. We all grew up in Flushing. This is a big day. We all took bets he'd never marry."

I pressed the black button to flush the toilet, again, so no one could hear me gulp. This was exactly what made me crazy! When I met men that no one thought would ever marry, they didn't disappoint. They completely lived up to their expectations. But for *other* people, people like Brooke…

Brooke meets a guy like Mitch Weintraub and… *Boing!* How does that happen? I had to find out. I unlatched the door, somewhat calmer than when I had entered, smiled at the women at the sink and joined in.

"When I first met Mitch, I thought, boy—if this guy were dating me it would be another hit-and-run. Another three-month dating accident," I said, clicking open my purse to gloss my lips with a color called Flirt. "But with Brooke, it was IT from the start. How does that happen?"

The older woman stood back and watched. True, she had initiated the original question, but she was just being friendly. This much information she could live without.

The other one, my peer, looked at me and said, "Easy. Brooke is exotic. That Waspy look. A gorgeous, blond *shiksa*. Mitch never thought he'd get a girl like that growing up. How could he? Look who was in his class…me!" She pointed to herself in the mirror. Dark hair, a bump on her nose, a little plump. But she was attractive, and she looked like she felt that way.

"There's got to be more to it than just looks," I said. "Though I know what you mean. I know the type. I grew up near all of you guys in Queens."

"Yeah, but you…" She surveyed me closely. "Could be weird for you, you know. You're in the middle. For those guys you're not like me, but you're no *shiksa* goddess, either."

My upstairs neighbor, Mr. Schindleheim, a retired gar-mento, had the tendency to sermonize in the lobby, keeping me up-to-date on modern Jewish ways and culture. Most recently Rabbi Schindleheim—a name I believe he's earned—told me that based on current statistics I had a bet-ter chance of getting run over by a truck than finding a nice-looking, successful Jewish guy in my age group who would want to marry me. This breaking news came as he held open the door to the incinerator while I was throwing out my garbage.

"So, what you're actually saying is… What *are* you actually saying? Uh, excuse me, what's your name?"

"Susan."

"Karrie. Hi."

I heard the bathroom door swing open and shut behind us as the other woman escaped back into the safety of her cluster.

"Never mind," said Susan who seemed to be losing points in trying to make hers. "Maybe you'll catch the bouquet."

"She's not throwing one."

Susan swung open the door and left the ladies' room. My perplexed image stared back at me from the gilded mirror. If I could only get out of this bathroom.

The impetus to move finally arrived, but by the time I exited, everyone was being ushered into a huge banquet room for the ceremony. I set my champagne flute down on the nearest table and followed the crowd. Two sides of the room had floor-to-ceiling windows that faced the Hudson River, now sparkling, since the rain had miraculously stopped and the sun was shining. The sunshine elevated everything.

I stopped and looked around. Gosh, it was beautiful. White-and-gold chairs, the long white aisle, white candles, and… Why was I so surprised to see a white *chuppah* up front?

The traditional wedding canopy was beautifully draped in white silk with rose petals strewn over it. The rabbi presiding would stand under it and wed the couple. And there you had it. Exotic, my ass.

Mitch may have originally been blindsided by Brooke's Bostonian beauty, but now that he was getting married he chose to do it in a conventional Jewish way. As for Brooke, she was an Intro to Judaism class graduate from their early courtship days, so from the beginning she had readily agreed.

How exotic was that? I thought, while my eyes searched for a row with an empty seat.

"Karrie Kline, you look great, girlfriend!" The voice made me jump, and I swirled around when I felt a hand tap me on the shoulder. "Hi!"

"Oh my goodness! Diane? What are you doing here?"

"I'm friends with Brooke, from commercial shoots. I know her for years. I did her makeup today."

"That's an amazing coincidence! Hey—what do you think of mine? I ran out and bought all the colors you used on me that day." I fluttered my eyelids for her to see.

"Very good," she said looking at me from a few angles. "See how that yellow shadow makes your blue eyes pop!"

"I thought you did a terrific job, you and Tina. What a great photographer she is."

"Well, I'm very happy for you," said Diane. "We totally loved your show! And the article was awesome."

"It sure helped sell tickets!"

"Have you heard anything new?"

Although there was nothing available, Diane still looked to the right and the left for a seat near to her. I took the opportunity to check out her makeup and her perfect French braid, curious to see how a real makeup artist made up when she was the one going out.

"It's going well," I said. "The *Wow Women* piece made a gigantic difference. We have reservations now!"

I still couldn't believe what was starting to happen. I was afraid if I talked about it I might give it a jinx. I turned to the side so Diane couldn't see, and quickly made a fake spitting sound through my forefinger and middle finger as not to give myself a *kaynahora*. As not to give myself the evil eye.

"Everyone reads *Wow Women,* and with that glamour shot of you on the roof of your theater, I think you're going to get a real run off-Broadway. Hell, I think you're going to get a movie deal, girl."

"Well, making a living might be a good place to start, but Ryan, the head of MTW—My Theater Workshop—decided to keep it going since *Wow Women* came out, and now I'm getting a cut from the door."

Boy, who knew Jay Kohn would turn out to be so helpful? When I saw him on opening night I could never have believed that he would have been able to get a huge magazine like that to do a story on me. He even told me he's trying to get the *New York Times* to come down. Ryan hired him, but he'd been pushing hard for me in exchange for a couple of dating tips. Since he saw the show he thinks I'm a dating how-to. The truth is I'm a dating how-*not*-to. But he and The Girlfriend reconciled, and now my show was getting hot. One girl's frog was another girl's prince…and another girl's publicist.

"It's gonna happen for you," said Diane. "I can feel it. Can't you?"

"I just think it's amazing that I was able to turn all those stories into something besides torture," I said. "I mean it was just a fluke that I even put it together. You know I was supposed to do another one-act, but the director got a gig and the show got canned. Speaking of happy endings, do I get to meet your husband?" I searched the row for the face I thought might be Diane's husband.

"He's working today. On Sunday. Life of a freelancer. Hey, so where are you going to sit? There's no room in this row."

I surveyed the room that had suddenly opened up with possibilities and saw one seat on the other side. "Over there," I pointed, and blew her a kiss. "I'll see you later." Then I slipped into my seat, noticing that the whole view had changed.

★ ★ ★

Craaaaccccckkkk!!!!

Mitch stomped on that glass like a jubilant hunter, before claiming his catch and sealing it with a kiss.

"Mazel tov!"

Cheers.

Applause.

Standing ovation.

The six-piece band burst into "New York, New York" as I made my way to the bar for a glass of Pinot Grigio picking up a crusted crab cake, two goat cheese truffles and a bite-sized cheese-and-pesto pizza along the way. I couldn't imagine what would be served at dinner. There was so much incredible food. Brooke's dad was going to be footing some bill! Unless he'd been saving since she was a kid.

Growing up I didn't have a lot of chores to do at home. It was not out of my mother's utter kindness. More compulsive than kind, Millie always felt if you wanted something done right you should do it yourself. I didn't mind. It took most of my concentration to just get my one chore of setting the table done on a nightly basis. Henry, my stepfather, took out the garbage. Millie would come home from work and cook, either she or Henry would do the dishes, and when there was no way out I would dry.

When I went over to visit my friend Rachel, it was another story entirely. Rachel's mom, Esther, had her hoppin'. Rachel was the only girl in a family of two other boys, and she was the oldest. As an only child I always envied Rachel, except for when I would go over to her apartment to play and find her sorting laundry, or even worse, ironing.

So one day I was over at Rachel's, lying on her bed that was covered with a loose-leaf notebook adorned with flower-power stickers, and Nancy Drew's *The Hidden Staircase* and *Secret of the Old Clock* that I shoved up to the side of the wall so I could sit and watch Rachel separate the whites from the darks, something in life I've still yet to master, let alone do, when Rachel told me about her wedding.

"I want a lot of bridesmaids," she said. "And flower girls. And I want all the girls to wear red velvet dresses. And I want to get married in a church or a *shul,* I don't really care." I will interject that Rachel Smith was a half-Jewish and half-Christian combo through and through.

"And I want it to be really, really romantic and I want to do it when I'm twenty-one," Rachel continued, as she threw her father and brothers' underwear into the white pile, which kind of confused me because there were light-colored stripes in all of the underwear which I thought had qualified them as a color, and that is probably why to this day although my apartment remains clean, my whites tend to be very gray.

"So what about you, Kar? What is your wedding going to be?"

"My wedding? How do I know? I'm twelve."

"But don't you think about it all the time? Don't you have a wedding fund? I'm the only girl in my family and I'm not getting a Bat Mitzvah so my father made me a wedding fund."

"I never think about it and I don't have any wedding fund." Was that because I was going to have a Bat Mitzvah? "I have a Christmas Club," I told her.

Millie had me make weekly deposits at the bank in a Christmas Club fund so I always had my own money at the end of the year to buy presents. But we weren't making weekly deposits to save for any wedding! Never gave the *thing* a second thought. But I certainly thought about boys. I thought about boys all the time. I always thought about boys, but I never thought about the other *thing*.

"You can throw in a few cubes of ice," I told the bartender as he poured my wine and I looked for a place to dispose of my newly acquired toothpick-and-napkin collection.

The couple to my left had just wrapped their arms through each other's and clicked their glasses together. I wondered if, perhaps, you needed a wedding fund to think a wedding was a viable thing that was going to happen. A build-it-and-they-will-come type thing. My Grandma Rose had left me her wedding band to be married in. Millie had it locked in a vault for safe keeping. Was that the same thing?

"There she is," someone called out, snapping me back to the moment. Who was that? A blue-haired, slightly robust woman came barreling towards me accompanied by another woman I didn't know.

"You're her, right? You're the girl in that show? The one about the frogs."

"Uh—yeah," I said. "How do you know that?"

"We saw you!" said the other woman. They looked like each other and they both looked like matinee ladies. "My sister and I went into the city to see a show and we couldn't get anything we liked at TKTS, and someone handed us a flier and we figured, if *Wow Women* went for it how bad could it be? So we walked over. It was great! You were great!"

"I, myself, have had a few dates like that," said the first woman. "My sister's married, but I never did. We're Mitch's side. We live in Rego Park. In Queens! Where you grew up!" They were so pleased to be privy to this information that had been revealed in my show.

They were beaming. At me. This was the first time I had been sought out. In public. For my performance. In my show. My little solo show that just started snowballing.

"Thank you," I said. "I'm so glad you liked it. I really, truly am," I said, amazed these people had come up to me. What a hoot.

"Can you give me your autograph?" asked the second one, taking a cocktail napkin from the bar. She pulled a pen out of her black purse and pointed to a spot under the gold-embossed *Brooke and Mitchell, June 12, 2005* for me to sign. "Write it to me. Rhoda. I can't wait to tell Stanley," said Rhoda, turning into the crowd and pointing to a faraway spot where her husband was apparently waiting.

"Let me ask you something..." The single sister started her question as I signed my name on the napkin for the married one. "How much of that was really true?" she asked. "I may be a little older than you, but *believe* me, I could relate. I went out with plenty nuts, too, in my day."

"Oh, you can't believe some of the frogs Becky went out with," Rhoda chimed in.

"But you didn't have that, right?" I asked Rhoda, pointing to her wedding band. "You got a real prince, right?" I figured Rhoda to be married fifty years if she was married a day.

"I like to think so," Rhoda said, reaching past me to the bar to pick up a few more napkins for me to sign.

"My brother-in-law's a real prince," said Becky. But the moment Rhoda's back was turned she mouthed to me, "Frog!"

Rhoda turned around with the napkins, having just missed the innuendo and said, "Sign one for my sister. Write that it's never too late for her to meet her prince."

I winked at Becky while signing her napkin—*Just one last kiss may be all it takes! Karrie Kline.*

Becky took it from me and smiled. "So what's doing with you, now? You have your show, you look so nice... *Beautyful!* Are you here with someone?"

Ah—life's ironies.

"Me? No. I'm here alone."

"That'll change," said Becky.

"Doesn't my nephew have any friends for you?" asked Rhoda. "You must be a friend of Brooke's because you're an actress like her."

"We met in an acting class like three, four years ago."

With that I spotted Brooke and Mitch for the first time since they had become Mr. and Mrs.

"Brooke!" I called out. "I'm so happy for you!" I ran over and hugged her, feeling the beading of her white dress against the palms of my hand. It was a sensational dress with a princess-style neckline, a bodice of teeny, tiny beads and a bottom that flowed to her ankles in panels of soft white chiffon. "You're stunning!" I told my friend.

"I'm just relieved everything is going well," said Brooke. "Look. There's my husband."

"Wait, is this the first time you said that?" I asked. "The words 'my husband'?"

"Yes! And it was with you!"

We squealed like two cheerleaders in a locker room for a quick second before Brooke and Mitch were surrounded by more and more well-wishers.

I left the bar and went down the stairs to the outdoor terrace. The sun was soothing against my bare skin, a warm contrast from the rainy morning. I walked towards the white railings overlooking the river. One foot in front of the other. Quick steps that changed tempo and became a melody that played as I moved across the promenade and saw him see me.

He was standing there, in the sunlight, near the railing. A drink in his hand, his dark slacks hanging like the bottom half of an updated zoot suit. Talking to another man. He saw me, left the conversation and the man, and walked towards me in slow motion as I stood and waited.

He was coming. Closer. Sauntering. Slim and athletic with short, light brown hair. And when I saw him in full, from his devilish grin down to his black leather Kenneth Cole shoes, I saw he was wearing a chic yellow T-shirt under a stunning sports jacket. He showed up at this black-tie affair in neither a suit nor a tie. Not even a real shirt. But you could see he had taken pains with his clothing. He looked great. Cool and rebellious, making sure he stood out. He commanded attention. And he had just received mine.

Two

Having smelled food, a frog will immediately make mouth-opening movements, despite the fact the object of desire may, indeed, be very far away.

"Hello," he said. "Who are you?"

I followed him over to the railing, ready to be led.

"Are you a relative? Brooke's cousin?" He leaned back against the railing and in with his eyes. They were very green and very bright in the sunlight.

"Not related. Brooke's friend. You?"

"Friend. Mitch's."

We smiled. He had a nice one.

"So. No cousins," I said, indicating both of us.

"Nope."

I took a sip of wine. His glass indicated he was drinking something harder.

"I met two of Mitch's aunts, though. Rhoda and Becky."

"Aunt Rhoda and Aunt Becky! How *are* they?"

As if on cue, I turned to my right and saw that some of the clusters had relocated outside to a spot a few feet away.

"See for yourself. They're right over there." Rhoda, Becky and what was most likely Stanley were across the promenade sitting on dark green deck chairs. Becky waved. We both waved back, but noticed Rhoda give her a quick swat that seemed to say, "Shush! She's talking to someone male!" The gesture did not get past...

"What's your name?"

"Doug."

I liked that name. It was strong, it was simple and it was sexy.

"Karrie," I said. "With a K. Derivative of Karen."

"But better. Karen once removed."

"Just better. I don't do once removed."

Doug laughed. "That sounds very L.A.," he said. "Are you from L.A.? You look like you could be."

So far he thought I could be Brooke's cousin or someone from L.A. I decided not to tip him off. Not too soon.

"Lived there once for a couple of years."

"For what?"

"Work."

He looked at me. Finish the sentence, said his eyes.

"Actress stuff." He didn't pick up on it, didn't ask if I was in anything now, and I was glad to move the conversation along. "Where are you from?"

Doug leaned in seductively. He turned his body as if it were holding on to some great secret it was dying tell. "You have to promise not to hold this against me." Then he bent over and whispered into my ear, "Queens."

"Ohmygod." Here was a boy from my own heart, harboring the same feeling about the illustrious hometown borough. "Where?"

"You know Queens?" he asked.

I nodded. Still not tipping him off. Not completely. Not yet.

"The armpit of the borough," Doug said. "Flushing."

Oh man, I could not contain myself.

"I trump you," I said, pointing a finger at me. "Sunny-side!"

"You think?" said Doug, my personal intrigue coming to an abrupt end. "You think that trumps Flushing?"

"I don't know. Sunnyside Gardens with the wrestling. White Castle hamburgers on Queens Boulevard. Home-town of James Caan. Hmm… Maybe not."

"Well, at best it's a draw."

A draw. I liked that.

"And now?" he asked.

"Upper West Side."

"Uptown girl. Ouch."

I tilted my head towards him.

"Soho," he said, I think with pride.

"Got it," I said, pointing to his outfit.

"Cool." With that he reached into his breast pocket and pulled out a cigarette. He didn't even think to offer one to me. *No one* smoked anymore. Yikes. I hadn't dated a smoker in…ever! I hated cigarettes. I mean, I *hated* them. But I didn't say a word because I already liked Doug.

As he lit up, I turned my head to avoid the smoke and caught the eye of Susan somewhere behind me on the promenade. Standing next to a balding man with an affable face who had to be her husband, she watched Doug and I talk while waving her right hand back and forth, like, like…*forget it?* Doug turned and saw her, and she caught her-self just in time by screaming to him, "Fox! What's up?"

"Later," he called back. He turned to me, murmuring under his breath, "She's been after me since junior high."

"Why did she call you 'fox'?"

"It's my last name," he said.

"Oh. So, it's not like a weird nickname or something?" I asked, hoping I could deal better with a fox than a frog.

"But I didn't go to the same high school as everyone else." He told me his mother sent him to some artsy-fartsy private school to avoid drugs. "We had all of these special programs. Had to build things with clay and create environments with words and blocks," he recollected, inhaling deeply and blowing the smoke out over the Hudson.

"So, now I'm wondering if I can guess how everything you learned in high school impacted what you do for a living today," I said.

I was having fun with this guy. Screw the cigarettes. I slid my feet into the bottom of the railing, grabbed the middle bar of it with my right hand and swung myself backward. I felt happy and free.

"I'm guessing…" The water stretched out for miles in front of me. I had no idea what was I was going to say. "I—bet—that—you—are…" I hung on to the railing, on to each word and on to the miracle of this man standing next to me, loving how the tides had turned.

"I—think—you—became…" I stretched each word out slowly and deliberately. "A residential architect!" I declared, much like Henry Higgins' pronouncement that Eliza Doolittle had successfully passed as having been born Hungarian!

"You got it! How did you do that?" he asked. Stunned.

"You're kidding." I jumped down from the railing. "That's wild."

"I'm impressed," he said, giving me a high five.

Things were going swell.

It had gotten quieter out there on the terrace, on the promenade. We had both noticed but pretended we hadn't.

However, when the announcements of things happening inside were made, I indicated that we probably shouldn't miss it.

"Okay," he said. "But come over to the bar with me before you go to your table. I need to drink a lot when I come to these things."

"Oh! I do know what you mean, but I don't think they're *so* bad," I said, forgetting all about the girl who had locked herself in the bathroom an hour ago. "Hey, did you know, Brooke had her dog, Mason, come earlier to be in the family portraits?"

"I hate dogs," Doug told me, stamping out his cigarette before we went in. "People and their pets. I just don't get. You have to make too many concessions, you know?"

"I, uh, have a dog," I said, stopping Doug in his tracks. "A little guy. Nine pounds. Doesn't take up much room. Maltese. Very animated. More like a cartoon character than an actual animal."

"Oh."

Doug got embarrassed, and I thought I should not have mentioned it. But Charlie was my family. I broke the strange moment of silence with complete candor. "I remember feeling afraid of getting him just in case I met someone who might not like him, but I really wanted him. I, uh…I wanted the love."

"You did the right thing," said Doug. "It's just that I once dated someone who was so tight with her dog, I'd be there feeling like, hey—where do I fit in?"

"You fit in. But someone has to let you know that," I said, remembering to remember that.

We got to the bar just as they asked everyone to put their hands together for the new Mr. and Mrs. Weintraub. Doug asked if I wanted anything to drink and I decided to switch from watered down wine to Perrier. He thought I should load up on alcohol like him, but I said if I drank a lot I wouldn't remember any of this—would he? And he said I was what he wanted to remember.

Happy, I scrunched up against the bar next to Doug when a woman rushed up next to me holding a pen and asking for my autograph. She told me her daughter had tickets for my show and everyone at this *thing* was talking about it. In fact, she had seen it last month when I was only supposed to do it those first few weeks—she actually knew someone at my workshop and had just come—and she was thrilled I had gotten the great article and it continued to run. Her daughter was definitely going to die laughing because she had so many awful dates and had dated so many frogs, just as I had, and it did create a *Frogaphobia,* and was that how I came up with the title?

She opened to a page in her little notebook for me to sign, and I felt Doug's eyes on me the whole time, the whole time she talked, and the bartender shoved a piece of paper in my direction for an autograph thinking I was really somebody. I felt Doug's eyes still on me while I saw his hand return the paper to the bartender, and then the woman left and I met Doug's eyes. He stared at me quizzically until he finally spoke.

"That's you? You're in that?"

"Ummmm… That's me. Yeah."

We walked away from the bar and up a few steps into the ballroom. The band was now into *klezmer* music. Out of the corner of my eye I watched as the Morgans, the Weintraubs and the newlywed Weintraubs all sat on chairs that were lifted into the air, everyone dancing around them being thrown up and down. I looked away, grateful not to hear any alarming screams over the next few minutes.

"I know about that show. I was going to see it. I just read

a piece about dating attitudes and someone quoted that show. Why didn't you tell me?" Doug asked.

Because I didn't want to wind up talking about bad dates? Because I was having so much fun talking with him about nothing? Because I was afraid he would think I was only talking to him for material? And who was it that wrote that piece and quoted my show?

"Well, Doug, you already told me you didn't like dogs, I figured it could only go downhill from there."

He laughed. His laugh was spontaneous and smart.

Good. Let's forget this. I hadn't met anyone I liked in a long time. Today was a complete surprise, and I wanted it to only get better from here.

"Do you feel like Carrie Bradshaw now?" he asked.

"Sort of. Except she's TV fiction, and I'm real!"

"You know," said Doug. "I'd really love to talk to you to about all this. About why men and women can't have relationships."

Nooooooo.

"I've been thinking about this a lot lately and I think you'd be a great person to talk to about why men and women don't connect," he said.

Ohhhhh, noooooo. I didn't want to talk to him about *dis*connections. We had just been talking because we were connecting.

"I already talk about it onstage, and I don't want to talk about it conceptually. I'll be happy to talk about it with you, Doug, but only if it pertains to you and me."

"But you and I seem to be doing fine, so far," he said, taking my arm and leading me towards the edge of the dance floor. "We're connecting just fine."

He ran his hand down my bare back. His fingers were so light it felt electric against my skin. Oh, yes, this certainly was a connection.

Just then Susan danced by, pulling me into the gigantic circle. Doug grabbed the Perrier from my hand, and before I knew it my eyes waved him goodbye while my feet were suddenly jumping and kicking and dancing the *Hora*.

"Listen," Susan shouted over the music, her voice matching the staccato, dissonant, defiant chords that played as she spoke to me with warning. "He's trouble. He's dangerous. He doesn't want a relationship. You better stay away from the Fox!"

Hava Neranena Hava Neranena, the orchestra responded.

"Hey, Susan, that means rejoice and be happy. So, I CAN'T HEAR YOU, OKAY?"

Strappy sandals were not made to dance the *Hora*. Without missing a beat I threw them off and over to Doug, who caught them with the athletic prowess I knew he possessed and always find so appealing, and pulled Brooke into the center of the circle. Our arms entwined, we circled to the right, and right on back to the left. Everyone clapped while Brooke and I did circles upon circles until the music momentarily stopped.

I walked back to Doug, grabbing and gulping the Perrier before putting it down on the floor while he handed me back my shoes.

"How cute you are!" he said looking down. Strappy sandals come with very high heels, and barefoot I was only five foot one.

"Oh, right. I'm not actually that tall," I said, looking up.

"I like it."

"Me, too," I said, deciding to stay that way. Doug touched my hand. Looking down at his hand on top of mine, I noticed that the Perrier glass was perched at the edge of the step next to his left leg.

"Be careful," I said, pointing to the glass.

"How soon it begins," he said.

"What?"

"Here you go," he said, reaching down and picking up the glass and handing it to me. "Anything else you want?"

"Excuse me?"

"You're already asking me to do things for you!"

"I just said to be careful," I said. "I didn't want you to step on the glass."

"Oh," he said, taking it back from me and putting it down on the floor. He looked a drop sheepish. "Ribbit. Ribbit."

"No ribbit. No. A tiny misunderstanding."

Was Susan right? I was tallying a list in my head. But in my list of pros and cons the pro column took the lead because I no longer felt a need to explain or defend chemistry.

Doug walked me over to my table where only one place setting remained. Mine. Sadly, the seats that belonged to Jane and William were not available as I had hoped. He carried my shoes over, and deposited them on the floor while he pulled out my chair and guided me into it with his hand. The touch and tingle of his palm lingered on my back, and would sustain me through the dinner until later. The time we had agreed to meet up again.

I was seated with family. Mainly Mitch's. First, second and third Weintraub cousins completed our table. Everyone was part of a couple, except me and the fellow on my right. He had been quite attentive as he watched Doug seat me, and now that Doug had moved on this guy felt he was able to move in.

"Well, hello, there," he said, breaking his bread and adding a huge slab of butter. "I know who you are!" he said, shoving half of the roll in his mouth and talking to me while he chewed. "I'm Leonard. Call me Leno. Leno Feinstein,

Mitch's mother's first cousin's son. I live in Bayside, Queens. I'm in telemarketing, and I know what you do," he practically sang.

The cachet of this whole *thing* had suddenly diminished. I felt like Cinderella running down the steps from the ball. I was afraid the clock might have just struck midnight and panicked that Doug had not kept one of my shoes.

"Oh, really?" I said, looking down at the soup and the salad that must have been served while Doug and I were still outside. I chose to skip the soup that was now cold, and go straight for the salad. I reached for my napkin. Leno sat and stared.

"So tell me some of your frog stories," he said, watching while I stabbed two teardrop tomatoes with my fork, noticing that little pieces of bread were stuck between two of Leno's teeth.

The Jewish wedding had turned into a Jewish singles event. The tomato felt like a lump in my throat, and I only wished Susan wasn't married so I could cut to the chase and send Leno her way. No one else was talking to me. I got the feeling the table had anxiously been awaiting the arrival of the person who belonged to the vacant chair, and when Cousin Leno's drab eyes lit up, everyone felt it best to let him take the lead.

"Maybe later," I said, pushing the finished salad off to the side, and retrieving the curried corn crab soup that tasted just great cold. I ate. Leno watched. Well, actually, Leno was also waiting. For later.

"So now you can tell me one of your frog stories," he said, after the entrée had been served and he attacked the roast chicken, while I nibbled on the duck, a leg and a breast drenched in sweet, peachy compote.

Leno regaled me with tales of how he didn't take the hang-ups personally in his line of work, it was kind of numbers game, just like dating. I didn't know why anyone ever thought that love was a numbers game. Love caught you off guard, it compelled you, it was emotional. If I were to meet another hundred Lenos, the hundred and first would not inspire anything more than a complete nervous breakdown.

"Just one story, okay?" he practically begged. "Just tell me your worst frog story."

Could I tell him I was devising it as we spoke?

"Ummm…okay," I conceded. "Once there was this guy and he called me to go out on a date and he was very excited about seeing me and he made a big deal about it on the phone, and then he never followed through and he never called."

Leno contemplated. "He just didn't call?"

"Nope. He just didn't call."

"Oh." Leno pondered. "So what do you think? You think something happened to him?"

"I think," I said, turning to Leno for dramatic effect knowing I was going to use my punch line, "*I* think the guy must have burst from anticipation!"

Leno thought this over. "You think? You really think that's what happened to him?"

"Oh, yeah, Len. That's what I think happened. Just like a big balloon."

"Oh." No further reaction. "So tell me another one of your stories. Or do you want to dance?"

Given the choice I chose to be a moving target.

Everyone from our table had vanished, and when we made our way to the dance floor it seemed that practically everyone from the wedding was on it. I located Diane, who was dancing with a few women. Keeping myself a safe distance from Leno while we danced, I made a face to Diane, who had figured out the back story. Leno got creative in his moves, pinching his nose while he wiggled downward like he was trying to keep above water. I smiled a frozen one that alternated with the real ones that emerged every time I caught Diane's eyes.

"You like this dance?" he shouted over the music.

"Yes!" I shouted back. "It's pretty interesting!"

"My sister taught me this dance. You know what it's called?"

"What?" I couldn't wait to hear.

"The Frog." Leno squiggled his body up and down in a dance movement that indicated that he might have drowned, but then like a tadpole swimming upstream, suddenly came back to life. To prove the success of his resuscitation he cried out, "Croak. Croak."

Diane also heard, and we lost it. But Leno thought he had done something really good.

"Croak, croak," he said again, leaping to another part of the dance floor. "Croak, croak," he blurted out when he leaped back.

Croak, croak was right. I couldn't wait for the dance to end. Later, for Doug and me, would be dessert, and I hoped that was just around the corner.

"You're a very fancy dancer, Leno Feinstein! Great moves! Just like a real frog."

Feinstein. The Frogstein.

Out of the corner of my eye I saw my would-be prince having a blast dancing with some pretty girl he had obviously met during the entrée. A frog by any other name can still smell prey! I was getting out of this swamp and leaping back to the other pond. By the time dessert was served I was seated next to Doug, who was perfectly charming and even managed to brush his hand on my knee when he bent down to retrieve a fallen napkin.

The sun had moved on past the Golden Hour as the party moved into its final phases, winding down while people got ready to leave. I wondered what would happen now. My assumption was that Doug would ask if he could call me, take my number and *adios!* I was anxious to wrap it up and get going.

"Looks like it's just about ending," I said, watching Doug polish off the last of the delectable butter-cream cake. Cue. Cue. Doug, pick up your cue!

"It's still early," he said, eating and sipping whatever it was he was sipping now. Doug may not have been into these *things,* but I had discovered he sure was into parties and he wasn't going anywhere.

"Well, I was thinking of heading on home."

"It's still early. You don't want to go yet, do you?"

"Well, I can hang for a while I guess…I mean, if you feel like it," I said, consoling myself that it was okay not to sound like a grown-up in these situations because these situations were not very grown-up.

"Stay," he said.

He talked me into it.

"Okay, but walk me to say goodbye to the aunts."

We made our way over to Rhoda and Becky, who both winked at me and said they had remembered Doug from when he was a little boy, or at least they thought they had. Then out of nowhere, Stanley spoke.

"I'm going to drive this young lady home," he said, pointing to me. "I have my Caddy here. You'll come with us, Karrie."

"Oh, thanks so much, but I'm staying a little longer."

"I'm going to take her home," Doug said, triggering six female eyes to flip over to his.

"Do you have a car?" asked Stanley.

"I'll take her home in a cab. I'll see that she's okay."

I was okay now. I was better than okay.

The catering staff had started stacking chairs. They rolled

the big, round tables to the sides of the huge, now almost empty ballroom. Everyone from the wedding party was outside on the terrace. We joined the open shirts, ties in pockets, sandals in hands, and the lighthearted laughter that indicated a party well partied. Brooke and Mitch looked happy.

"She's shivering," Doug explained, pointing to me. I wore Doug's jacket over my bare shoulders as it had gotten colder. "It's time to get this girl home."

My eyes were shining when I hugged my newly wedded friends. I collected a dozen white tulips as we made our way through the hall and out the front entrance, exiting through the same parking lot I had entered, with great trepidation, hours earlier.

Doug beckoned the last yellow cab at the end of the taxi line, and opened the door so we could climb in. The driver sped up the West Side Highway, while I finally allowed myself to get drunk on this after-party with Doug. We both leaned back against the upholstery, our heads leaning in towards each other's, almost touching, while our legs, looser, fell next to each other's at the knees.

"Some people are meeting up later at the Soho Grand," said Doug. "You want to come?"

"Oh. I would," I said. "But tonight I have a show. Another time?"

"I want to come see your show. I want to talk to you about men and women. I want to understand it."

Now that we were here, in the cab, away from the wedding, it didn't sound as ominous. Maybe the Fox really did want to understand. Maybe he just really wanted to do better. And maybe he wanted to do better with me.

I breathed him in amidst the scent of the flowers that lay across my lap and fell on to the backseat of the cab. He tilted his face towards mine, and kissed me. His lips were warm and the kiss was short and full. We broke, but not away from each other, and smiled.

"I believe in very traditional male/female roles," he said, pulling me back into him by gently and seductively pulling me by my hair.

"I believe in them, too," I said. I did. I do.

"Would you like to have dinner with me?" he asked.

When?

"I'd love it," I said, as the cab headed up Seventy-ninth Street to Broadway.

When??

"I'll call you during the week," he said, releasing me from his touch, but not until the taxi deposited me in front of my building, just off Amsterdam on West Seventy-eighth. The cab stopped but the engine didn't.

"I don't have a card or anything to give you."

"Me, either," I said. "You have a pen?"

Doug pulled one out of his jacket pocket while I got some receipt paper from the driver. He kissed me while I wrote down my name and number. Then I turned and kissed him back. I really kissed him. God, how I had missed romance, and was always surprised and unleashed by its sensations.

"Okay," he said, breaking away. "I'll get embarrassed in front of the driver."

"Oops," I said, flushed, embarrassed myself. I handed him a tulip. "Here."

"Thank you." He grinned. "I'll call you during the week."

"Great," I said, gathering up the tulips, a little too slowly. "Thank *you*."

I got myself out of the cab, though not quite as gracefully as I would have liked. He smiled from the backseat, and I smiled back from the curb. Holding on to the pink raincoat, the unused umbrella, the beaded purse, the tulips and the promise of Doug's call.

Three

If you can't keep your frog, see if you can give it away, as there will most likely be someone, somewhere, who wants your unwanted frog.

The June Before

I removed my slightly sweaty T-shirt in the fitting room and waited a minute to cool down before taking the dress off the hook and trying it on. The pavement outside was hot and sticky, and this first Sunday in June seemed to promise one helluva hot summer. Beads of sweat had collected under my hairline, and the silver bracelets on my right arm jangled as I twisted my hair and raised it up behind my head, as if someone were standing behind me with an electric fan. The fitting room was in the back of the small and elite boutique, with only a purple velvet tasseled curtain shielding it for privacy.

Charlie and I had been taking a walk when he pulled me over to a dress rack in front of the store deciding whether or not he wanted to mark it as his territory. When we got there it was clear we had landed on mine. I'd often drift in and out of Truffles, doing more looking than buying. The clothes were chic, the prices steep.

But the sales rack had beckoned. The shiny metal rack on Columbus Avenue was filled with clothes marked down so low they were practically free. I plucked off four items like I was a contestant in the *Supermarket Sweep* of sportswear. Facing them, now, in the fitting room I felt my competitive shopping gene emerge. I knew I was going to get lucky.

It would be about time, I thought, pulling the first item off the hook and unclasping it from the hanger. Beyond the curtain I heard the French salesgirl cooing.

"Can I give him a biscuit?" she called to me.

"Sure." Charlie had every vendor in the neighborhood wrapped around his four paws. This dog would never starve. In his worst-case scenario he would be at a highway exit wearing a sign that said Will Dance For Food.

I slipped on the dress, my heart beating a bit faster as I reached behind me to zip it up. I took one step back in the tiny room to get a better view, and in that second I knew it was a winner.

Strapless with a velvet ribbon under the bust line, hanging straight down with a ruffle falling over the knee, the thing that made it unique was the fabric. Wool. A sexy, strapless, burgundy and brown winter plaid. It would be perfect for some holiday party. Maybe even for Thanksgiving. With a little cashmere cardigan casually tossed over the shoulders. I could just picture myself going home with him to meet the folks, helping out in the kitchen. She has such style, they'd all say while I graciously scooped the cranberry sauce out of the can and decoratively arranged it on small seasonal plates.

I would buy this dress. Why, this dress in my closet was practically a guarantee that the next six months would be better than the first. This dress encompassed the optimism of last New Year's when I had looked ahead hopefully, feeling the warmth of this season penetrating through me, while tasting the texture of a passion that was waiting. Right! After a washout of a winter and not much of a spring, the only summer warmth was the city sweat, and the only texture was this wool against my skin.

Okay. From now on I wasn't going to just visualize. I would put together every detail, construct the big picture. When I would think ahead I'd be visualizing myself in an incredible designer outfit. Surely a girl in a great outfit had someplace great to go. If you buy it he *will* come. Won't he?

Charlie was chomping on a biscuit when I walked over to the register to pay for the dress, skirt, slacks and sweater that would sit tight all summer and be waiting in my closet come fall.

"I remember you from last week," she said, taking my Visa card before ringing up the stuff. She wrapped each item in lavender tissue paper, and placed them in the Truffles shopping bag with the long purple string handles that made the bag itself a definite keeper.

"I'm addicted to the sales rack," I confessed, thinking that as addictions went this one was inexpensive and even improved my appearance.

Not wanting to go right home, we headed over to the little park outside the dog run by the Museum of Natural History for some quiet time on the park bench. But no sooner were we settled, a big young woman sat down next to us with her big white Bijon who yipped and yapped at Charlie.

"Chaos, stop!" she yelled. "Chaos, quiet!" she hollered, as a yappy Chaos ran over to pounce on my dog. Startled, I dropped the leash allowing Charlie to pull a Houdini by slipping in between the bars of the black iron fence that wrapped around the garden. Charlie, now in his own private park, twirled in the grass taunting Chaos, who had put his face up to the fence to squeeze his way through. Except Chaos couldn't fit.

"Ohhhh…" Chaos's owner emitted a long sad sound as if she were going to cry. "You have to get your dog out of there. Chaos will be so jealous because he can't fit. I can't do that to his self-image." She pointed to herself. "Chaos and I suffer from similar insecurities."

You had to wonder how Chaos got his name.

But I suddenly seemed to have plenty of my own when back in my apartment, sorting through the mail, I opened an envelope with a Save-the-Date card for Brooke and Mitch's wedding that set a panic right through me. It was going to be next June. *Next* June. In a year.

I thought about running back to Truffles and splurging on some magnificent dress in order to create one infallible visualization to absolutely ensure I'd have a great date for the wedding next year. But my pragmatic side took over as I had to convince myself today's purchases would still be in style this fall. Those people who always tell you that things never go out of style are wrong. They do.

I took another hit when I opened a letter from the accounting department at my talent agency expecting a check for the next cycle's holding fee, but instead received a release notice telling me that my Yippee Yi Yogurt commercial had gone kaput. So much for the splurge. So much for anything. Losing the income on a national commercial before its expiration was bad news. So bad that I couldn't even think about it, folding the letter and only hoping the next envelope would be better. It was a card, but my heart dropped when it turned out to be a belated birthday card from my most recent bad and banal blind date.

Written in tiny script after the Hallmark message was, "Is this what you want? Happy Birthday, Stewy."

"It's always the ones you don't want to hear from that remember," they say. I looked around my kitchen to silence this negative chorus, but it was hard to locate as it existed in my head.

My downstairs neighbor had insisted for months that I meet her boss from Yonkers, Stewy Stein.

"He's so polite, he's forty-five, recently divorced. He likes restaurants and movies and sports and ballet," she said, pronouncing the word ballet by putting heavy emphasis on the second syllable making it sound more like a trendy dessert I hadn't yet had the opportunity to try. "And this is the best. He looks *exactly* like Tom Selleck."

"Really?" I found this only slightly incredible. "With or without the moustache?"

"Both. Except better! Better than Tom Selleck! I see you in and out of the building with these guys and, I don't have to tell you Karrie, nothing works out for you. But wait till you meet Stewy. He's super."

"Well, I'm not sure it's such a good idea, Faye. I mean me and your boss? Me and Stewy Stein?"

"You're really being close-minded and I thought you were so open," said Faye, who mainly knew me from our lobby dissertations of our favorite soap opera, *All My Problems.* "I thought you really believed in getting out there," she said in the elevator the fifth time this came up.

What's in a name? Call me shallow, but whatever was in his already told me stay home. Albeit for the stage, I had changed my name from Klein to Kline, and I just didn't think it would ever work out with me and someone named Stewy Stein.

"So Faye says you like restaurants and movies and the ballet," Stewy had said on the phone, also putting heavy emphasis on the second syllable leading me to believe if you spoke to anyone in that office they would all pronounce it the same way. Perhaps they had a group subscription to American BaLay Theater.

Stewy and I had met and gone out. He suggested an Italian place in the village that sounded nice. When I told him it was lovely he asked, "Is this what you want?" He told me about the cardboard box business and when I told him about being an actress he asked, "Is this what you want?" Stewy had been divorced five years and I said I'd never been married, which prompted him to ask, "Is this what you want?" At which point I told him yes, yes it was exactly what I wanted, and then Stewy told me his marriage had ended because whatever he did he could never please his wife.

A week later when Stewy called to ask me out, I politely conveyed the message that I didn't quite think we were a fit.

"So maybe we *are* a fit? Is that what you mean?" he asked.

"Well, Stewy. In truth I would have to say no."

"You women. You don't know what you want," he said, hanging up the phone, his confusion countering my relief.

And now this birthday card. Well, I didn't have to respond, did I? There was no law that said I had to go out with Stewy Stein. With great annoyance I revisited the scenario I had tried to avoid in the first place, thankfully interrupted by the ringing of the phone.

"Hello, Missy," said Fred when I finally picked up on the fourth ring. "Am I interrupting something?"

"Fred…! I need pork chops."

Fred and I had met twenty years ago in acting class. Early on, we were rehearsing a scene for an actor's showcase and we couldn't get it right. We took a break and baked pork chops. When we went back to work we were brilliant. Or so we thought. Now, whenever the going gets tough, the tough get pork chops.

"Eat in or take out?" asked Fred, with a new lilt in his voice. "What are you doing later?"

"Watching the Tony Awards. With you. Hey, you didn't call me back," I said. "You're coming over. Right? I'm having a really shitty day, and—"

"Step on the brakes! We're doing the Tonys. But not on TV. We're going in person. Save all questions for later. I have two tickets and a tux. Do something fabulous and formal with yourself and I'll pick you up at six," he said before abruptly hanging up the phone, this new Tony version of Fred.

I left the mail on the kitchen counter moving directly into my room to rummage through my closet to get ready for the night. The Tonys! Is this what you want? You bet.

Except there was nothing fabulous in my closet to do anything with. I went through it for the third time, examining and reexamining every item of clothing as if I was expecting one piece to step up and take center stage, if for no other reason than to get out of the closet.

It didn't.

At five-thirty I sat in the living room, hair washed and blown, makeup fresh, jewelry adorned, wearing a bra, panties, shoes and no dress. By five-forty-five my Fairy Godmother had not arrived. At five-fifty I went back into my room to see if anything new had entered my closet.

It hadn't.

I tried on the maid-of-honor dress I had worn to Jane's wedding for the third time. It was a long, lacey platinum capped sleeved A-line dress. Sweet, simple and simply out of style. But it looked like the only option. As I pulled the dress over my head, my arms got caught inside both sets of threads that attached the sewn-in slip to both shoulders of the dress. I did not realize this until I looked into the full-length mirror and saw myself wearing only the slip, the lacey rest of the dress hanging over my shoulders, behind me. It was six p.m. And the buzzer rang.

The cab shot down Central Park South, making a right on Seventh Avenue. Knowing that Radio City Music Hall would be mobbed with reporters, cameras and onlookers, Fred asked the driver to stop when we got to Fiftieth Street. I reached into my purse, but Fred pushed my hand out of the way as he reached into his pocket to pay. Then he gallantly glided out the door to hold it open for me while he extended his right hand across to mine and escorted me out.

"What's going on? You turn into Fred Astaire?" I said, really enjoying the attention as I looked down to make sure I didn't get the heel of my shoe caught in a pothole.

"I thought we'd take the bus here, but when I picked you up, Karrie, you looked so beautiful, I couldn't do it. You deserve the star treatment," he said, extending his right arm to be linked inside my left while we headed down the block to Radio City. "I thought you left me a message that you had nothing to wear. Where did this little number drop down from? The sky?"

"Just about," I said, truly elated how it had come together. When the buzzer rang, I whipped around and ran to the door causing the dress to get caught on a hook on the wall behind me. As I opened the door, I discovered I was decked out in a shiny platinum slip dress!

With Fred's hair gelled into hip, his angular features softened into handsome. He sure was looking handsome in his tux, and even more handsome in his assertiveness. It made me wonder, for the first time ever, what Fred might have been like if he were straight.

We made our way into the spectacular Art Deco foyer that never disappointed, and always created the same thrill I felt the first time, thirty-five years ago, with Grandma Rose. My expectations were wildly surpassed when the stage show convinced me my calling was to be none other than a Radio City Rockette. The short and sweet fantasy came to an end, when, among other things, I stopped growing and was just too short.

Fred led me across the red-and-gold carpeted floor and up the winding grand staircase to the next level. "You know I have three brothers, and on Tony night I was the one wearing the boa and acting out all the musical numbers, while everyone else was in the yard playing ball."

Killed by a feather boa, images of a straight Fred quickly died.

We had to arrive early so the audience could be briefed as to what to expect since the show would be televised live.

"I always wanted to work in television," said Fred, when we entered the huge, glitzy theater and took our seats. We were sitting up in heaven, close to the gold-leaf ceiling and closer to the TV monitors that offered the closest view of what would be happening on the stage.

Still, it was a thrill. Once settled into the cushiony red velvet seat, I pulled out a pen and the scrap paper that had both my bets and Fred's on who we thought was going to win. I was most interested in the category of Best Performance by a Featured Actress in a Musical because I had had two callbacks for the role of the fledgling actress who came to Manhattan to take the big city by storm in the height of the Great Depression. I didn't get it, turning it into the stormy story of an actress in Manhattan who just wasn't making it big and fell into a great depression.

"By the way, Fred, whose seat am I in? Or whose seats are we in? How did you get these tickets?"

"You know that show I did in February at the Square Peg Theater Lab? Remember Trey? The designer who did my caveman costume? Well, he and I have been in and out of whatever, and he's been working in Broadway costume shops and got these tickets and asked me. Of course I said yes, but this morning *something* came up. I can just imagine what it was, too! So he just offered me the tickets," he said, leaning back, carefully placing the *Playbill,* tomorrow's newest collector's item, on his lap. "I've had worse that didn't work out *this* good," he said, lightly running his fingertips over the words Tony Awards and the picture of the coveted trophy.

"Did you ever dream of winning a Tony?" I asked him.

"Did I? I still do."

I think that had to be every aspiring actor's dream, and made me think back to the first time I set foot on a real Broadway stage. I had gone to an open call for a national tour of that long-standing hit about a bunch of teenagers doo-wopping their way through high school in the fifties. Unfortunately, the part I was right for was already cast. Then out of the blue, I received a call that the actress who was supposed to play the beauty-school dropout had dropped out. Could I come in and sing?

Two days later, I was backstage waiting to audition. I sat on a small bench with Malcolm, my voice coach, who I paid to play the audition so the accompaniment would be just the way I rehearsed it. We sat among all the girls auditioning who not only looked like my type, but could belt their hearts out. From that bench you could hear the competition sing. I was going crazy waiting.

"Karrie Kline. You're up."

Malcolm squeezed my hand and whispered that the job

was mine. He walked down to the orchestra pit to take his place at the piano, while I followed the stage manager. I stole a peak at the cafeteria trays, cigarettes, and 1950's movie magazines on the prop tables as I was led to my spot on stage. I was on the set on the stage. In front of the cafeteria table, downstage of the gym lockers, gazing out at the elegant Broadway house from the stage. The magical dark stage only lit by the lone work light beside me.

A nod from me, a wave from Malcolm, an arpeggio, and the audition would begin. I jiggled my body singing the "wa-oooh oooh ooooh-oohs" that got me a reading, a call-back and a final dance callback. Three days later I was in the home stretch, but my feet and my mind were at complete odds. I was sure all had been lost, until the dance captain told me to push for the character's personality instead of trying to get the steps right. I did.

"Thank you."

But it was over.

My heart froze as I went back to the small bench, bending down to change out of my character shoes and into the snow boots I had worn for the blizzard. I felt a tap on my back. The stage manager was standing over me, asking myself and another girl to follow him again.

I walked back on stage in one dance shoe and one stocking foot, two sweaty hands tightly gripping one snow boot.

"Are you both available to go out on a national tour in three weeks for a year?" asked the producer. "We rehearse in New York for ten days before opening in Baltimore."

And everything was different. Now I would become a member of Actors' Equity. I got the job. My first union job. How fitting that the offer was made while I was in one stocking foot.

It turned out there'd be a production number where I would sit at the edge of the stage as my feet, unseen by the audience, dangled into the orchestra pit. After the tour had ended, I went on to do the role in the Broadway company, receiving my initiation when, during my first performance, the bass player took off one of my shoes and tickled my stocking foot! I always hoped he wouldn't, but it was a prank he would continue to play every night he played the show.

The lights in Radio City suddenly went dark, bringing me back from that show to this one. The countdown from ten. Action. And the music soared.

"Live from Radio City Music Hall in New York, it's the 58 Annual Tony Awards!"

Fred looked like he had died and gone to heaven, and to be honest we were already pretty close. The opening number began. I turned my head to the monitor to watch.

"I thought you said we weren't going to watch these on TV," I whispered to Fred, who gave me a jab with his elbow as he leaned forward, an invisible feather boa twirling around him.

The host was dazzling. It was exciting seeing the actors and actresses present the awards, and more exciting to watch as each winner accepted. Riding the emotional wave of the moment, trying hard not to ride out too far as the music would suddenly play, cutting them off and ending their speech.

As the Featured Actress in a Musical category approached, I couldn't help but fantasize what might have happened if I had been cast and it was me sitting downstairs now, waiting to see if my career would elevate with the prestige of winning a Tony. Everything about it swung on the side of desire, except having to accept the award and remember everyone with style, grace, and humor in under thirty seconds.

A TV star and movie star who had both gotten their start

on Broadway came out to present the award. I rooted for my actress, deciding that if she won it'd be an omen I would get a great acting job soon. But if she lost...well, she was going to win. I saw the show, she was great and she was going to win.

I nudged Fred to look up at the monitor as they announced each nominee and came in for a close-up on each expectant actress's face. I thought it a good opportunity to practice being a nominee. I was going to sit, fully composed, and practice a generous smile that said I would be happy with any outcome because just to be included in this elite group was an honor in and of itself. There were five women nominated in the category, and as they announced each name I knew they were saving the best for last.

"And the last nominee for the Best Performance by a Featured Actress in a Musical is..." said the female TV star in her canary-yellow halter-cut gown.

The camera zoomed in on the nominee who was beautiful, fully composed and wearing a generous smile that said she would be happy with any outcome because just to be included in this elite group was an honor in and of itself. And why wouldn't it be? Because sitting next to her, leaning into her with love and admiration, not to mention looking totally gorgeous in a trendy tux, was Broadway musician Jeff Broder, who had unceremoniously dumped me in a letter this past New Year's Eve stating he had "unresolved issues" with his "ex-girlfriend," who I knew to be an actress. And clearly this was her!

I dug my elbow into Fred in the split second they were both on the screen, and in a loud stage whisper cried into his ear, "Broder!"

He spun to face me, understanding the full impact of the moment, and when the movie star announced the winner and it wasn't her, I stood up and yelped for joy. Fred grabbed my dress from behind and pulled me back down. No one in heaven had been that responsive to any winner so far.

"You never told me he was that cute," Fred said over the applause that followed the winner up to the stage to make her speech. "I sure wouldn't throw him out of bed."

"Well, he's obviously taken," I said. I had just been hit between the eyes that were already filling up with tears. "Does she have to get everything?" I asked as the winner thanked her co-stars, her crew, her agent, her parents, her teachers, her pets and her mailman. "I mean she got the part, she got the nomination, she got the guy. My guy. My almost."

"Well, she didn't get the Tony," said Fred, pointing out the obvious that did not make me feel any better.

Once it was over and we were out on the street I let it rip. I walked through the crowd over to a side street, Fred trailing behind, leaned up against a gray Volvo with Jersey plates and cried.

"If I had a handkerchief I'd give it you," said Fred.

"Fred Astaire at least would have a hankie," I said, reaching into my purse, pulling out a tissue and blowing my nose. I pulled out my compact to check on my eyes. The eyeliner had smudged, and I had to use another tissue to smooth it out so Fred wouldn't get pulled over for assault and battery on the way home.

"She didn't win," said Fred, for probably the fiftieth time that night. But, in my eyes, he was wrong. She most certainly had. "Kar, I mean, it's not like he was really your boyfriend or anything."

"It's the 'or anything' that really drives me insane. Why does everyone turn out to be either nuts or not anything? When is someone that I like going to turn out to be everything? Or at least something."

"They do turn out to be something. Something to talk about," said Fred, taking my hand and swinging it an attempt to cheer me up while we went on our unmerry way. Fred's damsel in distress.

"What do you mean?" I took back my hand. I wasn't ready to move on but I couldn't cry anymore because I was out of tears. The truth is I was over Jeff Broder. I had been since it happened. But it was the picture I saw that pointed up what I didn't have. My empty frame.

"You have so many funny, interesting stories, Karrie. More interesting than if you were happily married."

"If I was unhappily married I'd probably have interesting stories, too. But then I'd have to suffer in silence and keep them private."

"That's the point, Little Lulu."

"What are you talking about now, Fred?"

"Oops, you missed a spot," he said, pointing to my left cheek where the black eyeliner had dribbled down. Taking out my used tissue I took pleasure in one last giant sniffle, and as I wiped it clean I heard a familiar, famous voice.

"Hey, why are you crying? They kick you out of show business?"

I looked up, in much less than all my glory, to find myself face-to-face with The Famous Television Star. Dressed in a tux, he was walking east down the street with a small entourage. The last time I had seen him was in L.A., at least seven years ago. He was much older than me then, but now he really looked it.

"That's you, right?" he said, walking a few steps over to the car on which I was leaning. I quickly pushed the tissue back into the purse and smoothed out my hair, like it mattered. Even though Fred knew the, *ahem,* funny, interesting stories starring The Famous Television Star, I could see he was slightly star struck. I watched Fred smile, stepping off to the side, smoothing out his hair, too.

"I never forget a face, but I never remember a name," said

The Famous Television Star as he walked closer to me. "Who are you again?"

"Karrie Kline," I said, finding it amazing how quickly things could go from bad to worse. The Famous Television Star was someone I planned on never seeing again. If I had to see him I wanted to be doing a show and doing great. I did not want to be standing in front of a parked car crying because I wasn't.

"Karrie Kline, Karrie Kline. I remember you," he said. "I do remember you."

I wondered what he remembered. Did he remember that he cut my part down to shreds on his TV show because I didn't respond to his confusing pass, when he barked in order to get me to bite? His idea of foreplay was to literally get down on all fours to paw me! Lucky for me I got away without ever giving him a treat.

When I got Charlie I did a lot of research on the bond between man and his dog. It seemed man had established a special relationship with dogs because he desperately needed their help in solving man's sexual problem. After I read that I felt incredibly lucky that The Famous Television Star had not made a traditional pass by kissing me in front of the fire that night. I might have actually responded, only to have found myself in his bed as part of some particularly peculiar pack of two.

"Well, I remember you, too," I said, feeling that perhaps this was good. We both could remember what we chose. Water under the bridge and all that. "This is my friend, Fred Grennon," I said, making a formal introduction to The Famous Television Star as the two men looked at each other and shook hands.

I looked at his entourage for an intro but they had backed off into a small cluster, as if waiting for The Famous Television Star was another of their daily activities.

"You know, I should have been nominated," The Famous Television Star declared, looking at Fred and me with undisputed certainty about this statement. "Did you see my show?"

I wanted to say, "No, I was out of town that week." His show practically closed before it opened, but I simply shook my head.

"Well the critics destroyed us," he said. "We really deserved a good run. I mean that show wins tonight about a cross-dresser during the war, and my show, a contemporary look at pressing political problems closes? The critics ruined us," he said, looking at Fred.

We were all standing on the sidewalk, but I had to look up to see The Famous Television Star because he was now several feet higher, giving this speech from atop his portable soapbox. I knew the only reason he had stopped in the first place was because he had spotted an audience that had not yet seen this show.

"I read interesting reviews," said Fred, shooting a quick look at me while he spoke. "I think you're right," he said. "I think you were robbed," he continued, egging him on.

"Who is this guy?" The Famous Television Star asked without waiting for an answer. "I like this guy," he said. "So we agree. No one knows a good play anymore today on Broadway. I want to know what's going on nowadays. You're either owned by Disney or you have to be Shakespeare to get nominated?"

It's never enough, is it? He had won more than one Tony, in addition to Golden Globes, Emmys, Obies, Clios and Outer Critic Circle Awards. And he had just worked.

"I really wouldn't know what you have to do get nominated," I said, speaking the truth. "I'm just trying to get a job."

"Well, yeah. A job is a good start," he said, perhaps taking a moment to see that he'd been lucky, but more likely just catching his breath. "So, back East for good? Back from L.A.?"

"Back six years," I said.

"What have you been up to these days?"

"Not anything spe—"

"That she wants to talk about just yet," said Fred, jumping in and saving me from my own honesty.

"Yes," I said, quickly recovering. "I'm not ready to talk about it just yet," I said, seeing that maybe honesty wasn't always the best policy. Omission was a pretty good one, too.

"Let's just say," continued Fred, when I thought the subject was wrapped, "that Karrie's in the middle of creating a one-woman show of all her dating stories inspired by Wedekind's *The Lulu Plays.*"

"How impressive," said The Famous Television Star. It was impressive. It was one, big, terrifically impressive lie. "Karrie, I never knew you had it in you," he continued. "I didn't take you for that kind of a girl. You were so demure when I knew you. Lulu was quite the heroine," The Famous Television Star expounded, eager to show off. I certainly didn't mind, because I had no clue about Lulu or her plays. "Yes, Lulu was the original femme fatale." The Famous Television Star got a nostalgic chuckle at this. "Tragic, but with a voracious sexual appetite under her waiflike facade," he said, sounding like a voice in a movie trailer. I turned to look at Fred. What in the world…? But he seemed pleased as punch, as did The Famous Television Star as he went on. "Hmm… I'm seeing you through new eyes, Ms. Kline," he said, smiling for the first time.

"Yes, it's all quite interesting, isn't it?" I said, enunciating each word as I spoke them directly to Fred. "But it's in the very early stages," I told The Famous Television Star. "The early very early, early stages."

The Famous Television Star shook Fred's hand, then leaned over and kissed me gently on the cheek. "Let me know when you do your show. I'll be there," he said, before he blew away like the wind.

Fred and I waited before we moved. The crowd had thinned out a lot by now, and we could see clear to the corner.

"'Splain it to me, Lucy!" I finally said to him. "That was some fancy dancing! What are you talking about, Fred?"

"You should do your own show," he said.

"Of what?"

"Your stories. Tell your dating stories."

"Right, just like that." I acted like I had never heard it before, but people had been telling me that for years. I would tell some dreadful tale from my dating swamp "anxiety and sympathy" making it funny to keep the spirits high, and then everyone thought all I needed was a couple of tweaks and a little scenery and I could take my show on the road.

"Think about it," said Fred. "Promise me you'll at least do that. Everyone's doing their own show these days."

"Okay," I said. "I'll think about it seriously," I said, knowing I wouldn't.

I did not want to do my own show. Who was going to raise the money? Who was going to give me a space? Who was going to direct it? For God's sake, who was going to write it? And who was going to be in it? Me? Just me? All alone up there playing me? Wasn't the joy of acting walking in someone else's shoes? Creating a character and living someone else's life? It was hard enough being me and now I was going to create a show about it? Forget it.

"I'll give it some really serious thought, Fred," I lied. "Okay?"

"Good. So. Where to, Little Lulu?" he asked. "How about

we drop into a bookstore and pick up a copy of *Your Name Here: An Actor and Writer's Guide to Solo Performance.*"

"My name where? What are you talking about now, Fred?"

"It's a great book about how to do your own show. And then I'll tell you all about Wedekind. He was a German expressionist."

Oh boy. Fred was really into this. It would be a while before I could get myself out of that conversation and back into the one about Broder.

"Okay. But how about right now we skip the bookstore and we find a diner where we can get some eggs and then ride the bus home so we have lots of time for you to 'splain."

Little Lulu and Karrie Kline. That would be a lot of 'splaining.

Four

The first two weeks of July are peak frog-calling time in France.

"Art imitates life," Brooke said to me, pointing to the copy written on a cue card inside the little studio where we were auditioning for a wholesale bridal factory commercial. Brooke and I were signed with the same agent, but being completely different types we sometimes wound up reading for different parts at the same audition, like today.

The casting assistant had just taken our pictures. We stood against a blank wall while she snapped a Polaroid of each of us to be stapled to a size card we had filled out listing all of our measurements. Decades of commercial auditions and thousands of size cards later, I still didn't understand why it was necessary to go through all that paperwork. Save the paperwork for the callback, I say.

"Hey—you know how sometimes they sell you the

clothes you wear on a shoot for half price?" I said to Brooke while we waited for the casting director, who was in the lobby yakking with some actors. "Well, if you book this, maybe they'll sell you the gown for your wedding. Wouldn't that be a hoot?"

"It would be more like a hootenanny. I actually checked the place out."

"Brooke, honey, let me see that ring!" Carol James, the casting director burst through the door, making a beeline to the glitter that had caught her eye. "When did it happen?" she asked, turning Brooke's left hand over and inspecting the perfect emerald-cut diamond.

"Last summer," said Brooke.

"I wanted the princess cut when I got engaged," said Carol, raising her left hand and showing off hers. "But if I had to do it all over again I'd go with the emerald. Your fiancé has great taste."

"I'm lucky," said Brooke. "I have ma*zel.*"

Brooke said the new Yiddish word slowly. It sounded like she was using the word in a sentence for the first time, because she put the accent on the wrong syllable instead of saying *ma*zel. Carol caught this quickly.

"A *shiksa* marrying a Jewish man," she exclaimed. "Just like me!"

Brooke shot me a quick look of apology.

"Now," said Carol, getting back to business. "In this vignette everyone has been fighting over this one gown, but only one girl gets it. Brooke is the bride who gets the dress. Karrie is the salesperson. Brooke, you have only one word—fabulous. It's written in red," Carol said, pointing to the cue card that was sitting on a tripod positioned just to the right of the camera. "It's up and happy. Karrie, your line is, 'You can never be early enough to be the bride of your dreams.' It's the line written in green, and you're envious. Got it?"

The audition had now accomplished the double duty of pushing two of my buttons.

"Let's try one," said Carol as she went behind the camera to shoot the first take. "And remember, Brooke, you're a bride-to-be and you're happy, and Karrie's character is a little bitter. Okay, get ready to slate your names and your characters. Brooke, first, and…action!"

I waited for Brooke to finish and for the camera to point to me. I wondered if I should present me, Karrie Kline, as a nice, happy actress who would be easy to work with if hired to do this job by giving an upbeat slate with great big smile, when I said, "Hi, I'm Karrie Kline." Perhaps it would be better to slate in character as the bitter sales clerk, which at the moment would not be much of a stretch. But if I did that, would the client think I'd be a pill to work with?

Every moment counted.

There were so many, many less auditions for women in their forties. Jane and I had recently gotten together for a mutual coaching session to figure out if there was something—anything—we could do to give ourselves an edge.

"They're looking at hundreds of women on tape and let's face it, everyone can do the job, right?" said Jane, while we were sitting in her den in New Jersey at our recent get-together, using the camcorder she and William had bought to record little Eve, hoping that seeing ourselves on tape would help us figure out how we fit into the cool I-could-care-less new trend in commercials.

"It's a type—that's one thing—but the slate is how you introduce yourself, right?" said Jane, analyzing this in the hope it was something that even deserved analysis and would therefore be worthy of a conclusion. "So that perky slate we used to do that got us all that work twenty years ago really has to go. That's definitely out."

Jane had just booked a big national commercial promoting the wonders of a depression drug and swore she got it from her warm but bland how-do-you-do new slate.

"I used my authority but also acted as if I had a million other things more important to do that day than be at that audition," she said, making direct eye contact with the camera, smiling an ambivalently superior smile when she said Jane Murphy. "Now you try."

Jane operated the camera. On action I looked directly into it, smiled and said, "Hi! I'm Karrie Kline!"

"No," said Jane, turning it off. "That slate says my agent never sends me out and I'm thrilled to be here at this stupid audition because I really need a job. Let's see some edge. You know what, Kar, next time you have an audition, don't even wash your hair. Be casual. Don't be so perfect. Try again. Action."

The whole show of the whole business was starting to annoy me, I thought, looking at the camera like an acquaintance I'd just met on my way to some better place I had to go. Identifying myself with a self-effacing grimace I stated, "Karrie Kline."

"Wow! That was great, Kar!" said Jane when we watched the tape and played it back. "That's a much more interesting person than that outdated perky girl."

"I see what you mean" I said, and this time when I watched the playback I did. "Ambivalent. Cryptic. Kind of off. But cute," I said, hoping to open a new slot I'd fit into.

In the world of advertising, Jane, at five foot five with a voice that was sultry cosmetic, had always been able to play women you would trust. My agent insisted I would never be taken seriously at five foot one with an offbeat voice. No one with severe headache pain would ever buy an aspirin from me. If you want to know what acting had to do with it, I'll tell you. Not much. Acting was in the theater. But the money wasn't, unless it was Broadway. My stakes for book-ing a commercial grew, while the volume of good auditions shrunk. Much like dating.

"Okay. Now, Karrie," said Carol, aiming the camera at me. "Slate your name."

I looked ambivalent, cryptic, kind of off. And right on cue, "Hi! I'm Karrie Kline!" popped out of my mouth! Perkier than ever, perhaps even the perkiest, my same old slate just popped out causing me to feel distracted and upset throughout the entire audition.

We did two takes. Carol announced it was fine. Worse than when they just say thank you, was when they tell you it was fine.

"When's the wedding?" Carol asked Brooke as she walked us to the door.

"Not till next year."

"Mine's next week! Then a two-week honeymoon in Paris," Carol chatted to Brooke as we left. "I bet next time I see you we'll be barefoot and pregnant."

"If she waits as long as she did this time to bring me in for an audition we will be," said Brooke as we waited for the elevator that always took forever. After a small eternity, we stepped in, but as the doors were about to close, an actress wheeling a baby stroller came running towards us yelling, "Hold it!"

"Old home week!" I said when the woman with the stroller turned out to be Jane. Little Eve looked up at us with the casual hipness of a one-year-old, wearing pink-and-green capris with a matching tank so cute I hoped it came in my size.

"Hi, honey," I said to Eve, kneeling over and giving her a kiss. "What were you here for?" I asked Jane.

"A credit card company," she said, slim in a light gray business suit and made up in what she would call her audition face. "I was supposed to have a sitter but she canceled last minute. William almost stayed home from work, but I just drove in from Jersey and brought Eve with me. Her first audition. A quick coffee?" Eve let out a sound saying that she readily agreed.

One Chai Latte, one iced Caffè Americano, and one Mocha Frappuccino later—ranging from small to tall to gigundo—we scrambled for tables, chairs, spoons and straws to sip java beans that were overpriced and overblown. But we finally settled down with a little time left to dish.

"Did you do the slate the way we tried?" asked Jane, rocking the stroller with one hand while sipping the medium iced coffee (yes, let's face it, that's all it was and all it would ever be) she held in the other.

"No, I did it the same old stupid way," I said, annoyed with me but loving the Mocha Frappuccino that I treated myself to on special occasions. Today I was celebrating my complete inability to try out a new slate.

"Don't be so hard on yourself," said Brooke. "I was with you. You were fine."

Even Brooke thought I was fine.

"We're all on automatic pilot having done the same thing for decades," said Jane. "It's not easy to change," she said, making me wonder what I should change first. My slate, my hair, my attitude, or my career.

"I want to feel the way I felt when we met on the road," I said to Jane, fondly remembering the fun we had on that first national tour.

"We were so young. It was the beginning. It can't stay that way forever," she said, looking at Eve. "Are you going to grow up to be an actress?" she asked her little girl.

"Oh, boy," said Brooke. "I love it, but I don't think I'd want it for my kid." I saw that Brooke actually could not wait to be barefoot and pregnant.

"You miss theater, Karrie," said Jane, hitting the nail on

the head. "Maybe you have to be more open about working out of town."

I sighed. You practically lost money when you worked in regional theater, not to mention how you had to uproot yourself for months at a time. On some level I even blamed working out of town on my lack of a relationship. It seemed that every time I met someone I liked the lift improved my life as well as my auditions, so shortly after I got into the relationship I got cast in a job out of town.

"Well, it would be different if it was a role that I was dying to do," I said. "I don't know. Fred says I should do my own show. Perform my dating stories like a solo show. How's that for a laugh. Urban femme fatale goes loco!"

"That's a fantastic idea!" said Jane, jumping on this track and steering the train. "What a great idea. Take it into your own hands!"

"I'd love to do something like that," said Brooke, "but I'd be scared to death."

"Excuse me," I said, using my two hands to point to myself. "And you think I wouldn't?"

"So do it *and* be scared. So what?" said Jane, someone good at following her heart.

I'd have to give it some more thought. Not the scared part. That had already been well thought out. The "so what" part. I'd have to think about that.

"Hey. What's everybody doing for the Fourth?" asked Jane.

I was brightened she asked because the holiday weekend was coming up, and I didn't have a thing to do. Anne was going home to Philly for the weekend and Fred had finagled a way to thank Trey for the Tonys.

"Anyone up for the beach? Want to watch the fireworks from my roof?" I asked.

"Well, I'm stopping in Boston on my way to the Cape to

do a shopping trip for wedding dresses for me, my sister and her girls," explained Brooke. "Then we're all going to my folks in Hyannis Port."

"We're going to my parents' for a barbeque and the rest of the time will be spent doing home improvements," said Jane, wiping a little dribble off of Eve's little face. "What are you up to, Kar?"

When Henry was still alive he and my mom had a summer place in the Catskills. I always had a place to go. Sometimes, then, I looked at it as a consolation prize. But now with just my mom in Florida I see it was the prize.

"Nothing."

All eyes were upon me.

"Well, MTW's having a party and some people talked about getting together," I said, thinking if I checked it out it might actually be true. "I'll be fine." That word again. Well, I would be. I might be a little lonely, but I would be fine. "So are all the bridesmaids' dresses going to match?" I asked Brooke, eager to change the topic.

"It's up to my sister. Kristen is matron of honor and we're taking the lead from her."

"Kar, you still have that maid-of-honor dress from my wedding?" asked Jane.

"Sort of." I smiled. Saved by the bell. Someone's phone was ringing.

"I never was a maid of honor," said Jane.

"Me neither," said Brooke.

Always the bridesmaid. Never the bride.

"Whose phone is that?" we all seemed to ask out loud at the same time. Everyone bent down to check their bags and it seemed the winner was me.

"Jerry!" I suddenly grew very animated, pointing my finger at my phone and nodding my head up and down so everyone knew my agent was calling me on my cell. "Wait a sec—let me get out my book. Anyone have a pen?" I asked, as I grabbed my date book with my right hand and a pencil from Jane with my left.

"Okay, I'll wear my hair clipped up for the callback, baggy shirt… They're making the character more frumpy for the callback," I cheerfully whispered as an aside to the table. So thrilled was I to find out I had a callback for a big spot and was *finally* considered to be cast as one of those funny, frumpy, forties housewives Jerry kept telling me it was so hard to get me seen for. "And I'm on first refusal for the third week of July. Got it. Great… Oh, today? The bridal thingy? Oh… Yeah, I read with Brooke… *Fabulous!*" I said, giggling with the gals as I hung up hopeful and happy.

Five

Frogs do not conform to one uniform means of mating, making this aspect of the frog fascinating.

I was on a commercial shoot for a major home appliance company at Silvercup Studios in Long Island City, Queens. It was just over the Fifty-Ninth Street Bridge, a stone's throw away from my old high school. We were on an extended break while the crew rebuilt the door to the laundry room on the set. In the spot my character, Wife, not only washed the pants in the family but also wore them, as her husband deferred to her about which washer and dryer would be best. In our last take when Husband flew through the door announcing to his honey he was home, the door flew off its hinge.

The women on the set could not ignore the irony that we had been employed to create this scene of domestic bliss. All of us were living single in Manhattan without husbands or boyfriends or, in some cases, a washer and dryer in one's apartment building, let alone one's abode.

"Well, it's not over yet," said Jenna, the copywriter on the commercial who was dating a man she had met buying the paper at a newsstand near her subway stop. She accredited this meet to resituating a plant in her apartment and throwing out a photograph of her most recent ex, thus creating better feng shui.

Jenna called all the single women on the set together for a crash course on how to feng shui your apartment. Gathering the wardrobe girl, her assistant, the makeup woman and me, Jenna had us draw the layouts of our apartments on the back of the day's shooting schedule so she could advise how throwing things out would bring romance in.

"You want to make sure that between your floor plan and where you have your stuff the energy is flowing and creating good chi," said Jenna, as she looked over each shoulder, supervising our drawings like a foreman in an architect firm. "If the energy in the relationship/marriage corner in your apartment is blocked, it's not going to work for you in love."

She stood at the head of the table showing a chart of the feng shui bagua, illustrating how an apartment could be sectioned off into nine areas. Each area was responsible for another part of your life.

Health was located in the middle of one's apartment, putting the state of mine inside a wall. The wealth spot was in the upper left area of the apartment. Lush green and red plants would help bring in money. I would have to start a greenhouse in my shower, in order to get rich quick. Jenna went on to tell us that the bathroom door should always remain closed and with the toilet seat down, as not to flush your money away. Known to kill off every plant I ever had and having enough privacy to leave every door ajar, I made a mental note to pick up a plant and lock the loo.

"Everyone show me the relationship/marriage corner of your apartment and tell me what you have there," said Jenna, holding up the feng shui bagua and pointing a finger to the upper right hand side.

Okay, think…the relationship/marriage corner of my apartment.

I mentally walked into my apartment through the front door realizing I had yet to decipher if it was facing north or south, already forgetting which side was good and how it affected the yin and the yang. Jenna had talked about the specifics, but I hadn't listened. So what if I faced the wrong direction, or if Gomez, the super, had messed up the chi in the lobby when he cracked the mirror with his mop. What was I going to do? Move? Let's face it, there was feng shui for apartments, and then there was feng shui for New York apartments. And if you lived in New York and were lucky enough to even have an apartment, let alone one that was rent stabilized, you already had some pretty cool chi.

I waved Jenna over to show her my drawing, pointing to an asterisk that located the relationship/marriage area of my apartment which turned out to be the corner of my kitchen that housed the stove.

"An appliance!" I said, thinking it serendipitous that I had booked this spot. I counted my blessings as to just how fortunate it was going to be. Although the commercial would not be running national, it was a buy with two of the three major markets, New York and Los Angeles. And it would earn enough money for me to qualify for health insurance. Between that and my unemployment I would be fine for a while, not to mention the added benefit of my friends on both coasts getting to see me on TV.

"Oh," Jenna said, gazing down. "You have a very nice apartment," she said, looking over my shoulder at my blueprint.

"Wait till you see it by someone who can draw."

"So, what's around the stove?" she asked. "Any pictures, plants, colored potholders...what?"

"Nothing," I said, picturing my window and next to it the stove. "Oh wait, I do have a picture hanging on the wall over the stove."

"Great! Of what?"

"Clinton. Bill Clinton's up there."

"Still?" asked the wardrobe assistant, pleased that her bed was in her relationship/marriage corner even though it was pushed up against a wall allowing for only one night-table, a no-no for anyone lobbying to be a twosome. "We're coming up on the second election without him. Let go, Karrie. It's time to let him go."

I had not been able to let go of Bill so easily. And I loved the autographed color photo the White House had sent to me because of a letter I wrote when I worked on his campaign. I'd kept it up all these years as more than a memory, but as a reminder of better political times to come. To this day, whenever I heard him speak I was overcome with a sense of pride and well-being I'd lost. I missed the Clinton years profoundly, and his picture created a yearning as if Bill were the one that got away.

"I can't do it, Jenna. I'm too attached."

Jenna did not move. Jenna's face froze. After she composed herself she pulled up the chair next to me, taking my hand and talking as if I were in counseling.

"You have to get Clinton out of that corner," she said in a low steady voice one might use on a mental patient. "Tonight. As soon as you go home. Bill Clinton's photo cannot hang in your relationship/marriage bagua."

"But why?"

Aside from everything else, I thought the picture suited my old-fashioned kitchen adding just the right touch of

Americana; the flag waving in the background behind, and Bill, in a navy suit, adding an extra splash of blue to the already blue-and-white decor.

"Do you want to attract a man like Clinton?" asked Jenna, illustrating the severity of my feng shui faux pas.

"Gee, let me think about that. Handsome, sexy, brilliant, accomplished, funny, family-minded, compassionate, rich... Nah. Why would I want to attract a guy like that?"

"You left out an intern," she said. "*And* a wife."

"Oh, please."

"Karrie, I do understand," she said, and I believed that she did. Living in New York City was thankfully to be living among like-minded souls. "I'd vote for him again in a heartbeat, but we're not talking politics. Tonight, when you go home, get Clinton out of the kitchen."

I didn't answer.

"Karrie. You want to meet someone *available*. Change your karma and change your chi and get Clinton out of that corner."

"But he's so cute, and I like looking at him when I cook."

"What's going on?" The actor who played Husband swaggered up behind us, putting a hand on my shoulder as he leaned over it to look at the drawing.

I had been surprised when I arrived at work that morning and saw Dirk Benson sitting in the makeup chair next to mine. Dirk mainly lived in Los Angeles, but considered himself bi-coastal. While we'd run into each other at an audition now and again, I'd mainly hear from him a few times a year, early in the morning, when he'd phone with a flirtatious wake-up call. I hadn't actually seen him for a while, and suddenly there he was.

"Karrie!" he had said, throwing down the *Daily News*, leaping up to give me a big hug. His dark blond hair was still tousled from sleep. He wore an oversized sweatshirt with "Montauk" written across the front that hung with the perfection of a model in an ad. "Wow. Today's going to be cool."

We had not seen each other at the callback, and I was surprised and excited to spend the day playing Dirk's wife. With a casually honed charm, Dirk looked like a TV star you might see hanging out in the Hamptons. Someone who claimed his fame playing a good boy gone bad. I could picture him on *The View*, captivating the ladies while plugging a new one-hour drama. But today he was here, plugging washers and dryers, and captivating me.

"Hey—it's you!"

"Sure is," said Dirk, not letting go of the hug right away, holding on to me in that touchy-feely way that is often the tendency among actors. "So you're the one who got booked to be my wife. How about that?"

"They say it's better the second time around," I told him, both of us grinning, clearly remembering when we had first met.

We shot a commercial together almost twenty years ago for an insurance company. Dirk and I played a young couple planning a family and buying their first house. That morning, the van picked us up and drove us to a bowling alley on Long Island where we shot. We spent the day giggling, bowling, working and flirting. For every gutter ball thrown by Wife, Husband scored a strike. We knew he would strike right when choosing insurance, and score as a big provider.

On the return trip home, the production assistant made the first drop-off on the East Side, to deposit Dirk. He and the P.A. had gotten stoned in the van on the way home. About the time we exited the Queensboro Bridge, Dirk had passed the joint to me, and to be polite I took a toke. A few minutes later he asked if I wanted to jump out with him

and grab a bite. After the toke he didn't have to ask twice.
I jumped. I grabbed. I was a goner.

"So, we made it. We're still married."

"Yes, we are, Dirk. And we finally saved up for a new
washer/dryer."

The morning shots had been going well, the door thing
aside. Dirk was a goofball and fun to work with. We chatted between takes. He'd come back East for the summer. He
wasn't married. And he wasn't dating. Anyone.

"Want to join us?" asked Jenna, who gave Dirk a brief
rundown of what we were doing.

"You have feng shui for couches?" asked Dirk, who told
us he was spending the summer sleeping on his brother's.
"You think if I rearrange the throw pillows I'll attract some
big movie role?" Dirk asked the women before shifting his
attention back to me. "So, Karrie, you really think you have
to move all your stuff around to get a little action? Come
on."

He flashed that sideways grin that got me going. Almost.
While Dirk as pretend husband wasn't such a hardship, it was
definitely pretend. Over lunch I got the real scoop about
who got him away from L.A.

"I went out with this woman who owns her own Internet business and she makes a lot of money, and I haven't
been working as much, so she had the money. And because
she had the money she was very controlling," said Dirk as
we finished the cold poached salmon and endive and goat
cheese salad, saving room for a taste of the pesto ravioli before diving into the peach cobbler for dessert.

Note—the importance of major markets extends beyond making major money; the better the buy on your
commercial, the better the catering will be on your shoot.

"So every time I didn't do something the way she wanted,
she withheld sex. But the sex was the best thing we had. So

why'd she do that? She wanted it, too. Why couldn't we have enjoyed the good things, instead of posturing and pretending? We weren't ever going to get married. I didn't want her. She didn't want me. But we had a good time. I wasn't committed to her, but I wasn't running away, either. And believe me, if she would have dropped the control and allowed herself to get what she needed, we both would have been happier and maybe...who knows."

On the one hand, Dirk usurped this woman's power by telling her they would never marry. On the other hand, her money had bought her a certain power with Dirk, and their sexual rapport had brought her another. So all she had to do was continue, and it *might* have turned into something more. But she couldn't because Dirk said they would never marry, which made her resent him. And withholding sex made Dirk resent her, which happened because of his withholding words about commitment. They canceled each other out, and nobody won.

"And so you came East, young man," I said. "Is that it?"

"That's it," he said. "And that's over." He paused. "And you? Who's got you?"

"Ah. Sadly, no one. Most boring year of my life," I said, feeling this scenario to be only slightly dramatic. But I told it to Dirk who loved to act.

"A girl like you not seeing *any*one?" he asked after lunch when we got back into wardrobe. "My little Karrie, all alone," he taunted as hair and makeup reclipped my hair and unglossed my lips. "You've got to be kidding!" I heard between takes. "A sexy girl like you not seeing *anyone?*" he whispered, while I stayed on my mark, surrounded by laundry.

Dirk continued to ask, continued to taunt, and continued to whisper. Sure. It was easy for him to say! Easy for Dirk to flirt since all he had to do was bustle through the door. Home from work in a Brooks Brothers suit, I was the one with the disheveled hair and the baggy shirt who spent all day doing housework. I was the one surrounded by laundry. Dirty laundry. So overwhelmed by our loads of dirty laundry, that if hubby didn't break down and buy me a new washer and dryer soon I was just going to pull every disheveled hair out of my head and, believe me, it felt anything but sexy.

"Come on," said Dirk in the charming voice when I told him I simply hadn't met anyone I liked. "I know you've met men," he said, somewhat missing the point. "You always attract men," he said, when the director called it a wrap. "A woman like you can get plenty of male attention. But you already know this," said Dirk. I think as a compliment.

Have you ever noticed when men give a compliment they often package it with the assumption that it's something you already know? Sometimes I think my compliment has made its rounds to other women in the city. But it goes to waste as no one ever takes it, because they don't think it was ever meant for them to begin with.

"It's not about male attention, Dirk," I said, an hour later when, taken in by Dirk's good looks, attention and compliments, I agreed we share a cab back to the city, where we wound up in my apartment, allegedly, to take Charlie for a walk before heading out to eat. Finding myself in this position, I headed straight into the kitchen to remove Clinton from that corner. I found Dirk blocking my exit when I turned around.

Gazing down through his huge hazel eyes he pulled me into him. I could smell the fabric softener on his sweatshirt. He was tall, his arms were strong. He nuzzled his mouth against my ear and whispered, "So…you been auditioning a lot lately?"

Huh?

"It's kind of sucked here since I'm back from L.A.," said Dirk, slowly, seductively.

He turned me so my back rested against his chest. The top of my head almost reached his shoulders, and he reached down so he could rub mine.

"I told my agent I don't want to waste my time going for these print gigs that pay a day rate of five hundred bucks." Dirk circled his lean fingers into the top of my neck, as they slowly worked their way down. "And I read for a line on *Law and Order,*" Dirk cooed while he complained. "A line. Two years ago I was guest star. I played an executive who murdered his wife. Now I'm supposed to run down there for a line. What kind of bullshit is that?"

He had touched a sensitive spot. I wasn't much in the mood to talk about Dirk's career, and I certainly didn't feel like talking about mine. Dirk went on to touch another, but this one sent a chill down my spine.

"That felt good," I said, rolling my head around in a circle, letting go of the kinks in my neck, in my career.

Dirk picked me up and brought me over to the couch, laying me down on my stomach and straddling me so he could continue to work on my back.

"Show hubby where it hurts," he said, lifting my T-shirt so I could feel his warm hands climbing up. "You worked hard today, honey!" said Dirk, in a 1950s sitcom voice while his fingers massaged away.

"I did," I said, letting the relaxation take over. Letting Dirk.

He stopped talking while he pressed his fingers into me, each touch breaking up more tension. His touch reminded me how good it was to be touched, and also saddened because I hadn't been but for a few weeks at the beginning of the year. Sex is a lot like money. It's only a problem if it isn't there.

I must have dozed off under the spell of Dirk's magic fingers, because I awoke to find Charlie's white tail covering my eyes. The dog was perched on the arm of the couch and had fallen asleep by osmosis.

"Awake?" asked Dirk, talking when I finally stirred. "Relaxed now?"

"Yes," I said, in a mixture of sleep and seduction. "Better."

As I turned my head Dirk pulled me up by my hair, turning me on my back to face him before he leaned in for a kiss. The kiss was nice, it created stirrings and that was nice, too. I smiled. The less I said the better. I wanted to hear from Dirk. I wondered what was going on.

"Feel good?" he asked.

I nodded. Still relaxed. Still good. Still unclear.

"Hungry?" I asked, wondering. Were we going to lie down, get up, go out, *or what!*

"For…?"

Dirk moved in a little closer. The dance had really begun.

"Thai?" I asked, purposely making the misstep. "Unless you're up for Chinese."

"I'm up for… " Dirk kissed me again. "Karrie," he whispered in my ear. "I'm very turned to you right now."

He tucked me into his tall, toned frame. I suddenly felt safe. Cared for. Attracted. And it became important to know if all this was a beginning, or just a means to an end.

"You're very turned on to me right now," I repeated. "*Now* being the operative word in that sentence?" I asked, leaning in and kissing Dirk before he could even answer me. Total mixed message, very coy, shouldn't have done it, great kiss, who cared, so what?

"Now being the moment," Dirk mused. "Now just being now," he said, still kissing my lips while massaging my neck.

Not fair, I thought, liking Dirk, liking his touch. Not fair at all, I thought, lunging into him and making the most of the moment, the most of the now. Enjoying the neck rub, enjoying the kisses that were very okay for now, but would have to be closely monitored as not to turn into later.

"I can talk to you like this, Karrie, because we're friends," said Dirk, knowing me and reading my mind. "And we just spent a nice day and… Hell, this feels good and… Man, I haven't had sex in a really, really long time," he told me, "and I just like being here with you. I'm lonely."

"Me, too," I said. Okay, if nothing else, the lonely part made it all make sense. My head, my heart and my body were in conflict, but Dirk and I now had something in common. We'd been lonely. "How long for you?"

"Oh," said Dirk. "Let me see, a long time. Like…" He paused to give it some serious thought. "Two weeks."

"Two weeks? Are you kidding me?" I sat up, quickly moving away. "Two weeks? That's nothing. That's only days," I said, annoyed, I said, jealous, I said in disbelief.

Men.

I spend the two weeks they're spending without sex waiting for them to call. I think they're just on hiatus, spending the time thinking about me. But they're not thinking about me. There is no hiatus. They have just moved on. They have moved on and are now calling new women, so at the end of those two weeks, with any luck, they're dating someone new. Back in the fold, back to having sex. While I have only just figured out that they are never going to call.

"How long for you?" asked Dirk.

"Two weeks."

Dirk grunted, shooting me a look like I was a sly little devil.

"Two weeks times whatever adds up to like almost six months. Not fourteen days, Dirk. Fourteen days is not exactly a very long time."

"Well you must really feel the need to be touched then, Karrie."

"How altruistic of you! I'm good enough for today but not for tomorrow?" I called out having picked myself up off the couch, moving across the living room. "Do you think that makes me feel less lonely? Screw you."

"Hey," said Dirk, jumping off the couch and coming after me. "Do you think we're going to walk off into the sunset? Look at me," he said, grabbing my hand as it swung by. "No bullshit, we're buddies."

"Right, what's a little sex between buds," I said, pulling back my hand, going past him into the kitchen and opening the fridge to find one cold KISZ beer on the top shelf. Have your first kiss on us, said the ads. Figuring the one with Dirk had just been my last, I took the beer out of the refrigerator holding it between my legs while I pulled open the drawer to find a bottle opener.

Dirk flew into the kitchen. He pulled the beer out from between my legs, twisted it open, took a swig and set it on the kitchen table before turning around and pinning me up against the wall.

The last time I remember being pinned up like that was in fifth grade. Lee Loran held my arms against the chain-link fence in the school yard and wouldn't let me go until I told him exactly how many movies I had seen in my life. Local theaters only, I was not allowed to include TV. Lee Loran. What in the world ever happened to Lee Loran? Lee Loran, Dirk Benson. One little boy and now one big one.

"Karrie," said, Dirk, keeping my arms pinned against the wall while he looked into my eyes, his body towering close and above. "I'm going to ask you something now, and I want you to be honest, okay?"

"Okay."

"What do you need now?"

"For you to let go so I can get a sip of the beer. I'm thirsty."

"Karrie. If you could have sex now, nice, good, friendly sex with someone you like that would make you feel great, no feigned romance, just a nice satisfying time that would make your day better and give you a little glow for auditions, why would that be so bad?"

"And if it's so nice, Dirk, so friendly and so satisfying, why is it just for now? Why can't it also be for later? For tomorrow. Please, I don't want to make you think ahead or anything, but God, what about next week?"

Dirk and I had each other pinned. We had each other up against the wall.

"Because you and I are buddies."

It made me wince. He was right. We were. Buddies with attraction. What in that moment made me think it could be different? Then again, why not? Weren't those the main ingredients for a relationship? What was the spice that made it more?

"Come on, you know I don't want a life like that. You know I don't want to be accountable to say I'm bringing the coleslaw on Thursday when I could be on a plane to Madrid to shoot a spot that day."

"You're on hold for a commercial that shoots in Spain?" I asked, accountability looking like a number-one answer.

"You don't want me. You don't want an undependable actor who's married to his dream. You want a more dependable guy. A nice, reliable Jewish guy."

"But you're nice and aren't you Jewish? You are, aren't you, Dirk?"

"Half," he said, reminding me again he was raised as a military brat and his only real foray into Judaism was his Bar Mitzvah in Ethiopia. "Listen. You know what you need," he said, using his voice and his fingertips to stroke me.

The soft touch up and down the inside of my arm was increasingly persuasive.

"Ohh," I moaned.

"So many women are uptight because they won't take some pleasure for themselves. Come on."

Dirk threw in a few soft kisses. I think he had a point.

If I waited until I was sure, and I waited until I met a man I could be sure of, I could live out the rest of my life waiting.

"Ohhh…"

And it felt so good.

"Ohhhh!"

After all…I had my head on straight about Dirk. I really did, I thought, as, "Ohhhhh!" he started on the other arm.

"And the beauty of it," Dirk spoke between kisses, "is that I can still be calling you for the next twenty years."

OHHHHHH?

My stomach tightened at the thought of living through this dating pattern for another twenty years. In the state I was in now, I wasn't sure I was even going to make it through the next twenty minutes. I exhaled, deeply, staring up to the heavens.

"You look great, right now," said Dirk, excited by something he saw in me. "Wow."

"Distress agrees with me?"

"Don't move. Just look up. Look right there," said Dirk, pointing to a spot.

The actress in me, used to taking direction, looked up, and the woman in me, grateful for a man taking any initiative, did the same.

We stood, silent, breathing in and breathing out. Dirk let go of my arms, instead pushing my shoulders gently against the wall, and quietly kissing my elongated neck before leading me to sit on his lap at the kitchen table.

"Now, listen up. I'm going to exit. And when I come back into the kitchen, you hand me the beer, and say, 'Hi, honey, home from a hard day?'"

"What? Are you kidding me? Suddenly we're in an improvisation class? I didn't sign up and I don't want to play."

"Indulge me," he said, sitting up quickly, causing me to stand as he exited the set he just built. "Okay…" called Dirk from the hallway. "Action!"

He sauntered into the kitchen, pulled up a chair and mopped his brow while I, please do me the great courtesy of not asking why, handed him the beer and said, "Hi, honey, home from a hard day?"

Dirk grabbed me by the waist. He pulled me onto his lap with one hand and took a swig of beer with the other with the intensity of an actor living his life at a kitchen table in an Arthur Miller play. Like a good actor, Dirk's motivation was clear. The sudden intensity made me feel important. I felt his passion, and while I knew it was not really for me, I could still feel my body respond. Great acting is often referred to as "moment to moment." Dirk was in love with all of them.

"Cut!"

"What?" asked Dirk, surprised I stood without a cue. "I was just getting into it."

"And now I'm getting out of it. This has been great day, Dirk, my bud, my pal, but it's over."

"Oh, come on, Karrie," he said, walking towards me. "I could feel the heat between us all day. I know you did, too. Wouldn't it be fun to do it like an acting scene? Think of it as research in case you ever have to play a character in this position."

He was acting like such a jerk, but he was so darned cute. Part of me just wanted to let go and feel good. I knew if I could, I would. But truthfully, I wasn't in good enough shape to do that. I knew the only thing I'd wind up feeling was bad.

"I can't be with you now, Dirk."

"Why? You could still be open to a real connection with someone else and you won't even feel needy because I can take care of that."

"I can promise you that you can't. It's the moment, Dirk, and then you're disengaged. And that won't take care of my other needs. I don't think there's anything wrong with living for the moment, except that it's wrong for me in this one. Get it?"

"Got it," he said, moving up and moving on. Dirk walked out of the kitchen and I followed him to the door. "Okay," he said. "I have an audition tomorrow, anyway. I should go."

We stood there and looked at each other, each feeling bad for our part of the mess. We *were* friends, we had had a fun day and now we had each gone too far. I didn't want it to end like this.

"What's your audition?" I asked, knowing it would get him to talk.

"A play. Off-Broadway," he said, crossing his arms in front of him. To show me we were off-limits. We weren't going to touch.

"Reading from the script?" I asked, shoving my hands into the pockets of my jeans. Two can play this game, I thought, feeling adolescent.

"Monologue."

"Which one?"

We both laughed out loud when he told me, knowing the play was a struggle between a woman and a drifter involved in an on-again, off-again relationship for fifteen years.

"I bet you're great," I said, picturing him. "Great character for you, Dirk."

"I love the piece. Gets me a callback every time." He

paused. "Hey—you want to see it?" he asked, suddenly turning from the door, walking back to the living room, and moving a chair to set up this set. "You can give me notes if you want, but the first time I do it just let it wash over you, okay? Let it just be the first time, as part of the process, and then we'll work on it. And when we're done I'll take you for tacos, okay?"

"You got it," I said, pulling up a front row seat on my couch.

And so did I. I was ready, but Dirk was not. If only Dirk had the same passion for the process of love as he did for the process of acting. I sipped the beer and watched. I watched Dirk act, while watching him work in the process he loved. I witnessed Dirk doing what he loved, as I witnessed Dirk when Dirk was in love.

Six

All your old frogs should be quarantined anytime there's an arrival of a new one to be sure it will not contaminate any healthy frogs in your collection.

"I love the pheromones that are released when you dance," Anne told me as we approached the pier.

Pier 25's Sunday Night Moondance was a definite summertime perk in Manhattan. The August night was steamy, and it felt like we had run off to a paradise on some other island. We walked past people eating and drinking around small candlelit tables, as we made our way down to the dock that held the dance, floating on the Hudson. The breeze blew off the water, and the beat of the music swung through the air. If you wanted, you could dance the night away.

Anne was a terrific dancer. A professional, she'd gone back to school for a CSW in her thirties, making certain she'd have an age-friendly career waiting for her in her forties. We met a few years ago at a swing dance on a night when a man shortage forced the women to partner with each other. When it came to swing, Anne taught me everything I know. She taught me well, making sure I learned the importance of the basic step and a good outfit. If something about your outfit said swing, you probably would.

Dressed in a navy-and-white sailor skirt, a matching headband pushing back her auburn curls, Anne looked ready for some fancy footwork. And it was only moments until a serious dancer—you can always tell by the shoes—scooped her into his arms and led her off to dance. I watched her petite body whirl. She looked like she was flying, and I knew how badly she wanted to cut loose.

On the subway ride down, Anne and I were seated next to two sixtysomethings who, we couldn't help but overhear, had just dipped their toes into the icy waters of online dating. Okay, so we were eavesdropping. But we couldn't help it.

"So when he came back after his call waiting I think he just wanted to get off." The voice was loud and screamed New Yawk! "But I wanted to finish the call. And he didn't even remember me he said so many women are writing him. Believe me, his profile wasn't so hot and neither was his picture. But after all that we decided to meet. So I said to him, how am I going to know you? What will you be wearing? And he says jeans and dirty white sneakers. So I said you have to meet someone the first time wearing jeans and dirty white sneakers? That's the impression you want to make? That's what you want to wear? So then he says maybe he won't wear the dirty white sneakers, maybe he'll wear black leather shoes, but he's definitely wearing a hat. He says how would you like if I wore a red hat?"

"Save me from this fate," Anne murmured, under her

breath, her self-expressive body shivering as if it had just been chilled.

I wanted to go on the date. I wanted to sit at the table across from them on their date. Wearing a trench coat and hiding behind a newspaper, watching her talk to the guy wearing jeans and dirty white sneakers, a maybe on the shoes but a definite on the hat.

"So I told him just to wear the black leather shoes and not to wear the dirty sneakers and to definitely *not* wear the hat, and then he tells me that he's going to wear Ray-Bans. I said to him what are you going to wear those for? It's going to rain. Why are you wearing sunglasses in a hurricane? And to top it all off he's from up in God's country. Poughkeepsie. And I thought what am I doing this for? How in the world could a guy like this enhance my life?"

"He sounds crazy," I said, poking Anne.

"But she sounds a little insane, no?" she replied, poking me back.

"Online dating," I snickered.

"I met Carl online," Anne reminded me. "And we went out for ten months before he heard his religious calling," she told me even though she made me promise not to let her talk about him.

Sometimes talking was the only thing that helped heal. But sometimes it made it worse. It all depended on who you talked to. Anne listened to people's problems all day. But when it came to her, she didn't always want to talk. Tonight Anne preferred to dance it out, releasing it through her pores.

I, on the other hand, was another story.

Considering I hadn't even had a date for the past six months, I had quite a lot to say. My saga finally came to an end with the recent non-date day with Dirk. And I had been feeling sad since. It wasn't about Dirk, but what he had stirred up. I realized my yearnings had been lying dormant because there was no one to open them. I used to meet men all the time. Okay, maybe I'd been kissing frogs, but at least I'd been kissing. I wasn't meeting anyone anymore. Use it or lose it. And the pond was dry.

"You really need to give online dating some serious thought," Anne repeated, moments before she danced away. She had told me she was back online looking and urged me to do the same.

I had given it some thought, but it was hard to give it serious thought. To me, online dating was the antithesis of romance. Romance was spontaneous and this was the complete opposite. Despite the myriad of press promoting the merits of online dating, I did not feel that trying to meet someone for a romantic relationship should be hard work, a numbers game, or approached in the same way you went about looking for a job. But maybe that was only because I was an actress, and I never really had one.

"Shall we?" asked an older Chinese man who appeared out of nowhere.

"Would love it," I said. He escorted me onto the wooden dance floor as he placed one hand on my waist, taking my right hand in his other.

I got hooked on swing from that first snowy night at the Y. The ballroom felt transformed into another era with a live band playing forties music, people wearing period clothing, and cookies and punch served on the side. The storm added another layer to the charm, making me feel like we were at a USO dance during the war. Weather conditions were detaining some troops, but when the men did finally arrive, the gaiety of the crowd and the music filled the warm ballroom on the cold winter night.

The element, however, that made it so lovely was the ritual to the dance. A ritual mutually respected and mutually understood. It was clear that the men did the asking and the men would lead. And when the dance was over, the men thanked you before moving on. The dance between men and women clear.

"A five, six, seven, eight!"

The Chinese man and I bobbed up and down in time to the music. He was a strong leader who danced more by rote than inspiration. When I danced it was pure instinct, and I was only as good as my partner. We clapped when it ended, and he kissed my right hand before he walked away.

Next was a swarthy Hispanic guy with highly developed muscles who spun me in circles before dipping me back for a big finish. There was a wiry, bland young man whose hand in mine felt like I was holding a dead fish. And a heavyset control freak that held me way too tight, continuously calling every move into my ear as he chanted, "Basic step, basic step, turn, turn, step, step."

I got away the moment I could, moving as fast as my feet would carry me, and colliding into a spry fellow with a very full head of wavy black hair.

"Dance?" he asked, taking my right hand and leading me to a spot in the center of the floor.

With the wave of the musical wand it began. From the very first step I entered a new world with this stranger, my body giving itself over and moving in ways I did not know I could be led or even know I could follow. He was a strong, passionate leader with turns and timing to beat the band. Our feet jittered and bugged and our bodies swung. His was pressed close to mine and our arms, entwined, moved over and down like two figure eights clandestinely meeting in the dark. The river splashed against the dock, and the music flooded the space as the blood rushed up inside me. Alive. Then in one clean motion he pulled me up from the dip. It was over.

"Thanks," was all I managed to say.

Could that word convey the thrill and sensations? I spontaneously stood on my toes and gave him a kiss.

"You're welcome." He made sure to smile to thank me, before turning on his heels and quickly walking away.

I felt like I'd been punched in the stomach. Unable to move, I stood still until a guy who looked like Hollywood's idea of big bad blind date came up beside me.

"You're one good dancer," he said, salivating, having watched me move in that way I never had before. "Want to dance?"

Yes. The box of desire had been ripped wide open. I wanted to dance. God, I wanted to dance, but not with him.

"I'm wiped out, but thanks," I said, running away, running behind the dance floor and behind the stage to the quiet that lay at the end of the dock.

A sofa, an actual worn-out couch, was sitting near the edge and I plunked down, a few feet from the water, staring out at the small waves, reliving the dance, reliving the touch. I stayed like that until I heard the ringing from inside my pocket. I always wore the purple flair skirt with the zipper pockets so I didn't have to carry a bag and had a safe place for my money, my cell, my MetroCard and my keys.

"Hello?"

"Where are you? You're not home," Fred accused.

From the ambient noise I could hear that neither was he. He was outside where someplace, nearby, someone was having a fire.

"Move to the side and let the red truck go by," I instructed.

"I'm not driving, Karrie, and I'm not in a cab." By the time he finished the sentence the noise had subsided and the truck had sped far away. "Where are you?"

"On the couch," I said, not lying. "On the river," I said, and explained.

"Oh, well, better to have danced and lost than never to have danced at all," he said, moving on to ask questions about the turbulence of the water. "Are you on that pier with the boats? They have free kayaking in the summer."

"I know all about it. I took Charlie last year."

"How Holly Golightly of you!" said Fred. "So, listen to this. Trey got back in town, finally, after his summer stock designer stint at a little theater in the Finger Lakes. Summer *shlock* he called it, the budgets were so low Trey said the whole cast practically had to share one costume!"

I could hear that Fred was building up to a big finish, and I hoped it would be the dip that he deserved.

"And...?"

"Anyway, fences have been mended between me and Babalou, my newest pet name for him. Even though he's a WASP his hair looks just like Ricky Ricardo's. We didn't talk about it, we didn't discuss what *happened*. We just... Let's just say I'm on my way back over there now. I don't like to kiss and tell."

"I just like to kiss," I said, that dance and Dirk having unleashed feelings that had been hidden all year.

Tonight the dam had burst, and it all came pouring out. The feelings bubbled up inside me flowed over, spilled to the floor, and I didn't know what to do with them. The feelings of desire had been relegated to a box marked Unfulfilled Yearnings. The fear of them remaining that way struck me with panic. I didn't know what to do, and when I turned my head and spotted my phantom dancer standing a few feet away on the dock, leaning against the railing chatting up some other girl, I decided I should just do what I could. I left.

Saying good-night to Anne, Fred kept me company on the cell until I got far enough in my travels to duck into the subway, losing my signal and ending the call.

When I got home, I took Charlie out for a walk on Columbus. The outdoor cafes were filled with couples back from their weekend away having a late supper, or winding it down over a drink. I couldn't help but wonder. Why wasn't I one of them?

There had to be a reason. If I looked back at the very beginning of the dating dance maybe I could figure it out. I thought about the beginning of boys. Back then I was part of the pack. But the leader was somebody else.

At our fourth-grade Christmas party Joni Wolf said she thought it was time we all went steady. Joni told every boy he needed to ask a girl. The announcement came in the middle of the party. All the girls wore go-go boots, and danced on top of their desks to the theme song from *The Monkees.* The classroom looked like an underage episode of *American Bandstand.*

Rachel and I walked home from school that day, plotting how I could get Lee Loran to ask me. I listened in on the extension when she called to tell him she got me to admit that I liked him. Rachel also told Lee that if he asked me she would pay him back by going steady with Marty, his best friend…if only Lee wouldn't mind asking Marty to ask her. Lee said he'd definitely ask Marty, but he couldn't ask me because Joni Wolf had already asked him to ask her, so he was taken.

The next day when we got to school Joni was wearing Lee's ID bracelet around her wrist, but it looked more like she had him wrapped around her little finger. Marty did ask Rachel and the four of them sat together during snack time while I watched, alone, a few rows away eating a stick pretzel and drinking my container of homogenized milk.

Later, Rachel told me that Lee told her that he really wanted to go steady with me but he never thought I would want to go steady with him. He only said yes to Joni so he wouldn't be left out. Then three different boys asked me to go steady but I didn't like any of them, so I told them all no. Rachel said I should go back and say yes to one of them, so I'd have somebody I could break up with when someone better came along.

Joshua Perry was my very first frog. But his jaw jutted out in a way that made him look more like an ape. He was scrawny, wearing top and bottom braces that had the kids calling him Metal Mouth. While I accepted his ID bracelet hoping that would make me feel more accepted, it kept the other kids away, thinking we always wanted to be alone. I felt more alone going steady with Joshua than I had when I was just alone and not going steady.

Once we broke up, Joni and Lee broke up. So Joni made a new announcement that everyone should break up. When I told Lee I was happy that he and Joni really had, he asked me to go steady. Joni got mad. Joshua was so hurt he wouldn't look at me. And since none of the other boys were going steady anymore Lee and I broke up, our relationship lasting from the beginning of the "Star Spangled Banner" through the end of Assembly.

"Happy Valentine's Day!"

I had found my way back to my building and came out of my trance when I was greeted by retired garmento aka Rabbi Schindelheim, standing out in front as if awaiting the arrival of a congregation.

"What are you talking about?" I asked, slightly distracted, as I couldn't help but feel I might have spent my adult life duplicating a dating pattern that started in the fourth grade.

"It's Jewish Valentine's Day. Are you aware of this?" he asked, smoking his cigar, imparting knowledge between puffs.

"A happy Jewish holiday? How come I never heard of it?"

"Well, *Tu B'av* is fairly obscure, but one of the most important. The girls of Jerusalem used to go out in borrowed white dresses and dance in the vineyards. Then the men would come down to the fields and pick a bride."

White go-go boots, or white dresses? What was the difference between a pronouncement from a fourth grader telling you to hook up for a while, or a village telling you to hook up forever?

Was commitment fate, or just a decision one chose to make at a certain point? Did love propel commitment, or was it the other way around? And if that was the case, what's love got to do with it?

"Tell me more, Rab— I mean, Mr. Schindleheim," I said, catching myself as this rabbi didn't even know he'd been ordained.

"Well, it's a day for flirting. *Tu B'av* is about hope and continuity, even after the worst of things," he said. "It's about getting on with life, and getting on with love. What do you think?"

I was going to find out because I just got an idea. My hope suddenly resurfaced, refueling me to continue the mission for that thing called love. Besides, if this kept up I had a feeling I'd soon be attending services in the lobby.

I went room to room after entering my apartment, flipping switches to turn on lights, the computer, the A/C, the TV and the answering machine. Alerted of my one message, the familiar sound of Millie filled the room.

"Hi, it's Mommy. I have to ask you something, so call me when you get home. But if you get in in the next fifteen minutes turn on the TV. I don't know the name of the show or what channel it's on in New York—its channel ten here…"

I pictured my mother sitting on the sunporch watching whatever it was while decoding the daily cryptogram in the *Palm Beach Post*.

"You may be interested. It's one of those reality shows where the girl sees everyone she's ever dated in her whole life in one room. They all tell her why they broke up with her and didn't want to get married, and then when it's over she has to marry the best of her worst. I thought it might appeal to you."

It didn't.

Aside from everything the whole reality trend had gone way past getting on my nerves, not to mention all the jobs that were being taken away from actors and writers. It was less and less interesting to watch regular people interacting in the non-reality of their reality show. All this reality was not stimulating entertainment, stimulating anybody's imagination, or giving breath to anything original or new. Besides, your average Joe really was pretty average, especially without charisma, acting skills, or a script. Television was falling way below average, and that was the biggest reality.

But I sure was fascinated with those bachelors and bachelorettes. I would love to understand the reality of falling in love in six episodes, or tying the knot in the new fall season lineup. I plopped down in a chair and opened my *TV Guide* to try to find the show my mother was talking about. The cover included a series of photos promoting the feature about couples who had met on TV. Little bubbles hovered over each couples' heads filled with blurbs that read *Dumped?* or *Headed for Divorce?*

Yet one photo caught my eye. I studied the face on the girl. Her blond, curly tresses fell around her happy heart-shaped face, her newly betrothed looked on, content and sincere. But really! Was this what Americans wanted to watch? Was it fate to fall in love on national TV? Was that someone's destiny? Perhaps I was only ready now to see the reality. I had to face the harsh reality that I could no longer leave it up to fate or destiny. I had to make it happen. I would need to search.

The high-speed DSL quickly connected me to Dogpile, my search engine of choice. I typed the letters B–A–S–H–E–R–T and quickly received eighty-four results! A novice in the unfated serious search for lasting love, I made my first double clicks on the heading, *BASHERT 101: How to Get Hitched for Dummies,* and began to read.

The word *bashert* means fate, destiny, or what is meant to be.

So far so good.

According to the Talmud, Rav Yehuda taught that forty days before a male child is conceived, a voice from heaven announces whose daughter he will marry!

Well, I hadn't dated anyone deaf but there sure was a whole generation of guys out there that obviously couldn't hear.

Your soul mate is generally referred to as your *bashert,* but the person meant for you is your *basherter.* How do you know if you have found that person?

One clue might be that he would call you again after sex, I thought quickly skimming the page until something alarming caught my eye.

Although a first marriage is considered *bashert,* or meant to be, sadly two people can still ruin it. Judaism allows divorce, making it possible to have a good and happy marriage with a second spouse.

Therein lies the problem, and it was so disturbing I had to go lie down. So much for my mission.

I lay on my bed, staring up at the ceiling, realizing I'd had it all wrong. I had never before considered that maybe it wasn't a question of *who* was *bashert* for me, but *what* was *bashert* for me?

Already well into my forties, was a first marriage between two late bloomers what was meant to be? Or was it *bashert* that I remained single all these years because my *basherter* was not yet even available? I threw the covers over my head, drifting off while contemplating how much longer I'd have to wait.

Maybe my *basherter* was only in the middle of ruining his first marriage, the one that was *bashert*. Maybe I had to wait until they separated, until he moved out, and filed for divorce. Maybe I would have to wait until he had one rebound relationship, one transitional relationship, and a handful of flings. Then I'd have to wait for his kids to adjust to the idea of their parents' marriage ending. Maybe I even had to wait until they were old enough to go to sleep-away camp in the summer so my *basherter* actually had some free time to hunt me down, date me, and mate me. And would that mean our marriage was *bashert* only for me and just a good and happy second marriage for him? Forty days before my *basherter* was conceived whose daughter's name was announced? Hers, or mine?

I was afraid my name wasn't ever announced. The fear was soon echoed by a sudden crash of lightning that jolted me. Sitting up in bed, I listened to the rain and pondered. What if my name was never whispered into anybody's ear?

I got up to go to the bathroom. When I turned on the light I was surprised to see I was wearing a white nightgown. Funny, it didn't even look like one of mine, I thought, before I flushed to leave the loo. But who cared? I was nothing more than a runner-up. The bachelorette unchosen.

"Hi!" said a geeky balding man who greeted me as I came out of the bathroom. "How are ya, today, Kar?"

"Aaaaaahhh!" I screamed, before running from this man and down the hall.

But there were men everywhere! On the sofa, on the chairs, in the doorways, on the floor.

"Ohmygod!!! What's going on?" I hollered before feeling a reassuring hand on my arm.

I looked up to see it belonged to a man in a Hawaiian shirt who was leading me to the center of the living room. He smiled a big *GQ* smile that made his white dentures gleam.

"Good morning, Karrie," he said. "I'm Rick and I'm the host of your show! Welcome to *The Basherterette!*"

The *Basherter*WHAT?

"Uh, listen, uh, Rick, is it? Something is wrong. Something is terribly wrong. This must be part of some very big mistake. I would *never* go on a show like that! Besides, my agent wouldn't even be able to get me an audition."

"Oh, it's no mistake," said Rick. "We're a brand-new show and forty days before the network picked up the pilot, the producer was driving his Porsche and out of the blue he heard your name announced to kick this baby off!"

And to prove he was right, Rick opened to a page in my *TV Guide.*

*The Basherterette—*Reality
Debut: A perennial single
seeks love in Manhattan.
Starring: Karrie Kline

What could I say? I finally got my name in *TV Guide.*

"Now that that's settled, let's begin. O-kaaaay!" said Rick, sounding like a game-show host. "Look around your apartment, Karrie, and you will see we have brought you twenty-five eligible men who all want to be your *bashert.* Are any of them your *basherter?* Ask us if we know. Ask us if we care. Let's face it, Karrie, you may be looking for your *bash-erter,* but we're just looking for ratings."

"Wait a sec," I said, skipping over that to get to this. "Back up. You're doing the show here? In my apartment?" I looked around the crowded room. "Don't you know this is only a one-bedroom?"

"Sorry. Your show doesn't have much of a budget. Now, gentlemen," continued Rick as he addressed the men. "One of you lucky men will be selected to have a serious monogamous relationship with marriage potential with Karrie. Due to the size of the apartment, this will be an accelerated version of the show. Every two hours we will hold a PEZ ceremony that will eliminate several of you wonderful men. Karrie will give each man she hopes to get to know better a Charlie Brown PEZ dispenser. If you don't get a Charlie Brown PEZ dispenser, we'll hail a cab for you on Broadway that will take you back to work. If for any reason you don't feel Karrie would be right for you, you do not have to accept the PEZ dispenser and you are free to go. Now let's get this show on the road."

For our first group date we went down to the basement of my building to do my laundry. A widower who worked in construction told me if things worked out he expected I would move into his house in Patchogue, Long Island, where he's built a great laundry room.

"But isn't that, like, two hours from the city?" I asked, finding it as difficult to separate the men from the boys as the whites from the darks.

"It would only be for another ten years. Just until my four kids grow up," he said, sketching a picture of the house on a pad to show me. "You do want a family, don't you?"

Thinking this scenario seductive, he made a move. In front of all the other men, right in the middle of the spin cycle, he kissed me. A big one. A big slobbery wet one. To his dismay, Reggie got eliminated at the PEZ ceremony.

"She made out with me in the laundry room, dudes" were his parting words. But he wasn't the only one to go once the ceremony officially began.

"Excuse me," said a nervous fellow with thinning hair. "I have an important client coming to my office in half an hour and I really don't have time for such a long courtship. Besides, tonight's my night with my kids."

"That's okay," I said, shooting Rick a look to let him know I didn't feel bad. "He wasn't really my type."

To tell you the truth, no one was, but I didn't know how to get out of this. I was stuck, I thought, sadly looking over at the stack of balding Charlie Browns. With that a round man with pocked skin stood.

"I just thought this would be an easy way to get laid. I didn't realize I was going to have to stick around. No offense to you, Karrie, but I don't want to have to jump through any hoops."

"I have two cats."

"I'm allergic to dogs," said another.

"But the Maltese is a hypoallergenic breed," I said, I didn't know why.

"Anyone else?" asked Rick. "Is everyone else here able to stay?"

The best-looking man in the room got up to go.

"I'm married," he said, slipping out the door. "Sorry."

Two men jumped up from behind the sofa just as he left. "I'm gay."

"I can't see anybody for more than four to six weeks. I didn't realize I'd have to keep it going *after* the show."

"Hey, Rick," I interrupted. "I thought you said you had twenty-five eligible bachelors. But you found twenty-five unavailable available men."

Man, what a nightmare! I concluded the first and last ceremony by handing out one PEZ dispenser to a real estate lawyer who only got in under the good graces of Charlie. But it was one PEZ too many.

I was not good at this show.

Riiiiing!

"And now it's time for Karrie to bring you home to meet her mother!" Rick announced.

Riiiiing!

"Since we cannot fly you to Florida we will show you a photo of her mother, Millie, and you'll have the opportunity to meet over a nice long chat on speaker phone!"

Riiiiing!

I didn't know how to get off the air.

Riiiiing!

I only hoped we wouldn't go into syndication.

"Karrie, pick up!" Millie's voice came through the speaker phone loud and clear.

Charlie was barking and barking while the phone was ringing and ringing. I would have to answer it. Then I'd have to stand by and listen to Millie chat it up with...what was his name again? Oh, I couldn't take the ringing in my ear. I reached for the phone.

"I was getting worried," said my mother. "Are you okay?"

"Uh-huh," I mumbled, somehow feeling drugged with sleep.

"Did you watch the show?" she asked.

"I'm on it."

"Oh. You. You're always on," she said. "What did you think of the *Best of Your Worst?*"

"The best of your who? You're mixed up, Ma. You mean *The Basherterette.* I don't think it'll make it."

"I don't know what show you're talking about, Karrie, but I don't think we're talking about the same show."

I opened my eyes, and with a great, big sigh of relief I was happy to see that we weren't. Talk about reality!

When we hung up I was, thankfully, alone in my apartment, but I was alone. I went back to the computer and logged on to a Web site, hoping my heart's desire was just a search, a click and Visa card away.

Within seconds I saw pictures of men and women hugging, kissing and holding hands. Sprawled across their smiling faces it said:

Welcome to the J-Spot
The Hot Spot for Jewish Singles To Meet

Barring the bang of blaring music, I felt the same anxiety I might feel if I had just walked into some massive singles events. But I took a breath and moved my mouse in the direction of love.

Seven

While no two frogs have the same call, the loudest calls are made by the male frog when he is seeking a mate, coming to be known as an advertising call.

The home page said there were eight thousand seven hundred forty-two people online right now. I wondered if there was always such a crowd or if it was just a seasonal thing.

Three days had passed and I still hadn't signed up. I had started, but stopped when I saw what it involved. It was such an elaborate process. The last time I had to answer such complicated essay questions I was applying for college.

No sooner did I sit down to do it I was back up on my feet, walking aimlessly, thinking about all the people, and contemplating the other eight thousand seven hundred and forty-one. Passing a mirror I noticed my hair was uncombed and I didn't have on any makeup. Well, I absolutely could not meet anyone looking like this. When I returned to my desk I had well-brushed hair, glossed lips, a bagel, a cup of coffee and three bottles of nail polish, unwilling to waste any window of time that allowed for a good drying opportunity.

It was now or never.

I entered my e-mail address. KKline2@uh-oh-l.com.

I entered a password. CharlesK.

Easy. I moved on. Create a username. Okay. Now I was stumped.

I had to create some cute little name that would instantly make someone want to either read more or click on. So what was I? WestSideWhy? ResistTense? CyberDoubts? I needed something clever. Catchy. I looked over at the names of the nail polishes. They all seemed plausible...Rudely-Nude, BerriesInTheSnow, ClearWillpower...for a porno site! Who knew nail polish could be so seductive.

BlueEyes. BlueEyes? Okay, not clever but I liked it. After typing it in, I found out that so did three hundred and twenty-four other blue-eyed girls. Yet when I was given the option of BlueEyes325, I agreed. My first J-Spot compromise, and not a bad one at that.

I checked that I was a woman in search of a man and read my options of Hot Spots: a friend, a date, a long-term partner, a marriage. A date sounded fine but I had heard that it is sometimes online code for just sex, something that managed to happen without prodding. Choosing not to advertise for it I checked both a long-term partner and a marriage. I felt a surge of hope after checking those boxes, as if the acknowledgment alone could make it happen.

Date of birth, astrological sign, occupation, schooling, height, weight, body type, eye color and hair. I said I was Reform, went to synagogue sometimes and did not keep kosher at all. The J-Spot ranged in people that were very religious and orthodox to those who were completely secular and unaffiliated. But I had chosen the J-Spot in the hope that meeting men in my tribe might add something familiar to the unfamiliarity of dating in cyberspace.

Anne had met Carl on Catch.com. However, Carl, now in his Chaim stage, had made a point of telling her that he'd transferred. He left Catch for the J-Spot where he searched only for women who described themselves as Religious, Very Religious, Very Orthodox and Very Very Different from Anne.

I glided through bunches of checklists and questions until I got to the first dreaded essay called "Who Am I." It was supposed to represent the way I would introduce myself to someone. Okay, let's be honest, not only would I never introduce myself to someone with as many words as it was going to take to write this essay, I would never *even* introduce myself to someone unless they were cute, or I made some cool eye contact first. But I wasn't out and about. I was online, and I was expected to present myself *authentically* in a one-hundred-word essay that would show who I was. *Oy.*

I should have signed up on Catch.com. Catch probably wasn't so demanding. I bet they didn't make you do so much work. Everyone on Catch was probably outside right now playing and having fun, while everyone on the J-Spot was stuck at home, only up to word fifty-eight on the stupid one-hundred-word essay. The J-Spot was probably dating for overachievers, and I was afraid if I didn't do a really good job on my essay my date and I would never get into a top restaurant.

I decided to bag it, until a little pop-up appeared on the screen.

Did You Spend Last Night Wishing For Love?
SIGN UP NOW

Don't Just Make A Wish—
Make Your Wish Come True

I reexamined the odds and decided they were in my favor. Online: Eight thousand seven hundred forty-two. My apartment: One.

Two hours later, here I was.

Who Am I
You'll find a smart, funny, pragmatic and romantic soul if you can tickle the right spot. Sometimes it's hard to find, but my itch to connect has brought me here, and I hope you'll be the one with satisfying hands. As a professional actress I've played roles in many fictional relationships, and feel ready for a reality of my own. I hope dating online will help me meet a like-minded man who'd be a great friend and lover. I am in good shape and take care of myself. I enjoy all the usual stuff, cultural and athletic, activities indoors and out! I have a funny dog, and what I may lack in culinary skills I make up for in my ability to eat out and order in.

I didn't know if the essay was good or even good enough, but the next part said to upload a photo. A picture is worth a thousand words, and I was going to post two. I had the feeling that would be my calling card, and if a guy liked my looks it wouldn't matter if I wrote a prize winning essay or couldn't tell a noun from a verb. I took out my actor's head shot, hoping it would land me more dates than it had auditions.

For the second pic, I removed a photo from my fridge held in place by a magnet shaped like a chocolate chip cookie. Anne took it on our way home from that Bat Mitzvah. Surrounded by buckets of daisies outside a Connecticut flower stand it was pretty, and in my favorite blue dress I thought it showed my figure without looking like I was trying. The shot possessed the added bonus of the wind blowing my hair. Slipping the photos into a clear little pouch, I scanned them into an e-mail and sent them off to the J-Spot folks to post and complete my profile. Blue-Eyes325.

But I was hardly done. With three more essays to go, it felt more like writing a dissertation on dating, or spotting, as they called it. I had to delineate my views about a good spot, a perfect spot and the spot of my dreams. I thought it safe to say it was one that came with a stain removal that worked faster than the time it took to get through this profile.

At long last they wanted to know what I had learned from my prior relationships. With gusto I typed my answer.

From The Last Spot
I've learned that you have to kiss a lot of frogs.

Bleep! Unaccepted answer! Unaccepted? What? I was crushed. I looked closely at the screen. They wanted more. More information. They needed more words. My God, this was *so* demanding, not to mention slightly humiliating. They obviously felt I'd not learned very much. However, judging from my dating history they were probably right.

I started out this year resolved with my dating past, feeling complete, and making a resolution that completely committed me to carpe diem mode. Having come through the New Year's breakup with Jeff Broder with flying colors, I was hell-bent on seizing a day, or quite frankly anything before it had a chance to seize me. So despite freezing forecasts I went running on an eight-degree Sunday in January.

Dressed in more layers than I knew I owned, I ventured

up to the reservoir that crystal-clear, numbingly cold day. Extra careful not to slip on the icy path, the run was taking longer than usual. But at a certain point turning back became equidistant to forging ahead. I forged on, only slowing down when I heard someone call behind me, "What are you doing here?"

Running alongside me, suddenly, like a package dropped down from the sky was a man. Underneath his wool cap, his triple layered sweats and even beyond his runny nose it was easy to see he was a cute one.

"We both must be crazy," I said, taking off my glove and extending my hand to shake hello while we continued our run.

Two nights later at dinner, Albee told me that was the moment he knew I was someone he wanted to know.

"I thought it was so endearing in that frigid weather you actually removed your glove to shake my hand," he said, pouring more wine from the bottle of Merlot he had ordered. We were in a sweet Upper West Side restaurant that looked like a room in a house, and was practically a private party. With temperatures hardly rising to ten, everyone else stayed in, while Albee and I went out. "Plus for a while I was running behind you and you looked pretty good."

"The frostbite must have gone directly to your brain. How can anyone look good in all those layers? Maybe I had a better shot at your attention cause I was the only other person on the path!" I said, sipping the wine, warming up while warming up to Albee.

It was a really good beginning to a new year. Albee was nice, fun. Bright, energized and wanting to bond. He was back in New York after a decade in Los Angeles. He liked his job and his apartment—conveniently located just a few blocks from mine—he liked his life, and he liked me. His twin teenaged daughters still lived in L.A. with their mom, but Albee felt New York was a better place for his sales work. Since the girls would soon be off to college—"Even in-state, it sure isn't cheap"—he felt as long as he stayed in close touch, all would be okay.

Albee had designs on me and quickly began painting me into his life. We fell into daily contact immediately, and though it felt like too much too soon, my break-up with Broder helped me appreciate an available guy like Albee. After two weeks he told me he was considering a move to a larger space, but nothing had come up as yet. He also asked how I felt about relocating back to Los Angeles and, though I swore I never would, I told him it was possible. I wanted to keep all the possibilities open, even though Albee had slammed the door shut on one.

Children. No way. He was done.

"You'll have two wonderful stepdaughters you can be-friend," Albee told me the third week over margaritas at a local Mexican hang. "You'll love them and they'll love you. That relationship will have great potential for you, Karrie, just like ours. But I don't want more kids. I know what it takes. I'm also older than you, and I just don't want any more," he said, making sure to add that if this talk seemed premature it was only because he was mature, and feeling clear about us he also felt the need to be clear.

"Think about it," he said, again, later that night when we kissed on the couch. "No babies. Okay?" he asked, all sweet-ness and sincerity. His kisses grew even sweeter and more sincere as I thought about that and also thought about whether or not he should stay. He had his terms and I had mine, and the potential of a sexual attraction was something I needed to know fairly early on. "I promise you I won't let you miss out on anything else," said Albee, physically re-sponding to my thoughts. I knew what that would be. And Albee didn't disappoint.

The next morning I sat at my kitchen table watching him make pancakes, staring at the paper and allowing my head to wander as I thought about last night. Still a little high, I was unsure if it was the tequila, the time in bed, or the talk. It was a big talk. A lot of talk for not a lot of time. But the cards were on the table, and I had to choose my hand.

I looked up at the clock, looking past Albee, past the paper and past the pancakes to see the time. My baby clock was running a race against time. While I had to admit it was a race I had never acknowledged, it no longer mattered whether I chose to run it or not. It was a race that was running without me. For all I knew it was over. I was in my mid-forties and I'd have to start galloping this second if I wanted to see if I could still win, to see if there was any chance that I would show.

That would never happen with Albee. Other things would. Or I could leave him. I quickly calculated my odds of meeting a man who would date me and mate me in record time, and saw they were odds that no one would bet on. Not even me.

I really liked Albee. There were many ways to become a family. And there were many ways to be a parent without having to give birth. Besides, if things really did work out I'd gain two stepdaughters without having to lose any sleep or any weight, not to mention bypassing all those years of laundry. It made a lot of sense for me at this point in my life. Albee leaned over the table to feed me his pancakes. They were warm and good. Comfort food. The maple syrup reminded me of the sweetness of last night, and in that taste my decision had been made.

The days that followed were wonderful. It was a romantic week—light and carefree. A week of romance had started off the month of February, making me happy it was a leap year and Albee and I would get an extra day.

Getting ready for a date one night, Albee phoned asking me to meet him for dinner at his apartment instead of our original plan to go out. When I walked into his living room I was standing amidst a sea of boxes. Boxes here and boxes there, boxes, boxes everywhere.

"I'm moving!" Albee jumped down from a stepladder where he had just removed a suitcase from the closet. He put his arms around me and gave me a big kiss while handing over some packing tape and a list of items that needed to be boxed. "We'll just order pizza tonight," said Albee, before climbing back up the ladder to bring down something else.

I loved the close proximity of Albee's apartment to mine and was disappointed he'd be moving, but for all I knew it would only be downstairs to that bigger place he had told me about in his building. Looking forward to pizza and packing and Albee and me, I pulled a piece of tape across the cardboard and sealed the box like it was my fate.

"So tell me about this new apartment," I said a few minutes later, going to the closet and taking some camping equipment off Albee's hands. I put it down on the floor thinking that maybe this summer we would camp. I'd only gone camping for a day, which most people don't qualify as real camping because you hadn't slept outdoors, but napping and peeing outside were enough of a qualifier as far as I was concerned. With Albee, though, I thought an overnight would be fun. Maybe his daughters would come and we could all do it together.

"Well," said Albee, as he stepped off the ladder, walking down the hall to the kitchen. "The new place has two bedrooms and two full baths," he said, his back turned to me while he spoke.

"Two bedrooms and two full baths," I said, following him down the hall. "That's incredible." I was hoping it would be in a neighborhood I loved, like this one, because if things worked out it looked like that's where I would be headed.

"It's close to a lot of shopping," he said.

"What isn't?"

"And you'll like this. It's got a room with its own washer/dryer and outside there's a nice little deck."

"Washer/dryer? Where you moving to? Nice little deck! What did you do? Buy the top floor of a brownstone! It sounds amazing. Where is it?"

"Colorado," said Albee, suddenly jumping on top of the kitchen counter as he gave his answer.

"I can't hear you," I said, catching up to him in the kitchen in time to see him standing above me and beyond reach atop the Formica countertop.

"What'd you say, Alb? The Coronado? That's right near here! Where's that building, again? Seventy-first or Seventy-second? I know they have a gym, but I didn't know they had decks. Where's your place? Top floor?"

Albee, still up on the counter, quickly reached over to a collection of kitchen utensils hanging on the wall and grabbed a spatula when he told me that I had misheard him and he would need to repeat his answer.

"So what'd you say?" I asked, finally facing him in the kitchen.

"Co-lo-ra-do," he stated, blurting out each syllable while holding the spatula in front of him like a sword for protection. "Colorado. Aspen, Colorado," he repeated, waving the spatula in front of him as if at any moment I might start fighting back by lobbing him with a ladle.

"I'm leaving on Saturday, on Valentine's Day, and I'm sorry I lured you over here but I wanted to tell you in person, which I thought was pretty decent of me all things considered, however, if you want you can just leave now. But if you promise not to hit me I'll come down and order a pizza and then maybe you can stick around because I'm out of here in three days and, if you wouldn't mind, I could use a hand and would love it if you'd help me pack."

I looked at him standing barefoot atop the kitchen counter, holding the spatula in front of his groin, protecting the only thing left of his manhood. I watched him diminish before my very eyes. Albee no longer looked like a man. He looked like a punk. Like a kid in a schoolyard. There were many things I could have accused him of in that moment, but all I saw when I looked up was a boy. A little boy. A baby.

"You are *so* irresponsible," I said, trying hard to negotiate my emotional life of five minutes ago with this new reality without having to go through all of the stuff you always have to go through, that I'd just gone through with Broder, and didn't want to go through again. "You are *so emotionally irresponsible!* You played two hands against the middle for reasons now I don't even care to know. And aside from everything else, you were *not* mature. You are so *not* a grown-up. My God, Albee! You behaved like such a fucking baby."

Albee was offended, but he was also too wrong to fight back. Instead he stood there, guarding himself with the spatula, ashamed. It was hard to tell whether it was due to the compromising position he'd put himself in emotionally, or the one of standing on a kitchen countertop choosing to defend himself with a spatula.

He finally spoke. And when he did a baby's voice emerged.

"What man is *not* a baby?" asked Albee.

Did he think that question was an answer? Was he right? I didn't want him to be right. Sometimes it felt like almost every man I met was a baby. A tadpole. A baby tadpole that grew into a big grown-up frog. Was there something in the food? Some bacteria floating in the pond? What made the development stop? What was it?

Was it, by chance, in direct proportion to their attraction? If their attraction was powerful, did it make them feel like they had lost their power? Did that make them feel too vulnerable? Powerless? Like a baby? Would that make them seek a lesser attraction that was, perhaps, less satisfying but something that felt powerful? Free? Powerfully free. There had to be a reason why this happened again and again. And to so many women.

"So why are so many men such babies, Albee? I need an answer to this question. I need to know and I need to know now."

Albee didn't know, and, sadly, neither did I. But I needed an answer. Women needed one.

We need the answer to this question because we run out of eggs. We run out of eggs and we run out of time and we need to be with someone, and before it's too late. We each need to find a man who's not a baby so we can make a baby. How can you make one with one?

I need a strong man that I can baby. I am strong, but I want to be somebody's baby. Yes, sir, that's my baby. No, sir, don't say maybe. Yes, sir, that's my baby now. It's always now. It's always just for now. And then now ends.

I went back to the essay with a clearer sense of what I had learned.

From The Last Spot
If you have to kiss a lot of frogs, that's just the easy part. I've learned that we are the choices we make. It doesn't matter what people say, it matters what they do.

Accepted! Good. I would find out if I had learned my lessons well. I would sign up for six months. Opening my wallet I typed in my credit card number, hopeful there'd be someone great by the time my subscription expired. I was done. I had enough for one day.

"You've got mail!"

The computerized voice drew me back in, just as I was about to turn off and shut down. There was already a message. One message. I had sat all day without so much as a shower, and there was already a man sending a message that he wanted to meet me. As I went to retrieve the mail, a musical introduction of sorts blasted out of my speakers. A small square box appeared on the screen alerting me I had an instant *hot* message. All this attention and my pictures weren't even yet posted.

In the right-hand corner of my screen inside the instant message box was a photo a of man. He was good-looking in a manicured sort of way, dressed in a button-down yellow shirt and sitting on a fancy white couch. Not quite, but the photo was nice enough that I guessed I could possibly be attracted to him on the outside if I liked who he was on the inside. His username appeared, and in tiny little writing I read that he was typing. SirLaughALot, this man on the white couch, was suddenly typing his way into my apartment.

SirLaughALot: Hi there!

Oh my! This was weird. This was incredibly weird. Without even a scene change, my apartment had been turned into a virtual singles bar without drinks.

"What should I say?" I asked aloud, running into the bathroom to check my hair in the mirror while I gave it a little thought.

SirLaughALot: Are you there?

BlueEyes325: Hi.

I must have dazzled him with such a sparkling, witty response.

BlueEyes325: What's your name? You look familiar.

Not much better. But he sort of did.

SirLaughALot: Don.

BlueEyes325: Hmm... I guess I don't know you, Don.

SirLaughALot: Yet....

BlueEyes325: Oh!

SirLaughALot: New beginnings can be very exciting, don't you think?

BlueEyes325: Yes.

Oooh, he was smooth, I thought. He must do a lot of this.

SirLaughALot: Sooooo....playing hooky from work? Enjoying your day?

BlueEyes325: Yeah.... you?

SirLaughALot: Well, I just returned from Del Ray Beach after visiting my parents.

Oh, so he just got back from traveling and he's home sorting mail, checking e-mail and checking out women online.

BlueEyes325: My mom's in West Palm. The Holy Land.

SirLaughALot: I read your profile. You seem nice.

BlueEyes325: So do you!

Was the exclamation point too much? Did the exclamation point make me seem desperate? I didn't know whether to keep it or delete, but clicked and sent it hoping the point would help me make one.

SirLaughALot: We should meet!

BlueEyes325: What do you suggest...?

Oh my, I was so bold! Ellipses! All wrong. Too suggestive. But he was asking. He was asking with an exclamation point!

I bet he wanted to meet me tonight. I bet he wanted to have a drink later. His profile said he lived in the city. Should I go to him? Not chivalrous, but at least he wouldn't know where I lived. I looked at the photo. He might turn out to be a frog, but I sincerely doubted he turn out to be a murderer. Better for him to come to me. Should I even be available on such short notice? No. Definitely not. Too last-minute. But so what? Could be... Spontaneous! I waited while the tiny writing told me SirLaughALot was typing, but his reply written in red, looked like a waving flag.

SirLaughALot: How about you call me when you feel like it sometime this week? 917-555-8228.... Where in the city do you live...me, Upper East.

Call *him* sometime this week? Maybe thinking that we'd meet tonight was jumping the gun, but if he was really interested wouldn't he ask if he could call me? Call him? Forget him!

BlueEyes325: Upper West.

Maybe I was supposed to give him my number. But why would I give him my number when he didn't ask? Was he just uncomfortable putting me in that position? Should I offer? I didn't know the online etiquette. Well, online or off I wasn't especially comfortable just handing out my number. Especially when he approached me.

SirLaughALot: Cool. Parting is such sweet sorrow....

BlueEyes325: Until tomorrow, I think they say.

SirLaughALot: Ahhhh, mysterious, I love it....

Maybe he thought I was being mysterious because I didn't give him my number. Is that what he meant? Should I give it to him? I guessed I could, kind of like an experiment. I could just put it out there and see. I typed it in the box, but when I clicked to send I was told that SirLaughALot was no longer signed on.

What?

Where did he go? Why would he say "we should meet" and then disappear? And he didn't just say "we should meet," he said "we should meet" exclamation point! Did I say something wrong? I thought SirLaughALot was interested. Was just getting any old attention enough for him? Was he juggling several conversations up there on his screen? Or did the Sir already have a Lady in Waiting?

I was only dating online eight minutes and I was already more confused than I'd ever been when dating off. I decided that having something to look forward to might be good for me, so I *x*'d out of the J-Spot and chose to save the new e-mail for later. If SirLaughALot wanted to find me I was sure he would, but my guess was that I had heard his last laugh.

Eight

In an experiment to teach frogs to discriminate, the frog became confused to the point of actually ignoring the flies he loved in favor of the insect he loathed.

"You were great!"

"Bravo!"

"Yay!"

We were all backstage seeing Fred, who had just finished a grandiose performance playing an arm in *Body Parts: The Musical*. Brooke, Jane and I all went to see the original play that had its first public performance at My Theater Workshop, where Fred had joined me in becoming an MTW member.

The irreverent play was set in the bed of Mr. and Mrs. Bellows, while an ensemble of actors played their body parts. Arms, Legs, Eyes, Nose, Mouth and Tummy groped around in the dark navigating their way through sex, love, nightmares, midnight snacks and a good night's sleep. With a TV on throughout in the background, the incidental music within the play was parodies of jingles from well-known commercials.

"Fred, you were fantastic," said Jane. "I loved how they mirrored the changes in the relationship with the media."

"It was great," I said, throwing my arms around him. "You were soooo good!"

I was delighted at how terrific the play turned out, especially since everything I had heard had indicated otherwise! And though I was happy for everyone involved, I had to admit it made me feel disappointed for me. I was called back for Tummy, originally set to be a waiflike Tinker Bell, but at the last minute the director decided to go Hispanic.

"And when you got inside the television for the commercial break and sang. I loved that!" Brooke stepped back to demonstrate. "Let your fingers do the walking through the Bellows' rages," she sang. "I always loved that Yellow Pages spot."

"I think you were the only one who got that." Fred threw a tissue in the trash after wiping the makeup off his eyes. "No one even reads the Yellow Pages anymore unless it's online."

"Well, we laughed," said Brooke. "The show was so much fun. It really made me want to do something, but I'm so busy planning this wedding."

"How many months away is it?" asked Jane.

"Nine," said Brooke. "I could have a wedding or a baby."

"On that note—" Jane pulled out her cell phone, walking out the open door onto the fire escape for privacy "—I'll meet you at the party, I just want to call William and check in on Eve."

"So tell me what it's like to be a bride!" Fred said to

Brooke on our way down the narrow hall to the small theater that housed the opening night bash.

It was a theme! Everywhere you looked were masks and
mannequins. A TV in the corner of the room looped a
bunch of famous commercials from the sixties, seventies
and eighties. Brooke, Fred, and I each took a bottle of beer
before walking to the food table to get something to eat.

"Ooohh, I love a buffet," said Fred, handing us plates to
load up on crudités, chicken wings, salsa and chips. "The bridal buffet," Fred sighed, as he led us to a spot where we could
sit and eat while waiting for Jane.

"Being a bride may be fun, but planning a wedding sure
isn't," said Brooke, as we sat down on the floor in a corner
of the room.

"Glamour problem," sang Fred, motioning his head to
me. "What do you think, Kar? Any J-Spots sticking?"

"Oh, it's not to be believed!" I said as I tore into a chicken
wing, where at least I knew I'd get a satisfying bite.

Jane snuck up behind me, placing a hand on my shoulder as she sat down with her plate of food. "Scooch over,"
she said. "I want to hear this."

"Well…" I moved, as I reached for my bag. "You can read
all about it," I said, pulling out the four handouts I had pho-
tocopied that included printouts of all my online dating activity. I passed one to each of my friends.

Each person received a thirty page stapled handout with
this on the cover:

WELCOME BlueEyes	325!
Members Who Have:	
E-mailed you:	59
Hot-Messaged you:	16
Hot-Spotted you:	4
Spotted you:	102

"I can't believe this," said Jane, as she flipped through the pages. "How long have you been signed up?"

"Exactly three weeks now," I said. It was mid-September and easy to calculate.

"Oh my! How'd ya find the time to put all this together, Little Lulu?" asked Fred.

I took a gulp of beer.

"You are both so lucky you don't have to do this online dating thing," I told Brooke and Jane as I ignored Fred.

"This guy's cute," said Brooke. "Page two, four down," she instructed the group, as we heard the swishes and whishes of turning pages. "What happened with him?"

She pointed to the handsome BrooklynBoy. The Brooklyn Heights writer, divorced, one kid, two cats who said he was able to offer the perks of a bad boy with the stability of a good one.

"He didn't write back."

"I like SkyHigh," said Jane, reading aloud. "Still single, I'm a liberal Gramercy Park architect who believes creativity keeps life interesting."

"Wrote him, too. *Nada.*"

"*Ooooo la la!*" said Fred, pointing to—

"Nope," I said cutting him off. "The cute guys are on pages one, two and three. I wrote to all of them and didn't get back one response."

"What about the fifty-nine guys that e-mailed you, Kar?" asked Jane, referencing the cover page. "It seems like a lot. Are you saying there was no one even okay out of fifty-nine guys?"

"I anticipated that question, which is why I brought along my show-and-tell," I pompously declared, pointing to the handouts. "Begin on page four and go as far as your stomach will carry you. My profile's on the last three pages if you want to take a look."

I couldn't wait see my friends' faces as they got a backstage look at the lunacy of online love.

"Ohmygod!" screamed Fred. "Page seven, near the bottom."

Everyone roared at MakeULaugh. In his photo he was standing on top of a desk wearing a business suit, a fedora and a cape. He said he was a paralegal turned actor and wrote that he mainly got cast playing idiots.

"I love these names," howled Jane. "RussianRuLips, BagelsnLove, BeaverBill."

"Page twelve, top!" shrieked Brooke. "LaughingGas?"

Everyone reacted to the green-eyed gaze in the slightly crossed eyes of LaughingGas. He was in a white lab coat, posed on a dental chair as his rubber gloved hands rested on his hips.

"Read the instant message," I said.

"Okay," said Brooke. "I'll read LaughingGas, and Jane, you be Karrie."

"I always wanted blue eyes," said my brown-eyed friend.

LaughingGas: I'm on a break till my next patient, what are you up to?

BlueEyes325: I'm writing to you!

You hear about people who marry after they meet on the Internet, but I kept coming across men who disappeared once you even responded to them. SirLaughALot was the first, and he had not left me in stitches. Each time I opened an e-mail and followed up with the person's profile I was filled with an expectation so vast it flooded me. But each time I opened the profile I saw something in the photo or essays *so* unappealing, I felt left with no choice but to instantly pass.

LaughingGas: Do you want to meet and get a drink?

BlueEyes325: That's a very kind offer, LaughingGas, but I would at least like to talk before we set up—

LaughingGas: My next patient is numb, gotta go. E-mail me if you want.

"And that was it?" asked a stunned Brooke as she came out of character.

"That was it!"

But Jane continued reading.

"Listen to what he wrote in his 'Who Am I' thingy. 'I am comfortable wearing both casual clothing when walking on the beach and a tux when I go out to a formal event.'"

"Oh. You shouldn't have nixed him," said Fred. "You never would have had a fashion emergency. That's quite an accomplishment, you know. For a straight guy."

"Right," I chimed in. "Imagine my despair if I fell in love with someone who had to wear a tuxedo when we went to the beach and workout clothes to his cousin Sheila's wedding."

"But what if Cousin Sheila got married on the beach!" said Fred.

"Fashion emergency!" shouted Brooke and Jane, as we all laughed.

LaughingGas. I guess he was. He was just a regular laugh riot. Go know! Perhaps I had missed my golden opportunity. Speaking of—

"Oh dear!" said Fred, pointing to page seventeen and a picture of GoldenBoy, one leg up on a stool, wearing a suede vest and possessing a handlebar moustache. "He says it's his mission to become a champion of the one true God? What is that?"

"Keep reading," I told Fred, who continued to do so aloud.

GoldenBoy: BlueEyes, it's important to IM you first because I cannot ask you out unless I understand your position on the Messiah. Talk to me.

BlueEyes325: Sorry. I don't feel comfortable talking about the Messiah behind his back.

"Here's a switch," said Jane. "YouthToUseYa. 'I am really a twenty-five-year-old guy but advertise as forty-five to attract and develop a sexual relationship with a woman in her forties who knows her body and herself. I am a monogamous and sensual lover.' Hmm... What did you think, Kar?" she asked, having a younger, but not that much younger, younger husband.

"If the answer to where were you when John Lennon was shot is a fetus, it's not likely," I said. A twenty-year age difference in any direction had never worked for me. In my twenties when I met men in their forties who liked me just for that, I always felt a little sorry for them.

"So did you actually meet anyone?" asked Brooke.

"Well, two," I said. "Almost."

"And?"

"TexasTed, Soho software salesman. Said he had gals chasin' him like a runaway coyote. We had three dates and one kiss that got cut short after I ran my fingers through his hair and found them glued together! It was a rug. It was embarrassing. It was also sad, because Ted had fallen in love."

"With you?" asked Brooke.

"With Charlie. He wasn't into me, but he did want to spend a weekend with my dog. Offered to pick him up and take him round-trip in a cab. Said he'd bring him to Washington Square Park, a few outdoor cafes and then walk him around the city."

"Nice. Sounds more romantic than the dates you had," said Fred.

"Who was the almost?" asked Jane.

"Page twenty-two. I'll read me and Fred you can be—"

"PingPongPoet?" he yelped.

"The back story is that we were supposed to meet at 7:30 and I left him a message at 7:25 on his cell to tell him I was running ten minutes late."

"How's this?" asked Fred, changing his voice so Ping-PongPoet sounded like a nerd in drag.

PingPongPoet: hi

BlueEyes325: Hi.

PingPongPoet: looks like we missed each other last night

BlueEyes325: Seems so.

PingPongPoet: i guess you got there around 8?

BlueEyes325: No!

PingPongPoet: when?

BlueEyes325: My cell phone said 7:47, but it was 7:53 when I called you for the second time. I looked around a few minutes before calling. I had told you if I couldn't find you I would call, so it was surprising that not only didn't you have your phone on, you didn't even leave me a message to tell me you had left when you knew I was on my way.

PingPongPoet: it was on

BlueEyes325: Was it broken?

PingPongPoet: no. the signal didn't get through

BlueEyes325: But you got my messages?

PingPongPoet: yes

BlueEyes325: And there was no thought to leave a message back for me? Since you heard from me but I never heard from you until just now, it's my assumption you were a no-show.

PingPongPoet: i was there early and stayed till 7:50

BlueEyes325: That's doubtful.

PingPongPoet1: what were you late?

BlueEyes325: I don't understand the question.

PingPongPoet1: why were you late

BlueEyes325: Does it matter since I called to tell you I was on my way?

PingPongPoet: since we are talking about this...there are 2 sides...

BlueEyes325: There always are. So what went on from yours?

PingPongPoet: one is that you were late and one is that I didn't wait

PingPongPoet: long enough

PingPongPoet: so

BlueEyes325: I didn't leave you wondering. I called you. Twice. Yes, I was a little later than I said I'd be. The place was pretty far west and it took longer to walk from the subway.

PingPongPoet: you did leave me wondering

BlueEues325: About...?

PingPongPoet: how long for a blind date should a person wait?

PingPongPoet: you could have showed up in an hour.

BlueEyes325: You put yourself in that position by not answering your phone and not giving me any benefit of the doubt. I called and said I was on my way. I would wait half an hour without a call, with one I would know the person was showing up. You had two calls within half an hour. You just weren't there, were you?

PingPongPoet: you claimed it would be ten minutes late and it could have been an hour.

BlueEyes325: You know what—we're actually not talking about this at all. I hope your poetry has more insight and depth than this conversation. It's a waste of my time.

PingPongPoet: right...you waisted my time enough already

BlueEyes325: Good thing we didn't meet, it would have been a bigger waste of even more. See ya!

PingPongPoet: not likely

"How romantic," said Brooke. "He's horrible."

"Ten minutes late, fifteen...I've dated men who showed up a week later...when I was lucky," said Fred, as himself, jolted out of character.

"Can you imagine sitting through one of his poetry readings?" asked Brooke. "There's a night out for someone you'd really want to get back at."

"What's with the grammar? That's telling in itself," said Jane. "What's PingPongPoet?"

"His two favorite hobbies," I said.

"Oh, brother," said Brooke.

"I actually liked that," I admitted. "I love Ping-Pong and the poetry thing sounded sensitive and creative for a guy in real estate."

"His sister probably told him to do that," said Fred. "He could have been DiverDouchebag, or SkiShmuck, but his sister must have told him that PingPongPoet would get him more dates."

"More dates to ditch. He was a no-show. He was probably double-booked. Down the block on another J-Spot and if he didn't like her he'd have left to meet me. I'm lucky I didn't have to deal with him, but this whole online business is just dreadful, and one big dreadful waste of time."

"Maybe you're just culling more material, Little Lulu!" said Fred.

"Who's Little Lulu?" asked Brooke.

"Remember I told you about the solo show Fred thinks

I should do using all my *facockta* dating stories that have been breaking my heart?"

"Except that it's not broken, Karrie. It's still beating, and they're good stories. Besides, Lulu is the perpetrator, not the victim," Fred reminded.

"Well, I don't necessarily think that's been true," I said.

"Oh, *I* know who you mean!" Jane said raising her arm with such enthusiasm the long-sleeved satiny shirt dipped itself into the salsa. "Darn it! If I don't have Eve spitting up on me I do it myself.'"

"I still don't get it," said Brooke.

"Those plays…that German playwright…what's his name, again?" asked Jane as she reached into her bag and pulled out her cell.

"Wedekind," said Fred.

"I'm impressed," said Brooke. "You want me to get you some club soda?" she asked Jane, handing her a napkin.

"I'm impressed I can remember anything above toddler age these days. Dry cleaners tomorrow," Jane spoke into her cell, leaving a memo on her answering machine without missing a beat as the conversation moved on.

"*The Lulu Plays* were a series where Lulu was a protagonist that broke her lovers' hearts. The original femme fatale," said Fred.

"Right," I said. "That's me!"

"But this seemed to hold your interest," said Jane, pointing to the handout. "You had enough concentration, and desire I may add, to create a cast of characters and edit this little script with the PingPongPutz. Imagine if you turned that energy into Lulu."

Everyone liked Jane's remark. I could tell, because they all turned their heads to acknowledge Jane for the good comment before turning back to see what I'd say next. But

I was grateful the moment was intercepted when Ryan, MTW's artistic director, came over and joined us. His wild red hair was held together with a ponytail holder. Ryan, himself, was a holdover from the seventies.

"Great show, Freddy," he said, crouching down to join our circle. "Love that piece. You were great, man. Funny shit, Grennon." Eloquence wasn't his strength, but on the over-all he had pretty good taste.

"Thanks," said Fred, simply and humbly. For all Fred's camp, when it came to his work he was a dedicated actor who appreciated being taken seriously. "Meet the friends, Brooke Morgan and Jane Murphy." Both women extended their hands to Ryan for a quick shake hello.

"I know both of you," he said, eyeing my two beautiful women friends. "Those were very cool commercials you did, especially for a middle-American department store," he told Brooke, leaning in when he spoke. "Always wanted to meet the girl behind that big Spheres smile."

"How nice of you," said Brooke, deliberately brushing her blond bang off her face with her left hand while she spoke, allowing the dazzle of her diamond to dampen Ryan's hope. It did the trick, and Ryan turned his attention to Jane.

"And whatever happened to you on *One Breath to Take?* One episode you were having Casey's baby, the next time I tuned in the baby was behind bars for attempted murder of his mother. But he never went to trial and your body has yet to be found."

"Ryan, you think you have a little too much time on your hands during the day?" I said, not that I had a right to talk with *All My Problems!*

"Oh, yes, the world of daytime dilemmas," said Jane. "It got weird but my husband and I had a baby, I mean in real life, so it didn't really matter."

"Cool," said Ryan, turning to me to chat after striking out with both of my friends, having struck out with me a few years earlier. "Bummer about Tummy," he told me, "but for sure we've got you doing the one-act fest in the spring. Putting it together now." Ryan stood to leave. "Okay, everyone, *ciao!* Karrie, I'll call you." And he was off.

I immediately got up.

"You're going to tell him you can't do the one-acts because you're going to do your own show?" asked Fred.

"I'm going to get more food. Anyone want anything?"

"We want whatever you want, dahling," said Jane.

And I wanted one person, not a one-person show.

I had to get away from everyone. I could feel their eager eyes upon me. Take the initiative. Grab the bull by the horn. Like this was the ticket. If I had to stand alone in front of an audience dragging my dating stories through the muddy water it was going to feel like I had drowned.

People think being an actress is vulnerable, but you are just the vessel to give life to a character in a story of someone else's creation. Besides, if you didn't get the part someone else would. But they wanted me to stand alone on a stage and talk about how I was alone. Talk about vulnerability. It was one thing to do a show about not having a guy if, in real life, you really had one. I not only didn't have a guy, I didn't have an acting job either. I knew that was exactly why they wanted me to do the show, but it was also why I didn't want to do it.

My head felt like it would burst by the time I got home. My anxiety level was climbing. I needed something great to happen. Preferably before I went to sleep. It was twelve-thirty in the morning. From what I could see, there were no auditions in my apartment. I was tired but I couldn't go to bed. I looked over to the computer.

Oh no. Not now, I thought. It was too late to start with *that* now. But as bad it was, it was always something. A constant merry-go-round of men, and every time I thought I'd get off another ride was about to begin. I turned on my PC to reenter the Dating Olympics where I had finished last in the Online Competition.

Was I destined to arrive at my romantic future via a link online, or had destiny already gone ahead and enlarged someone's photo for the big picture? Forty days before a male child was conceived was an announcement of who he was to marry still made, or did someone in heaven just send out an e-mail?

My J-Spot mailbox was filled with three new messages. One from a man whom I would never write back, a second from a man I had not written back and a third. Three's the charm, they always say. I clicked to open the mail and hoped they were right.

To: BlueEyes325@jspot.com
From: Beyond@jspot.com
Subject: CONGRATULATIONS: You Hit The Right Spot!
Hi BlueEyes,
Finding myself in my law office working, again, last Sunday I thought it time I got a life.
I am new to dating in cyberspace and while I am finding the whole thing a bit daunting, after seeing your profile I thought maybe I should come here more often!
I'm sure you have many online admirers, but I hope after reading about me we can get in touch and be off.
Looking forward to hearing from you.
Beyond

As I waited for Beyond's profile to appear I felt surprised, again, to feel hopeful. The feeling was so nice I only hoped it would not be lost to disappointment in a matter of seconds, and that Beyond would not be beyond my approach.

There he was. A personal injury lawyer who lived on the Upper East Side, divorced, no children, athletic. Loved ethnic food, nature, theater and film and smart, funny women. With dark brown curls at the bottom of a hairline that receded, he wore glasses and seemed smart, like his well-written, witty essays. I didn't have any hunch of what it would be, but, finally, I had a desire to find out.

To:　　　　Beyond@jspot.com
From:　　　BlueEyes325@jspot.com
Subject:　Re: CONGRATULATIONS: You Hit The Right Spot!
Hi there, Beyond!
You have a nice writing style…a definite plus in the world of cyber-dating. And I liked your pictures, too!
Yes, I have an overflow of pursuers, but look forward to just one putting that to a much happier ending.
Write back.
BlueEyes

After my commercial audition the next day—it was for a new cable company that coaxed you into choosing them by keeping their customers locked in a bullpen in order to prove their rates would not go up—I skipped my workout to rush home to see if Beyond was within my reach.

To:　　　　BlueEyes325@jspot.com
From:　　　Beyond@jspot.com
Subject:　Re: CONGRATULATIONS: You Hit The Right Spot!
The Enigmatic BlueEyes,
What will I find beyond those baby blues? I have yet to meet a woman online who has confessed to a bevy of pursuers.

Am I probing? I do mean to...you have stirred my imagination.

By the way, I'm Edward Smith. What is your name? Are you comfortable corresponding through your personal e-mail address? If so, I will enclose mine.

Beyond

To: edward_smith@bslaw.com
From: KKline2@uh-oh-l.com
Subject: J-Spot

Hi Edward,

As the agent in *Tootsie* says, "I field offers!" And though I do receive my share of mail, it's not as much fun as you may think.

While we are both e-intrigued, in-person chemistry is a whole new ball game.

Don't you agree?

Karrie Kline

PS—Are you, perchance, related to my childhood friend Rachel Smith?

To: KKline2@uh-oh-l.com
From: edward_smith@bslaw.com
Subject: Re: J-Spot

The Intriguing Ms. Kline,

I think you are lovely, Karrie, and most likely out of my league, but may I call you? You will have to give me your number in order for me to do that...if, of course, you are willing.

Edward

PSS—My grandfather came over from Russia and had lost his birth certificate on the boat. When he arrived at Ellis Island he asked for an American name, hence Smith. But please send Rachel warm regards.

To: edward_smith@bslaw.com
From: KKline2@uh-oh-l.com
Subject: Re: J-Spot
212-555-4321

    I enjoyed waiting for Edward to call, knowing as I did that it would not be a very long wait.

Nine

Although frogs love rain, a factor that stimulates the frog to mate and to breed, torrential downpours should be avoided.

To: KKline2@uh-oh-l.com
From: edward_smith@bslaw.com
Subject: Rain

Turns out I'm not going to get home to change and so I'll be wearing my lawyer costume, though as I said you shouldn't hesitate to go as casual as you like.

To: edward_smith@bslaw.com
From: KKline2@uh-oh-l.com
Subject: Re: Rain

Do you think it will stop raining before our date? If not, can we pretend it's sunny?

To: KKline2@uh-oh-l.com
From: edward_smith@bslaw.com
Subject: Re: Rain

Karrie, I'm certain your smile will provide all the light and warmth I'll need.

On a less gooey note, I expect the company and the food to be quite good—the restaurant has the highest Zagat rating of Turkish cuisine in the city. However, based on Turkey's past behavior they might serve us but make us sit in the restaurant next door!

I hate to be cliché, but I can't resist, so here goes. How will I know you? What will you be wearing?

To: edward_smith@bslaw.com
From: KKline2@uh-oh-l.com
Subject: Re: Rain

I'm not sure. I was going to wear a linen skirt and pumps, but due to the storm I may need to change. Needless to say this is probably TMI...Too Much Information.

To: KKline2@uh-oh-l.com
From: edward_smith@bslaw.com
Subject: Re: Rain

What exactly are pumps while we're on the subject? I've never really understood what sort of shoes qualify as pumps, or where the term comes from. Would it be too much to ask you to come to dinner able to explain that to me?

To: edward_smith@bslaw.com
From: KKline2@uh-oh-l.com
Subject: Re: Rain

Rest assured, I will come prepared!

Dressed in a silk blouse, plaid pants, black boots, a trench coat and a black beret, I hailed a cab to take me uptown. I enclosed a folded umbrella and folded a printout into my bag about the history of women's footwear that illustrated dozens of styles, taking in all the possibilities. Doing the same, I rode up Broadway ready to meet my match.

I arrived a few minutes past eight to find Edward in the waiting area. In an immaculate dark gray suit and red power tie he was the picture of a respectable New York lawyer waiting for one of his personally injured clients. I considered tripping over a chair and falling, just to make him feel at home.

"Karrie?"

"Edward? Hi! Here," I said, handing him the envelope with the printout I had downloaded from the Internet. "I think you'll find everything you need to know about pumps and women's shoes in general," I said, smiling.

Though his big smile back was kind of held back, I noticed the monogrammed E.S. on the cuffs of his shirt because his handshake hello had lingered on.

"Thank you, Karrie," he said, slipping the envelope into that mysterious pocket sewn inside men's suits. "I'll review this later. Our table will be ready in a minute."

"Great."

Middle Eastern sounds and smells wafted through the curtained partition that divided the restaurant, and the waiting room from the dining room. We took our seats on the velveteen settee as I removed my raincoat, tucking the beret inside a pocket, and closing up my umbrella.

"I think it finally stopped," I said, looking at the umbrella to indicate the rain.

"I'll check these things for you, okay?"

I watched as his medium athletic self carried my stuff over to a woman dressed in a belly-dancing outfit at the coat check.

You read the essays of people online and they often share

a piece of themselves in the writing they would only share with someone they felt a sense of connection, or intimacy with. Just because you both respond to what you read does not mean you will be able to connect, or access that intimacy from each other. But no matter what you think, you do show up expecting. The sight, the smell, the sound, the feel of the two of you together—live and in person—almost obliterates all that was said and all that was read before.

If you could connect, that background would serve as a delicious subtext. But if you could not, it would be as if all the emotions behind all those words you both had written never even existed. Without an in-person connect, everything else gets deleted.

"You're having fun?" he asked when he returned.

"Yeah. I'm having fun. Are you?"

"It's too soon to tell," he said.

I laughed, thinking it was a joke, but I wasn't quite sure.

"We can show you to your table now."

I got up and followed the hostess while Edward walked behind and followed me. Our walk through the white gauzy curtains transported us not just out of the city, but out of the country into a new culture. The dimly lit room was tented. It was as if we had walked onto the set of *Ali Baba and the Forty Thieves.* Sheaths, scarves, gilded paintings and lanterns adorned the restaurant, the white linen tables lit up with white candles.

Edward ordered a bottle of Shiraz and a waiter dressed as a sultan put a feast of different spreads and salads before us.

"Complimentary, on the house," the sultan said to Edward, placing a round meat pie on the table and taking our order, or Edward's—I let him order for me—before moving on.

"Dig in," said Edward, cutting off a piece with his knife

to put on his plate. "I think you'll like this. Turkish pizza. It's called *lahmacun*."

"*Lahmacun*," I repeated. "It's good," I said after tasting the textured, tomatoey meat on the thin crust.

He lifted his goblet. "To meeting." We clicked our glasses and each took a drink. "You're beautiful," said Edward sincerely, and with a longing that almost seemed a bit sad.

"You're kidding." It was the last thing I thought he would say.

"You don't think so? I bet you already know that."

Oy vey, I thought. Here we go with the compliment that probably started downtown and has now made its way through Turkey.

"No, not that," I said. "Not that I don't...or that I do..." I brought my napkin up to my mouth as a polite way to check and see if my foot was dangling out of it. "Thank you, Edward. That's, that's nice. Just—"

"What?"

"Just that this...us, meeting this way, it's kind of...difficult. And I like you, but I feel like I can't find you," I confessed.

"So let me help you," said Edward, who after taking a drink and a breath proceeded to be delightful company, telling me the condensed but somewhat personal story of his life.

"Kate really didn't want to work. She just wanted to be a stay-at-home wife and mother," Edward said of his ex, as he cut into his lamb casserole. "The food here is very good," he said, approvingly. "You seem to be doing okay with that." Edward dipped his fork into my moussaka for a bite. "You mind?"

"Be my guest," I said, as I dipped my fork into his lamb.

"You can really eat," he said, chewing heartily.

"As opposed to what?"

"You really eat a lot for someone so slight. Where do you put it?"

"In here," I said, pointing to my brains.

I did eat a lot. At meals. And I didn't eat much between them, but I didn't want to discuss food. I wanted to hear more about Kate so I used food to steer the discussion back in the direction I wanted it to go.

"Did Kate have to watch her diet a lot when she was doing ballet?"

"Kate. Yes." Edward was back. "And she stopped watching when she stopped dancing. Good cook though. Anyway, after dancing she had to do something and she hated interior design and became bitter and a bit of a bore."

"Well," I began, wondering if that description was really more about him. "Sounds like she would have been a great mom," I said.

"I wanted an equal partner."

"A woman running your home and raising your kids is pretty equal, don't you think, Edward? I mean, it's a traditional setup, but I confess to being a pretty traditional girl myself."

"How? You're in your forties, you've never married, you live alone in Manhattan and you pursue a career in acting. How are you traditional?"

"Well, when it comes to the American Dream I don't believe in the white picket fence, but I do believe in the white picket co-op," I said. "I just think since we're different, men and women, and we're going to stay that way, the traditional roles work the best. But I don't believe in holding each other back. In the world of the white picket co-op you allow each person their dreams."

"We had our moments. One really nice thing about being married to a *shiksa* from Nebraska was always having a real

Christmas. But it's been four years and it's time to get on with my life. What about you, Karrie?"

By that point we had polished off a few more courses, ending with the baklava, while a Turkish belly practically danced her way right up the nostrils of Edward's nose. We decided to walk home, walking all the way down Broadway from Hundredth Street, as we told tales to entice and tales to entrap.

"I think you would be happier being married," said Edward, waiting for the light to change at Seventy-ninth, stepping in front of me to take the splash of a cab speeding down the street through the remaining puddles.

"So you are a traditional kind of guy, after all," I said of the sweet and chivalrous act.

"And look, he managed to miss me!" said Edward, smoothing his hands over his perfect suit that had miraculously remained dry. "Cabbie probably knew I'd sue him for damages," he said, seductively pulling me into him. "I'm very conservative, in general, but I do pay a lot of money for my suits."

"Let me feel the fabric." I ran my fingertips down his sleeve. "Nice," I said, as he reached for my hand.

Edward pulled me down on one of the benches on the little island in the middle of Broadway. He wrapped his hand around mine, running his fingertips over the top of my hand and under my palm. I looked down, watching the movement and the motion, jutting my head back to get a good look at his eyes.

"Ouch!" A sudden pain soared through my neck. It felt like I might have pulled something. "Wait a sec. It hurts."

Edward gently massaged my neck. It let go along with the rest of me.

"You might benefit from having a boyfriend," he whispered into my ear.

"Oh yeah? Of the traditional sect or the non?"

"You J-Spot girls need to know everything, don't you?" Edward said, and then he kissed me.

It was either romantic, or it wasn't. You either remembered the first time someone kissed you, or you didn't.

And that's what I thought about all night when I couldn't sleep because I was thinking about Edward. I liked him, but felt somewhat troubled. I couldn't quite put my finger on it, the troubled part, so I'd put it aside, placing it on the empty pillow next to mine so I could relive the untroubled kiss.

"I thought about you last night. Sent you an e-mail this morning," he said when he called the next day. I was happy to discover Edward had felt the same. "Did you get it?"

"I didn't even get up till an hour ago. And I didn't go online."

"Right. You live on actress time," said Edward, while I turned on my computer to see what Edward had written in his mail.

"What time is it on your lawyer watch?"

"I'm at work," he said. "Getting ready for a case. In fact, I came off the lawyer clock right now because I don't have any billable hours allotted for dating."

"You used them all up?" I asked, seeing that Edward had written me three e-mails starting at 8:11 that morning. By 10:59 he wrote he was on his way to work and left the number for me to call him there.

"I know you're a traditional type so you probably don't like to call men. Is that correct?"

"Guilty as charged. Not at the beginning. But I do like to call back," I said, calculating that Edward had told me over dinner that he had found himself in his office thinking he needed to get a life on a Sunday. Today, a Saturday, had also found him at work. I did the math and it added up to the possibility that he could be the type that worked seven days a week.

"But you didn't call me back," said Edward.

"Do you want to hang up and I will?"

"Do you want to go out later instead?"

"Okay."

"Then I'll call you," he said, and hung up.

"Something is off," I told Jane two weeks later on a shopping jaunt to an opening of a new children's store in my neighborhood Janey thought worth the trek into the city. "This is cute," I said, holding up a little orange-and-white poncho that was scaled down to fit Eve, who was playing in the supervised play area of the store.

"Is he insecure? He sounds insecure," said Jane, chasing after Eve, who was chasing an inflatable Nemo so she could hold the poncho against her to see if it would fit.

"Kind of insecure, but who isn't? Self-contained. Sort of abrupt, overly sensitive. Interesting. Quick. Very smart. Uh—sexy."

"But?" asked Jane.

"I don't exactly know yet and I'm afraid I'll find out. I like him. It's not like he's a prince and I could care less. But I need him to be a good guy. You know…a good frog."

"So you do like him. I haven't heard you like anyone in a while. That's a good thing, isn't it, Kar?"

"It could be. It really could. Let's hope so," I said.

It most definitely felt like it was when Edward and I sat entwined in the movies that night. Throughout the film his tantalizing, feathery touch kept me on the edge of my seat. It found its way up my arm, under my neck and around my collarbone before moving down my bare leg back up under my skirt and along the inside of my thigh.

When the lights came back on, I felt a dozen eyes on us of women whose seats surrounded ours. But I moved closer to Edward, not caring what anyone thought or saw, hungry to live my own movie moment. Loving the feel of Edward and I close, him breathing his kiss into mine, lips to lips, light, gentle, entrancing.

I wished that I could make something along the lines of a public service announcement telling the women if I could be sitting there tonight with Edward—Edward who I didn't even know two weeks ago, Edward who I had met *online*—then indeed, anything *was* possible.

A few nights later, Fred and I were leaving MTW when my cell phone rang and it was him. Still at work, a little after nine, just calling to say hi. It was the first time he called me directly on my cell.

"So what does the stalker want now?" asked Fred, holding open the door on the lobby level as we left the building, walking out into the somewhat chilly night air. It was the end of September, and the first night you felt as if it had fallen into autumn. Fred was wearing a hooded sweatshirt, and I had gone all out, grabbing a denim jacket to put on over a cotton sweater.

"He hung up," I told Fred as we walked towards Ninth Avenue.

Every day from the get-go I'd have messages on my machine that said, "It's Edward, just calling to say hi." I was happy he was calling, but found it confusing when I called back and he had to go. He wouldn't talk. He just wanted to say hi.

"Hey, where's a Citibank, Fred? I don't think I have more than a ten in my wallet," I said, walking to where I thought I had seen an ATM. "He got a phone call from L.A. It's still business hours there."

"Maybe he's a workaholic because he keeps the same hours as businesses everywhere. Global warning, Missy!" said Fred, who was happy I felt chemistry, but hoped I heeded the message he felt the phone calls had signaled.

"Maybe he——" My phone rang. "Excuse me," I said to Fred. "Yes, Edward," I spoke into the phone, recognizing the number, not needing to recognize the voice.

"Meet me tonight. Now. At a hotel."

"What happened?" asked Fred, who could not hear what Edward had said but heard my exhale, as it rushed through my body and out my mouth when I heard Edward's words. Meet him at a hotel? We weren't even lovers. But it sounded *so* romantic.

I looked over to Fred. Okay, I did have doubts. Should I clear them up before we became lovers? Yes. But what if I couldn't? I knew. Maybe the doubts would get cleared up in bed *after* we became lovers! Gee, I missed the days when I could talk myself into that one. I thought of Edward's tantalizing touch. Well, until it felt clear I would have to pass on being lovers. And, I would. Just not in this lifetime.

"Don't do anything I wouldn't do," shrieked Fred as I left him flat, ducking into the first available cab. "And that's not much!"

The taxi shot across Times Square to the Algonquin, the legendary hotel where Dorothy Parker downed martinis at the Round Table; her romantic angst giving way to great literature. In her day if a woman my age was single she was considered a spinster. And if she was single and sexual she was considered a whore. What would Dorothy have thought of women now?

When it came to men I didn't even know what I thought of us. Aside from the workplace, I had to wonder how many gains we had really made since the time of "liberation." Having come of age during the woman's movement I had never known any difference. But I always wonder what it was really like *before*. And though our meet was for no more than a drink, as we sipped Courvoisier tucked away in the corner of the Blue Bar, I felt grateful to Ms. Parker for her part in paving the way.

"Dorothy could have been the perfect woman for me," said Edward. "She was brilliant, independent, a writer, made a nice living." He listed Dorothy's positive qualities with confidence. His. He had me where he wanted me. Relaxed, Edward kissed me ever so slightly as he spoke.

"She also wrote *A Telephone Call*, so just keep that in mind next time you get on my case about the calling thing," I murmured as I ever so slightly kissed him back.

"God, I like you, Karrie!" Edward practically declared, pulling me in close, excited. "Yes, the girl in it waits and waits and you never know if he calls her or not. She should have just called him instead of waiting."

"Somehow it doesn't work that way."

"Sure it does," insisted Edward.

I didn't answer, hoping never to find out that I was right and he was wrong. In a new relationship when it came to calling, men called you when they wanted to. And didn't, when they didn't. Were there exceptions? You bet. Could you call them? Absolutely. In the end would it make a difference? Nope! But you could always pretend that it did.

"If she wrote that piece now the girl wouldn't just be sitting by the phone. She'd be checking her machine, checking e-mail, calling voice mail, looking up the missed messages on her cell phone…"

"Going through the list of caller IDs," said Edward. "I don't even use an answering machine at home. I just review the caller IDs."

"I'm glad you told me that. Now I know I can never call you and hang up."

"You don't do that? You do that?"

"I used to. I just stopped."

I leaned back in my chair wishing we were in a room upstairs.

"Tell me what you're thinking."

"I bet that you can actually guess," I said, leaning back, far back, my back up against the wall.

"I want to feel you," said Edward, his voice dissolving softly in my ear. "I haven't behaved like this in…" He suddenly jumped. "Hey. I'm a lawyer in a public place."

"Prove it," I said, sitting up. "Show me your briefs!"

"You…" Edward gazed into my eyes. "This is great. Hey, how would you like to go for a ride in the country and see the leaves change?" Edward paused. "Maybe we shouldn't plan dates ahead. Maybe we should do one at a time."

"One date at a time," I said, loving what seemed to lie ahead. "Maybe you can show me where you grew up? Do you have family left in Pennsylvania?"

"My brother's in New Rochelle, but I don't really ever see him."

"Oh. Are your parents still in Atlanta?"

"I don't have much to do with my parents," Edward said, pulling back from me. "I don't like them much," he said, as I watched him break away and retreat.

It felt as if I had just been cut because Edward's comment slayed me. There are reasons, sometimes good ones why someone would choose not to be around their family. But certainly by this point in life there needed to be a real understanding of that wheel. It not only informed who we were, but how we would spin off into other relationships, especially intimate ones. In my travels I had learned that when a man I was dating shared information like that, *like that,* there'd always been something fishy at the bottom of the pond.

"Oh," I said, taking it all in. Wanting to make Edward comfortable enough to talk to me without him feeling pressured. In what I hoped was a gentle voice I asked, "Did something happen?"

"No."

Perhaps if I told him about my family he'd relax? After all, my father had run away to join the circus and become a clown. Whatever went on with his family, that piece of info could surely help to put him at ease.

"Let's drop it," he said, on the stern side. "There's no reason now to discuss families." Then seeing the look on my face, Edward hugged me. "Come on…." he said, cajoling. "It's just a few weeks. We just met."

"Okay," I said, my body now feeling somewhat stiffer next to his. Perhaps he had what he considered a shocking story, and only shared if he came to trust someone. I would give him the benefit of the doubt. I had to. I wanted this to go further.

"How are you getting home?" asked Edward, having other ideas. "Would you like me to treat you to a cab? I'm happy to do that. It's getting late and I'll worry about you."

I could see the air gush out of me and zip through the Blue Bar as I watched it all collapse. What had just happened? Was the night now over? Was everything?

"I'm not ready to go," said Edward, as if he had read my mind. He pointed to his unfinished drink. "I was simply thinking ahead. For you."

I smiled while I looked at my watch. It was just a few minutes past ten. I didn't want to go looking for a cash machine tonight and I had spent my money on the cab over, but I did have a MetroCard. If I left within the hour it would not be that late and I could just get the bus uptown. I loved that Edward felt concern for me and would treat me to a cab. But he had made such a fuss about independent women, equal partners and now all this stuff with family. I thought it best, tonight, to fend for myself.

"As long as you're sure," he said, when I thanked him but said it wasn't necessary. "It's not a problem for me."

We found our way back to each other as we talked and talked. Edward could not understand how I could have made a creative choice that had kept my funds limited. His income was ten times mine. But he was drawn to the passion of my choice, as I was drawn to the steady motivation of his.

"But how do you live?" asked Edward, the creativity applied to my accounting lost on him.

"I live well, but I cut corners. Cooking instead of ordering in, half-price tickets instead of full, buses instead of cabs," I said, the words suddenly serving as a cue to glance at my watch. I had to look twice. I couldn't believe it was coming up on midnight. We had found our way back and lost track of the time.

I wasn't going to ask Edward to walk me to an ATM. The thought of waiting for a bus at this hour when they came every thirty minutes was unappealing. I had an early audition, I had to walk Charlie and I suddenly felt very, very tired.

"What's the matter, Karrie? Did something just happen?"

"Nothing."

"Tell me. You can tell me," he said. "Did I do something to upset you?"

"No. Not at all. I'm embarrassed to tell you." And that, of course, had paved the way for telling.

"So…?" asked Edward, seductively, like I would ask to take him home.

I ran my finger up the side of his sleeve.

"You generously offered to treat me to a cab earlier and that made me feel very good. But I felt a little awkward to say yes, and… Well, I didn't leave when I should have and now it's late to wait for the bus, and I didn't get to the bank

earlier so I don't actually have enough cash on me for a cab."
I was hoping he would interrupt me, I felt vulnerable and
not in the good way. "So now I wonder if it's not too late
to take you up on your offer? I really did appreciate it before, Edward. It warmed my heart and I felt…nice. You
know, taken care of."

Edward looked at me for what seemed like an eternity
before he spoke. And when he did he wasn't speaking to
me. It was as if I was receiving the words that belonged to
other people, other women, other family members and
other situations. But my words were the ones to set Edward
off, and when his came out they stung.

"I like you, Karrie, but I don't need another person in my
life to take care of. It was manipulative of you to refuse me
and say no and then say yes. Did you want me to fight you?
Did you want me to beg you to take a cab? It felt coy, demanding and it reeked of Jappy."

Edward got up, indicating with his hands that he would
be back, and I sat there shocked while Edward walked away.
I thought I should leave, but instead I waited. The troubled
part had been revealed and I waited for Edward because I
did not have the desire to go.

Why Edward, who liked me, had become hostile was
something I didn't know. Why I would want to stick around
and find out was probably the bigger question. But having
that desire was enough for me to see it through. I'd find out
more in time. But here was a chance to think about me. So
I stayed and I thought while I waited for Edward.

It was new for me to be called a JAP. I wasn't a *shiksa*. I
guess I had to be something, but I did not know any Jewish American Princesses whose fathers were clowns.

Had I been manipulative? I didn't feel I was, but Edward
had felt differently. I had thought he'd feel pleased I did not
want to take advantage of him. But it created other feel-

ings. Who did Edward have to take care of? Who made him feel obligated, manipulated and used? Would he ever tell me? Could he? Would he even call again? Just to say hi?

He returned. Sheepish and embarrassed as he walked to the table, Edward grabbed my hand to bring me into the lobby and out the door. If there was a high road leading out of the hotel it seemed we both hoped to take it.

"Look, I did not in any way mean to make you feel manipulated and for that I do apologize. I guess—"

Edward stopped and faced me. He made a motion with his thumb and forefinger that zipped up his lips. He twisted his fingers like he had turned a lock, and then he threw away the key.

"Finished," he said, walking out to the deserted midtown street and hailing a cab. "Okay," he said when it pulled up.

"Okay, then, Edward, 'night," I said, walking away.

He pulled on my arm, pulling me back.

"It's for you, get in," he said, opening the door to put me in the cab.

"Huh?"

"Here," said Edward, shoving a ten-dollar bill into my hand, guiding me into the backseat and closing the door.

Looking at each other through the opened window I mouthed the words thank you. His eyes were intent on mine, and his lips caught the last syllable in a quick kiss. I didn't move, unwilling to do anything that might be perceived as coy.

It was midnight and the spell had been broken. I hardly felt like a princess, Jewish American or other. And regardless of Edward's frog-prince potential, I felt I was leaving him less than enchanted. He stood waving as we drove away. It was midnight and I had to get home. I wanted to get there and fast, as I feared any minute my coach might turn back to a pumpkin.

Ten

Touch, the most intimate and up close of all the frogs' sensory input, is transmitted directly into the senses.

It stopped. Time. Space. The room and the world. All that was left was his touch. Full. Elongated. Stretched out and suspended. Like a soft wave, rolling towards me, into me, and through. And when finally, it reached me, I gasped.

I had been sleeping. I had fallen asleep inside the curve of Edward. His muscular arms around, Edward behind. Me sewn inside, floating like a raft. Him holding on for dear life.

How long had we been sleeping? How long since we had made our bed and loved in it? An hour or two? Four, perhaps, five? We had rolled over and in, my head falling, my hair combing his chest. His hands reaching to reach down, between. Soft strokes, hot and warm, finding the middle, the middle of me in the middle of the night and then… there…the touch.

"Aghhh…"

To soar and be still.

I wanted to touch. Back. I tried to lift my hand, but a languid attempt kept it hidden.

"Shhhhh," he whispered. "You deserve this pleasure, Karrie. Take," he said and continued to give.

I did. But I did not just take. I relished, I responded, I swirled, I rode, I gave myself over. I flew.

We fell back to sleep.

In the morning I awoke first, surprised at what I felt when I felt Edward next to me. Surprised how much I wanted to give to him the same way I had taken before. He was not yet awake, but he was ready.

I kissed his lips and then brushed mine across his cheek, down his back and back on down, down, down and under. I took him, taking him in, and while I did I felt his hands on my head. Pulling me over him by my hair, setting me down, and setting us off. Like a top. Spinning, gaining momentum, swerving. Whirling into a quiet frenzy that peaked, topped and toppled over, giving way to a quiet collapse. An assortment of sparklers emblazoning the bed before they would subside.

"I think you're my sexual soul mate," Edward said when he spoke. I was lying next to him thinking about nothing, my skin still pulsating, enjoying the heat. "I have never felt anything like this before. This is amazing."

"I know, neither have I," I said, turning into Edward. "How did we get here? Let's stay. I like it." I waited. "I love this."

"Me, too."

"And…" I started.

Silence.

"And, you, Edward, I love being with you."

"Good," he said, but said no more. Until after more talk and more touch he said he had to get up and go to work.

"It's Sunday. And it's just…" I looked at the clock. The red neon numbers flipped from one to the next like enemies in a line up. "11:35. Let me cook breakfast," I said, wishing we could stay in bed, shower, get the *Times* and read it across the table from each other at a cafe on Columbus over Bloody Marys, Eggs Benedict and scones.

"I know you like to have a date in the bag," Edward stated.

He was leaving. His body out the door while his hands stayed behind, moving themselves up my back and over my chest. He kissed me twice and told me he'd call.

When I had gotten home from the Algonquin that night there was a conciliatory message from Edward waiting on my machine. It was clear he had not wanted the wrong turn we had taken to change the course of where we could be headed. And good or bad, neither had I.

"I can't stop thinking about you," said Edward on the phone, calling me from work. He continued to call every day. "Just the sound of your voice." He lowered his. "God, it makes me crazy!"

"I know," I said, or do confess I purred back into the phone like a kitten as I responded to Edward's verbal strokes. "You get to me, too, Edward. You got me."

"You got me…you have me… You," he said when we were together. He said with breath into my ear as he leaned over, parting my legs, opening me while opening me up. "This is for me, right?"

"For you. Just for you. Only you."

It was. It could not be for anyone but him because he had been the one to find it. Others had searched, but Edward knew just where to look.

"I can't believe the actress likes me. Why me?" Edward told me he had asked his friend Lynn, a songwriter, as he pondered his good fortune.

"And why me?" I asked back, a talk we continued to have.

Over the empanadas, asking each other the same question. Trading admirations over tandoori chicken. Asking on the street, under the umbrella of a Sabrett hot-dog stand. Wondering again, as his foot slid out from his shoe, up my leg and under my dress, under a table of stuffed shells and whole shrimp. Still asking in my bed, high on each other and a bottle of wine.

"I haven't heard from you, Karrie." Millie's voice sounded concerned on the answering machine when I played my messages the following day, after Edward had gone. "I know if something was wrong you'd call, but call me when you get this. I want to hear your voice. It's Mommy."

"I'm glad you have someone," Millie said when we spoke.

"We have great chemistry," I told my mother, and while it might have been too much information to give a mom, it was what I knew for sure I had.

"So it's going well?" asked Jane, with whom I hadn't spoken in weeks, certainly more than a month, not since the day in the clothing store.

"Yes."

"No more sleepless nights?" she asked.

"Better," I answered.

I wished I had talked to her the week before. The week before I would have given Jane a different answer, a happier one, because today when Jane had called I jumped. I picked up the phone, it ringing classic Edward time, and my heart dropped down to my toes when instead of his voice I heard hers.

"So the stalker hasn't called for a few days," said Fred at dinner that night when I told him I hadn't heard from Edward. I looked at the table next to us and saw what appeared to be a real couple eating together, one that wouldn't have to worry after they said goodbye whether or not there would be another hello.

"No."

"Maybe he's just busy. Maybe he's working," said Fred.

"He's always working and he was always calling. No, something has shifted. Something's not good."

Edward had broken a date because he had to work, but he wouldn't reschedule. His tone was brief, off-putting. He would not talk to me and he would not stay on the phone. All he would do was say he would call. I chose to take him at his word. His word turned into a week, without one. I could not call him now. Perhaps some other woman could, but I could not, and I didn't know how to manage my feelings.

I sat still on a chair in the kitchen while, inside me, everything was in motion. The quiet eating me alive. I had to get out and I had to go. So I left the apartment and walked. I walked the streets until I found myself standing outside a neighborhood community center. There were tons of people standing outside. I walked down the steps to peek in, but when I went to open the door I practically shrieked when the hand of a goblin reached over my head and stopped me.

"Boo!" he said, scaring the bejesus out of me! "Happy Halloween! Wanna dance?"

I threw off my coat and my pointy black shoes. Shoes, whose heels were too high for walking, let alone dancing. I wanted to join in. Jubilant was the only word to describe it. I wove in and out of the crowd until someone picked up my hand to include me in a circle. Round and round we danced past faces of all ages. Faces masked by scary costumes, but bodies that were dancing happy.

The two of us became four, six, eight, as a woman grabbed my other hand and others grabbed hers. Our line was wild across the floor, shooting through the crowd, me barefoot and free. I was free-falling and it felt good. So good the feelings had replaced thinking, and I forgot about Edward.

The music halted and the dance ended, sending me home. Home to be haunted by another sleepless night, greeting morning with the familiar anxious feeling, hoping it would be put to rest when the phone rang. And this time when I answered it was.

"You didn't call me all week," said Edward, disarmingly putting me on the offensive.

"You canceled our date and wouldn't reschedule and you told me you would call me, so I waited. I'm very literal, Edward."

"Why did you wait? Why didn't you call me? What if I never called you, then what?" He paused. "You never would have called me, would you? It would be over because you're such a girl you just wouldn't call."

Later, when we were together we knew we'd lost more than an hour when we turned back the clock. And still later, when it turned dark too quickly, we dragged ourselves out of bed to get something to eat. After the lust, after the promises of more, and after things between us had changed and changed into something better. I could see Edward felt the unspoken test he had put me through had brought about the results he desired. So he asked if, now, I would call. Call him first. I did.

I did. And as the weeks rolled by, he did not.

"What time is it?" he mumbled into the phone, groggy. Still asleep when he answered.

"Six thirty," I said, waiting until 6:30, until the first glimpse of light to call Edward, who had not called to wish me a happy Thanksgiving, and now, the following week, had not even called me back.

Edward, whose plans to see me would now be made closer to the last minute. And though in his last minute with me he would still allow his touch to linger, he was quickly out the door. Not available for more than a quick cup of coffee, traveling very, very light. Letting go of everything, unwilling to be weighted down, it becoming way too heavy for him to make a date in advance, let alone have to carry it around for any length of time in a bag.

"Stop that," he had practically cried out at dinner when the salad we had decided to share had not been split in the kitchen, and I dished half of it onto his plate before putting the rest on mine.

"What did I do?" I asked, looking around the restaurant to see if anyone heard.

"Don't ever serve me." He grimaced. "It reminds me of my mother."

"How?" I asked, a big clue to Edward landing in my lap. But he would not talk. He ate in silence, while I'm sure his stomach churned.

The only good times left were in bed. The communication potent only there, the language spoken in bed the one we both understood. It made it even more powerful, and ultimately more painful. In the light of day he shut down as quickly as the door that closed behind him, resistant to discuss what felt crippling, disinterested to make any acquaintance with my darker side while running as fast as he could from his.

Time was the culprit. Edward and I were no longer new, and the time that had passed required a more intimate reality to set in. And while it was practically impossible to locate the trust to find a friendship, the wanting never wavered.

To: edward_smith@bslaw.com
From: KKline2@uh-oh-l.com
Subject: To dip or not to dip?
Christmas came a little early at My Theater Workshop with today's holiday bake-off. My hot artichoke dip won Best Ap-

petizer, and my prize is two tickets to *Abandoned*, that play, off-Broadway, you wanted to see.

I know how you enjoy theater and hearing about the growth of my illustrious career.

To: KKline2@uh-oh-l.com
From: edward_smith@bslaw.com
Subject: Re: To dip or not to dip?
I have always, always said that your dip was hot.

To: edward_smith@bslaw.com
From: KKline2@uh-oh-l.com
Subject: Re:To dip or not to dip?
Always, always hot, but seems not enticing enough to devour.

Loss of appetite? Dieting? Full from junk food? Attention Dip Disorder? Too spicy, better eating bland? Maybe *too* good, and can only indulge on occasion?

Should dip be kept warm in oven? Perhaps only delicious to dream of, tucked away in fridge where others can taste, then served with a slight chill.

Cravings; need to eat well and often. Willing to experiment with recipe.

Please advise.

To: KKline2@uh-oh-l.com
From: edward_smith@bslaw.com
Subject: Re: To dip or not to dip?
Wear a slip. With nothing underneath.

Edward walked into my apartment and lifted me above our problems. He carried me into my room, awash in candlelight and anticipation. Pulling down the straps of the slip, the silk riding up with his hands, getting closer, coming near, laying me down on my bed. Ready to dip in.

"Don't look at me like that," he said the next morning when it was time for him to go. "It was a great night, Karrie, let it go. You don't know how to let things go. That's a problem of yours, do you know that?" he said, as if the emotional problems might vanish, if only I could let them go.

"I'm only asking questions. I want to know you, for you to know me. I haven't learned anything more about who you are since the third date."

"We're at that point where you want what you want, and I want what I want."

"So what do you want?"

"I want you to let it go," he said, and he was gone.

The night before we went to the play, Edward called to invite me to a party afterward at his friend Lynn's. However, the triumph of being introduced to his close friend was wiped out when Edward proceeded to tell me that *Abandoned* would be one of the last social engagements he would be able to plan with me for some time.

"What exactly does that mean?" I asked, knowing I should call it. My call, the one to end it, and I should call it over now.

"It means just that and nothing more."

I was watching my self-esteem, power and all that crap fly out the window because I was unwilling to do it when it wasn't what I wanted.

"I am asking you to be a friend and talk to me," I pleaded to deaf ears, angry at myself as I dug into Edward, searching for the nonexistent buried treasure. Knowing all the while *Abandoned* would only be a prelude to what was going to happen, and the actress in me had made the choice to play out the scene.

It was a night like any other. Edward could not keep his

hands off me. His touch served as a firewall blocking the messages that pleaded with me to stop, and I ignored the pop-ups that tried to get through to my brain. We sat close in an engaging tête-à-tête at the party. Lynn was a gracious hostess, charming as she sang her songs before coaxing me to sing along.

"Edward will be so impressed," she said.

After my plaintive solo rendition of "Moon River," Edward—dutifully impressed—and I left for home.

It was raining. Hard. Cold, dark, hard rain. We walked for blocks and blocks before it became remotely possible to even try to hail a cab. We rode uptown in silence, two drenched drifters after the same rainbow's end; the dream maker successfully breaking my heart. Edward paid the driver before we walked into my apartment. Then I left to walk my dog. Coming back I found Edward undressed in my bed. I took off my clothes and joined him.

It all felt the same as Edward told me how beautiful I was and how much he had wanted to make love to me at the party all the time we were sitting on the club chair by the side of the radiator. I allowed Edward's words and Edward to fill me up because I wanted to get full. Very full. So full I wouldn't be hungry again for a very long time. Because even I could no longer pretend, when Edward left in the morning and told me he would call.

Eleven

A female frog finds her mate by answering a frog's mating call.

My aunt Cookie and uncle Sy became engaged three weeks after they met. They married three months after that. They started a life together in the same time frame mine often felt like it just ended. I never understood why three months was significant in the dating arena. But it seemed when it hit that time, it was often the tendency for the man you were dating to vanish like a cloud.

Blessed with a window seat, I stared out at the sky. The plane plowed through clouds that were bold and beautiful before they disappeared, and I calculated that my last date with Edward was practically three months to the day we had met. It made me think about the lecture I attended last week for single women in Manhattan to find out what they were doing that drove the men away.

"What happens at three months, ladies?" the female speaker asked from the podium, intending to teach women to take responsibility for their lives without betting on the prince.

I thought it safe to say I'd never bet on the prince. I couldn't because I didn't believe in him. Besides, he wasn't all that interesting. Even in fairy tales, with his chiseled perfect looks he was without personality or humor. But the frog was funny. The comic relief, quirky and cute. The frog wasn't all bad; he just had to be good for you.

"Is three months the first time he doesn't bring you flowers, and instead of letting it go you get in a huff? Is that the first time he wants to kick back and says he'll wait till the weekend to see you, and instead of being easygoing you demand he see you before?"

I wanted to be a woman torn up over no tulips and dateless Tuesdays. To me, the inability to plan another social engagement for an undetermined amount of time did not say kick back, it said back off.

"Is the familiar disappointment of men what you are in love with the most? Do you keep choosing the wrong men so you don't have to end up with them, ladies?"

It was easy to blame both the frogs and the frogettes! But there was something else. Something she wasn't addressing. There was no reason to jump from lily pad to lily pad *that* fast if you had made a substantial connection. She was making the assumption a relationship started because both people really wanted to be in one, and I didn't believe that was necessarily true.

"At three months you still need to have your own life. You need to have your own plans. You always do."

I agreed with her there. Okay. So you bought and decorated your apartment, you took that solo vacation. You threw yourself a birthday party and would see a Saturday night movie alone. What then?

"Learn to have a man be just one part of your life. You have a full life. Live your life and *he'll* pursue you. Let *him* call."

I left. Grabbing my coat and purse I got up and fled the cubicle-sized lecture room so I could be free to think outside that box. Love was not formulaic, I insisted to myself, breathing fresh air when I got outside, filling up with relief and exhaling some of the blame I felt had been laid on women.

I walked west across Fourteenth Street, the boom boxes blasting. At Seventh Avenue a young Hispanic man handed me a flier for bridal gowns starting at $39.95. As I stuffed it in my pocket it occurred to me that the problem was not what happened when it got to be three months. The problem was what had *not* happened during them. My God, had I figured something out?

During those three months a man was either courting a woman with intention—he wanted a relationship and his actions said so—or he was dating her, without.

Bear in mind he could be dating her with intention; the intention to date in order to have steady evenings out, companionship and sex. Still, when it hit three months something would intrinsically shift. Something that said to both parties it needed to become something more emotionally connected to continue. To become something you could count on. And if it didn't start out with relationship intention, at three months, even if he was just kicking back, it would not kick in.

Note: It's fair to say that women do that, too.

I thought about Edward. Aside from never e-mailing back in the first place, once involved I didn't know how I could have managed it better. I supposed if you knew you felt legitimately interested, the trick would be to understand his intentions while keeping the wings on yours open and, at the same time, self-protective. Hats off to anyone who can pull off that trick!

We landed. Deplaning with my new theory tucked inside the shopping bag of gifts, I thought there was nothing like going home for the holidays to make a breakup feel a little better and a whole lot worse. I tried to wheel the disappointment of this unromantic holiday season out of the airport with my luggage, and allow myself to be soothed by the balmy West Palm air. I didn't know whether or not the change would be good for me, but I knew it would be different.

"Hello." Millie jumped out of her sparkling clean car, unzipping the jacket on her pistachio-green warm-up suit, her face all lit up. "Did you have a good flight? Did you eat anything? Come here, let me hold you," she said, bypassing me and walking, no running, directly to Charlie while I popped open the trunk and put my stuff in the car.

"Hi, Ma," I said, leaning in to give her a kiss.

"You were a good boy under the seat?" she said, holding Charlie, who gave Millie a big lick hello. "Did you ask them?"

"Yeah, I asked," I said while I buckled my seat belt, sticking a piece of Charlie under the strap. "They made me pay for him and he got his own confirmation code but they won't give him miles. I said my dog is a frequent flier, but they only give miles to the pets that go in cargo."

"Oh, no," Millie said, giving Charlie a little pat as we drove past the palm trees and onto the main drag. "My grand-dog doesn't travel in cargo."

I wondered what life would have been like if I had married young and given my mother a two-legged grandchild. If I had had a life more like hers. Whenever I came to Florida and spent time with the people in my mom's retirement community, I was struck by the different steps in the mating dance of the post World War II world.

"I made *flanken* with the pea soup like you like," Millie told me when we stopped at a red light. I looked out the window and noticed there was no one out walking on the street. "Tomorrow, if you want, I'll take you shopping and at night Aunt Cookie invited us for dinner. Cookie and Sy have a big anniversary coming up, you know."

I knew. I couldn't even imagine. But their courtship completely proved my point. Plus it was one of my all-time favorite stories.

In August of 1954, Sy Gottlieb took his maroon Pontiac sedan for a ride up to the Catskills to spend a weekend in the Jewish Alps. He was a wiry, athletic guy, living at home in the borough of Brooklyn, and gainfully employed after the war as a salesman for a growing medical supply company. Everything was on track except for the one small detail of a wife. Handsome but shy, Sy did not go out too often. A few months back there was the prospect of a blind date, but that had been put on hold. Seymour's would-be match had an older unmarried sister, and under no circumstances was the younger sibling to be married off first.

Every Saturday, Grandma Rose and Grandpa Lou had game night with a handful of couples from the neighborhood. They took turns playing in each couple's house, also taking turns hosting the evening with freshly brewed percolated coffee and home-baked cake. The men played gin rummy in the kitchens; the women occupied the living rooms playing Mah-Jongg. Everyone played and talked. The men only talked about the game, but the women talked about everything else.

"So, Rose, what's with Seymour?" asked Hannah, picking up a tile she hoped would be a good one and discarding another. "Five crack," she said, putting the patterned tile face up in the center of the bridge table.

"What could be? He goes to work, he's healthy. Who

knows what else? He's secretive. Not like Millie," said Rose, picking up a tile and slipping it next to another on her green rack before discarding one to complete her turn. "Soap," she said, placing the tile with the picture of a white dragon on the table. Then she turned to look at Emma. "Go."

"Don't rush me," said Emma, taking her sweet time to pick before even deciding what to discard. "Go. You're always telling everyone but Hannah, go."

"Well you don't go fast enough. Go," repeated Rose.

"I'll go when I go," said Emma, pausing long enough to take a drag on her Camel cigarette. Emma inhaled as she studied the tiles on her rack. Slowly and deliberately she blew out the smoke, picking up one tile, changing her mind, and then exchanging it for another. "Okay. Now I'll go," she said, ready to discard. "Two bam."

Everyone looked on with great annoyance as the tile with the blue bamboo sticks finally landed. Next was Frieda, who made an announcement before starting her turn.

"I have news. News that was bad that now is good," she said, everyone's curiosity peaked while Frieda picked.

Frieda was a very quiet player, but Frieda was a shark. In addition to whatever it was she had to say, it was also possible Frieda was set, and might have picked the one tile she needed to make Mah-Jongg.

"I don't want to hear no bad news," said Rose, who was highly competitive and always wanted to win.

Every week the biggest winner was omitted from having to contribute money to the *pushke*. Both the men's and women's games collected money, and they saved until there was enough for everyone to go out for a celebratory dinner.

"Don't worry, this won't hurt," said Frieda. "I can finally introduce your Seymour to my neighbor's daughter. Her sister, Evelyn, *kaynahora,* just got engaged. Mah-Jongg!" she said, flipping over the tiles to show her winning hand.

Frieda collected her winning chips from the other players. Each colored chip had a hole in its center in order to slip through one of the four posts attached to the side of each rack. With her fleshy fingers Frieda slipped the chips through the appropriate posts, watching her winnings stack up.

Emma rotated out, and Charlotte, who had been on the side quietly observing, came in. Starting a new game, the four women at the table turned each tile face down so only the smooth, shiny ivory was exposed. They used their hands to mix them all up, swishing them around and around. They clacked against each other, the cigarette smoke filling the room. At the same time the shuffling of cards and the ping of pennies filled the cigar smoked kitchen.

The front door opened, and in walked Seymour.

"Sy, come 'ere," called Rose, as he averted his mother's eyes, hoping to avoid the living room and go directly down the green linoleum hallway into his bedroom. "Frieda has something nice to tell you."

"Forget it," he said, after he heard. "I met someone up in the mountains and tonight we got engaged!"

"Engaged! So fast you're engaged? Who is she?" shrieked Rose.

She didn't know if this was good news or bad. What could she compare it to? Rose never had any courtship. Lou was her first cousin, five years her senior. He moved into his aunt's and uncle's Lower East Side tenement when he arrived from Poland at seventeen years old. Cousin Lou fell in love with Cousin Rose on first sight. Rose was twelve, standing in the parlor while her mother, Lou's aunt Reba, braided her hair. When she turned thirteen, Lou told Rose when she grew up he would marry her. And five years later he did.

"How long ago did you even meet?" Rose asked her son.

"Three weeks ago," said Sy. "In Kiamesha. The Lakeview Hotel. You'll like her, Ma, she's coming for dinner next week. Cousin Molly's bringing a diamond to show us for a ring."

"Oh my God, what am I going to cook? Where's Millie? She's too young to be out so late. Lou, get in here, your son just got engaged. What's this girl's name? Do you know anything about her family? Sy, where are you going? Come back in here and talk to your father."

The women continued to talk while they picked, each filling their racks with thirteen new tiles. Then Charlotte, who hadn't said a word all night, came to life.

"Frieda, if the girl's so nice, how about she meet *my* nephew?"

In those days, if a man saw you every weekend and told you how much he liked you and you found you liked him back, you didn't have to second-guess his intentions. You knew. But I bet some of the urgency of what you did do came from what you didn't. In three weeks' time people today just started having sex. Back then they got engaged so they could. Nowadays, we all get the milk for free. And, yes, that has changed the course of commitment but at this point its one that's moot. Today we have the luxury to think about who we are and what we really want. But then, who had time for that *mishigas?* Life wasn't so easy. It was better to do it with someone.

You grew up, got married and raised a family. Unless you couldn't and if you couldn't, you didn't. Perhaps you'd adopt. Otherwise, that was that. No fertility drugs. No surrogates. No in vitro. No one froze their sperm for a rainy day or stored embryos for after the big promotion. The work day ended at five, instead of never. Stores closed on Sundays. The city did sleep. There was more time, less options. Was it better? I don't know, but it was clear. And maybe that part was better.

"Karrie!" my aunt shouted the following night when we rang the bell. "Sy," she yelled into the house. "They're here. Where's your mother and Charlie?" she asked as I pointed to a nearby patch of grass where Charlie had dragged her so he could sniff and do his stuff.

It felt good to be with my family. Without any plans at home I thought I'd stay on through New Year's. Tonight, the development, Kensington South, was having a Hanukkah party in the clubhouse that would be starting soon, leaving us very little time to digest before we'd be eating again.

I was stuffed to the gills after two helpings of my aunt's legendary stuffed cabbage. My mom and I had driven the three cul-de-sacs over here for dinner, and would drive two back to the clubhouse after dessert. I'd really have to bump up my running time if I was serious about staying on longer, I thought, reaching across the table for another of Uncle Sy's *puggies,* the sourdough cookies he had baked just for me. The dishes had been done, and now just us women were dawdling over some decaf.

"Okay, Aunt Cook, tell me now," I said, like a kid, to my aunt who had promised during dessert she would tell me the rest of the story I never tired of hearing. I pictured everything like I was watching a play; the set, the costumes, the characters, the plot. "So then what happened?"

"You could use these for hockey pucks," said Mille picking up a *puggie* like it was one.

"They're good," I said to be nice. Though not actually disagreeing with my mom, I dipped the *puggie* cookie into the coffee to soften it up enough to be able to take a bite.

"It was your Grandma Rose's recipe. But when my mother baked you wanted to eat," Millie said, getting up from the table. "Excuse me for a minute."

"Karrie, you want to hear the story or want to talk about cookies? Now that night came around," my aunt began, somewhat theatrically. "I was already engaged to your uncle, and—"

"Wait. What made you decide in three weeks he was the one?"

"Well, I'll tell you," said Cookie, taking a moment to go back in time. "First, he was very nice when we met at the Lakeview. Well dressed. Very complimentary, he made me laugh. And he gave me a ride back to the city."

On occasion I've been accused of being picky, but I would seriously consider anyone who offered me a ride.

"In the car I was talking about my dog, Buster. Sy said he liked dogs."

So far I completely understood my aunt's decision-making process.

"He talked well about his family. Sy had a good job. And he made a date with me when he dropped me off at my house. A few days later he took me to Ben Marden's Riviera on the Palisades, in Jersey. Now that was a very, very fancy nightclub. That was the limit! If you really wanted to impress someone—that was the date."

So Uncle Sy made plans on the spot and in advance. I was quite certain that how a man made plans was in direct correlation to his availability.

"We had a very nice time, and he asked me to get together again during the week. When he came to pick me up I was crying. Buster was sick and had to go to the vet. My sister and I were very worried. The vet was far away, we didn't have a car and neither of my parents drove, so your uncle volunteered to take Buster. When he asked me to marry him I figured anyone who would go out of his way like that for me couldn't be all bad."

I made a mental checklist of the things that had first attracted my aunt:

- Good looks
- Good dresser
- Good job
- Funny
- Family-oriented
- Complimentary
- Owned car
- Generous
- Liked pets
- Planned special date, and in advance!
- Did favor and went out of his way
- Drove her home to front door (instead of depositing on street corner to fend for herself, but let's not get into that right now)

"Okay, so what happened that night?" I asked.

"So the night came, I was already engaged to your uncle—"

"Oh *that* story?" interrupted Millie, who had just returned to the table. "I try to forget all those stories, and this one only wants to hear them over and over. It wasn't so blissful, Karrie, believe me," she said, as she sat back down.

My mother had taken quite the detour when she married my father. Mel appeared to possess qualities similar to Sy, except for the well-concealed fact that Mel was somewhat of a con.

He didn't know it. It wasn't intentional. His image was a mirage. The Mel Mirage literally disappeared before my very eyes when I turned four, never to see him again until the bizarre chance meeting six years ago in L.A. I had always remembered my father as a hero who had saved us before running away to the circus to become a clown. Six years ago I stumbled on to a man posing as a butcher in a studio storefront on a Hollywood lot. It turned out to be Mel. That meeting ended the Mel Mirage. After that, it became clear that Mel's future whereabouts would, to me, remain unknown.

Men like Mel somehow managed to get by. For them it worked out okay. What they didn't realize was how it affected others. The other people standing on the dirt road would be blinded by the cloud of dust that appeared when a Mel would saddle up his horse and ride away. They rode off to places unknown, leaving you alone on the road, the dust clouding your eyes.

A few clouds could help camouflage some hurt of a failed relationship, until you were ready to see through clearer eyes. But it could also distort how you saw others riding by. Nothing and no one was flawless. The acquaintanceship of each other's flaws was the beginning of an authentic relationship. I felt Edward's phobia to deal with any of his or any of mine was more than a flaw, it was a defect. He taught me that a defect in a legal document could render it invalid. And that's what we had created, a relationship null and void. Without working through our combined flaws our relationship ultimately amounted to nothing more than a passing storm, a blast of wind. And while that may have cleared the dust from the road, it left it empty.

For my mom the dust had settled when she met Henry a few years after Mel had left. Millie had a good marriage with him. A happy one. Marriage to Henry Eisenberg had filled her with pride, and a sense of feeling complete. Henry was a good man. How strange he passed on just months after my finding and, once again, losing Mel. It was a double loss, Henry's absence still missed, it all still hard to believe.

Listening to my aunt, I was trying to find my way back because even an empty road led somewhere, and there was always an opportunity for someone new to ride through.

"Let me finish the story already, Mil," said Cookie, passing the platter to my mother. "Here. Eat. Make your brother happy."

Millie obligingly took a *puggie* from the plate, putting it directly into her coffee before putting it into her mouth.

"So," I said.

"So," repeated Cookie. "Sy brings me over to meet his family and to pick out which diamond would be for the ring. We had dinner out, and later we went over to the house on Wyona Street. Now we walk in, and it's a Tuesday...I'll never forget that because it was the night Milton Berle had his show. And your grandparents had a seven-inch Philco television. It was a big deal in those days to have that, no one had a TV. So we walk in and the whole neighborhood is there. Everyone came over to watch the show. Mind you, I hadn't even met anyone in the family yet, and now I had to pick out the stone in front of everybody."

"My brother," my mother said, shaking her head back and forth.

"You were there, Ma?"

"Of course I was there. Where else would I be?"

Seymour led his girl into the house and into the living room. Rose was on pins and needles. Relieved from having to make dinner, she spent the whole day baking her coffee cake with the raisins, and baked enough for the army of people who had come over.

"She's so pretty," Rose said to her husband. "I'm so impressed Sy could get a girl like that. Aren't you, Lou?"

Lou shook the new fiancée's hand and brought her around the room to meet Millie, his sister, Raizy, her daughters, Mina and Molly, and all the neighbors from game night. They went around and he introduced. Chair to chair, sofa to sofa, *mazel-tov* to *mazel-tov* until they got to the Silvers. Frieda Silver stood up.

"Cookie Cohen?" she screamed, then she sank back into the sofa as if she was going to faint.

"Mrs. Silver, what are you doing here? The Silvers are my neighbors," the newly engaged girl explained to the crowd that was watching to see if Frieda was okay.

"It must be quite festive in your house," said Frieda, when she recovered, "what with Evelyn just getting engaged and now you!" She reached into the large pockets on her house-dress and pulled out a white lace handkerchief to wipe her brow. "I passed your mother in the street today she didn't say a word."

"You know my mother's not much of a talker."

"*Oy,*" Frieda said, finally catching her breath, sucking it up and finally letting it all sink in. "Let's get it straight. You're engaged to Seymour. That's the boy I told you I wanted I should make the introduction. But it happened on its own. So it's better. It must be truly *bashert!*"

"What?" Rose stepped into the conversation. "This is the girl?" she said pointing to her future daughter-in-law. "Well, Frieda, maybe I won't doubt you so much next time. Maybe you can look for Millie."

Charlotte popped up from somewhere behind the TV and into the conversation. "So if Cookie's taken, then who's going to be for *my* nephew?"

All eyes turned to look at Millie, a young working girl and not yet hitched.

"I never knew this part," I said to my mother. "So did you go out with her nephew?"

"You know this story," Millie said. As she distastefully re-membered the date, a look came across her face reminiscent to some I've seen on my own.

"Who was he? What happened?"

"You know," Millie said. "The one we called The Pro-fessor. He knew I was deathly afraid of mice, and he hid a white mouse in his jacket pocket and he told me to reach inside because he had a surprise, and I did and I pulled it out and then I had a mouse in my hand. I was mortified, I was screaming. Don't ask what went on. I ran away and I never talked to him again."

It made me wonder if somehow this all had been passed to me through the genes.

"Let me finish, already," said Cookie. "We have to go to the clubhouse soon. So Cousin Molly worked as an accountant in the jewelry center and she was able to bring over three diamonds," she said. "She brings them over to the dining room table for me to see. Now everyone leaves the living room and comes around the table, and I have dozens of eyes on me while I have to decide. And I just met these people!"

Molly pointed to each of the stones like she was the owner of a store. She had done her homework, brushing up on the value of each of the diamonds in order to present them in their best light.

But for the TV in the background there wasn't a peep out of anyone as they oohed and aahed, watching Molly carefully unwrap the stones. She removed the crinkly tissue paper to reveal each diamond.

"Oh, they're all so beautiful," said Cookie, lightly rolling her hand over each of the stones.

"You can pick whatever you want," said Sy.

He had already gone over the pricing with Molly, and narrowed it down. Within the range of these three diamonds, Cookie could have whatever she'd want. Cookie made a quick decision, pointing to the big one in the middle.

"But that's not a gem," said Molly. "This one's a perfect diamond," she said about the smallest stone.

"I don't want a perfect diamond. I don't want a gem," said Cookie. "I just want the bigger stone!"

"And that's it?" I asked, touching my aunt's left hand. "That's the same stone?" I looked at her ring. It was so pretty. The big round stone still shone, it had a baget on either side, and it was set in platinum.

Early in the year I had gone out on a date with a divorced divorce lawyer. Somehow the topic of engagement rings came up, and he told me he had never bought one for his ex. He said he'd never spend that kind of money on a gift. He was far from broke, and at the time of their engagement he'd been working in a big firm. But the romantic decision to marry came the day his lease expired, and he realized that his girlfriend's Morton Street apartment was a lot nicer than his.

"I love my ring," said Millie, extending her left arm and admiring the huge rock that Henry had bought back when. "Henry had great taste," she said of my step-dad, now having a jewelry box full of beautiful baubles.

"I want a ring," I said, feeling left out.

"Okay," said Millie. "Go get one. No argument from me."

"Me, either," said Cookie.

"Me, too," said Sy, who snuck up on us and was standing in the doorway. "What are we talking about? Whatever it is, count me in."

"Sy, why are you wearing your pajamas?" asked Cookie. "We're getting ready to leave soon."

"You girls go without me. I'm not feeling well," said Sy.

A quiet came over the table. This was far from the first time that Sy had to beg off because of his sagging health. In the past year his diabetes had been acting up, causing numerous problems with his eyes and his heart that, thankfully, had been regulated and fixed. Now there was trouble with his feet. Sy had neuropathy, and I knew the short trek out from the bedroom into the kitchen had not been easy.

I looked across the table. Nothing had happened, but we

all felt scared. My mother's eyes looked down, and my aunt's looked somber. As we got older, it all became increasingly fragile. In the story my aunt just told my grandparents were about my age. The chain of life continued, but at some point people stopped.

Did it help to have children? To know you had contributed to the continuation of the chain? Evelyn's sons were the ones Cookie and Sy considered to be like their own. And they were the ones I considered to be my cousins. But Cookie and Sy had never had kids. They couldn't, so they didn't.

I looked at my uncle and tried to picture him more years ago than I am old now, driving his Pontiac into the Lakeview, a swagger in his walk as he approached Cookie for the very first time. Not knowing what she would say, or that a month from that day they'd be taking a hall. Not knowing what lay ahead but feeling fearless, knowing it was safe not to know. It was so important to enjoy the now, and to be able to enjoy it one step at a time. Literally.

"We're going through your *puggies* like hotcakes, Uncle Sy. So before you go back to bed, sit down here and give me the recipe."

He seemed to like that idea. Settling into the chair, he took a *puggie* from the plate.

"This is your Grandma Rose's recipe," he told me, biting directly into the cookie without softening the blow. "Pretty good, I think," he said, chewing the cookie that brought back sweet memories.

I wanted to be able to bite into a memory one day. The memory of tonight and the memory of the story I had been told. I got up from my chair, opened a drawer and took out a pad and a pen. Bringing it to the kitchen table I told my uncle, "I want the *puggie* recipe. You dictate and I'll write."

Sy gave the instructions and I wrote them down. He had

substituted yogurt for sour cream. Maybe I, too, would modify the recipe. One day when I baked maybe I would make a change. But at the very least, I knew that in my own way I would continue the chain.

Twelve

Having a keen sense of smell, the stronger the odor, the greater the frog's excitement.

The phone rang as we were getting ready to walk out the door. It was my aunt's next door neighbor, Gladys.

"No problem, we're just leaving now," I heard Cookie say as I finished loading the dessert plates into the dishwasher. "Meet us outside in five minutes."

We went out into the cool Florida night. I zipped up my denim jacket, but it was still quite mild for December. Especially for the snowbirds that had moved down south to escape the winter storms of the north. We waved to Gladys as we walked the short distance down the narrow path to Millie's cream-colored Toyota Camry. With the exception of the license plates, it looked exactly like the five other cream Camrys in the lot.

"You know my sister-in-law, Millie, and this is her daughter. My niece, Karrie," said Cookie, climbing in the front passenger seat next to my mom.

"Hi," I said smiling, climbing next to Gladys in the back.

"Oh, she's lovely," Gladys announced. "I have a son, Karrie, he's divorced, but he's seeing someone now. I love him to death, but I wouldn't even think to fix you up with him the next time he's *between,* as he likes to call it. You wouldn't need the headache. Where's Sy tonight?" she asked, as we rode to the clubhouse.

"Lying down," said Cookie. "What can I tell you?"

"Lester's lying down, too," said Gladys. "There's nothing wrong with him. He just doesn't want to go to the party. He says it's boring."

"It is!" said Millie, pulling into an empty spot in the lot.

I still couldn't understand why we never walked. Not only was it good exercise, it took more time to get in and out of the car—what with the waiting for everyone and the production of the seat belts—than it did to do the whole ride.

A three-foot *dreidel* made of colored oak tag greeted us, as it hung on the front door of the clubhouse. The *dreidel,* a symbol of Hanukkah, was a four-sided spinning top. A Hebrew letter on each side signified how much you won or lost when you played the holiday gambling game. The letter facing out was a *nun.* Translated into English it meant nothing. I didn't take that to be a very good sign.

Cookie, Millie, Gladys and I walked to the front desk to hand in our tickets. We were greeted by Arlene. I knew this because it said so in giant letters on her name tag, pasted on the front of her lavender twin-sweater set.

"Where's Sy tonight?" asked Arlene. She stood up from behind the desk giving us a big hello as she took the tickets.

"Home," said my aunt in a way that indicated why he was there, but she really didn't want to talk about it.

"Okay, tomorrow will be a better day." Arlene looked past Gladys, searching for Lester.

"Also home," said Gladys, but to this Arlene simply smiled.

"Here," said Cookie.

She opened her pocketbook and handed over a small envelope that contained her ticket. Arlene took two red tickets from the envelope, as her eyes registered Gladys and my aunt at the same time.

"Wait, let me get mine," said Gladys reaching into her purse.

"Doesn't matter," said Arlene, waving the two red tickets. "You can go in on these."

Cookie nodded, Gladys thanked her, and they walked inside. Millie and I were behind. My mom had her two red tickets out, ready to hand to Arlene.

"These are for me and my daughter," she said. "Karrie, I don't know if you've ever met Arlene? Arlene, this is my daughter, Karrie, from New York."

"Hi," I said.

"Nice meeting you," said Arlene, taking the tickets from my mom. She paused a moment to look at them, and then looked up. "Millie. You really can't use these tickets."

"What's the matter with them? They're dated. They have today's date."

"Yes, but these are two homeowner's tickets. Karrie is a guest. You really need to use one of your green guest tickets for her."

"Why?"

"These are just for homeowners," Arlene pressed, shoving the tickets back into Millie's hand.

"Karrie is a homeowner," Millie said. "Her name is on the deed."

"But it's not in the Kensington phone directory. She

doesn't live here. She's a guest. Don't you have a green ticket?"

Red tickets, green. I was not in the directory, but my name was on the deed. The thought of how I would come to own that house was not only sad and terrifying, but this kind of welcome did nothing to make me think Kensington South would be the place I'd enjoy spending my golden years.

"What's going on?" said Cookie, who walked back to the desk to see why we were delayed.

"Don't ask me," said Millie.

"Oh, that's ridiculous," she said when Arlene explained. "You just let Gladys in on my other homeowner's ticket."

"Well, that's different," said Arlene. "Sy is sick so he's not using it, but with Millie, she doesn't even have a—"

She caught herself, because Arlene stopped before she got to the heart of what she was going to say. But Millie finished for her.

"I don't have a husband, so I'm not allowed to use my other ticket?"

Arlene did not answer. She stood as if she was the one who had been wronged, but just for the record my mother set her straight.

"I pay the same money for the season's entertainment as each household, and in addition to the guest tickets each household receives two homeowner's tickets per show. Are you telling me I can't use my other homeowner's ticket when I bring someone, because the person I bring isn't Henry? You'd discriminate like that with a widow, when you didn't think anything of letting Cookie use Sy's ticket for Gladys?"

"What *chutzpah!*" said Cookie.

The one with the *chutzpah* was Millie, and I was proud of her. Arlene's face was red, but I felt her embarrassment came more from having been confronted than because of what she had done.

"I didn't realize," she said, taking back the two red tickets, the closest to an apology as she would get. "I have a lot on my mind."

Sufficiently made to feel like we were on the standby list for Noah's Ark, we entered the clubhouse and walked on in.

"What nerve, really," said Cookie, but I could see the worry for my uncle's health ride a new wave as she contemplated the ramifications of living in a coupled community without a spouse. Everyone was quick to say how beautifully the widows managed. Just so long as they didn't have to be one.

"Ma, save me a seat. I'll be right back."

I wasn't ready to join in and be merry, and excused myself to the ladies' room to take a few minutes for myself. Some of my best thinking was done escaping events in public bathrooms. I went down the hall to my office to work.

People were often dismissive to women, not to mention women alone. In Arlene's defense, I could only think that she really did have a lot on her mind, or that thing with my mom possibly triggered her own fear of being widowed. I've observed that one of the great perks of coupledom was that it made people feel comfortable. It didn't matter much about the couple. At face value it was a shield they could hide behind, it fit people into a box that was easy to understand, and it was a lot less threatening. Singledom. The Scarlet *S*.

I used to fight my mother on this thinking it was only her generation. That mine was more enlightened, and none of it mattered. That was when I was younger and had more single friends and expectations were different. In my twenties, my landlord would not allow me to have a dog. I had pleaded with him to no avail.

"But I found such a sweet dog in need of a good home. Why won't you let me have one, Mr. Biofski? Why?"

"You know, I rent to all you young girls thinking I can

get a quick turnover on the apartments because you'll move out and get married. And instead, you want a dog? Don't get a dog, get a boyfriend!"

Although still single, things still changed, and with changing expectations. Like friendships. Your girlfriend's privacy bond was with her husband, not you. Social circles shrunk, and without your own family, holidays were up for grabs. Saturday night's date night, couples date each other. If you're not part of one, don't expect to eat with someone that is. And on a more interesting note your friends' dads. They used to look at you with the hope that you'd soon meet a prince who'd whisk you away. Now there was the hope that *they* might.

That's not the great news. But I am not romanticizing couples. I have had dinner with some that sent me hopping back to my worst blind date. While coupledom was not all great, singledom was not all bad. And when a coupled woman treated a single woman unkindly in a social situation, I could only think she somehow felt threatened, or was not one of the happy ones. From the view of coupledom being single could look sad or terrifying, but it might also look quite desirable and romantic.

For me it's never been about marriage, it's only been about love. Some have assured me that what I want doesn't exist, my expectations are off. Perhaps they are even right. But those are just words in a conversation. I'm the one who would have to live with the guy. I'm the one who needs to be true to myself. And if I wasn't, I'm the one who'd have to stuff it because, after all, to the world I'm the one who was happily married.

Even with their different lives, single, married, divorced or whatever, your close friends will always be just that. If ever married I hoped I would remember life B.C.—Before Coupledom. It only took a moment for anyone to be back there. No one was immune.

While being single had not changed, my view from sin-gledom continued to. But always constant was my freedom, my possibilities and my hope. It was not only envied, it was among my most valuable assets.

"Karrie, over here," Millie called in a loud whisper, wav-ing her hands when she saw me coming out of the ladies' room. She was sitting with Cookie, Gladys and two women I didn't know. Widows, I wondered. "I got for you," she said, pointing to a paper plate with a purple menorah that was filled with three deliciously greasy potato *latkes.*

I sat down, quietly waving hello to the other people at the table as the singer had already started her act. Holding a hand mike, dressed in black sequins and false eyelashes, she crooned "Rock of Ages," number one on the Hanukkah Hit Parade. She was accompanied by a very small man on accordion. I looked up from the singer and back down to the table. Next to the *latkes* were two bowls, one with apple sauce and another with sour cream; toppings for the holi-day's traditional potato pancakes. I'd had enough with the *puggies,* it made my stomach hurt just to look at the *latkes.* Except they sure looked good.

"Didn't we just eat?" I asked my mother.

I resisted the *latkes* by taking only one onto another plate, still deciding. I wasn't hungry, but how could I pass? I thought I could be content to eat one with a little drop of apple sauce. Or maybe a little drop of apple sauce and a teeny dollop of sour cream. That would work, I thought. I reached for the bowls but suddenly, as if possessed, I found myself slathering two huge spoonfuls of apple sauce *and* sour cream all over the one lone *latke.*

"Can I join you?"

A tall man with glasses dressed in a navy-blue warm-up suit came over to our table. When he smiled at Millie she pointed to an empty chair.

"Mmmmmm," he said, as he sat. "Get a whiff," he said of the fried potatoey smell. "Isn't that something?"

He reached to the center of the table taking the two *latkes* that were left, finalizing my decision to eat just the one. I watched as he ate one *latke* with apple sauce and the other with sour cream. He wouldn't put a topping on the next until the first was finished, obviously keeping his foods separate.

It was interesting to watch how people ate, and more interesting to see what they did with the food. Passion or necessity? To hog or to share? A taste off the plate, or cut and hand over? Save the best food for last? Anyone for seconds? The lowdown on leftovers—to keep or to throw? Perhaps on my next date we'd skip the talk and go directly to a taste test.

I liked to taste each food individually before I combined. But combos often led to new recipes. My favorite was the tuna-chip, where you put some chips from the side inside the sandwich. A crunch on every bite!

"Come on everybody! Let's hear it! Put your hands together! This song is for everyone who uses an electric menorah!"

So absorbed in the *latke,* I hadn't noticed that bit by bit everyone had begun talking over the singer who'd been singing her little Hanukkah heart out. To the tune of "I Have a Little Dreidl," everyone joined in singing like they were part of a holiday concert.

Oh lightbulb, lightbulb, lightbulb
It helps save energy

Millie wasn't a joiner under the best of circumstances. But the man at our table was having a ball.

"Come on, Millie," I said, egging her on. "It wasn't easy getting into this shindig. I think we should have some fun!"

Oh lightbulb, lightbulb, lightbulb
Come save the world with me

They repeated the verse over and over while I caught my mother's eye. Soon we were laughing. We were laughing so hard I thought they'd have to call the paramedics, and considering our location they were probably very nearby. Between the *latkes* and the lightbulbs, not to mention the sour cream and the *puggies,* I thought I would burst wide-open. I got hiccups. I was laughing and hiccupping and hiccupping and laughing, and then the hiccups got so bad they hurt. I was sick to my stomach as I sipped water in a glass through a cloth napkin I had to hunt down in the kitchen. I'd like to say it helped, but it didn't.

"Your daughter sure knows how to have a good time," said the man.

He had gone to the main table and brought us back cake. When I came back from the kitchen Gladys got up with the women, leaving me, my mom and my hiccups at the table with the man.

"Take a whiff of this," he said, pointing to the warm cherry cheese strudel. I couldn't smell any more food. I couldn't deal with any more. But it was all over the place. More food. More cake! Chocolate cake, pound cake, cheesecake, and strudel. Let *them* eat it, I thought, as I absolutely could not manage ano—(hic)—ther bite!

"Marv," the man said to me, extending his hand. "And you are…?"

"Karrie," I said, saying it slowly and trying to regulate my intake of air. "Nice to meet you," I managed.

"Your mother talks about you all the time at bowling," he said, pointing to my mom, who was drinking her tea. "She's a good bowler. Too bad she's not on my team."

My mother was a good athlete. Growing up in Brooklyn

when they'd choose sides for teams she was always first pick. She was the only girl, and they called her The Skirt.

"Do you bowl, too?" asked Marv, smiling at my mother, who had yet to say a word.

Marvin was chatting me up. He wanted something, but thankfully I knew it was definitely not me.

"A little. But I'm not as good as my mother," I said, tossing her the ball though she was curiously out of this conversation.

"If you'd like, maybe I could take you girls," he said.

"We have a lot of prior commitments," Millie now chimed in. "We have plans, we have the book club."

"But I'll be staying right till after New Year's," I said, confirming my decision to change my ticket and stay a little longer before I went home.

"Then it's a date!"

"It's up to Karrie," said my mother.

"Okay. I'll call you," Marv said, before he got up and self-assuredly sauntered away.

"Karrie," said Millie.

"We'll set it up but then we'll cancel, and you can reschedule with him for when I'm gone."

"Karrie!" said Millie, her voice the beginning of a reproach.

"It's okay, Ma. Maybe he won't even call."

"Oh, if he said he'll call, he'll call," said Millie, with a confident annoyance.

But I thought it was great. A man said he'd call and you knew he would call. It was a Hanukkah miracle after all.

"You know what I wish for you," my mom had said when we clinked champagne glasses to bring in the New Year. I was going home in the morning. And another year would begin. What would happen now?

"So you think you'll go out with him on Wednesday?" I asked later, when I finished packing. We lay on her bed watching TV. I reached down to pick up Charlie.

"I'll do what I want to do, okay?" said Millie, who was far from enthusiastic about the prospect of Marv.

"Okay! But what are you so worried about? He's very nice."

Millie sat up. I could see she was finally going to talk.

"Marv makes a very nice appearance. He seems comfortable, he drives at night. He's fine. But since he's widowed he's been involved with two of the women here already. One was my friend."

The intrigue of Kensington South. The people were seniors, but dating was the same as high school. Dating didn't change, but each generation gave it its own spin. Fifty years from now, twentysomethings living in Kensington South would probably make a dinner date by sending a text message.

"So what happened?" I asked. "Marv break her heart or something?"

"No, nothing like that," Millie turned away from the TV to look at me. "But he's a sexy man."

"So you are attracted to him."

"What makes you think I'm attracted to him? Who said anything about being attracted to him?" asked Millie.

"You just said he's a sexy man." It was self-explanatory to me.

"Yes. A sexy man," said Millie. "A man who wants to have sex. You understand now?"

"Okay." I didn't understand at all, but after the other night I could see that I didn't really understand anything.

I went with my mother to the Kensington South book club. It so happened that they were discussing a book I'd just finished and loved. It was about a young girl who fled her hometown after her fiancé came upon a tragic accident after their graduation. She ran away to New York where she became involved in a very passionate, all-encompassing, highly sexual relationship with a secretive, older man.

"What did you think of the character of Gibson?" asked Gloria, who moderated. "Who liked him?"

The room, filled with about twenty-five women, suddenly became electric and was quickly divided. Gibson made some swoon, while others thought him swine.

"I loved him!" I shouted. "He was soooo sexy."

"Oh, I wouldn't have minded knowing a Gibson," said Sylvia from my mother's bridge game.

"But why didn't he tell her anything about himself?" Gloria asked the women. "Why was everything such a big secret with him? He had to make such a *gedillah* when he brought her to his parents? He couldn't have just invited her home, like a *mensch?*"

"But he was starting to open up," I said. "It was his first real relationship."

"Real relationship?" asked Gloria. "Because all day all night they were with the sex?"

I thought about Edward and wished I could explain, but I couldn't. All day all night those characters were with the sex because it was emotional. It was their bond, an exquisite sensual duet. And it wasn't just sex. It was the most amazing sex I had ever read!

"Who has relationships like that?" asked Blanche. "That wasn't a real relationship. That was nonsense."

If that was nonsense, what was Edward? One big load of baloney.

"Well, I think he would have come through if she stayed," I said, defending myself through Gibson, though I was annoyed with him for not giving me more to work with. "I really think he would have stepped up to the plate."

"Oy, veissmir!"

"She's dreaming!"

"Karrie! That's why you're still single!"

"You don't think he would've changed?" I asked, wanting them to say yes; for me, for Edward, for unfortunate relationships everywhere.

"Of course he wouldn't change. Forget about that," said Gloria.

"That's right," said Gladys in a singsong voice, reminding me she wouldn't even introduce me to her own son.

"I have a question," said Marion Rosenblatt, the woman next to me whose full name I knew because it was written in script on the front of her book. "Why did the author have to write *so* much sex? I could have enjoyed the same story and it would have been enough for me to read it in one paragraph. I have nothing against sex, believe me, I am far from a prude. But I don't have to read where he touched her, how he touched, he touched her here, he touched her there, up, down, out and under, over, in...*oy vey,* why do I have to know all that? I ask you, is that any of my business?"

The woman had a point. Sex was your own business. But didn't people always stick their nose in someone else's? Inquiring minds *did* want to know. They wanted to know what you did and how you did it. And then they wanted to compare.

"So what happened with Marv and your friend?" I asked my mother. I wondered now if her friend had told tales of Marv's sexual gymnastics that had scared my mother off.

"Nothing. She was done with all that. She only wanted some company for dinner or a movie. And to be honest I don't think I'd want much more. At this stage in my life I don't want to start with that. I was very happy with Henry. That's enough to sustain me. I can't be bothered."

Is that what happened? You can't be bothered? I can't *not* be bothered.

"But he's kind of cute, right? Couldn't you, like, kiss him and see? Maybe you'd like it, Ma. Maybe you'd want to. A little sex isn't such a bad thing. It helps people live longer."

"I'll live long enough without it. If I don't have a special feeling, then forget it."

"But if that part is special, then can't you get the feeling?"

"Go ask the book club," said Millie, picking up the remote to turn the volume back on. "Discussion over."

I thought about Marv. His teeth were good, he still had hair and at night he could drive. It made a girl wonder.

"So, let me ask you something, Millie. If we had grown up together, if we were the same age, do you think we would have hung out? Do you think you and I would have been friends?"

"Somehow, Karrie, I don't think we would have been in the same clique."

"Do you ever think what your life would have been like if you were born when I was? I always think about grandma. What she would have been like if she was able to be independent. If she had gone to college."

Millie reflected. My grandmother had not allowed my mom to finish. She insisted she go to work. She was only a girl. She'd get married. What did she need to know from college?

"Well, I definitely wish I'd finished," Millie said.

"I think you could have gone to law school, Ma. I think you would have been a lawyer."

"Me, too. I think I would have liked that."

"Yeah. I bet you'd have made partner, you'd own a co-op on the Upper East Side, you'd have a share house in the Hamptons…"

"And I'd be single!" shouted Millie.

We laughed.

"Yeah, you'd be single," I said.

I was ready to hit the road after I hit the hay. My thoughts already turning from a Millie my age, to New York and tomorrows.

Thirteen

You should always put your frog through a test to see it eat, as difficulty with eating may indicate serious problems.

"Oh my God," I said, looking up at Brooke, who was standing on a small carpeted platform while a seamstress expertly pinned what was going to be a magnificent wedding gown. "You're breathtaking," I said, watching her blush under the compliment.

"It looks like it'll work out," she said of the sensational dress when we were leaving the store. "Can you believe it's only four months away? There's not much time left."

"There really isn't," I said, hoping there was at least enough to insure that I wouldn't wind up at the wedding stag.

"So, Karrie," said Brooke. We had walked a block in an uncharacteristic silence before she asked. "Has he called?"

"Oh, yes. He's called."

For all of his protestations, it seemed that what Edward liked to do best was call. But he had done more than just call. And so had I.

Edward had swept in after the New Year with resolutions I had swallowed hook, line and seduction. He had kept me warm and cozy in the year's first and most amazing snowstorm, my resolve to do nothing with him but talk quickly melting like snow. Drunk on the wine and the promises Edward had poured on over dinner, we left the restaurant to find the city painted white. Our feet making the first tracks in Central Park, we fell onto the Great Lawn making angels in a snow that continued to fall. Wet and wanton, we went back to my place and made love.

"What did he say? Was he apologetic? Does he want a relationship?" asked Brooke, as I thought ahead to the next time.

Two weeks later, after I received no response to an e-mail or my phone invitation to dinner, Edward called twice a day, three days in a row, to pave the way to a tryst. The tryst to nowhere. We blossomed quickly before wilting, just like the two dozen yellow roses he had brought me that night.

"Well, he told me he was unavailable to me and he didn't know why," I told Brooke, skipping over the sexy parts and going straight to the pain.

The pain that continued. One I felt every time I logged on to the J-Spot and saw that Edward was logged on, too. He was always there, constantly searching, causing me to do the same. But I wasn't searching to meet new men. I only searched to see if he was. Always hopeful his searching meant he was still free, and had not met someone new.

The J-Spot told you exactly what date and time the person you were searching for had logged on. Several times a day I did just that, in my search to find him. It was too much information. It was all too much, and it was driving me mad.

I'd been out of high school a long time, but felt like I was back. The J-Spot was practically a virtual high-school hallway where you continued to run into your ex during passing. Whether you were flirting with someone new, or just trying to get to class.

"He didn't know why he was so unavailable?" asked Brooke. "That's not good."

"Well, it's not really bad," I said, not wanting Brooke to know how bad it really was. "He said he was trying to figure it out, and maybe next time we talked he'd have an answer."

"And has he called?"

"Well...no."

No, he hadn't called and, thankfully, I had officially stopped. But it didn't stop me from hurting yesterday when the only flowers I got were from Fred, who insisted we buy each other pink and red carnations. Fred was stuck in a similar spot with Babalou, who canceled their Valentine's date because he was out of town and snowed in. Or more likely snowed under, said Fred...if I caught his drift.

"Well, I bet a lot of new people are on the J-Spot today. The day after Valentine's Day is probably great for business. Why don't you log on and try again?" suggested the always enterprising Brooke.

"You know, my subscription is up the end of this month and I was just going to let the whole thing go. Six months, Brooke. Half a year with that. I think it's time to log off and shut down."

We stood in front of the Prince Street subway station, preparing to go our different directions.

"I know relationships are hard, Karrie, and...it's just that...well you want to be with someone nice. Would you say that Edward is a nice guy?"

I looked at Brooke as I thought about Edward.

"Uh, no, actually. I couldn't say that he is," I told my friend.

"Oh, Karrie!" Brooke's voice came out more like a cry, as it was way too late for a warning.

"It happens. I don't have any regrets. That's why you date. It's not as if I married the guy." I paused. "It was very…compelling."

"I know. I've been there, too," said Brooke. "You remember Joe." Brooke looked away as she recalled the relationship I heard so much about when she and I had first met. "But you can't have a life with those guys. Go back online and give it one more try. And if you still don't like it, then just let the subscription expire."

I felt anyone who was going to be married in a dress like that was worth listening to.

I gave it one last shot, and when I logged back on I found I had mail. But I went through the same highs and lows as before when I wound up deleting the prospects before me. Then I changed my search by checking off that I only wanted to see the profiles of men who were five foot nine and over, eliminating all men five foot eight, eliminating Edward once and for all. The new search began, but it reminded me, again, of high school as the same familiar faces passed before me. And then I got more mail.

Looking up MatchMan I finally felt encouraged because for starters, in his photos he was really pretty cute. A cognitive shrink with partial custody of his daughter, he conveniently lived a little farther uptown. I composed a sweet response and sent it off. Maybe Brooke was right. After all, you never know.

Between the news I had booked a national radio spot for a wireless service and my anticipation of hearing back from

MatchMan, my spirits were high. It was a good thing, too, because they sank when I got a call from Ryan about the one-act festival.

"What do you mean I have to audition? Brockman said I was doing it. He said he wanted me. That I was the perfect actress to play Time."

"Well, you're not doing it. Neither is Brockman. He just got a paying gig to direct out of town. Regional thing. The show's off."

"So where does that leave me?"

I saw where that left me. Nowhere. I'd been so obsessed about my social life it hadn't occurred to me I'd lost my theater career along the way. That I could be this upset about a non-paying show in a workshop was more upsetting to me than doing the dumb play.

"It leaves you available to audition for *The Playmaker*. It's a cool piece and a good friend of mine, Ivan, wrote it and is directing. He wants funny, attractive women who can play a couple of different parts. One of the women is already cast, but he needs another one and I thought of you. So just meet him, okay?"

Ryan and I sat in a silent pause that sounded like no was my answer.

"Come on, beauty, I'll give him your number and just meet him. Ivan's really funny. He quit his day job and started doing stand-up. I think the two of you might even, you know…! And hey—he's Jewish. And I think he's even gotten like, *more* Jewish."

More Jewish. I knew what that was code for, even from an Episcopalian like Ryan.

"You know, Ryan, the play is one thing, but give me a break. You think I want to date some unemployed guy turned comic turned religious as part of some sort of mid-life crisis!"

"How'd you get all that? Wow—you're like one super perceptive chick."

Super perceptive chick! Hanging up the phone I thought how nice it would be to be wrong. How nice, for a change, to have a hope that Ivan would turn out to be together. What I had found amusing and odd behavior ten years ago was now just downright annoying. My social circle wasn't doing anything to elevate me. I wished I could slip into someone else's.

But a few nights later I found myself walking to the Star-bucks on Eighty-sixth to meet and discuss the script with Ivan. The days had passed without word back from Match-Man. I was trying not to let anything burst my balloon, yet I watched it deflate when I walked through the door. Be-cause I immediately knew that the skinny guy in the old flannel shirt, the one alone with a cup of coffee, the one who looked drained from life when his eyes shifted up to see who'd just come in, was Ivan.

I sensed when I sat down with the stand-up our time to-gether would be anything but funny.

"Karrie," he said, rising to the occasion. He gave me a shy once-over that indicated he approved.

"Ivan. Hello," I said extending my hand, receiving a limp response that made me realize good handshakes needed to be practiced. Don't leave home without one. "Nice to meet you."

"Do you want anything? I already have coffee."

"Come with me," I said, walking us over to the counter.

I ordered a small decaf, picked up the coffee and opened my wallet to pay.

"I can get that if you want," said Ivan, running his hands over his jeans and questioningly into his pockets. "I think. Let me see what I've—"

"Thanks, Ivan, but I have it, its fine."

Looking for Mr. Goodfrog

Oh boy, here we go. It was all *so* predictable. Ryan had obviously told Ivan of the romantic potential, as Ivan had that look in his eye. And here he was, wooing me by not being able to buy me a cup of coffee. What a way to a woman's heart. I could not stand this anymore. What could these men be thinking? Were they ever embarrassed? Maybe they needed to be. Maybe something should be said.

If we discussed the play fast I would get out in under half an hour. I thought that the easier option than walking out now, and having to get into it with Ryan. But I would need cake. I pointed into the glass casing to the decadent chocolate one with icing.

"That looks really good. Ivan, you want to share?"

"Oh, that's okay," he said. "I brought my own."

"What do you mean?"

"I brought my own," he repeated.

"You already bought cake?" I asked.

"Muffin. I brought my own muffin." He paused. "From home."

I took a moment to digest this.

"I don't think you're allowed to do that."

"Sure you are. I did it," said Ivan. "It's okay."

"Does Starbucks think its okay?"

"Who cares? Why wouldn't it be?"

"It's just that Starbucks is in the business of selling muffins, not having people bring them here to eat them for free. You're allowed to bring your own laptop but I think your pastries have to stay at home."

I had only a coffee when we walked back to the table. It was unlikely I'd be there long enough to even drink it, let alone to sit down and eat cake.

"Well," said Ivan, back at the table sipping from the container he'd left. He was thirsty, but even if his hunger panged

I doubted Ivan would crack open his knapsack and pull out that muffin now. "I just come here for the ambiance. I have dietary laws prohibiting me from eating their food. I'm Orthodox. I'm very religious."

I observed Rabbi Ivan's attire.

"How religious?" I asked. "I mean, I'm just curious," I continued, wanting to understand this down to the very last drop. "You're not wearing a *yarmulke,*" I said, pointing to his uncovered head.

"I usually wear a baseball cap," said Ivan.

"But you're not. You're not wearing anything. How religious can you be if you're not wearing anything on your head?" I was on a mission, and I was going to bust his muffin wide-open.

"I know the *kashrut* and it doesn't include Starbucks muffins," said Ivan. "Only their coffee."

"I know the dietary laws, too, and I think the muffins *are* kosher. I think the *New York Times* said Starbucks *is* kosher. In fact, I think the rabbi at my synagogue made an announcement that it was. Look at them," I said pointing to a man wearing a *yarmulke* seated with a woman by the window. "Look," I said, pointing to the kosher couple. "Let's see if they got a muffin."

"Karrie, I don't want to talk to you about this anymore," said Ivan.

He was exasperated. I was making him crazy. On top of it, he looked as if he might just keel over from malnutrition if another second went by without him taking a bite out of his muffin. The muffin he brought from home.

"The coffee is in an urn and it's poured into a paper cup," Ivan explained, trying so hard to make his point and move on. "But I don't think that the ovens where they bake the muffins are kosher and that's why I can't eat them. And I don't have to explain to you why I don't cover my head.

Okay? Okay? Are you satisfied? Are you satisfied now, Karrie? We're here to talk about my play."

His play. Well, this audition sure wasn't going very well.

"Yes. Your play. Out of curiosity, are the women in your play Jewish?" I asked.

"It doesn't matter. It's generic. It doesn't say."

"Oh. I just thought that since you were religious you might write about women in that world. But, uh, I was wondering…do you only go out with religious women? I mean since you are."

Ivan stared at me before he answered. It was as if for that split second he had seen himself through my eyes. And then he became, rightfully, angry.

"You know, Karrie, it's really none of your business who I date, but no. I don't go out with religious women. The women I go out with usually aren't even Jewish."

"Oh, *I* see. So you're a religious guy who dates *shiksas*. Gee, I'd think it might be hard to date someone who wasn't kosher let alone someone who wasn't religious, not to mention someone not even Jewish. If you're so religious and all."

I didn't even know what I was trying to prove, I was just fed up. I had reached my limit. Constant hypocrisy, constantly going nowhere. Always running in place, always excuses. Tell me you already ate, tell me you're broke, tell me you date women you know you'll never marry because you know you never will. Just tell me something true. Don't use religion to back door your way out of what you don't want to do in life. And don't use it to back your way out of a dollar-seventy-five muffin.

"Why do you think you hate men?" asked Ivan.

"Men I like, it's dishonesty I have trouble with."

"My play is funny and I need a funny woman. Do you think you're funny?"

"I think I wouldn't be a great fit with your play," I said as

I stood. "I think I should go," I said, taking my coffee with me as I headed out the door.

Ivan was past thirty, he had past forty; he may have even shot past fifty. Fifty! What happened when a frog was still bringing his own muffin to the pond at *fifty?* Was there anything good swimming anywhere I'd want to catch? Where was a pond I could fish in?

I was never so happy to see Charlie when fifteen minutes later I was back in the safety of my little abode. I let him lick my face before turning on the computer, seeing there were no messages on my machine. My heart did an involuntary flip-flop when I saw my mail from the J-Spot. I took a breath. What was he up to? What did Edward want now?

To: BlueEyes325@jspot.com
From: Beyond@jspot.com
Subject: CONGRATULATIONS: You Hit The Right Spot!
Dear BlueEyes,
I confess to be in the habit of checking to see who has spotted me when I log on to the J-Spot. To my tremendous interest, I have noticed for the last few weeks that you, BlueEyes, have spotted me not just daily, but several times a day.
Are you sending me smoke signals? I can only surmise that you are obsessed with me.
While it is flattering, do know that the J-Spot has options for you to hide your profile if you don't want me to be aware of your activity. However, I think you do, so please feel free to call!
Beyond

I looked for a gun so I could shoot myself.
He was *so* arrogant. So insensitive. Hurtful and mean. But

it was even worse than that. It was unemotional. This was funny to him. It wasn't important. It was only sport, our time together nothing more than recreational. I felt humiliated.

"Look how he treats us, Charlie," I cried, including Charlie in my saga because it made me feel less alone. "Why did he do that to us?"

Poor me. Poor Charlie! He started whimpering and now he was sad. At least he'd never wind up on an analyst's couch complaining I projected my negative dating experiences on him. Hugging my sweet innocent dog only made me cry harder, my sobs almost drowning out the ringing of the phone.

"Hello?" I wiped my nose of the sniffles, picking up when it hit the fourth ring.

"Is this BlueEyes?" asked a squeaky voice.

"What?"

"This is MatchMan, from the J-Spot. I wrote to you a few days ago and asked if I could call and you e-mailed me your number. I was out of town, but now I'm back. Is this a good time?"

No. This was not a good time. When it came to the J-Spot there seemed to never be a good time. But I tried to compose myself in case this might be it.

"Yes," I said. "It's fine. I'm Karrie. I remember your e-mail. I really liked your profile. You're the shrink, right?"

"Yes. And you're the actress. I'm Bob. I was very drawn to your profile. So how are you today?"

"Good. How are you? How was your day?" I asked, trying to bring the talk to something easy and immediate.

"Fine. My day was fine and I'm fine, thanks. So, BlueEyes…Karrie. Before we begin our talk, I'd first like to know how you feel about your online dating experience."

"Are you doing a survey?"

"I'd just like to know your feelings about it so I can

gauge myself against that," said Dr. Bob, the shrink, already shrinking his experience of me into information he could analyze that would stop him from having a genuine experience.

"Well, frankly…" I wondered just how frank frankly should be. "Well, Bob, I don't think online dating and I have been a great match, and I know that's what we have in common so far, but maybe we can find something else."

"Like what?"

"Like…I don't know, anything… What did you have, tonight, for dinner?"

There. Maybe we could banter, chat about something light, innocuous. Yes, a light chat. Fun.

"I don't think that will take me in the direction I need to go. Why won't you discuss your feelings about online dating with me?" insisted Dr. Bob.

"Because they're negative and they're about other people, and you and I are brand-new." I wanted the statistics and information from all of the men to disappear into cyberspace. "My other online experiences have nothing to do with us."

"I believe every relationship is important. Tell me about your prior relationships. How many long-term relationships have you been in, how long did they last, and how did they end?"

I was silent.

"Why don't you like online dating, Karrie?"

I was silent.

"Please explain to me why you don't like it. I really feel we need to cover that question before we move on to your long-term relationships. Just tell me what's wrong with it. I need to know how you feel."

"So I had mashed potatoes with the skins, I made them myself, and I broiled a lamb chop. And you?"

I stroked Charlie's belly, relaxing for just a second, catching my breath and gaining my strength before I'd say goodbye and get off the phone.

He thought this would bring about a romantic connection? Could anything feel more disconnected? Could anything be less romantic, less fun? Had people come to believe they had a program running inside them that would elicit love if they successfully installed the software? Had they lost their humanity to such an extent, they thought they were interacting when they hid behind a formulaic checklist hidden behind technology?

"So since you won't answer me I assume you've had no long-term relationships, and your profile said you've never been married. Is that true?"

I was silent.

"Have you ever been engaged? Karrie? Have you?"

"No."

Dr. Bob was quiet. I sat on the phone line listening to the quiet between Dr. Bob and me. Dr. Bob. Divorced, one child who lived with him, sometimes. Dr. Bob. Looking for a friend, a date, a long-term relationship, marriage and children. Dr. Bob, quiet. Dr. Bob, incensed.

"I feel I have excellent perception into these profiles and I was going to make an exception in your case. Karrie. But I cannot date someone who has no idea how to be in a long-term relationship," said the socially skill-less, deluded Dr. Bob.

"Okay, but before we go, do let me tell you that you have really helped me here tonight, Bob," I said, hearing his attention shift into gear, while I sat up on the couch ready to go in for the kill. "I had gone back on the J-Spot to be sure, and after this call with you I can safely take myself off knowing I will not be missing a goddamn thing. I thought part of being a shrink was the ability to listen. I told you there was no productive purpose in discussing past negative online experiences, but you continued to press. You don't know how to listen, do you, Bob? Is that why you're divorced? I have learned a lot from my time on the J-Spot. And I have learned that one's ability to have a bad marriage is not a bigger success story than a person who has not yet found someone with whom to take that plunge. Thanks for the insights. Goodbye, Bob. Oh. Don't call me."

I walked over to the computer and clicked on member services to deactivate my profile and take it away. I didn't know what tomorrow would bring, but at least I knew what it wouldn't.

Fourteen

Having red eyes and orange feet, the Red-Eyed Tree Frog becomes stressed quite easily, and should not be handled unless absolutely necessary.

"So if I'm a *shiksa*," said Anne, "what's a guy who's not Jewish?" she asked, nodding her head in the direction of Fred.

They had come with me to the *Purim* party at my synagogue. Though it had been at least a month ago, I had not seen Anne and was catching her up on the tale of the Muffin Man. Everyone was in good cheer as the holiday was festive. God knew I needed that!

Purim was a kind of Halloween as people often came in costume. When Rachel Smith and I were ten we went to the *Purim* carnival dressed as ballet dancers. We dunked for apples and ate cotton candy, parading through the festival in pink tutus and hot pink tongues! On a more serious note, the holiday celebrated the time when the Jewish people living in Persia were saved from extermination. If it wasn't one thing it was another.

"*Shagetz,*" I said, looking at Fred.

"Ooooh, so what do you think of *my* costume?" he asked, doing a twirl in the center of the floor. Fred was dressed in his usual jeans and sweater having added only a black half-mask.

"What are you?" I asked.

"I'm a *shagetz.* So in case I meet some cute Jewish guy here tonight who wants to know what I am, I can tell him I'm supposed to be a *shagetz* and it won't be a lie. Besides, I'll go anywhere for free food."

Fred agreed to come when I told him there'd be wine and *hamentaschen,* the signature triangular cookies filled with preserves.

Anne and I were dressed as swing dancers. We were both wearing short flared skirts with sweaters, socks and sneakers. It was one of those noncostume costumes where it looked like you'd made a real attempt, but you didn't have to feel unreal masquerading about, in the event it turned out you weren't really in the mood.

"I always wanted to be Jewish," said Fred, while we stood to the side munching the cookies.

"Well, you've come to the right spot," I told him.

Looking around there was a smattering of people from other races, cultures and backgrounds.

"How come it's so multi-ethnic at this synagogue?" asked Anne. Her eyes darted around in what I assumed to be a lookout for Carl, but if he was still in his Chaim phase he was too religious to ever come here. "Did everyone bring friends tonight?"

"Could be," I said.

I observed a pretty Asian girl filling her glass with punch

and felt fortunate to be part of a liberal and progressive congregation.

"It's just a very open-minded place and it welcomes anyone who wants to be here," said a man's voice that seemed to rise up from behind, and fall in front of me.

I looked down to locate it, following it as if it had landed at my knees. Yet when I turned my head to the left, I saw the voice belonged to a pudgy pair of man's legs clad in bright orange tights. The legs belonged to a short bearded guy.

"Hi, Anne," said the bearded guy, talking to my friend.

"Hey! Look at you," she said, leaning in and giving the guy a great big hug.

Carl? We had never met, but who could it be but Carl? Oh my. I had pictured him completely different, but this was him and there they were. Anne and Carl. Carl and Anne. It took me by surprise that Anne would date anyone who would ever, under any circumstances, wear orange tights. Even as a costume; especially as a costume. Orange tights! My God, couldn't he have just come dressed as a cop?

"This is Rod," she said, introducing the guy who thankfully turned out not to be Carl. "We know each other forever, through friends and friends of friends. How have you been, Rod? I haven't seen you in ages," said Anne.

"Good," said Rod, sipping on a glass of wine as he entered our little circle. The burgundy color showed through the plastic cup, a nice complement to Rod's spectacular tights.

Rod joining our circle had suddenly brought the conversation to an abrupt halt. He was staring at me and it felt pretty uncomfortable. Fred and Anne carried the conversation, while Rod continued to stare. Rod the bearded guy, the guy in the orange tights. I knew he had come over to say hello to Anne, but now he was annoying me.

"What are you supposed to be?" I finally asked.

"Servant to the King," said Rod. "It was my costume. I was in the *Purim* play earlier tonight. I was the one standing in the back. Did you see it?"

"Yeah, we all saw it," said Fred.

I looked at Anne with a face that said at least there was a reason for the orange tights! Fred, meanwhile, was looking at Rod like he was trying to remember him from the play.

"I'm trying to place you. Did you have any lines?" he asked.

I was thinking that he certainly had not, because it would have been hard to forget a short bearded guy with pudgy legs in a *Purim* play wearing a pair of bright orange tights.

"One," said Rod. "I had one line. But it got cut."

"Well, I thought the play was fun, even though I already knew the ending," said Fred, whose curiosity, I could tell, was piqued as the orange tights hinted at the possibility that Rod could be pinch-hitting for Fred's team. "Did you two ever date?" he asked, throwing the bait to Anne to see if she would reel an answer in.

"No." Anne flashed Rod a big smile. "Rod's the only guy on the Upper West Side I never slept with," she said, completely out of character for her and completely joking.

"You look familiar," said Rod, turning from Anne to acknowledge me.

God, what in the world did this guy want?

"Why? Did *I* sleep with you?" I said, cracking everybody up, especially myself. I'd had my share of frogs but at least they were green, not orange.

"Where did you go to school?" asked Rod.

"What?"

"You look familiar. Where did you go to school?"

"Why?"

"I think I know you."

Anne and Fred perked up and looked at me while Rod, in all his orange splendor, again stopped speaking and continued to stare. This was ridiculous. This moment was precisely why I had brought my friends along. This was like dating online, offline! I was really sick of getting sucked into conversations with men I did not want to converse with, and now I was getting sucked into this one while my friends did nothing but watch and look on.

"You really look familiar," Orange Tights persisted. "You know I've been seeing you around here. I've been watching you. I think I know you."

"Well, I think you don't. Listen, I don't want to be rude," I said to the orange stalker. "But I just don't feel very talkative. I'm sorry, uh, Rod, is it?"

He nodded.

"Rod, we want to mill around a bit before we go," I said including Fred in my statement. "Anne," I said, looking at my politely astonished friend. "If you two want to catch up we'll come back to get you." I faced Rod. "I have to say, I really don't know you. Aside from maybe seeing each other here, you don't look familiar to me at all. I want to get another drink," I said to Fred, signaling the conversation was finished and I wanted him to come with me. "Happy *Purim*, Rod," I concluded, and turned with Fred to walk away.

But I didn't get far because I heard Rod call "Karen?" causing me to spin around and face him. The acknowledgment of my name created a glow on his face that matched his legs.

"How did you know that?"

"That's it, right? Right? Karen? That's you, right?"

I stopped short, looking at him from a few feet away.

"You're scaring me now. I don't know you. How do you know my name?"

"Klein, right? It's all coming back to me. Karen Klein, that's it, that's you, isn't it?" he said.

The bearded guy in the orange tights was beginning to look more and more like an anti-superhero in some Jewish comic book. I looked intently at his face. Nothing was familiar, but… The way he was looking… It was sticking to me. To my body. It was really sticky and it wouldn't let go. I wanted to scratch it off. The feeling was disturbingly familiar, but I… I just… I—

"What's your name, Rod? What's your last name?" I asked, praying to God it would not be memorable because the feeling was starting to itch and make me uncomfortable and it was beginning to remind of when I was in college and I lost my virginity to a guy named—

"Schwartz."

And… Oh, no…

OH, NO.

NO! NO!!

But that was this and this was him, and…

"Rodney? Rodney Schwartz? That's you? This is you?"

Anne was next to Rodney and Fred was next to me. Rodney moved towards me, as Anne and Fred moved towards him. Four corners of a box of confusion squished in and mixed together.

"That's me!" he said.

Proud. Pudgy. Triumphant. Orange.

"RODNEY SCHWARTZ! OHMYGOD!" I wailed. "I never wanted to see you again for the rest of my life!"

I was mixed up in the middle, turning in circles before running across the room, out the door, down the cement steps and onto the safety of the street. My head was suddenly pounding and I needed water. I needed something, something to drink. I felt sick, like I was going to throw up.

"I can't believe this," I screamed to Fred, who came running out after me, barreling down the stairs. "I just can't fucking believe this! Do you know that—?"

Fred pushed me down to the curb on West End Avenue. He put his left hand over my mouth so I couldn't speak, while he used his right hand to flag down a cab.

"West Seventy-eighth," he told the driver, opening the door and practically tossing me into the back of the cab. "And step on it."

"Rghhhh," I grunted, taking my hands to push away his. "Fred! What do you think you're—?"

"Listen up, Lulu, and listen up good."

We were huddled up together, but now both of Fred's hands were covering my mouth.

"You can breathe but you can't speak. You can't speak until we get into your apartment. Of all the stories you have ever told, this one is really a doozy. And I'll be damned if it gets wasted on the steps of your temple, and then later over a glass of wine, and then tomorrow on the phone, and then next week at the workshop when you complain to me, again, how there's no one-act for you. You want something to happen? You want to act? You want to be in a play? Okay. It's showtime!

"Now I want every gory, juicy detail about Little Lulu and Rodney Schwartz, and I want you to tell it to me right here," said Fred.

We were in my apartment, and Fred had planted himself on the oversized club chair in my living room. He pointed to the old Panasonic tape recorder he had me fish out of the top of my closet that was now plugged in and sitting on his lap.

"This will be the beginning of your one-person show," he said all cozy, as he put his feet up on the brown leather ottoman. "We will transcribe what you say and this is how you will write your script. Now, as your director, I am going to sit back and listen."

Fred leaned over the tape recorder using his two forefingers to press the buttons that would record.

"Okay," he said, looking at me across the room, busting and bursting out of my very own seams. "Now, tell me, Karrie, in your own words," said Fred as cool and collected as I'd ever seen him. "What the fuck went on in college between you and that guy in the hideous orange tights?"

FROGAPHOBIA

Just when you thought it was safe to date!

A TALE TOLD IN ONE ACT

Performed by Karrie Kline
Directed by Fred Grennon

Premiere:
My Theater Workshop
May 6, 2005
New York City

FROGAPHOBIA

The time is the Present.
We discover KARRIE, in bed, asleep in her bathrobe.
The stage is bare but for a bed, a table, and a chair.
The phone rings. There is a pause. The phone rings again.

KARRIE
(Sleepily looks at clock.) Eleven thirty-eight. Oh God. Eleven thirty-eight? Who's calling me so late? I just went to bed.

(The phone rings for the third time.)
Wait... Is it eleven thirty-eight tonight or is it already tomorrow? *(Thinks.)* I remember I watched *Sleepless in Seattle*. That was...

(The phone rings for the fourth time.)
I'm not getting that.

KARRIE
(voice on answering machine)
Hi there! It's Karrie Kline. Wait for the beep and do what you do!

KARRIE
(speaks over her outgoing message)
(Counting on her fingers.) Eleven. Twelve, one, two, three, fo— Oh my God! It's tomorrow!

JERRY
(voice on answering machine)
Good morning, Karrie, it's me, Jerry, over at Talent All-Too Limited.

KARRIE

I've been sleeping over twelve hours! I've got to get up.

JERRY

(voice on answering machine)

You're released from hold as the mouse for that voice-over for Cheeze Bitz. The client didn't think you sounded plump. 212-555-1234. Thanks.

(She throws the blanket covers over her head, then peeks out and talks to the audience.)

KARRIE

What a way to start the day. It's almost noon. On a Tuesday. Primetime time in the workweek. Other people, most people, are out. They're working. At the very least most people are dressed. Then there's me. Fast asleep.

I really think I would have a whole different life if I just woke up early. I once said that to a date. He said I would. He said I'd be more tired. But when you look at really successful people, don't you think that? Oprah has a talk show, a book club, a boyfriend, a movie company, a personal trainer, a cookbook and a book deal. And when I look at Oprah, all I can think is… Gosh, what time do you wake up?

(She throws the blanket covers off and points to herself.)

But I don't want to get up. I don't want to get out of my pajamas. I don't even want to get out of bed. And tonight is Marcy's bridal shower. I'll watch her open a hundred gifts on her registry so I get a good look at what I'm missing. It's all too much. I am staying in this bed and I'm not getting up until I get married.

(The phone rings. And the phone rings again.)

KARRIE

I just want to see who it is.

(She hears the voice on the machine and pulls the covers over her head.)

RODNEY
(voice on answering machine)

Hello, Karrie. This is Rodney. Rodney Schwartz. I took the liberty of looking you up in the phone book. I felt it was probably okay to take that leap after you've run into the woman who lost her virginity to you. Call me. 212-555-5678.

KARRIE

Well, this is turning out to be one red-banner day. If I knew that night in my dorm room that two decades later, a still-single me would run into Rodney Schwartz at temple, a Rodney dressed in bright orange tights for his part in the *Purim* play, I probably would've opted to "lose it" with some other guy. We met my freshman year at college. I was a theater major and Rodney was getting his Masters in film. Soon I was starring in his thesis, "The Geometry of Love." He directed me to run through the other girl's dorm with a knife screaming, "Where is she?" I had to douse him with a pitcher of beer when I caught them making out in the campus pub. And then there was the nude scene. Rodney directed me to be ecstatic, like I had an orgasm. And that's where my acting ability failed me because I couldn't act what I just did not know. In the end I refused to spend my spring break at school filming and left him to wait tables in the Catskills. "What are you interested in—art or money?" Rodney would scream, wild like his bushy hair. It was soon after I "lost it" but I lost it again and we broke up.

(The phone rings.)

KARRIE

It's so busy! Look. I'm still not married, but I do have to pee. You listen while I'm gone. Take a message. I'll be right back.

(She exits.)

MARCY
(voice on answering machine)
Hi, it's Marcy. I know we talked about you coming to Bloomie's with me to help pick out a couch for the new co-op, but Martin reminded me we have theater tickets tonight to see *Phantom* so I can't. Call me.

(KARRIE reenters wearing a skirt, tank top and flip-flops.)

KARRIE
(As if she's at a surprise party.)
SURPRISE! Won't Marcy be surprised to find out that tonight, instead of seeing *Phantom* she's going to see every important female she knows tell her, "I'm so happy for you. I told you it would happen. It happens for everybody. It just has to be your time." Do you think it happens for everyone?

(KARRIE asks people in the audience.)

Do you? What about you, sir? *(Points to someone else.)* And, over there...you? I think— Well, I'm going to need a very strong cup of coffee to tell you that. I know...if I'm making I should make

enough for everybody, but I just don't have a big enough pot.
Sorry!

(She goes to an area and makes coffee as she talks.)

I used to think if you kissed a lot of frogs one of them would
turn into a prince. But look at this. *(Picks up magazine article
from table and reads.)* "Some women turn frogs into princes, do
you turn princes into frogs? Find out, take this test." Well! Let's
dip our toes into the last fifteen years of my dating pond and
we'll find out.

(Pours a cup of coffee and sits.)

There was Donald the writer, who spent thirty-two hours working on a paragraph about snow. The Famous Television Star
whose idea of foreplay was to bark like he had four paws. Born-
again Christian comedian Jack Whitney was some match for a
Jewish actress. Instead of having the relationship we just sold
the movie rights. Publicist Jay Kohn left me flat in the dunes
of East Hampton. Elliot Lieberman, the photographer, changed
his mind as fast as he changed his phobias. Arthur was probably my worst date…almost. A total no-show, he must have burst
from anticipation. But it wasn't all bad. Some frogs had great
families. I pretended to be a shiksa to snare Dr. Alan Greenberg
for a place at his seder table. And I really loved David's dad. Jordy
the Hollywood agent, put the La into LaLa Land, and eating with
Bradley was a flavorful potpourri—his cheesecake a real delight!
Then there was Roman. *(Wistful.)* Now he was a holiday. The
cute Yaley stockbroker was transferred to Boston just as we were
getting hot. So let's look at these stories and count them like
sheep. Then you tell me if it's such a big deal. Maybe it's not.
Maybe you just have to kiss a lot of frogs.

Fifteen

"Jeremiah was a bullfrog—"

The song blasted through the theater after the show, the opening night party calling me to come on down. I was alone backstage but could hear the buzz down the hall like an electric current zipping its way towards the dressing room and coming to get me. I couldn't wait to go, but first I needed to take this moment to congratulate my cast.

Staring hard, I looked at myself in the mirror. I looked past the round lightbulbs and the makeup, to the woman underneath who was me. Me. Who stood on the stage alone for thirty-six minutes and performed her own one-person show to not *just* an appreciative audience, but an amazing one. An audience that hung on for the whole ride—laughing, crying and cheering me on.

"It's Mommy, can I come in?"

I was excited that Millie had flown up from Florida to be here, but now that she was standing outside my dressing room door I suddenly wished she wasn't. I got ready to face her with only just a little trepidation. When my mother usually came backstage I hoped she liked the show, and bought me as the character. But what was she going to buy me as now? After all these years, was I going to get called out on the carpet for going out with all those men?

I made a quick mental list of everything I talked about in the show that could be incriminating. The stuff about my father…should be okay. The stuff about my stepfather… would be okay. The stuff about her…could be okay. The stuff about sex…uh-oh. The stuff about sex was definitely *not* okay.

It suddenly occurred to me I had not thought this through!

I didn't think my mother had ever known when I lost my virginity but she sure knew now, and I sure was in really big trouble. I was going to get grounded. I would be sent to my apartment and I would have to stay there for the next fifteen years and I wouldn't be allowed to sleep with anybody. I wondered if the part where I paid tribute to my Judaism had been enough to redeem me.

"Karrie, I can't believe it." Millie opened the door and came towards me. I could hear her voice, but I wouldn't look up.

"I'm sorry I never told you about doing a nude scene in a movie in college," I blurted out to my mom. "But I mean, why would I tell you that? I didn't think it was something I should tell you. You didn't want me to tell you that. Did you? Did you want me to tell you?"

"Why would you tell me something that never happened?" asked Millie. She took a second to throw her arms around me. Then she broke away. "Listen to me, Karrie. You were great. Your show was great. And these days you have to have sex for something to sell. Danielle Steele does it. They all do it. I know it's not true."

I faced my mother.

"Ma," I began, looking straight into her brown eyes. "You're right. They all do it, but—" I paused for a long thoughtful moment. "It's just a show! I mean, come on— it's not like it's my autobiography or anything," I said, suddenly gaining confidence as I spit out each word. "And Fred said you have to do this sort of spin to make it more interesting. That's what you have to do when you do these things. Embellish," I said, as I did. However, my next thought was a little more than unnerving. "What if people do think it's all true?"

"Who gives a shit what people think? If anyone wants to know what's true you tell them *everything* and really give them something to talk about. Now, come on. Your friends are waiting for you down the hall."

They sure were. Everyone cheered when I walked into the little theater that held the party. The tables were covered in green tablecloths, and a variety of different colored plastic frogs were scattered among the finger food. Starving, I smiled at everyone as I made a beeline to the buffet where I picked up a few squares of cucumber and cream cheese sandwiches.

Ryan called out for everyone's attention.

"Hey, everybody! Thanks for coming out tonight. Let's take this moment to congratulate everyone in MTW's One-Act Fest. The whole evening was a big success, but tonight was also the debut of My Theater Workshop's first ever solo show. Let's hear it for Karrie Kline, who finally did something worthwhile with all those bad dates of hers. Way to go! And for Fred Grennon, who not only directed the piece, but also played a big part in its conception. Let's not forget our staff and the crew who kept the whole thing running. So tell your friends, bring everyone down, and now…let's party!"

I was completely elated as I looked around the room and
saw the supportive, happy faces of Brooke and Mitch and
Jane and William and Anne and Millie and…where was
Fred? I couldn't find Fred. Fred, the one I owed it all to. I
had to find him, I thought, and was on my way to do just
that when—*pop!*

A white flash of light popped in front of my eyes as if
someone had just taken my picture. It really blurred my vision, because it seemed that standing in front of me was Elliot, the photographer, who I'd not been in touch with since
the time we broke up.

"Hi," he said, the halting and tentative quality of his voice
reminding me that, indeed, it was him. "It's funny running
into you like this, Karrie. It's been a while. But this is really,
really weird for me. I mean, you were great up there, but I
have to say I really didn't appreciate all that stuff you said
about me in your show. I was a nice guy—I was supportive
of your career, why didn't you say that? At least you said we
had good sex. If you didn't say that I don't know what I
would have done.

"But you made me sound so indecisive. *Changed my mind
as fast as I changed my phobias?* And why did you say I eat
pizza every day for lunch? I don't eat pizza every day, I eat
tuna. Tuna for lunch and bagel for breakfast. Though now
I go to a diner every morning and sometimes I eat a muffin, but only blueberry, so if they're out of that I have to get
a bagel. Otherwise I have to get toast."

I was so glad Elliot had filled me in. But Elliot was not
finished.

"And I thought you liked it when I sang Broadway show
tunes in the car?"

"I didn't say I didn't like it, I just said you sang off-key.
That your conversation in the car was only to be alternated
with your off-key singing of Broadway show tunes. Off-key

is funny. I think it even got a laugh. It's just a show, Elliot. You only served as an inspiration for the character. God it wasn't *Elliot Lieberman: The E! True Hollywood Story.* So, hi back at ya. What are you doing here, anyway?"

"The publicist for your theater called me to come down and take pictures. I thought I'd surprise you, but the surprise was mine when the curtain went up. Jeez. Say cheese!"

He snapped away as I silently posed for a bunch of shots wondering who the heck the publicist was for the theater.

"Listen, can I call you? I'd like to see you again, Karrie, but I don't want you to think anything will be different. I don't want you to think anything won't be, either. I mean, I think about you and I'd like to call, but I don't want to… Well, I do, sort of. I just don't know if I…can you help me out here?"

I was only trying to help myself out of this same conversation I had walked away from four years ago. And I was about to tell him when I was intercepted by *Bradley?* Ohmygod! There he was, in the flesh. It had been a decade since I'd had the *delight* of seeing him. But Bradley was suddenly before me; tall, real and handsome as ever.

"Hello after all these years," he said, jotting notes into a small spiral pad while we spoke. "The publicist of your workshop called and invited me to come down, and when I heard it was you I did. My magazine has branched out to tell tourists not just where to eat, but what shows to see when they visit New York. I had no idea when I came down tonight that I would be in it. That was very sweet, I've never been immortalized in a show before," he said to me while I looked at handsome him and wondered. Wondering if this was all business, and whether it could be more?

"You look well," he continued. "Can I ask you just a few questions now, Karrie? I want to get this into the next issue. I'll be brief because my fiancée is waiting for me at home," said Bradley, answering my question while I continued to answer his. However, there was no time to sort out those feelings because *another* familiar froggy face suddenly appeared after Bradley's departure.

"I can't believe you remembered that I never gave you a ride back from the Hamptons!" said Jay Kohn, the publicist that left me behind in what was an almost-forgotten summer. "I bet you're wondering what I'm doing here?"

For someone to actually answer that question would be asking a lot. I never expected my opening night party to turn into a segment of *This Is Your Life.*

"Ryan hired me to be the publicist for MTW," Jay proudly announced. "And I've gotten a lot of people down tonight for my first shot," he said. (I didn't have the heart to tell him that I had dated half his media list.) "Hey, since I'm responsible for getting you so much coverage, could you do a little something for me?" asked Jay. "I was dating this woman for over a year and she kind of ended it, and I'm really, really upset and…I wonder if maybe I could pick your brain to see if I could get your take on it. See if you had any dating tips for me. I mean, since you're a dating expert and all."

"Dating expert? I'm an actress. When did I become a dating expert?"

And to prove my lack of expertise, my stomach tightened and the cavity in my chest hollowed out when I looked up to find myself facing Edward!

"My goodness! Edward Smith. How did *you* get here?"

"Well, BlueEyes, you never called me after I sent that last e-mail, and you disappeared from the J-Spot so I Googled you. There was a link that took me to the MTW site that led me here," he said, his dark eyes piercing.

Next time a guy tells me he didn't call because he lost my number I'll have to remember this.

"You were stunning," he said, with shock, awe and an almost begrudging tone. "I had never seen you perform. You were in your element. I had to tell you that. I had to give you that. I couldn't take my eyes off you."

"Well, it was a one-person play. There wasn't exactly anyone else on stage to look at."

"No. You were terrific. I mean that, Karrie. And I wondered—" He stopped. "I just wonder…"

What was he trying to say? And why did I even care? Oh, please, who was I kidding? So what was he trying to say? Had Edward had a revelation? Had my *Frogaphobia* cured him of his?

"I just wondered," Edward began again. "How come *I* wasn't in your show? Didn't you think me frog-worthy? I was so disappointed when it got to the very end and I wasn't in it. How come all those other guys got to be in it and not me? I want to be a frog."

"Edward, why do you want to be a frog so badly? Why don't you aspire to something better? Why don't you want to be a prince?"

"The frog status is so attainable," he said.

It felt like I'd just been hit! But I was. Right behind me stood Fred, whose enthusiasm produced too strong a tap on my back.

"You're a genius!" I said, throwing my arms around him. "How can I thank you? This is amazing. I think you're on to something, Freddy. And not just for me, maybe a directing career for you. I can't believe how this came together."

"And in such large portions," said Fred, basking in the mutual admiration club to which both of us were members.

It all happened within six weeks. The experience a real testament to the words—*Just Do It!* Once I committed, everything else had followed.

Even without a finished script, Ryan had agreed to give me the slot left open by the loss of Brockman's play. As MTW's first solo show, he made *Frogaphobia* the featured part of the One-Act Fest. Being produced by MTW relieved me of having to pay for a theater rental, lighting designer, stage manager and, apparently, a publicist! The set was sparse. It was Black Box Theater, and I mean that literally. Black boxes created my set of a bed, table and chair.

My show was the only one after the intermission. I was told it could run no more than forty-five minutes. I came in at thirty-six. That was far less daunting than creating a full-length solo show. However, it was still a lot of material. My first concept was to do it as a one-sided conversation—just give me a phone and thirty-six minutes could go by in a flash!

Fred was my director and, at the beginning, my dramaturge. But once I began to adapt my audio tapes into play form it became obvious that while I'd never written, I had analyzed, read and acted in enough plays so that when it came to structure I was surprised to find I actually had a few ideas. Once I got going it was fun, it was mine, and I saw that no matter what happened I'd always have that experience of creating. Ultimately I had nothing to lose.

"So," said Fred. "You did it, Lulu."

"I could never have done this without you," I said in all sincerity. "People say that all the time, but only you and I really know how true that is. I need to start collecting more material. And I think tonight's party has already given me enough for a whole second act. Hey—when are you free? You want to come over tomorrow? I'll set up the little tape recorder thingy and we'll do more. What do you think? What time is good?"

Fred did not answer. I thought, perhaps, he was running his schedule through his mind, but his unsettling silence seemed to indicate something more.

"Fred, did I do something wrong in the show? Did I forget some important direction or…I don't know, you look a little weird. Are you tired? Are you okay?"

"I'm fine," said Fred. Straightening up, opening his eyes wider when he spoke. "And you were fine in the show. I mean you were really good. Don't be so paranoid, Karrie, it was great. It's not that. I have something to tell you."

Who died, was the first thought that came to mind. Who got diagnosed with cancer, was the second. Something terrible had happened, but then suddenly Fred was smiling.

"Babalou, I mean Trey, I should really call him Trey, has decided to give up his philandering ways and he really wants to try." Fred sort of sang the word *try* as if it were a couple of syllables. "And," he said, also stretching that word out to show just how important the additional info would be. "He got this job as the Wardrobe Master for *Whistles and Whispers* at the Ahmanson. The national tour did such great business in their last stop in L.A., they turned it into a sit-down company and it's got an open-ended run out there."

"That's great," I said thinking, perhaps, I could work something out with Ryan so *Frogaphobia* could get an open-ended run. I could do it in the smaller theater, or since it was only thirty-six minutes maybe I could do it as a curtain raiser before the next show! If we could figure something out, I could always be performing. I'd have something I could invite industry people to if they wanted to see my work, and I was so absorbed in my thoughts I had missed the punch line because when Fred asked, "So you're okay about it?" I had no idea what he was referring to.

"What?" I asked, pulled out of my trance. "I'm sorry. What did you say?"

"That I've known for a few weeks but I didn't want anything to upset you before the show. I'm moving to Los Angeles with Trey. I'm leaving in two days."

"Oh nooooooo!" Tears spurted up in my eyes and involuntarily fell down my cheeks. "You're my partner in crime. My friend. What will I do without you?" I wrapped my arms around him and started to cry while I felt Fred, who I was never physical with, tentatively pat my hair. I looked up and saw that he was crying, too. "Oh…and I'm not a complete selfish shit. I'm really happy for you, Freddy!" I sobbed.

We stood there for a moment, in a moment we never thought would come, but had to. The point was to work towards these moments that propelled you forward in your life, not to be held back in the comfortable coziness of the same old same old. I didn't want us to say that everything would stay the same. That he would be back or I'd go out there or anything like that. Life was moving on, and in time we'd know what it would do. Right now it was going to be different and different felt hard, but different was what we were always lobbying for, wasn't it?

"Well," I said, using the napkin that had held the cucumber sandwiches to wipe away my tears. "I hope everything will exceed your expectations. You and I are friends. For always. And—" I had to suck the air in quickly before I spoke so my voice would not choke on the sob "—I'll miss you, Fred."

"Lulu," said Fred, holding on to my free hand tightly as I was now using the napkin to blow my nose with the other. "I love you."

"Well, I finally have a great guy telling me he loves me. I love you, too, Fred. We get to keep that part," I said, taking in a fresh breath of air. "And that part's really good."

Sixteen

When mating, some frogs may emit a release call telling the amorous suitor, essentially, to get lost.

To: KKline2@uh-oh-l.com
From: RYAN@mtw.org
Subject: Fwd: Saw You In *Frogaphobia!* Would Love To Talk!
Hey, KK!
E-mails are still coming in, beauty. From your newest admirer!
Ryan

To: RYAN@mtw.org
From: jerseyguy@uh-oh-l.com
Subject: Saw You In *Frogaphobia!* Would Love To Talk!
Would you please be so kind to forward this e-mail to Ms. Kline:
Dear Karrie,
May I call you that? I saw your show last Saturday night. I

brought a date from New Jersey and we got into quite a difference of opinion on the ride back to Englewood. She
thought men (aka me) don't really pursue women in a
princely fashion, while I tried to explain that what most
women don't realize is that men typically don't feel that they
have the upper hand in these sorts of situations. Most women
don't recognize the potential power that they hold over men.
Of course, every relationship is different, and you probably
know more than I do about this. Perhaps one night after your
show I could take you out for a drink and we could exchange
dating viewpoints.
Please let me know when I might be able to call to arrange
this.
Respectfully,
Harvey Weiner

I wondered how often *Dear Abby* got hit on?

Women were writing that I made them laugh. They felt
relieved to know they weren't the only ones who had trouble finding a good frog among their undesirable toads. Men
personalized and intellectualized. And some tried to use my
how-not-to insight to literally woo me. Had Harvey really
paid attention to my show he would have known his e-mail
pursuit was on par with the unprincely fashion of which
he'd already been accused. I suspected theorizing over a
drink with me was meant to lead up to a little more than a
new perspective. But for the first time in a long time I had
other things on my mind besides dismal dates.

It had been a couple of weeks since the show started. The
four weekend run of the one-act fest would soon be coming to its end.

Jay Kohn had managed the miraculous coup of getting
Wow Women magazine to agree to see the show this weekend and do a story on me. The magazine scheduled a big

photo shoot after the performance Friday night. I was pos-
itively ecstatic. Tina, the photographer, called today to get
my sizes because they would be supplying wardrobe and a
makeup artist, too. I was hopeful when the piece hit the
stands it would help drum up business. Ryan, already certain it would, decided to keep me up and running. His idea
to hire a publicist for MTW was a good one. Jay Kohn was
money well spent. Jay also had a vested interest, but it wasn't
in me.

The combination of being dumped by The Girlfriend,
somewhat deservedly as Jay had come to admit, and seeing
himself as a frog in my show gave Jay the desire for redemp-
tion. He had spent several nights at my kitchen table telling
me his tales of woe. To keep it balanced I shot a few frog
stories his way. Suddenly in the middle of his third scoop
of Ben & Jerry's Chocolate Chip Cookie Dough he said,
"I've got it. I've got an angle *Wow Women* would love. Listen to this! *She Kissed So Many Frogs She Did A Show About
It!*"

I didn't know how to thank him. Ryan was paying him,
so what he wanted from me was advice. But I was without
any further insights as to how he might patch it up with The
Girlfriend. Not wanting to come up empty, I suggested Jay
send her three dozen roses with a sincerely apologetic note.
It sounded like a trite move in a soap, but to both our surprise she agreed to meet him for dinner. After all the drama
the shift came down to thirty-six red, white and yellow
flowers, and one short and honest note.

When that happened I almost wished Jay could call Edward and tell him twelve monochromatic ones with no note
would do the trick. But then, without even knowing it, I had
a shift. I was so absorbed in my work, my thoughts of Edward were finally appropriate to what he deserved. Without

even realizing, they slipped and faded away. It felt peaceful to be free.

Dirk called last night. Dirk had been in Los Angeles all year. Oddly, he called to tell me he was free. That it was coming up on the year anniversary of his breakup with the Internet business woman and he knew he was finally free because he no longer thought about her.

"But you are thinking about her, Dirk," I said. "You're thinking about her right now," I said, lying on the couch with a glass of wine, thinking that I wasn't thinking about anyone because I was going over that night's show in my head.

It had been a small, but very responsive, Sunday night house. During the Dissecting Mr. Frogstein section I said while the average frog had four legs, only two species possessed "fingers," which could be a reason why most frogs could never pick up a phone and call. Right then a woman in the second row stood up and shouted, "You got that right. You go, girl!" Prompting everyone in the audience to cheer and jeer.

"No. I was just thinking about you," said Dirk, as I pictured him of the species *Chiroleptes platicephalus* that possessed an opposable thumb. I imagined Dirk swimming in a pond surrounded by palm trees under the Hollywood sign, coming up for air, and using only one webbed limbed digit to make this call. "I just passed the test, Kar, because of you."

"Okay. Feel free to clue me in anytime, Dirk."

"The old M.T. The masturbation test. I didn't think about her at all this time. And guess why? Because I was thinking about you!"

"And this is supposed to make me happy?"

"Well I'm happy for you," said Dirk. "It's empowering to do what you're doing. Hey, man, I would love to find something I could call mine where I didn't have to feel infantilized by the way these agents treat you in this business. It's worse for a woman, but it's not great for a man in our age group, either."

Neither of us spoke, allowing the harsh reality to settle in in silence. Unlike most other professions we had made a lot more money when we were younger. With the extension of *Frogaphobia,* Ryan promised me a cut from the door. That would probably cover the subway and my cups of coffee! But my commercials were running, and so was my show! One thing often led to another, and right now I was managing fine.

"Your agent come to see you yet? He must be pretty jazzed you're making this happen."

"Jerry's coming. So he says. It's weird. I'd thought he'd have been one of the first. But now I'm extended. He'll come."

"They all say that and then the show's over and where were they?"

"He will. I mean, he is, Dirk. He's away, and *Wow Women* will be out by the time he's back so it'll be perfect. I want to talk to him about getting casting people down to see me. Maybe I'll even come out next year for pilot season. I want something fantastic to happen."

"Hmm…I'd like something fantastic to happen, too. What are you wearing?" Dirk murmured into the phone.

Dirk. Why hadn't I thought of it before? He'd be perfect. He could be it.

"Hey, what are you doing two weeks from today?" I asked.

"Why? You coming out here?"

"No. Will you come here? Be my date for a wedding, Dirk. Okay?"

"Absolutely not."

"Dirk! Please. It's Brooke Morgan's. You know her, right? It'll be fun. Come to New York. Stay here." I paused. "With me," I said, I thought seductively but instead I felt it come out like a whine.

"No."

"I'll pay your plane fare. I don't want to go to the wedding alone."

"I don't do weddings, and I don't do Bar Mitzvahs. What day is it, again? I think I have to get a haircut that day. Oh, wait, *that* day? I think I have to do something really important *that* day. I think *that* day I have to take a shower. Karrie, even if I was back East you know this is not something I do. Even for a great bud like you."

With all my energy into the show, I had almost forgotten about not having a date for the wedding. But now that I remembered I was less than thrilled. Not quite desperate enough to enlist Harvey Weiner, it seemed I had to go it alone. Wait! Jay Kohn! Yes, he owed me after all those nights *kvetching* at my kitchen table. Ohhhh, but I remembered we even talked about it because that was the day Jay had bought tickets for the opera with The Girlfriend.

"I don't know how to thank you, Karrie, but it worked. She talks about those flowers all the time. Especially the colors! She says if they were all red she might not have called, but it was the multicolored theme that got her going."

The attention I received the following week, the week that *Wow Women* hit the stands, was as gratifying as anything I had ever known. I felt thrilled to open the magazine and see the beautiful, blown-up glossy shot on the roof of the building that housed MTW, backlit with the lights of Broadway. It was a sexy shot that glittered, just like the gauzy, green spaghetti-strapped dress I wore with shiny beads sewn into the fabric.

I looked at the smile on the face of the actress in the photo. The confident, carefree smile of that single actress who did the show about all her bad dates, and was loving every minute. Then I read the article that spun my life into a fairy-tale happy ending, and I could not believe that the woman in that photo, that actress, that woman, her, *me,* was stuck going to Brooke and Mitch's wedding alone.

So the night before the wedding when Jerry and I went out after the show, I decided I would ask him. I decided to ask my agent to escort me to the wedding. It was a little weird, but weirder things have happened.

Jerry and I had been close. I'd been signed with his agency for sixteen years. Jerry's mom saw me perform in San Francisco. He had visited me when I lived in L.A. He visited me on sets when I worked, and even came to a Passover *seder* in my apartment. A decade ago Jerry and I had gone away to the Poconos for a weekend at a mutual friend's house where the three of us made dinner cooking the fish we caught that day. Jerry would come with me to the wedding. It would be another event to remember another decade from now. Brooke said I could call her the day before with a date and it was the day before. And the best part was in the end there would be no confusion with Jerry because Jerry was gay.

"I loved your show," he squealed with his infectious laugh as we sat down for a beer in the nearby bar everyone always hung out at after the shows. "You were so funny. You totally crack me up, Karrie Kline. It was great!"

"I'm so glad, and I have a ton of stuff to discuss with you about how to promote me with it, but first I need to ask you something."

"Well, actually before you do that I feel there's something we need to talk about."

"Well, this is important. Can I go first?"

"Actually, Karrie, I took you out to do this in person. Would you mind if I went first?"

You wake up in the morning and you always think you know what will happen. You think you know what the day will bring. You have a list on your desk of things to do, and sometimes you may even do them all. But we don't have a list for the unexpected. The unexpected, that can often bring something better than what you had planned…or not.

So when Jerry, looking at me through the same green eyes that looked at me years and years ago when he had begged me to leave another talent agency to go with his, told me that my contract was up for renewal and put a manila envelope down on the table, it was with great embarrassment to both of us when I took out a pen and opened the envelope to sign the new contract, only to find that Jerry was returning fifty of my unused head shots because the agency had decided not to re-sign me.

"You don't fit into the category of the funny, forties, suburban housewife. Even though you look younger, the casting people all know you so they know your real age. You don't fit into that mom slot, you never grew into that," he said as if that were a bad thing, a definitive thing, a thing I had to be.

"But, Jerry—" I knew I would say this only once and let it go. Because after I said it I would never have a need to say it again. "I created something. My show. I created a character, a persona based on me in an original show. Don't you think it's possible to take me out of the box I no longer fit in, and sell me in this new package? Don't you think it's more exciting? Don't you think it's at least worth six months to try?"

But he didn't. Jerry said the casting people would never go for it. They remembered me a certain way and that era was over.

Elvis and Marilyn would always stay their type, but other people grew. They aged. They changed. And they changed into something else. I looked at Jerry and while I felt sad, I had to admit that I liked what I had changed into. When I realized that, it felt good to be cut free. I no longer wanted to be the actress, or the person, he thought the casting people would go for.

Jerry and I talked about how we would stay in touch. But when we said good-night we both knew we had said good-bye. And though I was disappointed, I was leaving the table with more than when I had sat down. My sense of self had grown. I owned it, it belonged to me, and I had made it happen. Without Jerry's permission—permission I would no longer need.

I went home and went straight to bed, but when I woke up the next day I did feel the loss. I had my show, but for the first time ever I was an actress without representation. I also knew I would miss Jerry. We could always laugh. Sixteen years was a very long time. It felt so cliché, but boy does time fly.

So here it was. Already June. An entire year had passed since the arrival of the Save-The-Date card. Today was the day. Brooke and Mitch's wedding. Sadly, this gray, drizzly Sunday matched my mood. And as I lay in bed looking out the window I hoped everything would clear up. Soon.

Sunday Night

And did it ever!

The Fox. From the wedding! Doug Fox. It was all I could think about when I went to bed. How happy I was to have met Doug this afternoon, out in the sunlight on the deck overlooking the Hudson at Brooke and Mitch's glorious, wonderful wedding.

"Would you like to have dinner with me?" he had asked in the cab, it skidding past the cars on the West Side Highway, later, when he took me home.

Tonight, the whole time I was onstage doing my show about the frogs, the day with Doug filtered through my mind as I felt I had finally met a good one! I drifted off to sleep picturing his face, his devilish grin, his short light brown hair, and the moment in the cab when he tilted his face towards mine, and kissed me. I fell to sleep, Doug's kiss lingering on my lips, and I slept. Soundly.

I awoke the next morning with the feeling all my frogs were in a well-organized row. And then I thought about Doug. Whoever said a kiss was just a kiss was sadly mistaken. But what made a kiss? What was it about lips coming together that created emotions that could send you falling or flying? Having spent so much time on stage talking about the kisses of the last fifteen years, I chose to lazily stay in bed, allowing myself to drift off and remember my very first ones.

Gary Waks was the first boy I kissed. Well, not exactly. But by the time I actually kissed Gary I felt amazed and relieved, since what I knew about kissing before him had done nothing but disappoint.

My very first kiss came from Lee Loran in seventh grade, at Joni Wolf's Bat Mitzvah. The reception had wound down when Joni brought out the empty wine bottle and suggested the game.

I always wanted to kiss Lee but it had never happened. In sixth grade we had an almost kiss, when after school one day he told me he liked the way my hair looked cut with bangs. I chickened out, taking off down the block to the safety of home. But now Joni wanted us to spin the bottle.

We arranged ourselves into a circle of eight boys and eight girls. I watched as Lee's turn moved him into the center. I watched this boy I'd known all my life, kneel down on one knee as he took the bottle to spin. This boy, who'd take my cake at birthday parties and mash it up with M&Ms. This same boy, whose voice now broke while his skin broke out. The bottle spun. I prayed and prayed it would stop in front of me. Until it actually did.

Lee—and—Kar—en, Lee—and—Kar—en—

I froze. Lee crawled to me on his knees. In front of the group he leaned over and kissed me. It was fast and furious, clumsy and strange, but it was something even worse.

"He smells like turkey," I told Rachel the next day at school, comparing notes in the coat closet.

Two summers later when we returned to our rented bungalow in the Catskills, I found out I was the only girl who had never made out. Peer pressure pushed me to make out with Stu Berry in Denise Critelli's bungalow one night when her father was in the city, her mother was out playing Mah-Jongg, and her brother was down by the lake blowing up salamanders. Denise and Gary Waks were making out on one side of the high-rise bed, me and Berry on the other. Berry didn't smell like turkey, but I sure didn't moan and groan like Denise did from whatever Gary was doing with her.

I was still talking turkey when my first night the following summer, I took a walk alone on the road where Denise and I had spotted Gary and Berry the year before. I jumped when I heard the noise. But it turned out to be Gary, riding by on his ten-speed bike, his brown hair long, his body lean and already tan. He was seventeen, gorgeous, and I felt in that moment he was destined to be mine.

"Whoa!" he said, parking his bike against a stone wall before coming to meet me. Rocks and pebbles crunched under his sneakers, and Gary eyed me closely as he walked.

The light illuminating the big yellow Edelstein Estates sign shone, revealing me in my cutoffs, my brown hair down to my waist, my blue eyes wide, and my heart practically popping out of my tight red polyester top.

"What happened to you this year?" asked Gary. "You've changed."

"I'm sixteen now. Do you think that's it?" I asked, unaware of the change, but for the awareness that whatever it was it seemed to be good.

Gary studied me hard before he stepped in, testing the waters to see if I would move away. I didn't. I couldn't. Something new was happening, as if invisible strings of desire were pulling us towards each other.

"You've gotten so pretty, Karrie," he said, as he took a piece of hair that dangled over my right eye and tucked it behind my ear. He grinned. "Who'd have thunk it?"

"You think?" My heart thumped away. Gary touched me. My hair!

"Very," he said. "And you know what else?"

His dark brown eyes penetrated through me. I had never seen a mouth like his. Soft lips, lush. The top lip curled slightly over the bottom. It affected me in ways I did not know how to describe. I had never even been so close to such a cute boy.

"No. What?"

"Voluptuous," said Gary.

I didn't know the word so I didn't know.

"It's like you're ripe," he said. "It's sensual."

"Sensual," I repeated. "Is that like…you know…" I felt butterflies. "Sexy?"

"Better."

Gary smiled. First he gave me a look to see if it was okay. Then his lips brushed across the tops of mine as slivers of sensations cut right through me. Gary continued to kiss me, very soft and very slow. And for the very first time I was kissing back. Until I felt something that made me giggle.

"Wait. Is that?" It made me stop. It felt like, uh…*tongue?*

"Yeah," he said. "Tell me if you like this. We don't have to do it if you don't want."

"I want. Show me."

"Nice," Gary whispered later.

"Mmm," I whispered back.

It was better than nice. It was what all the fuss was about. Yes, I had learned that it was much ado about *some*thing.

And no one ever tells you that it gets better as you get older. Especially for women!

I got up to attack the day. I needed to work out, work on the play, look for a new agent, and look at my calendar to see what nights I was available this week to go out with Doug. I was hoping for Wednesday or Thursday. If we had dinner midweek, perhaps he'd come see the show on the weekend. Or maybe it would be better if we spent more time together before he saw the show. It didn't matter. However it tumbled would be fine, but I couldn't wait.

I looked at the clock. It had just turned ten. I didn't take him for one of those guys who'd call first thing in the morning, but I did feel he was as jazzed as me. And I couldn't wait for him to call.

Monday Night

It was only a day. I mean, if I were him I think I would have called today. If I were him I would have made a dinner plan in the cab.

But I'm not him.

Well, it was only a day. I was pretty sure that tomorrow he'd call.

Tuesday Night

He was cool.

Doug was a very, very cool guy so he wasn't the type to jump it and call right away. Besides, I thought those how-to-get-a-guy books always said Wednesday was the night to call for a Saturday night date. This week I had a special show, for a singles group, but I supposed I could just see him after.

Okay, no problem. Wednesday. Wednesday's the day. I'm sure Wednesday he'll call.

Wednesday Night

He didn't.

Thursday Night

What's going on?

It's almost eleven. It's too late for him to call now.

And if he hasn't called by tonight, tomorrow's Friday and then it's the weekend so he probably won't call till next week.

He could have just been busy all week. Really busy. He could have had lots of meetings. For all I know maybe he had to go out of town. And when he's back next week he'll call. Or maybe even on Sunday. Sunday night would make sense. It's a decent time frame. Certainly not overeager, but still it's *just* a week. A respectable amount of time.

Okay. I'm fine.

I'm really okay. I'm busy, too. I have my show this weekend. I have people coming down, plans to go out. I'm cool, too. He'll call on Sunday. Everything's cool.

One Week

"I believe in very traditional male/female roles," he said, pulling me back into him by gently and seductively pulling me by my hair.

"I believe in them, too," I said. I did. I do.

"Would you like to have dinner with me?" he asked.

When?

"I'd love it," I said, while the cab headed up Seventy-ninth Street to Broadway.

When??

"I'll call you during the week," he said, releasing me from

his touch, but not until the taxi deposited me in front of my building, just off Amsterdam on West Seventy-eighth.

I rewound the tape, replaying it over and over in my mind as I tried to see what I had missed. What I misinterpreted. What clue I had lost that would help me understand what was going on. I felt so bad, so monumentally disappointed.

I really wanted him to call.

Two Weeks

One kitchen table: Jay Kohn's, and one pint of Belgian Dark Chocolate: Godiva's later, Jay—newest dating expert since he and The Girlfriend were as happy as two peas in a pod—told me that when a guy really, really likes you and has serious intentions he absolutely does *not* call for a first date right away.

Instead, *he waits two full weeks* before he calls.

The thinking behind that is he knows you are not some passing fancy, you won't be just a flash in the pan, and he has to get ready. He takes those two weeks to contemplate, getting ready for this major life change as he knows he will be taking a plunge.

Okay!

Well…

I guess we'd have to see.

At least it sounded hopeful.

I was heading downtown to do the show and then I'd come home. There would be a call.

Or there wouldn't.

Three Weeks

There wasn't.

And there would not be.

Seventeen

Frogs tend to be farsighted, having the ability to see objects fifty feet away but missing what's right under their nose.

Anne scraped the mozzarella cheese off the top of her chicken cutlet while I scooped it up from her plate, adding it on top of the sausage that was already added onto the slice. Vinnie's Pizza, an Upper West Side hangout from the early days, had been renovated to include black-and-white etchings of Italy and table service. Anne and I decided to bag an upscale cafe on Columbus for Vinnie's, a place we knew we could grab a bite before heading down to Lincoln Center for Midsummer Night Swing. Despite the new décor, I still folded the pizza in half and ate it with my hands. Aluminum tables and artwork were not motivation for me to eat a slice a pizza with of knife and a fork.

"So I guess for someone with a CSW, I'm an idiot," she

told me, placing a napkin over the chicken parmigiano to sop up the grease.

"Why would you say that?" I asked, watching the napkin absorb it with fascination. I never think to do that. If it's really bad I'll tilt the plate and let it roll off, but when I see grease I always assume the food's just still marinating.

"Well, you remember that Carl and I broke up last year when he became religious, but he really wasn't into it and he went back. So we got back together the beginning of this year. Sort of."

"Oh?"

I flashed back on the *Purim* party and wondered why she hadn't mentioned it then, but there was kind of a lot going on. Not to mention I kind of disappeared after the reappearance of Rodney. In general, Anne was fairly private and had been as evasive about her sort-of-boyfriend this year, as she had been last year about her sort-of-ex.

Carl was the first man Anne had really been sweet on in the five years since her divorce. Initially he had been neither her prince nor her ideal, but over time Carl became something very dear and important to Anne. And he seemed to be able to share everything with her except the ability to make a full surrender. Carl, a slightly overweight balding bachelor who just turned fifty, thought that everything about him and Anne felt right. Since he and Anne were so compatible and loving, he thought they might be able to move forward as a couple. And he was about to take that step, except for the gnawing fantasy that a more perfect, more beautiful and more fertile younger woman was just around the corner.

Carl felt any ambivalence he had towards a complete relationship with Anne existed because of the reality of the fantasy woman. And when that woman appeared, his ambivalence would magically disappear, making the road to bedding, wedding and bearing his offspring a piece of cake.

Sadly, in the eight months they were apart none of the women Carl dated worked out. In fact, none of them even got past a first date. Not when he was religious and dated religious women, not when he was unreligious and dated unreligious women. Carl dated various women of various ages and backgrounds that he met online, and when none of them worked out he dated a variety of women he met offline. Ultimately, he missed Anne. So Chaim was gone and Carl was back. Curled up on Anne's couch watching reruns of *Curb Your Enthusiasm,* his heart more appreciative, his door more open, but the escape hatch still unhinged for the possibility of when the really right thing could come along.

"So my fear," she began, as she cut the cutlet, placing half of it on my plate for me to pile onto the pizza, over the sausage, and over the extra cheese. "My fear, is that a year from now he really will meet someone else and then he will leave. I've tried dating other men, but he's so good to me, so caring and gentle, it's hard. He's just raised the bar."

Although this was sad, it sounded pretty good to me as this past Sunday officially marked a month that I had never heard from Doug. Even Jay Kohn was disappointed, but less for me and more for the flaws in the two-week theory. To lift my spirits, "After all, things with The Girlfriend couldn't be better," Jay promised if my show could only hold on through summer he would do his damnedest to get a reviewer down from the *New York Times.*

I confess that earlier today I actually thought about calling Doug. Okay, a thought is not an action, and fortunately for me I didn't have to think too hard because Doug was unlisted and I couldn't find him online. The added bonus was that I couldn't get his number from Brooke and Mitch because they were still in Italy. Okay, so they were not still in Italy. They'd been back from their honeymoon two weeks. But too much time had passed, and it was simply ridiculous for me to call Doug. And because Doug never called me I felt ridiculous calling Brooke, but that was really ridiculous so I knew I'd face that call sooner than later.

Still, they say every dark cloud has a silver lining and mine shone when the phone did ring late Sunday night. I picked it up, heard the hello and my heart raced to the finish. My mind created the male voice as Doug's, instantly creating some fictitious scenario that he had been called away on business, that he flew off to a family emergency to a land without phones devoid of all wireless towers, or that he'd been in a relationship that had taken all month to untangle, waiting to call until he was completely and totally free.

But it only turned out to be Edward. It's 12:12 a.m. Do you know where your ex-lovers are?

Taking resolution anywhere I could get it, I got Edward on his cell on a midnight walk home that followed his cathartic experience of becoming dehydrated from crying after seeing a new film billed as the greatest love story to ever caress your heart. And he wanted to call to say hi.

"You're so aloof," he said, with amazement. "Why are you so aloof?"

"I take the Fifth," I said, thinking that a snappy reply to this lawyer who could only deal with his emotional life in as far as it could be outlined and bullet pointed.

"You think about me," he said. "Admit it. Admit that you think about me."

"I think the evidence is in that you have been thinking about me."

It was a waste of time to deal with Edward because I didn't know him well enough to even know the real issues. I had moved on! And here I was, moved on and into the dither of Doug. Why hadn't he ever called? Better yet, why was I still hung up on a guy I had met a month ago at a wedding? I needed to understand these men, but how?

That, I believed, was the $1,000,000 question, and felt I had used up all my life lines phoning for the answer.

"I understand, Anne," I said, tearing off a piece of pizza crust and dipping into the red sauce on her plate. "It's hard to find someone worthwhile. Hey, remember that computer guy you wanted me to meet?"

"Oh, God. Forget that. With Carl being so iffy and you so excited after you met Doug, *I* went out with him. He pinned me up against my door frame for a good-night kiss and told me it would be okay to sleep with him, he was really safe sex because he couldn't have it! That he could only maintain an erection if I would *command* him not to come! I commanded him to get lost and gave my colleague quite an earful the next day. The men I've gone out with..." she said, finishing the sentence by taking a sip of her drink before she continued.

"I'd meet them and see that there was something a little off, and at first it wasn't alarming, but I knew, I just knew there was some big dysfunction. And I would try to guess, but I couldn't. And then when it would happen it was astounding. I wouldn't have been able to guess it. I mean each person's thing is so intricate, so incredible I wouldn't even know how to make it up. So are you going to see Edward?"

"No."

He called again last night and left a message saying I could call him if the spirit moved me. It wouldn't.

Anne and I left Vinnie's and walked down Broadway to Lincoln Center. It was the first half of the summer and New Yorkers' faces had that openness of the possibilities that could still lie ahead. I had been fantasizing about Doug and me going up to the Cape with Brooke and Mitch. The disappointment I felt because that would not happen made me feel both empty and silly.

"What if Carl actually proposed to me?" said Anne as we

passed a tall twentysomething blonde with a fortysomething nothing that neither Anne nor I would ever give a second glance. "I mean, wouldn't that mean he was just settling and that he would always feel that there was really the perfect person for him, and I just wasn't it?"

Did the men's inability to even be consistent ultimately save me, or would Carl's consistency ultimately bring him around to love?

"I think if Carl proposed to you, Anne, it would be because he really wanted to. That if he does it, it won't be his defeat and it won't be by default. It will be his victory of finally being able to come home."

Was I talking about Carl or was I imposing what I had hoped might happen for me? My guess was that if Doug did call and we went out and it was great, he would then run away for the same reasons that stopped him from calling in the first place. Yet unlike Anne, I was not in love. I had not fallen in love with Albee or Edward, with Dirk or with Doug. I had fallen in lust and I had fallen in like. But the most powerful was that I had fallen in hope. Falling in hope was very powerful, and the loss of that hope was more painful for me than actually having loved and lost. Hope. One of the true underrated emotions.

How did all this happen? How had these men become this way? If I ever came to understand could I do anything to change it? And if I couldn't, what could I do? Could I keep on believing there was one out there, warts and all, just for me? Did every pot really have a cover? What happened after you'd gone through the entire cupboard and nothing was going to fit?

Anne and I were both out there, trying. We were not looking for a bona fide prince, just our very own good frog. So why did it all go astray? What were you supposed to do with the encounters and the dates, the liaisons and the relationships? Where did they all go? And if they didn't go anywhere, where were you supposed to put them?

I walked with Anne, as I obsessively talked to Anne. My mind, my mouth going a mile a minute laying one thought out after another. I had to get it out. It was beyond a specific man, beyond seeing or not seeing someone again, and beyond the, "you should have known betters," because who says you should? It was simply about feelings and feeling appreciated. About understanding and being understood. So what if it didn't work out? It had mattered. And I needed to know that all of the things that had mattered to me had *really* mattered. And not just to me but to each of the men, to both of us, and to all of us.

"What do you want me to say, Kar?" Anne asked in the bathroom of Lincoln Center. The conversation had started at the corner of Seventy-second and Broadway where I took note that Papaya King had raised the price of their recession lunch special in order to accommodate their raise in rent. It continued down Broadway, past the Loews Cineplex Lincoln Square, across the promenade at Lincoln Center, and into the lobby of Avery Fisher Hall where we found out that the bathroom on the lobby level was out of service, only to have to walk two flights down to the basement to another that was jammed, then down a long corridor to yet another.

Anne changed into her dance clothes while I watched and talked. I had planned to go back to my apartment and change, but now it was late. On top of everything else I would only get to watch, because in my high-heeled slides I would surely not be able to dance.

"If these things don't turn into any*thing,* I, at least, need to know that what I feel is real," I said, watching Anne bend down to tie up the laces on her dance shoes. "I want you to tell me what *you* think." Having already exchanged her tailored work skirt for a short little flare, she put her pumps inside her black vinyl bag, zipping it as we got up to go.

"I think you and the person are the only people who have any clue as to what might have gone on between you," said Anne, as we made our way up the stairs and out to the promenade. The plaza was filling up as Wynton Marsalis and the Lincoln Center Jazz Orchestra played Count Basie's "Every Day I Have The Blues."

"Karrie, whatever you feel—that's inside you. But understand the closest you might get is in just honoring your own feelings, and owning your own truth."

Anne swung her black bag over her shoulder as she got ready to meet her dance friends on the other side of the fountain that I would either hang around or throw myself in. Honoring my own feelings. It wasn't much of a consolation prize. It was like missing out on the car behind door number one, and being sent home with a hundred boxes of Rice-a-Roni. But I guess no one could ever take away that you got a chance to play.

"Thank you, Anne. You're certainly no idiot with a CSW, I'll tell you that. So do what *you* say…not as I do. And do with Carl whatever feels right for you. Follow your heart."

We hugged goodbye and promised to meet again soon. I looked around. It was a beautiful night. The stars were out, people were dancing, the music was sweet and I decided to stick around and try to meet someone the old-fashioned way. I was going to make eye contact and smile; except no one would smile back.

I walked through the crowd, at first only smiling at men I believed could be prospects. When neither of my two smiles were returned, I smiled at men who would never be prospects. When that didn't work I wanted to make sure my smile still did, so I smiled at women. But they may have interpreted it differently because they, too, did not smile.

It was time to give it up and go to a movie. Lincoln Plaza Cinema was just across the street and I was sure there would be a torrid, romantic foreign film I could get lost in that would be a guarantee to keep me company, take me someplace new, and influence my mood.

I wove my way in and about all the people. There were just so many of them. All these people were out on a Tuesday night in July, and all of them made their way to Midsummer Night Swing without any intention of dancing. You had to wonder who they all were. These people with dreams and quirks and bills to be paid. *And another hundred people just off of the train,* I quietly sang out loud as I exited the dance finding my way off the promenade, walking along the side of Avery Fisher headed down to the street level via the marbled stairs.

As I made my way down the stairs, a man I considered smile-worthy brushed past me coming up. He was wearing tan khakis and carrying a soft brown leather briefcase. I got to the bottom, standing on the pavement no more than a second before turning back up. I followed him while I tried to figure out if I should go for the smile, or take a full fledged risk and say hello.

Smile Worthy walked across the promenade and got on line to buy a drink. A drink. That was a good idea. I'd get on line and I'd buy one, too. I stood in the back, a safe distance behind him. A little too safe, I thought, seeing him look at his watch and talking to a woman I guessed had a similar idea. Perhaps she moved it along more swiftly, incorporating the smile *and* the hello into, "Do you have the time?"

Stalling for some I walked to the side of the bar to check out the drink menu. I turned around, intending to strategically and nonchalantly join Smile Worthy in line before delivering mine. But I never got far because suddenly there she was, right in front of me.

"Oh my God! Don't tell me your name, I know it. Karrie! My God, it's been such a long time. I haven't seen you for years. I haven't been in the city for years. Maybe three, or maybe even four. How *are* you?"

Holding a drink in her right hand, she reached over to give me half a hug with her left. Her hand floated by and I saw the diamond I remembered so well. It was as beautiful today as it was a decade ago. The new DKNY perfume surrounded her, smelling both heavenly and expensive. I recognized both having recently been spritzed in Bloomingdale's before a promotional postcard with the price was put into my pocket.

"Cecilia Keats, how are *you?*" I sang, thrust into this new scene, while glancing out of the corner of my eye at the old one, trying to sneak a peak at Smile Worthy, on line, still waiting.

"Oh, I'm fine. In Connecticut. Still. Still living in Westport. Good ole Westport, Connecticut."

"I remember," I said.

I sure did. I also remembered running into her at an audition several years ago, three, maybe even four, and afterwards riding the subway together uptown. She was on her way to Grand Central to catch the 4:07 home, me en route to an appointment with the gynecologist. On the three stop ride from Twenty-eighth Street up to Forty-second she managed to work the words au pair, personal trainer, housekeeper and husband into the conversation.

"My girls are getting big," she said now, after telling me about a planned family trip to Nantucket in August where they'll just drive up in their newly leased BMW SUV, and how the show biz biz was so bad it was hardly worth the effort to commute in anymore for a casting…it wasn't as if she *needed* to work. Cecilia said all this with charm and ease, the faint traces of her silky smooth Savannah speech just catching me up on life's recent events.

"Let me introduce you to everybody," Cecilia said, stepping back to open up the social circle. "This is Charles Forester, a work associate of my husband, and this is his wife, Liz Forester." Charles and Liz each raised an eye and a glass in acknowledgment. "This is my husband, Buck Harmon. I think we ran into you once when we still lived in the city in that sweet brownstone on the Upper West, right?"

"Yes, I remember you," I said to Buck the banker, who reached out and shook my hand.

"And everyone, this is Karrie…" Cecilia paused for dramatic effect, looking at me as if the next question was crucial to her ability to finish the introduction. "Wait, is it *still* Kline?"

Cecilia smiled. In fact, I think she may have purred.

"Yes," I said, smiling at everyone and using up the last of my smile reserve because Smile Worthy was now gone and after this conversation so was I. I wanted to run into the crowd, and pull Anne out of her two-step to tell her this story. Because during the time we talked about the insensitivity of men towards single women, we had never touched upon how women could also pay equal time.

Did they even know when they did it? Did it make them feel better when they did? Someone like Cecilia could not have been feeling so great to begin with, because I believed it was a sprinkle of insecurity that caused the few drops of poison to drip from her saccharine smile. Yes, her words could be taken just as a comment, a throwaway for me to do just that. But I trusted my instincts and conscious, or unconscious, under the surface I knew it was more.

Did I do things like that? I'd assume some women somewhere must have thought that I had. I would be especially careful, because this subtle introduction just went into the core of me and churned and burned. I stood listening while Cecilia yapped away. Maggie the Cat. She was pleased as punch to have run into a fellow acting veteran. She had no idea how I felt. Or did she?

"So after the commercial strike the business just never came back, so I figured, why should I?"

Yes, it's still *Kline.*

"I can't believe I actually came up with your name, but I mean you do *still* look the same, Karrie, so when I saw you… *Bingo!*"

And Cecilia Keats, if names were so crucial to this passing conversation, why wasn't I corrected when I didn't call you Cecilia Harmon?

"I mean, I'm amazed I could come up with your name."

Did it help you to make me still *look the same?*

"I'm just brain-dead out there in the burbs. Just brain-dead," she said. Making a self-deprecating face, Cecilia took the pointer finger of her free hand and twirled it around pointing to her forehead, while giving her head a shake of disbelief.

Did you think that—wait, this was interesting. Very interesting.

"Yep. Just not thinking about much of anything. I really have to do something besides being brain-dead in the burbs."

She's apologizing! Not for a faux pas, but for her life. Why in the world would Cecilia need to apologize to me for her lovely life?

"So you *still* here, Karrie? In the city?"

"Yeah, just uptown. Seventy-eighth."

"And what are you doing? Same old, same old?"

I looked at Cecilia all dressed up in suburban swing. One of her first nights out in the city in a long time. She looked great. Healthy, hearty, taken care of and well-groomed, but

I knew that the short little skirt and matching headband must have looked a lot more hip and way cooler when she was standing in her driveway in Westport than it did when she arrived in Manhattan.

When I told her what I was doing, would that make her feel better about her life or worse? I *still* was Kline and Kline was *still* in the city. But the bigger question lurking was what I was doing there. Whether or not I was *still* acting? The dream. And if I was out there when she was not, what would that mean for Cecilia? Did our two lives together add up to perfect, or did each one stand fine on its own?

"Well, I'm doing this solo show over at My Theater Workshop called *Frogaphobia,*" I said. "It's about fifteen years of bad dates in the life of a single, Jewish actress. Well… Me! It's been doing well. *Wow Women* wrote a great story that changed everything, and now…hopefully now there're possibilities. It's been good. Great, actually."

"I heard of that show!" Cecilia screamed. "I didn't realize that was you! I heard someone talking about it in the supermarket while they were reading some woman's magazine on the checkout line."

I nodded my head and smiled because I was proud, and I felt that I had really earned this moment.

"I am so happy for you!" she said, and I felt she meant it. "God, I've got to do *some*thing. I am bored with the burbs and I'm going out of my mind. The truth is, after the strike I didn't leave the business," Cecilia confessed. "It left me. My agent dropped me."

"You're kidding," I said, suddenly forgetting every mean thought I'd had about her, feeling nothing now but camaraderie and compassion. "That stinks. You used to book a lot, too, more than me. But listen to this! Just a few weeks ago, my agent came to see the show and we went out for a drink after and I thought we were celebrating, but, instead, he took me out to drop me. Talk about crying into your beer."

"That slime!"

"I know! After sixteen years, can you believe it?"

"Well, I do have to move on and I do have to get myself doing *some*thing," she repeated.

"Cecilia, you know that thing they say about your hobby becoming your next career is kind of true, so take a look at your hobbies. I mean I talked incessantly about being single and having bad dates and look where it got me!" I laughed. Cecilia pointed to her skirt and her husband, and she laughed, too. We babbled about a few more things before saying goodbye and hoped it wouldn't be another three, or even four years, till we'd see each other again.

By now I had not only missed the smile op, I had also missed the movie. I pulled my cell phone out of my purse, making a call and talking while I did one last circle around the plaza before leaving. This time for good.

Fred answered on the first ring, telling me he had just left an audition for a Taco Hell commercial where he was up to be the salsa. He had done well, but thought vocally he might have added hotter tones to his bottom register when he read the copy. He really wanted to read for the taco shell, but they were only seeing ethnics for that part. Fred was on a public bus riding down Sunset Boulevard, the only person I knew who managed to live in Los Angeles without a car.

"She probably wishes she was you!" he said after I told him about meeting Cecilia.

"Today I wish I was her," I said, skipping over the Edward call and going straight to the one month update on what was now termed The Fox Fiasco. "So not only do I miss you, but no one will even smile at me anymore, Fred," I said, talking and walking past the first prospect that had ignored me, watching him ignore me again. He got up to leave the same spot I had spotted him upon my arrival. "He probably spoke to no one all night and now he's leaving here alone. And that was preferential to even smiling back at me? Maybe I'm giving off a very off vibe."

"Maybe. You are a little off."

"Oh, you have no idea how far. Maybe it is me. Maybe it's over. Maybe no one will ever smile at me again," I said, enjoying the lightness of the dark conversation as I left Lincoln Center.

I stepped off the curb and onto the paved road made for taxis to drop people off when they arrived. There were no taxis, but a guy on a bike rode by. I looked up as not to collide with him, and he smiled at me. Well, not just smiled. First he looked at me. Then he rode to the end of the road quickly looking back, and back again, in a double take fit for film. And from the distance he smiled, wide, genuine and generous.

"Okay, Fred, I take it back," I said, having smiled back at the guy while continuing to watch him ride, watching the bike move forward before it made its descent down to Broadway. "A guy just rode by on his bike and he smiled at me."

"So what did you do?"

"What do you think I did? I smiled back!"

No sooner had the words come out of my mouth, the guy and the bike rode back, stopping in front of me, smiling again, and—

"Hi."

"Hi," I said to the guy on the bike. "I'm on the phone to my friend in L.A. and I just told him that no one smiles at me anymore."

"What's going on?" asked Fred, both of us suddenly feeling like he really was three thousand miles away.

"Don't you think that's really weird timing?" said the guy on the bike or the guy *off* the bike; he wasn't on it anymore. He had jumped off and was holding the handlebars while he talked. His blond hair was combed back straight and he was wearing a silver Santa Fe bracelet, jeans and that same, big smile. "I mean what were the chances of me smiling at you just as you said that? What are the chances of something like that happening?" he asked.

"Pretty good, if you're me in my life," I answered.

"Oh, Karrie, please," said Fred, who I practically forgot about, and was overhearing this scene while riding a public bus in L.A. "Suddenly everything's coming up roses? Who is this guy? Give me the phone, I want to talk to him."

"Who's that?" the guy asked, pointing to my cell phone.

"Oh, that's Fred," I said, turning back to the phone as if I was at a cocktail party and had ignored one guest in favor of another. "Fred, I'm going to talk to this guy and I'll call you back later," I said before pressing End so I could begin.

"How soon they forget! Have fun, Little Lulu!"

"So who's Fred?" he asked, pointing to the phone. Looking at me, whoever I was, a new character in the next scene of his life. "Who's the guy?"

"Fred is my friend in L.A.," I said.

It was a hot night and at least five buttons on his shirt remained open, revealing a nice, strong chest. Looking at him more closely he looked a little like Kevin Costner, which was really like a pretty nice thing.

"Your friend," he repeated. "Your boyfriend?"

"My gay friend."

"Your gay friend. Cool!"

We stood waiting for the next batch of talk. It was imminent, as we could feel that neither of us would be walking away.

"So here you are, out tonight. You're alone."

He waited for corroboration. Instead of running over the fountain in the middle of the plaza, grabbing the microphone and making an announcement for everyone to hear that yes, I, Karrie-*Still*-Kline, was here tonight *alone,* I just nodded my head, encouraging the guy on the bike who had come off it to talk to me to continue, because he only wanted me to be alone so I could be free for him.

"Yes. I'm here alone." I smiled.

I could see he had a lot of questions and settled on the one that would give the most information fastest. "What do you do?"

"Guess," I said. I was curious to see what he would say and he answered quickly.

"Lawyer."

"Lawyer? Interesting." Those dates with Edward must have rubbed off on me! "No."

Lawyer? I chalked it up to the black tailored pants and the scoop necked black-and-white striped top. My mother liked that top. Jane said she liked it because it was smart, and looked like something you'd wear to go sailing on a yacht.

"Singer?"

"Closer."

From lawyer to singer. The guy had an interesting mind.

"Artist? Writer…? Actor?"

"Got it."

So what next? I knew. The question. The infamous question.

"So are you in anything now?" he asked.

Would *Frogaphobia* scare him? I hoped he wouldn't ask for dating advice; the idea of all that, again, sure as hell was beginning to scare me. But I had nothing here to lose. I spilled.

"That's *your* show? You wrote that?"

"Well, more like an oral history, but it's mine. Every word belongs to me."

"I know that show. I can't believe it. I was going to see that. This is unbelievable. You'll have to e-mail me," he said, as he reached into his pocket and took out a business card. I looked at it and saw an image of the New York City skyline with women's legs crossed across it. In the center it said, *Women and Manhattan.*

"What's this?" I asked, looking at the card long enough to see his Chelsea address, e-mail and phone number.

"I made a film. Wrote it, shot it, raised all the money. It's about this guy in this city and all his dates. His women. His stories. I have interest now from a production company in Europe. In fact, via a short holiday in France, I'm leaving for London for an extended time on Friday."

We looked at each other and began to laugh as if we were co-starring in an animated film and both saw the bubble with our dating potential burst.

"We have a couple of things in common, here, don't we?" I observed.

"This is pretty weird, huh…? Oh. I'm Paul. Paul—"

"Schroeder. I saw your card. Karrie Kline," I said, handing him mine.

The sun set that night like a ripe orange melon, and the luminous moon lit up Count Basie's music that could still be heard in the distance. I believed the elements of a romance dead-ended was what prompted Paul to ask.

"What is it with men and women? What do you say about it in your show? Why can't men and women connect?"

I wondered if men were going to ask me that question when they met me for the rest of my life. Women never asked that, only men. But none of them seemed to stick around to figure out an answer.

"I have to tell you, Paul, I met a guy at a wedding and when he found out about my show, well, it was similar sort of to you, and he asked me the same question and…" I told Paul the story.

"You know why he never called you?" Paul asked, leaning over as if to share a secret. "Because over the day he had revealed so much, it was like he saw the whole relationship like a movie in his head. And it had already gotten to the too intense part where he was about to get weird, so what was the point of even starting?"

"So what you're saying is that when I got out of the cab that night we had really just broken up."

His theory, however, made some sense to me. I looked down at the pavement and I thought of the guy from the wedding. Doug. The guy who couldn't call. The lawyer I met online. Edward. The guy who couldn't stay. I looked up at the guy on the bike. Paul. The guy already gone. Who were these guys? And who was I when I was with them?

"Let's say, Paul, you weren't going to London. Let's say, you were staying. And you took my card," I said, indicating that he already had. "And you told me you would call. Would you do that to me, too?"

I expected him to get back on his bike and ride away. But he laughed a big laugh. He looked at his watch and said, "We know each other, what is it? Seven minutes! Nine? Nine minutes and it's already come to that!"

"It gets there very fast."

"It's tormenting, isn't it?" said Paul. "And trying to get it can be worse."

"You got it," I said.

I laughed, too, but it was tormenting. It was wild. I lifted my head to look at him, and saw Paul intensely looking straight into my eyes.

"But you *can* get it," he said. "You can make it work for you. You seem pretty smart. You may not know what's good for everyone, but you know what's good for you, right?"

"Yeah…" I said, though I didn't yet know what he was talking about.

"Find out."

"I don't know what you—"

"I'm not giving you a plan. Figure out what works for you. You have questions, so go get your answers. Fuck what anyone else says or the *right* way to get them. Go out there like you did with your show and get what you need to get."

I looked at him, quizzically.

"You'll have to think about this, Karrie Kline, and figure out what it means to you, because there's no right way and there's no one answer." My phone started ringing on his last few words. "Don't get that," said Paul, putting up his hand. "I don't have a cell phone anymore. I got rid of it. I threw it in the river."

I pictured him riding there on his bike, taking the thing out of his pocket and chucking it into the water, as the sounds of his own drummer beat and rippled across the waves. I noticed Paul noticing that I had drifted off. He reached across to me with care and precision. Slowly, he used his thumb to sweep a piece of hair covering my eye off my face, over to the side. The gesture was simple. And it moved me. This gesture. My eyes began to fill, and I felt the brim begin to water. Paul noticed that too, and this time used his thumb to wipe away a tear. He kissed his thumb before placing it on my lips and smiled.

I looked at Paul through my less blurry eyes. I looked at this guy who came off his bike to talk, and watched as he climbed back on. I watched Paul ride away to another land. To a place he would ponder his questions on film, while I pondered mine here on stage. We would ponder the same questions, the same ocean between us.

I stood still, looking at the fountain and watching the dance in front of me. The dance between men and women.

I would try to get answers, but not just yet. Right now I could not move. So I stayed, touching my fingers to my lips as I relished this random act of romance.

Eighteen

A distress call may put a frog on red alert, but it will not spur him into action.

I just read one of those books that tells you how to hook a man. Well, not hook exactly, just how to set the bait to get him swimming to you. The book practically guaranteed that a woman who cast her line with flattery and flirtation could reel a man in, even if she later chose to throw him back. Fishing through the chapters helped tackle my doubts, and brought me around to the possibility that Doug Fox wasn't really off the hook.

Understand that the book did not suggest women call men. Nor did the book suggest if you met a man at a wedding six weeks ago and he had never called you, it would be any kind of a good idea for you to ever call him. Yet I'd been thinking intently about what Paul had said, and I did have a question. A monumental one to which I desperately wanted an answer. And desperate times required desperate measures.

"Karrie! Finally! It's been weeks and you haven't returned my messages. It's not like you. What's going on?"

How could I tell Brooke I was just embarrassed to call her because Doug Fox had never called me? It sounded so completely adolescent, especially the part that it was absolutely true.

"Oh, Karrie. Why would you feel that way? We don't think less of you because he didn't call, we think less of him! I don't want to tell you what to do, but I don't know if it's really such a great idea to get involved with the Fox to begin with."

I forgot to mention the other embarrassing part was after all this I still wanted to get involved with the Fox to begin with.

Then I got a brilliant idea.

"I don't want to get involved with him," I lied. "I just want to talk to him. Like, uh…*research*. You know. For my show. Yes! It would be great for my show! In case I ever need more material. You know in case I ever, like, want to…*expand*."

Truth? I had tried, again, to find Doug's number on my own. And this time I had even done searches with his name and architectural firms in Manhattan. Unfortunately, each one came up empty leaving me no place to go but to Brooke.

"Good," said Brooke. "It's just that I think he's in his forties and never married for a reason and I wouldn't want to see you get hurt," she said, giving me Mitch's number at work because she didn't have Doug's, so now I would have to call Mitch! Punching in the numbers I wondered if I'd even get far enough to get hurt. Well, if I did I'd just have to make sure that Brooke didn't see. But the shield of *re-search* was a good one to hide behind, and I made sure to have it up when I was holding for Mitch as the reception-ist in his office rang me through.

"Hmm…" he said, when I told him I needed the Fox's number so I could interview him to get some new ma-terial for my show. "I don't know if he would go for that," he said, pondering whether or not he thought it a good idea.

"Well, then, what do you think I should do?" I asked be-cause I didn't know.

"I think you should appeal to his ego. I think you should flatter him," said Mitch, causing me to wonder if everyone had read the guy/girl fishing manual but me. "If he doesn't go for being research you're sunk, but he might want to be asked out. If that fails, you can always pull out the research thing as backup."

"Are you kidding me, Mitch? How could I do that? I mean, for starters I don't call men and ask them out on dates. And I especially don't call men who not only never gave me their number, but never called me when they said they would. How could I do that? After all this time how could I possibly call Doug and ask him out for a drink?"

"Hi, is this Doug?" I asked after I called Doug's work number and hung up on his voice mail and then hung up when I called his cell phone so I could call back the work number just to be sure he hadn't come back to his desk be-fore I tried his cell again, totally surprised when after almost five rings he actually picked up. "This is Karrie," I said, when he answered me by stating his name. "Karrie Kline. We met at Brooke and Mitch's wedding. Do you remember me?"

"Yes," answered Doug, in a dark, dead monotone. "I re-member you."

Silence.

"How are you?" I asked, a little too perky. "How have you been?"

"Busy," said Doug. "Very, very busy. Lots of work. Very busy." He paused for a big one. "And you?"

"Oh, me? Busy. Really, really busy. Never worked so hard in my life. The show, you know…it's keeping me, well, busy."

"Good."

So far it was safe to say we were not having a very good conversation. It wasn't as if Doug didn't sound excited to hear from me. It was more like the only way I might have elicited any positive response was if I'd hung up. But I didn't.

"Is this an okay time to talk? Did I catch you in the middle of something?" I asked. I was not only polite, but hopeful I had caught him coming off a big fight with a client and he was secretly thrilled to hear from me. He just hadn't as yet gotten the chance to reveal it.

"It's fine," he said. "But could you call me back on the landline? The office number?"

He gave me the same number I had already called, which helped push away the fear that he had been cursing the caller ID with annoyance each and every time his work phone rang. I hung up and redialed. So certain I would be sent to voice mail and it was Doug's passive-aggressive way to get rid of me, that when he answered the phone and said "Hi," I had calmed down enough to recoup a little confidence.

"Listen," I said, before the smidgen I had might be washed away. "I just spoke to Brooke and Mitch today. For the first time, in fact, since the wedding."

"Really?" I took Doug's interjection to be a good sign. One that meant he now knew I had not been talking to them for weeks about never having called me. This, at least, was true.

"And I remembered what a great time I had at the wedding, Doug. Mainly because of you. How much I enjoyed meeting you, and I wondered if we could get together and I could take you out for a drink?"

Man. I was good. I was slick. Now that I did this I saw it wasn't such a big deal thing after all. Now that I had called and asked a guy out first I thought it felt kind of powerful. I wondered if men deemed it that way because it really was kind of fun.

"Well, that's very nice, Karrie, but as I told you I'm busy. I'm really, really busy. So why don't I take your number and if my schedule allows I'll call you and we can schedule something."

Well, it had been fun, but it wasn't anymore. And I had to see him. I had to ask him my question. What had Paul said to me that night? Forget the right way—just get out there and get what I needed.

"So do you think that might be within the week because I really want to see you, Doug. I mean I *really* want to see you."

"I'm not sure, I mean—"

"I can meet you somewhere, I'm flexible. It can be short. An hour is fine. I just want to see you. I mean I *really* want to see you," I said, suddenly laughing at myself as I spoke. "I *really, really* want to see you," I said, like I was playing a scene and I was also the audience and the joke was on me. This was all so ridiculous and by this point so was I. What was I doing? I needed to stop. I really needed to shut up. I must have sounded like a complete—

"Okay, how's next Wednesday?" asked Doug, totally shocking me. "Five o'clock. The Campbell Apartments at Grand Central?" he said, appeasing me, making a plan, and even sounding…nice!

"That's great," I said. "I'll be there. Wednesday at five. Thank you." I took a breath and for the first time felt the desperation replaced with a more familiar feeling. "I really appreciate this, Doug." I flirtatiously cooed into the phone.

"No problem. I feel flattered," he said, and then he hung up.

I kept the meeting to myself like a big, giant secret. I

could not believe I was finally going to see Doug Fox. And I made it happen by doing everything I felt, as a woman, I should not. In the end, what made him respond was flattery. But I spoke the truth. I did enjoy meeting him, I had a great time, I did want to see him, and I sure was looking forward to it. Flirtation and flattery! So it had been that simple, all along?

Perhaps I'd not been aggressive enough. Perhaps I should have been calling up men for years, buying theater tickets, making dinner reservations and taking them out on extravagant first dates. Hell, maybe I should have been sending them flowers. I came of age in the era of Women's Lib. I should have been more liberated and taken a stronger stand.

I went out and bought a new black skirt that looked just like the one I had in white except it was black, a color I knew I could count on to step up to the plate and be whatever I needed it to be for the drink. So confident was I of the color black, I bought it in a V-neck summer sweater and a pair of open toe high-heeled sandals. I tried my outfit on at home, practicing in front of the mirror with an empty wine glass, certain I would look casual but datelike. Like I wasn't really trying. Yeah, right. Even I couldn't believe that one.

The weather was beautiful come Wednesday. I ran the reservoir earlier to be relaxed and ready. So it was nothing short of one big mess of a disappointment when two hours before the date, right after I had showered and took pains to apply my makeup, my cell phone rang with a call from Doug telling me he was really, really busy and he really, really couldn't make it. He had appointments, he had a meeting, he had to pack for a business trip…I think he even said he had to take a nap! He talked on and on and I let him. Until I heard him say he would be in touch sometime after December 1, when his schedule was free, putting four months between me and another phone call I would never receive.

It was time to stop fishing and reel in my line. I took the bait off the hook since it obviously wasn't working as any kind of a lure.

"Doug. Listen. I need to see you because I have to ask you something. It's for my work, but…" The game had been fun but I wasn't a shrewd enough player to win. "It's also for me. I don't want you to think I'm some wacky chick because last week I was so flirtatious about a date and now I'm telling you it's about work. I'm genuine and I do want to ask you something, but the work just helped give me the confidence to call you. It gave me permission. I mean I don't call men as a rule, and I can see why because it obviously doesn't work."

"No," he said. "It doesn't. You got me going last week but today…" His voice trailed off and he didn't finish his sentence.

"You weren't interested to see me." I needed to know so I finished it for him.

"No," he said. "I wasn't. But I will do anything to help out an artist."

We made plans to meet at his loft for a chat. Trading the new black skirt and sandals for a pair of cargo pants and flip-flops, I hopped on the C train downtown to Canal. Walking east through the colorful neighborhood I realized I was no longer afraid to see Doug, just excited to ask him my question. Without the pretense of The Date, I felt I even had a shot at an honest answer.

Doug's loft was great. He kissed me hello, showed me around, and we both settled for big glasses of nonalcoholic iced tea before we settled in. He had a wild assortment of cool antiques; a spinning wheel, a turn-of-the-century desk and a bicycle built for two. I took a seat on the dark brown leather sofa, expecting him to sit across from me on the chair. But he sat down next to me, close, and looked into my eyes.

I had felt the electricity as soon as he had opened the door. Wearing a worn-out white T-shirt, jeans and flip-flops, he was tanned, toned and attentive. Despite the verbal protestations I heard on the phone, his eyes danced as they followed my every move.

You can't start those conversations right away, so we spent time talking about the summer, the weather, movies and the news. We talked about the new facade for a bakery he'd designed, about my show, and about the possibilities it all ensued. We each had our feet tucked under us. Sitting on his sofa, heads tilted. Talking and smiling in a delightful sort of way.

"So, Karrie," Doug finally said after taking a deep breath. "What is the question you wanted to ask?"

With a strength and dignity that surprised me, without recrimination and without any blame I smiled and said, "I wanted to know why you never called me?"

Doug was jolted like he felt a surge of pain. He leaned back to examine the situation with new perspective before telling me I was very brave.

"It takes courage to ask that and that's a very valid question," he said. "I know what it feels like to be on the other side of that question when I'm not called back. It sucks. It's rude. I was wrong. I apologize. And you deserve an answer."

An overweight high-school kid who couldn't get the girls, in his twenties Doug turned into a svelte, athletic man who could get any girl he wanted. And he wanted everyone, until his late thirties. Then he felt guilty. He had too many—too many options—and he didn't know how to choose. Doug stopped dating so he could stop choosing. He became complacent in his aloneness, comfortable in his lack of pursuit. Now he would only choose if he were sure the choice would be the one that would last.

This information supported Paul's theory that Doug hit the wall in our relationship just when the cabbie had pulled up to my front door.

"So, Doug," I began, trying the theory on. "Are you saying that when I got out of the cab it was like we had already broken up?"

"I didn't think you'd be the one. So it wasn't worth the dates, the sex and the disentanglement. I thought it would be easier to not even start, if it at some point it was going to have to stop."

I didn't react, forcing Doug to get a good look at me. His eyes burned close to mine. He seemed to care what I felt, trying to guess what I thought. I thought he was scared. I thought when Doug liked someone he became immobilized and scared. But he was well protected, because his theory would surely insulate him.

On the other hand…

"So you just weren't that into me," I said, coining a now well-known phrase from another well-known book. I said it lightly, with a smile, like it didn't matter, because whatever his reasons that was the case, so it really didn't. "That's cool. I guess I just liked you more that day than you liked me."

"Really?"

Doug was *very* interested to hear about that so I told him. I told him what led up to our meeting and how brilliant it felt when we did; at the beginning of our banter, out in the sunshine, over the railing overlooking the Hudson.

"It was fun," he said.

"Yes. It was," I said with finality.

But our conversation didn't end. We stayed on his sofa talking about everything under the sun until it went down, only noticing when darkness had filled the room. Because after the question was out of the way, after it became clear he just wasn't that into me and I wouldn't try to change that, after all the expectations had been ditched and diffused, we got to be two people who both had trouble finding a relationship. That alone had given us much to discuss.

"I still hate dogs," Doug reminded me.

"I hate cigarettes," I told him when he lit up his second. Doug prodded and asked why.

It wasn't just the dirt, the smoke and the smell. It was the babysitter who was watching me when I was four years old who fell asleep with a lit cigarette and set our apartment on fire. The babysitter who tried in vain to open the front door that was seconds away from becoming inflamed while a scared-to-death me hid under a table a few feet behind her. My father arrived home with my mother, as they say, just in the knick of time. Ironically, it was Mel who saved me when he valiantly bashed and thrashed and opened our apartment door. It wasn't long after the fire he left to join the circus. My memory of Mel always heroic, the memory fading and changing as life readjusted that picture.

And Doug didn't just hate dogs because they barked and they shed and you had to pick up their poop. Doug's younger sister had become competitive with him over the family dog, pulling Pete out of Doug's seven-year-old arms and yanking him so hard he turned on Doug and bit him hard on his thigh. Doug was rushed to the hospital, petrified.

"I have the scar to prove it," said Doug, as we both acknowledged our scars. Scars that had healed but had still left their marks.

He had to pack and I had to go. Doug leaned in, very close. I thought he would kiss me and hoped he would not.

I wanted us to leave this exchange intoxicated by each other. Not by alcohol and not by sex.

"I've learned something here tonight, Karrie," he told me, thoughtful, careful. "You have opened my eyes to something. Do you know what that is?"

"Me?"

"Yes. I really enjoyed talking to you and well…I don't know if it's true, that I'm just not that into you," he said. "What do you think?"

"That's not for me to say." I dipped my head up towards his asking another question I already knew the answer to. "Are you attracted to me?"

His eyes opened wider, and he brushed his fingers softly across my cheek as he nodded. That was all I needed. I was ready.

"I didn't know the ending of our story when I got out of the cab that night." I spoke clearly and gently. "I only knew I was willing to find out. Sometimes we're just *not* that into someone. But sometimes we could be. And we're just not that into finding out *why* we can't find out about them. We're not into finding out what stops us. Do you know what I mean? You can*not* meet anyone you're into, but you have to be *able* to be into it if you do."

Doug looked like he was studying me. I could tell he wanted to say more, but he would not do anything where he could not follow through. He would not ask me to have dinner. He would not say he would call. He would not pull me in for a kiss by pulling me by my hair, allowing himself a taste when he knew he would have to let go.

"You have opened my eyes and I think I have to open them some more. If I do, would I be able to call you?"

We stood in the front, at his door in the dark. A small light glowed on a desk behind us. The air conditioner had not reached that part of the loft. It was hot, and the heat rubbed up against us.

"You can call me anytime, Doug," I said, and meant it. "You'll always have a friend in me." He quickly kissed me, and I went out the door.

I did not expect to hear from Doug. It wasn't that I didn't want to; I just did not expect to. I also didn't need to. It seemed to me he just wasn't that into anyone because he wasn't into being in a relationship. That was the main reason, the missing piece, and that's where Doug was now.

And I was on the street. Cool and calm and buying a treat of chocolate ices to eat while I walked over to Canal to catch my subway home.

Nineteen

One's experience level is an important factor in determining the choice of your very first frog.

"Five minutes to places," said Ryan, who'd been acting as the stage manager during the extended run. Having applied the finishing touch of lipstick, my *Frogaphobia* face reflected back in the mirror.

"Thanks, Ry," I called back, and took a swig of water before I ran to the ladies' for a last minute pee before going out onstage. Jay had called me earlier to tell me the news. The *Times* reviewer would not be coming tonight.

"It was set," he said, upset when he spoke. "It was all set. For a week. I just called today to confirm a pair of comps would be at the box office, and he told me they cut back and could only review one off-off-Broadway thing a week and he could only send out one person and she was already assigned a different show."

"Which one?" I asked, as if that would have anything to do with anything. It just seemed easier than dealing with my disappointment. Losing the *Times* felt like losing everything. I had such high hopes for that review and now the option was gone. "Did you ask?"

"I did, and it's even in the same building as MTW. The Harrow Theater Company on the second floor is doing that show on war and they feel it's a better fit with the news. I'm sorry."

"Oh well, thanks anyway, Jay. I know how you tried."

What could I say? He'd been working very hard and I could see that doing PR was not easy. It's just that I was still *sans* agent, not having much luck getting any new ones to come down to the show, and I needed a shot of adrenaline to give things a push. We were well into September. Ryan had extended me for two shows a week for over three months, and I didn't want to quit until I had gotten ahead. But I would need people in the seats to make that happen.

"You know, this may sound over the top, Karrie, but I felt things were slipping a little with The Girlfriend, so I did the roses thing again, but this time I changed the colors. Light pink, hot pink, and mauve—I never knew there were so many different shades of roses, so many shades of pink! Anyway, you can't believe how good things are now. I really owe you. I'll make it up to you. Screw the *Times*. Next week—*People*."

"Places," called Ryan, popping his head inside the dressing room door. "There's a full house tonight. Should be great. Break a leg, beauty."

Tying the belt on the yellow terrycloth bathrobe I wore in the opening, I left the dressing room and walked onto the dark, bare stage. The green trail of glow tape led me to the spot on the set where the lights would uncover me when the show began. It no longer felt strange to be onstage alone. I knew the script upside down and inside out. It was odd how sometimes I could be completely in character and immersed in the show while my day's laundry list literally ran through my mind. I climbed onto the boxes that formed the bed, snuggling under the bright green comforter. The stage still in black, the opening music began.

The *Snow White and the Seven Dwarfs* soundtrack recording of "Some Day My Prince Will Come" played, while a series of different types of frogs were projected onto a screen behind me. The audience immediately started to laugh. I could practically rate how receptive the audience would be depending on which frog got the first laugh. If they didn't laugh till the fifth, I knew the audience would be a dud. The third was the standard response, and indicated a fairly decent house. Tonight got the biggest laugh ever on the very first toad. I smiled at the irony.

All week I'd been praying the night the *Times* reviewer came the house would be responsive and big. And tonight, as I worked, it was one of those magical nights onstage when the whole show felt brand-new again. I got laughs in new places, found new nuance and business, and didn't think I'd ever had more fun. The standing ovation I received during the curtain call lifted me over Cloud Nine. I assumed part of the success was because I'd been so relaxed, not over-working or pushing to impress the *New York Times* that wasn't there. In fact, I didn't even have friends in the audience. When I changed backstage into my street clothes, I felt content to go home and sink into a hot tub with a glass of wine and the knowledge of a job well done.

So it was nice to see someone standing down the long corridor with her pen out, obviously waiting for me and my autograph.

"Karrie! Hi. I'm Caitlin O'Conner from the 'Arts & Leisure' section of the *Times.* Can I talk to you for a minute?"

She stood before me: this woman, close to my build, close to my age, a short red bob, and thin red lips wearing a black shift and red sandals. Looking at her left hand I saw it was ringless, like mine. I hoped that would be a good sign.

"Hi, Caitlin. I'm so glad you're here. Did you see the show? I was told you couldn't make it," I said, wondering if I had said too much, but I had to know, because if she did see the show, and she actually saw *tonight's* show, and she was coming backstage to meet me, it could mean that, maybe, possibly, she really…

"*Loved* this show!" she said, talking fast like a reporter, spilling over with enthusiasm. "You know, they cut us back and I was supposed to cover the thing downstairs on the war, and I saw the poster for *Frogaphobia* when I came into the lobby, and to tell you the truth, I believe make love not war, and I'm so sick of hearing about what's a good fit with the news. Theater is entertainment and it doesn't have to correlate with the damn, depressing news. And I needed a few laughs—my boyfriend dumped me last week and…" She suddenly stopped, thoughtful and a little sad.

"I know," I said. "I wrote a play about it."

"Well, you start writing because when my review comes out you're going to get moved and you'll need to have yourself a legitimate full-length play," said Caitlin.

I lived, ate and breathed the show. The work, the theater, the stories and the frogs. I had no shortage of material, which was a blessing because with all I had to do there was no time left to date. A longer version was in the works. There had been calls and interest, but no offers…yet. I felt optimistic. A good review from the *Times* could change your life, or certainly the life expectancy of your show. I sent Caitlin O'Conner a sincerely thankful note to which she e-mailed and told me that her boyfriend had read her review, and not wanting to be thought of as a frog came back to her on bended *webbed* knee!

People came backstage and told me *Frogaphobia* had become the hot first-date date in the city. Jay Kohn was in love. Anne brought Carl to see the show and, by association, he felt so ashamed of his warts he asked Anne if they could begin again, for real. Everyone seemed to have spun a happy ending with their frogs or frogettes except for me. My dance card was empty. The only frogs I had now were immortalized in the show, plastic or stuffed. I had received so many frog gifts my apartment was littered with the creatures, adding new pizzazz to Charlie's life.

So on a night off, when the phone rang last minute and it was Rodney Schwartz asking me to meet him for dessert, I agreed. It had been over six months since I became aware of his orange legs, and I thought it took great courage for him to call. I gained enough perspective to know that saying I had been rude hardly said it. It would be good for us to talk.

I changed clothes, threw some money inside my purse, and as evidence of another season change, grabbed a leather jacket from the closet. I thought about Paul Schroeder as I walked north to the trendy dessert cafe where I was to meet Rodney. I'd recently heard from Paul when he sent an e-mail from London telling me things were moving along well with *Women and Manhattan,* he thought they might even get a distributor soon. He was staying on as he had also met a girl in the underground—Paul obviously had a thing about transportation and meets—that he had taken a shine to, and was having a less than tormenting time getting to know her! Had I found my answers? I wrote and told him that so far I had only found one question, but getting that answer was helping me to find more.

It was eerie seeing Rodney. I had brought along several photos from college. I placed them on the table, looking down at a twenty-one-year-old Rodney examining a piece of film. But when I looked back up to this grown man, the temples of his bushy hair turning gray, I could not find the boy I once knew. All I felt the entire time we made forced, uncomfortable, what-are-we-doing-here, stilted conversation, was the astonishment that I had chosen to give myself to this person. That decision alone made Rodney, who had been forgettable in most respects, unforgettable in one. Aside from us both still being single, and the small item of my virginity sitting next to the pictures out there on the table, Rodney and I had nothing in common. But I was there because I needed something from him.

I needed something badly, and I couldn't ask for it because I didn't know what it was. It made me nervous. It made me so nervous that I started tapping my fingers on the small, marble table. Tapping around the cappuccino, around the chocolate mousse pie, tap-tap-tapping around the water glasses, tapping with two hands just like I was...

"The typing!" we both said, at once. A memory, a shared memory, one nice shared memory of the time we had spent together so many years ago.

"You remember?" he asked, a smile finally coming to his dour face. He clumsily pushed his hair out of his eye and looked vulnerable, and in that moment I saw, well not completely and I was really trying hard to see, but I almost saw the boy I had met that day in the Fine Arts building. "Where did you do it? Wait," he said, reaching into his pocket and pulling out a pen. "I'm going to write the answer down on this napkin and then you tell me, and we'll see if we remember it the same way."

"Ready?" I asked before I said it. "I typed on your back," I said, turning the napkin over and reading Rodney's scribble that said "She typed on my back." We looked at each other, not speaking, only remembering how we would lay in bed and I would type him messages as if an imaginary keyboard was on his back. "What did you just write?" he would ask. I would tell him and he would kiss me, and then I would type some more.

While Rodney and I were awkward with each other as adults, while it seemed we should have more in common, while it would have made one heck of a happy ending had we been able to walk into the sunset, what we really shared was a mutual disconnect.

If I couldn't get more answers, I was at least beginning to formulate more questions. This next one was a little off the track but important, having gained just the smallest smattering of celebrity. With great trepidation I asked Rodney, who now designed Web sites for a living, what had ever happened to his film. Millie may not have believed I was ever nude in *The Geometry of Love,* but we didn't need to see it sold to *Entertainment Tonight* as evidence to the contrary.

"I lost it," he said, simple as that.

"You're kidding."

"No. Don't worry. I never even finished editing it. It was sixteen-millimeter film and I misplaced it somewhere and I lost it. I really didn't want to go into film. I suppose I didn't really care."

While I felt sheer relief, a wave of wistfulness I would never have expected swelled up inside me. As scary and painful as it might have been, I would have given anything to catch a glimpse on screen of the young woman I was when all this first began. And with that, I got another question.

What was I like when I was a little girl?

How many Lee Loran's could there be in America? If it worked it was going to be just as easy as that. And when I went online and typed in his name, it was. There were two listings for a Lee Loran in San Diego and I jotted down the numbers assuming it would be him. While I took Charlie out for his walk I pondered how you call someone up you hadn't talked to in almost thirty-five years to ask what they had thought of you when you sort of kind of went steady for two hours…when you were ten!

I memorized the numbers and called them both. It was clear from the outgoing messages that Lee was married, and both he and his wife each had a home business. But I didn't want to leave a message. I waited and called again, and then a man answered.

"Is this Lee Loran?"

"Yes. Who's this?"

"Ummm…don't hang up, I'm—well, I looked you up on the Internet and I'm not crazy or anything, I mean… Before I go any further, by any chance are you the same Lee Loran who perhaps grew up in Sunnyside, Queens?" Lee's family had moved when he was twelve and a half. It was one of my big disappointments that I didn't get to go to Lee Loran's Bar Mitzvah.

"Yes," said a man who sounded somewhat astonished, but had obviously grown up to be rather trusting.

"Do you remember a Karen Klein? I lived on your block. We went steady, sort of, in fourth grade. We were in Hebrew school, and then you moved away, just before your Bar Mitzvah?" I cringed as I spoke, the years peeling off me as I talked to this boy. This boy who used to sneak a peak at my panties in kindergarten, when I bent over on the step stool that helped me reach the water fountain.

"Oh my goodness! Yes, Karen!" said Lee. "Yes, I absolutely do. I am so fuzzy about that time in New York, but yes, I sure do remember you."

"Well, I remember you, too," I said. "But you sound really different. Well, I guess you would. I mean, let's put it this way, you don't sound twelve."

"And neither do you."

We settled into the talk, filling each other in. After we caught up on the elementary school memories, of which I remembered everything but Lee had mainly forgot, and after we brought the conversation into the present where we had even less in common, I asked my question.

"Can you tell me anything at all that you remember about me? From when we knew each other?"

I didn't know what Lee would say, and I waited a long while as he sadly explained his memories of the New York years had been left behind in the old apartment in Queens. However, he did remember one thing.

"I remember you were a very proper young girl," he said, me listening intently to a man's voice on the phone, though the face had remained unchanged from our sixth-grade class photo. "I remember you had light brown, blondish hair, blue eyes and bangs."

So he *did* remember the bangs! I was happy to hear that, and chose to keep quiet about the panties.

"I remember that you were very pretty, Karen, and that you dressed great. You had pretty dresses, outfits. You were always put-together, I liked that, and it made you stick out because a lot of the other girls were not."

We chatted about his kids and exchanged e-mail addresses and said we'd stay in touch. When I hung up the phone I observed how fashion represents who we are in society, how we are a product of the times. It was the expectation then that girls—big ones and little—*were* proper. But that was before Vietnam and before Kent State. After that girls gained permission to skip the skirts and dresses and wear pants to school. It took a little longer for permission to wear T-shirts, flannel shirts and jeans.

For the first time in history, men and women wore the same clothes. And in public! The change of that dress code was probably a big contributor to the liberal changes in dating and mating, the casualness of clothing representing the new casualness between women and men. But I wouldn't know because it all unfolded when I was an adolescent, alongside my first turkey kiss to Lee Loran. The mores of the world may have been considered new, but that was the world I inherited, the only ways I knew.

I would have been a whole different girl had I been born a generation earlier. But I wasn't. And by the time I was coming of age, proper was out, because Women's Lib was in. It was confusing enough to be in college, and the confusing times didn't help as I tried to find myself. I was hoping now to find out who I was when I had been looking.

In college I became friendly with a guy named Jed in my dorm who was friends with Gary Waks, my Catskills Kisser, from their high school in Brooklyn. When Jed and I got to playing Jewish Geography, I learned that Gary wound up at M.I.T. He and I had dated the summer I turned sixteen, but we had a parting of the ways that winter when I didn't make enough time to see him in the city. As part of an accelerated program I was only sixteen when I applied to college, turning seventeen just weeks before high-school graduation. I was very involved with school and a little overwhelmed. The train ride from Gary's house in Brooklyn to mine in Queens could take up to two hours. Not to mention the small detail that he began suggesting it was time I lose my virginity. I couldn't. I felt too young. I wasn't ready. Gary found someone in his local high school who was, and that pretty much was that.

One night, first semester freshman year, late after a long rehearsal, I walked into my dorm and allowed the smell of pot and the blare of the Rolling Stones to bring me down the hall to Jed Grossberg's room where I was stunned to see Gary, sitting on Jed's bed and getting stoned.

I was thrilled to see him again! Upstate New York and

Boston were farther apart than Brooklyn and Queens, but to me it was another chance. And while I still wasn't ready, I was closer.

My roommate was sleeping with somebody so my room was free. I had never taken my clothes off with a boy before, but I couldn't imagine that losing my virginity, doing *it,* having sex whatever that was, could have been any more exquisite than that night that I had spent naked with Gary. He told me no one was a virgin anymore. But I was. I guessed someone had to be. When I did it with Gary, it was going to be important. So I waited.

Weeks went by without word from him, until finally one night I went down the hall to the pay phone, closing the door tight so no one would hear, and I called. It rang three times, four, and then five, until a breathless Gary answered the phone. Lighthearted and laughing until he heard it was me.

"Hi," I said, sounding scared. "It's Karen. How are you, Gar?"

There were muffled sounds on the other end. He put his hand over the mouthpiece to tell someone he was on the phone. Then he came back and said, "Game's up."

Shattered, I threw down the phone, ran down the hall to my room, slammed the door, flopped on my bed and cried. The following semester I met a guy in the Fine Arts building and, sick of being heartbroken over Gary, decided I'd had enough. It was time, so I did it with a film student named Rodney.

I typed *whitepages.com* into the empty white bar, entering the name Gary and Waks and "All States" into the appropriate fields before immediately backspacing. Stopping myself from making another call I might regret. There were some things in life you didn't need to know. This was one of them.

I thought Gary was a special boy who didn't know how to tell me he had met someone at school, and he wasn't involved enough with me to feel that he had to. I had beautiful kisses from a young man I hoped went on to have a beautiful life. Even if Gary had called, even if I had lost my virginity to him, even if everything had been perfect, I don't believe I could have possibly sustained that relationship over the last thirty years. I could never have put down those kinds of roots at twenty, not even thirty. For me, it only began to turn around at forty.

I lost my virginity to Rodney Schwartz because I had lost Gary Waks. I had forfeited my prince and, instead, made the decision to go frogging. I never consummated my feelings with Gary, but I still got to have them. And I still had a pretty hot and heavy thing going with life, with love, with passion, and possibilities. Not to mention with my old standby—New York. I hoped Gary had found himself at a young age. I was still on my search. And once you really began to look, you'd just keep finding more.

"You know, that stuff is very powerful," said Jane, sitting on the edge of my bed watching me pack as she read Rodney's letter. It had arrived in today's mail, two weeks after I'd seen him, and a week since I got the call.

I was going to L.A. to meet with a producer who had seen the show when he was in New York and was strongly considering optioning the play to try to sell to film. He invited me to do a one-night-only invited performance of *Frogaphobia* to see if anyone might bite. Jane had come over to pick up Charlie and take him to New Jersey, and judging by the way he and little Eve were getting along I wasn't sure he'd be coming back!

"It's an incredible letter." Jane held it up and waved it in

Laurie Graff

the air. "God, what didn't you like about this guy? He sure can write."

The letter had been incredible. The letter was important. The letter also showed there was an amazing Rodney hidden inside the package he presented to the world, but alas, we had no chemistry or rapport compelling me to dig to find it.

"What stuff is powerful?" I opened the closet and pulled out two skirts. "For after the show…this or this?" I asked, soliciting Jane's good opinion. "I want to look savvy actressy, not funky actressy," I said pointing to the black skirt and the white that were identical.

"Kar, what are you talking about? The two skirts are identical," said Jane, catching me on one of my overly analytical moments of fashion analysis.

"Well, I guess I want to say I'm an actress who wants her show optioned, but I also want to say I would like that show to be optioned with *me!*"

"Oh, honey." Jane folded Rodney's letter before helping me fold the black one because you can never go wrong as a New Yorker dressed in black. "You know how weird it is out there. I don't want to sound like the voice of doom, but you know…it's hard enough for a female star to get to carry a film. Unless it's an indie movie they really would never go with an unknown," she practically whispered because she so did not want to hurt my feelings.

"Look, don't worry about it, Jane. I'm already in a winwin. I can't believe this much has happened," I told my friend while last week's conversation with the producer replayed itself in my mind.

I reserved a theater space for you. I'll fly you out, put you up, and with your permission I would like to tape it. It reads okay on the page, but it really comes to life with you.

I didn't say anything to Steve, the producer guy, because

I didn't want to get ahead of myself. But I felt that there was no way I wouldn't get to star as me in the movie version of a show about me that I wrote that was getting great attention because of the great work I was doing playing me in my show.

"It's just logical that if my show made a sale I'd be brought along with it."

"But we're not talking logic, Kar. We're talking Hollywood," said Jane, and then she changed the subject back to what was suddenly a more neutral topic—the guy I lost my virginity with. "You know, I really believe that first time sets such a precedent, not so much for sex but your attitude about it. I mean you chose Rodney almost at random and then you dumped him, and me, the good Catholic girl I was, practically got engaged to my guy just because he was the first."

"Yeah, and you're married now with a beautiful little girl and another on the way, and I'm trying to cash in big-time on all my wanton randomness!" We both laughed. "Where's that nude film when you really need it?"

That night on the plane I pulled Rodney's letter from my pocketbook, yet again, to read. Flattening it out on the tray table in front of me, I took a sip of the wine I was drinking to quell my small fear of flying. I used to be fearless, but it was not quite like that anymore. Life events, stories, terrorist attacks and the news had upped the ante. You didn't have to make every trip but if you longed for adventure, if you had that desire, if there was a place you needed or wanted to go, you had to brave it. You had to fly.

I looked down at Rodney's words that helped to heal so much.

While enjoyable to reminisce and see that old picture of me from the day, what was most poignant was the one little detail of our time together that was re-counted. That was when you talked of "typing on my back." The specificity of that memory, the uniqueness of that gesture all sent a big tear lolling down my cheek after I left you. I felt your fingers jad–jad–jing-ing on my scapula as you recalled doing that. How playful and sensitive, how perfect, and that odd thing sent all the memories flooding back.

I'm the first man to have made love to you and, for better or for worse, that will always be a singular event in your life. But nobody before or since has typed on my back and probably nobody ever will. Stupid, maybe, but means a lot to me. For that and everything that means, you'll always be special to me.

Your advent reacquaints me with a former self—a guy I realize I love very much. I hope you feel the same about a woman, who many years ago, gave herself for the first time for whatever reason to a man with wild hair and wilder ideas about art, a man who loved her on a tiny bed in a college dorm room in upstate New York.

I would write Rodney back. I would thank him. I would let him know what his letter meant. I would let him know that all of it had mattered. But now I would put the tray table back up because now I needed to get ready. Now it was time to land.

Twenty

When a warning is uttered that indicates danger, a frog uses his hearing to make love—not war.

I turned the key in the ignition for the fourth time, but it didn't catch. Beads of sweat broke out around my temples as I cursed Los Angeles for having put a car curse on me. I had to be at the theater for rehearsal for tonight, and the rental car would not work. The rental car just sat in its spot, while I pressed on the gas and turned the key, trying my best to coax the car to life.

"I rented the car from you because you were supposed to be number one," I cried into my cell while pacing up and down and around the car. I tried to relieve my anxiety by scooping up handfuls of purple flowers that had fallen from the bougainvillea tree onto the windshield, compulsively throwing them down to the ground.

In the ten minutes I went into Longs Drugs to pick up

a bottled water and mascara, the rental car's lights had automatically turned on. Apparently it was something that just happened on this model of car. Something that was impossible to note on a dashboard in daylight. And something you'd only notice once the battery had gone bust. But by that time it was too late, and now so were you because you're not on your way to where you were supposed to be because your rental car's not turning over, not turning on and just not doing whatever it was a car was supposed to do.

"I thought you were supposed to put me *in* the driver's seat!" I cried, looking at my watch that did work and reminded me as each second passed that time was slipping away. "I need another car. I need someone to come right here now with another rental car."

I need to catch a cab, I thought, looking up and down Ventura Boulevard and over yonder to Universal City, where driving down from the hotel I did not see a single one. I would have to find a cab company and have them pick me up. I would have to go back into Longs to find a Yellow Pages. And I would really have to calm down because tonight was my show.

"What are you going to do?" I screamed into my phone, anything but calm as my anxiety level climbed as high as the bougainvillea tree whose stupid purple leaves continued to fall. "How are you going to help me?"

"Weeeeellll, m'aaaaaaam," the Oklahoman on the other end drawled. I could have completed five sentences in the time it took the representative to get out her first two words. "I'm soooooo soooooorrrrrry for aaaaaany innnnnnnnnconveeeeenience—"

I inhaled on the count of three and exhaled on the same. I breathed in and I breathed out. In out, in and out. I didn't know anyone could talk *so slow!* I checked my watch allotting no more than five more minutes to get things squared away. But in the middle of everything the representative alerted me that her supervisor just told her she had to hang up, because her entire office was being evacuated to the basement as they'd just been informed they were having a tornado.

"Weeeeeee're haaaaaaviiing a tornaaaaaaa—"

I hoped she could walk faster than she could talk.

"How do you find a cab around here?" I shouted, desperate, across the parking lot, pressing End on my cell when I saw a man get out of his car. "I'm from New York!"

He shocked me when he shouted back. "Where are you going? There's a metro across the street!"

Any urban girl worth her salt knew metro was just another word for subway.

I couldn't have been happier when fifteen minutes later I found myself sitting on the Red Line that miraculously traveled to downtown L.A. where I was headed. My *Frogaphobia* script open on my lap, I was able to sit back, avoid traffic, and peacefully read in the air-conditioned car.

Why anyone would want to drive around all day when you could have privacy, reading time and people contact all rolled into one on the subway was beyond me. I got to experience all three when the elderly man sitting next to me struck up a conversation by telling me he admired my earrings.

"They look very rich," he said, as he peered at the Tiffany sterling silver knots that pressed against the bottoms of my lobes. "I used to be in jewelry," he told me. "Before I retired. And I am going now to the old neighborhood to meet my old partner for a little bit of talk and a little bit of lunch."

I could see him enjoy the fun feelings of a chance meet. Always heightened when it happened on public transportation where everyone had a destination, and conversed within the time frame of where they had to go.

"You look like a princess," he said, smiling back in response to mine. "Do you have a prince?"

I shook my head no.

He looked very sweet, his sparse gray hairs, his Eastern European accent, his brown trousers and his dark green vest.

"You will. You have to kiss a lot of frogs," he uncannily told me, and with a seriousness that was downright spooky! I practically choked, laughing and gasping at the very same time. "This now will be my stop," said the man as the quiet subway car approached Hollywood and Vine. "Three more stops for you."

He stood up, unfolding a pair of sunglasses that appeared from the inside pocket of his dark green vest.

"I have been happily married for over fifty years and have a married daughter and a grandson. So please take this the right way, and let it bring you luck," he said, reaching over and picking up my left hand. "Let this kiss from me bring you a prince." The doors flew open and in a flash he was gone. I touched the top of my hand and smiled, feeling I had, indeed, been touched by an angel.

Steve, the producer, was waiting for me at the subway when I got off the train to drive me to the theater. He was smart and excited, funny and tall, and originally a New Yorker, which made me feel at home.

"You have to put that in the show," he said, when I told him about my angelic encounter on the subway. "That's a great story. I've been living out here fourteen years and nothing like that ever happened to me," he said, showing me around the theater space that was set up exactly as I had requested.

Steve expected a good turnout and I was getting very excited, but nothing topped the moment I felt a tap on my shoulder and turned around to see that the person behind me checking props was Fred! Fred, who helped make it all happen and who I hadn't seen in months. He was already there, having come down early to work with me and do a run-through.

"Ohmygod! Look at you!" I said, throwing my arms around a confident, happy and healthy-looking Fred. "I love these pants!" I tugged at his cool chinos. "You look very L.A., but I mean that in the very best way! Where's Trey? The infamous Babalou?"

"He won't be here today or tonight, he has to work," said Fred, causing me to wonder for the first time about the man's existence. But he had to be real, and even if he wasn't, something very real had Fred very happy.

Steve took a seat in the modern little theater, while Fred reviewed the light and sound cues with the tech crew.

"You guys are great!" I said, going backstage to the small dressing room to under-dress in the skirt and tank top that the yellow bathrobe hid.

"So let's see how this frog has grown," Fred called out from the booth.

The house lights dimmed, "Some Day My Prince Will Come" went on, and I was off. It was rumored if you had a bad dress rehearsal you had a good show, but that afternoon was a good dress rehearsal, and that night was a great show!

The sweet, small house had filled with laughter, friends from my L.A. days, industry people and a bunch of actors who took the freebie tickets passed out at Equity. After the show we all went to a nearby bar where the good news was that there was something to celebrate! The bad news was that I could not do it with a drink because I would have to drive.

Steve was animatedly engaged in a conversation with all the suits at the table, except for the one who was totally engaged by Fred. Fred had somehow captivated the creator of *Occasional Husband,* a new sitcom that had just debuted and seemed destined to become a hit. About a single gay man pretending to be married to make headway at the office, whenever a work function arose he had to find a male to pose as his permanent partner.

"But if one week 'Larry' is his husband for Client X and another week 'Barry' is his husband for Client Y, he has to remember who's who in order to keep up with what's what...*unless* there was a small rotating stable playing the husbands who wound up making his real dates jealous!"

"Oh my!" said the creator, listening to Fred as he chomped on his calamari. "So you're not just another pretty face who directs, but you also act?"

Fred and I exchanged a quick glance acknowledging this to be the very first time anyone was ever excited about meeting an unemployed actor. The air of being "already taken," had made Fred someone that someone else wanted to take.

"The buzz is great!" Steve whispered when he turned to me, holding out his glass for a toast.

"So what happens now?" I asked as I clinked.

Steve felt good enough from the feedback to sign an option deal with me in the hopes of making a film sale so that *Frogaphobia* would become a major motion picture.

"Starring me!" I blurted out loud.

The suits at the table turned to look, laughing out loud at what they'd just heard. One of them gave me a wink, like I had only made the preposterous joke because the clear water in my glass had to be a little vodka, of which the little New York actress had consumed a little too much if she actually thought her show, the show she wrote and starred in, and the show that was a success *because* of her would ever turn into a movie *with* her!

Steve was on me the second he heard me sputter the words, getting me up from the table to lead me away. He quickly suggested we go outside, suggesting we take a look at the brand-new Hyundai Sonata the car rental company had delivered to the theater during the day.

As Steve ushered me out to the parking lot I heard Fred's voice behind me, coyly networking in a way I'd never before seen nor heard.

"As an actor I could stand to be a stand-in lover," he said. "Let's just say I have a little real-life experience that had me on *both* sides of that fence!"

"I like this guy!" The creator laughed along with Fred. "I really like him!"

"Why did you say that?" Steve asked me the second we got outside. "Those guys in there might be very interested in the project, or they know people who know people. I'm glad I caught you in time to do a little damage control. You don't want to joke around, Karrie. Not like that. It can be taken the wrong way."

"And what way is that?" I asked, leaning up against the Hyundai Sonata that I had to admit was way nicer than that other car. Its elegant exterior and lush blue interior made this midsize car appealing to the eye, reliable *and* enjoyable to drive…but who cared about a dumb car because now I would never, ever get to play Karrie Kline in *Frogaphobia!*

"Will Fred get to play Fred?" I asked, thinking it was time to change everybody's names in the show. It was getting to be too much. Life was imitating art that should have been imitating life but was…whatever.

"No, Karrie, he's not. Depending on the sale we'd go with names. Movie people…actors with series credits."

I looked at Steve, silent and incredulous.

"I don't make the rules—that's just the way it works.

Look," he said, taking my key, opening the car doors, and getting in on the driver's side. He was showing me how to adjust all the mirrors, while I was only still trying to figure out how to turn on the radio. God, why was everything so complicated?

"You wrote a terrific piece, and if we sell it you get on the map and make a little money. Those are two good things, right?" said Steve, now taking over on the radio end as well.

"Yeah. Those are two good things." I sat back on the passenger side wishing I was in the driver's seat.

"And I might be able to get you a couple of lines if it goes," he said. I thought he was making a joke, but then I saw he was serious. I quickly turned my head away, looking out the window and hiding a few tears. I stayed that way, for a bit, waiting to pull it together before I spoke.

"Gosh, Steve. I don't mean to sound ungrateful, but…I mean *Frogaphobia* is my baby and what I am supposed to do? Turn it over to Michelle Pfeiffer?"

"No, Michelle's too old for the role," said Steve, clicking on the hazard lights while we sat in the car, staring out the window like we were at a drive-in without a movie. "Look, Karrie. Try looking at it like this." Steve turned to face me. "Your show has a great chance now at getting an off-Broadway run…*with you!* And if it gets made into a movie you make money. Money buys you some freedom, and your show gets you a new agent and more theater jobs. I can get an option deal drawn up and all you need is someone to look at it. What do you say?"

What could I say!

What could I say? This was amazing! It was more than I ever thought would happen, and while it wasn't everything I hoped for, in so many ways it was already more than I ever hoped to have.

"Yes," I said. "I say yes. And thank you. I say thank you, Steve."

We got out of the car and walked to the door in the parking lot that was the back entrance to the bar. I stopped before we went in.

"Just one more thing. Do you think if I used my pull with the producer I could maybe get an audition? For a small role?"

"Karrie, after seeing you tonight you won't have to audition. I have complete confidence in your ability to play Woman Number Two at Bridal Shower!"

"Woman Number Two?" I shrieked. But this time I didn't have to look at Steve to see if he was joking. I already knew he wasn't. I could like it or I could lump it.

"Woman Number Two at Bridal Shower is the role of my dreams," I told my producer, who chuckled as he opened the door, escorting me as we found our way back to our group.

I couldn't believe if he made a deal I would be Woman Number Two at Bridal Shower. A few lines in a scene for one day… *If* I was lucky.

We sat back down to the table that more people had joined; more people who had personalized opinions and points of views and reactions to the show. It was then I began to understand what was really going on. The conversation bounced from one person's story to another, and it was only then I was beginning to see that it was bigger than Woman Number Two. It was bigger than the number of lines, and it was bigger than an acting job—be it a day, a week, or months on a set.

It was no longer about creating a role for me. It had become about creating a work, and creating a world. The world of *Frogaphobia* moved people. However it did, for better and worse, it made people feel. Many actresses could play

"Karrie." Someone would always get the job. But if not for my creation, "Karrie" would never exist and there wouldn't be a *Frogaphobia* set. For anyone.

Twenty-One

Frogs are part of the ecosystem meaning what happens to them will affect even us, as we are all connected in the web of life.

The new set was slick. The one-night-only performance in Los Angeles had everything going in a new direction. Forward!

Steve had been right. The people there knew people who knew people. And someone knew someone who knew a producer that backed the show, moving me to a 99-seat house on Theater Row, just down the block from Times Square. I'd been working on a full-length script since last summer and was ready to roll, especially when a hip female director I loved won the job. She competed against a more established director I was happy wasn't hired, not just because he and I had once dated, but because that date had also earned him a frog-worthy mention in the show.

Everything at the Lillian Hellman Theater was impeccable. The production team hired was terrific. The set designer kept the same bare stage but the laminated floor was bright blue, the backdrop was painted as a pond, and *Hallie's* bed…yes, for the two-act, full-length, seventy-five-minute, off-Broadway production I had changed the names of all of the characters, including mine. *Hallie Hine's* bed had a headboard shaped in the face of a frog, and a footboard like two webbed feet.

Each night I felt lucky when I went to work. But when I walked into the lobby and said hello to the stage manager and crew, turned the knob on the door with my name, and went into the dressing room to prepare it still didn't seem real. Even though the show was listed in the Sunday "Arts & Leisure" section of the *Times!* However, when I received a paycheck at the end of the week I knew it was. And while the stakes could always be higher, I also knew this was as good as anything got.

I felt proud, and while it didn't go to my head it might have gone to Charlie's, the only character that had not undergone a name change. After a write-up in an Upper West Side weekly, Charlie's popularity soared to such an extent we could barely get down a block without someone stopping to ask if he was the dog in the show about frogs!

In the months since Los Angeles things had really accelerated. By the time Thanksgiving passed I already had a lot to be thankful for. I had just signed with a new talent agency. Rich's Artists would not only represent me for commercials and theater, but their West Coast affiliate office had a department that did the movie rights deal with Steve. The great deal between us led to another great one. A major network would be producing *Frogaphobia* as a TV movie that would serve as a pilot for a television series. And if *that* happened, Steve promised I'd get a shot at a guest shot playing Woman #1 at Singles Event!

Grateful as I was, with new representation I did hope after *Frogaphobia* closed there might be better acting jobs than that in the offing! But it had only just opened a few weeks ago. The holiday season came and went with no time to deal with being dateless, mistletoe and menorahs submerged in *Frogaphobia*. When the ball dropped, the curtain went up on this New Year with unabashed optimism.

On the work front!

When I came home after the show I was too wired to sleep and there was no one around to go out with. I got into late-night TV, watching reruns and paying closer attention when I watched, trying to understand how the shows were written, wondering if it was something I could do. It was not only a good skill to learn, but it also kept me company.

I would get home from work in New York just as Trey left to go in L.A. The three-hour time difference gave me more time to spend talking with Fred. The night of my show he had made quite the impression on that sitcom creator. Good enough to get a recurring role as Dave, Occasional Husband #3 of the three-man husbandry stable. I'd watch and wave at the TV. So proud I was of my own Fred Grennon. He had been on twice so far, and next season both he and the show would be back for more. And with a little money to burn, he was *très* excited about the big surprise he had planned for Trey for tomorrow.

An expectant Jane would be spending the night at home, while Brooke expected that the romantic night might father her familial expectations! Anne was ordering in for Carl, and Millie was eating out with Cookie and Sy…and Marv! They weren't dating, she kept insisting, but it seemed Marv had spent all last year giving Millie more than a few helpful tips at bowling, patiently showing her what to do so she could score. Or he could…if you asked me. But another Valentine's Day was upon us, and no one had.

Totally immersed in rehearsing the show I had emerged from this last holiday season unscathed. But here we were just six weeks later and the Hallmark hoopla was back, with romantic expectations to beat the band. Because of the show, instead of having my weary feelings remain private I got to go public. Opening today's *Post* to the section called "Pulse," mine raced, as I gulped my coffee and read:

Ditch the Date! Celebrate Valentine's Day in a Frog Pond…
With Frogaphobia's Karrie Kline

BY YVONNE CAREY
"By comparison the whole holiday season's a piece of cake," Kline said, chuckling. "At least then you can cling to your friends and family and hide behind them. But Valentine's Day—that's just a direct, 'Hey! You have no one! And there's no place to hide!'"
Fifteen years of bad dates could put a damper on anyone's outlook, except maybe New York City actress Karrie Kline. Kline put the litany of losers, Casanovas, weirdos and plain old bad choices to work for her in her new off-Broadway show, *Frogaphobia.*
Share your Valentine's Day drama with Kline, who will perform an excerpt from her show and share her thoughts on dating dilemmas.
Tonight: Tuesday, February 14, CLUB ERRATICA
Door opens 10 p.m., $15, 42 West Sixty-ninth St., Cash Bar, Music, Snacks

The photo wasn't half-bad, I thought, rolling my eyes suddenly having something in common with those actresses you see on talk shows talking about how though they had everything they couldn't get a date. And while I was a far cry from telling it to Letterman, I had a glimpse into the feelings behind it.

I went through my closet searching for the right outfit for this singles event I'd be doing after tonight's show. If I wouldn't be making love, I'd at least be making people laugh. And I planned on doing it with panache! I passed over a pair of black pants, too dull, a cashmere cowl neck, too covered up, and a bland tweed skirt. Outside it was bitter cold, but I wanted to wear something that said hot.

I went through the rack, using my hands to flip through the hangers before backtracking to an unfamiliar one. Unzipping the white plastic cover revealed a dress I not only didn't remember, but didn't even remember I had. It had been sitting in the closet forever. I'd never even worn it. How long ago did I buy it? Not last summer...the one *before?* Yes. The day I went with Fred to the Tonys. The night he first told me about Little Lulu. It was amazing to note how something seemingly insignificant could become life changing.

I looked at the dress. I still liked it. The sexy, strapless, burgundy and brown winter plaid was still perfect for some holiday party. It was destined to be worn to tonight's Valentine singles soiree. If you buy it he will come, I remembered thinking when I did. Well, he didn't. And I wanted to wear it now. For me. Tonight I would.

I had second thoughts after the show, when I was backstage changing. Layering two sweaters over the strapless dress I hoped I'd be warm. The wind had chilled down to a single digit that was practically enervating. Wearing my new green coat, I tied a big pink pashmina across my shoulders covering half my face and most of my eyesight.

I left the dressing room and walked through the lobby to go out the front door. Through my peripheral vision I saw a man holding his *Playbill* while leaning against the bar. He was completely engrossed, reading a review that was framed and hanging on the wall beside him. A quick sideways glance was enough to see that he was around my age and quite handsome. It looked like he was waiting for someone. I wondered if it was me, but I went by unnoticed. Not to mention I was covered to the point of practically being unrecognizable! Anyway, it was doubtful this handsome guy was here alone on Valentine's Day. Please! He was probably waiting for his date that was probably in the bathroom. Just as well, I thought, bundled to the point I could barely open the door as I ventured out and up to the event.

So wrapped up, in my thoughts and my clothing, I almost missed him. But I didn't. I recognized the shape before I recognized the face, but there he was, a few feet off to the right of the theater doors, right in front of me, holding a pen and—

"Can I have your autograph?" he asked. The fur collar of his black wool coat turned up at the neck, his hat pulled down to his forehead. But I knew those eyes, the quality of his voice and the unmistakable current that added heat through the cold air.

"Hi!" I said, smiling, feeling flushed, as I pulled down the pashmina and tried to sneak a peak to check if he was there with a woman. I didn't want to act too familiar if, perchance, he had brought a date.

"You were great!"

Pause.

I could not believe it. I stood as my mind clicked ahead, watching frame after frame of this ending to our movie.

"Thanks!" I said.

Pause.

It was as if we were sitting on a stick of dynamite. The conversation was tucked inside ready to go off, but when? Who was going to light the match? It had been a while since

I'd seen him. I didn't think I would again. I had stopped thinking about him. But wasn't that how it worked? When you let something go it came back? Was he on his way?

"So. I read about your show since the move. I wanted to congratulate you, Karrie, and well…I wanted… Do you have a minute?"

"Sure. It's great to see you. I have time," I said, though I didn't. The event began at ten. It was ten of. But I wouldn't be on until at least ten-thirty. Plus they knew I was coming from a show.

Okay. Take a breath, Ms. Kline. Chill. Well, maybe not. It was already so cold.

"I really thought a lot about what you had said that day in my loft," said the Fox, leaning in a little closer, doing the leaning in close thing he always did that made me feel like I was the only one in the world he wanted to talk to. "And I may look a little different to you because my head's a little smaller."

I looked at his head. "It's hard to tell the size. Maybe when you take off the hat," I said, pointing to the wooly black cap.

"Well, I've been getting my head shrunk the last six months. And it's been working."

"Really?" I beamed. I was pleased. Since I last saw him, Doug Fox had been seeing a shrink! How about that? In fact, I didn't even notice—

"And I quit smoking," he said.

"Wow! This is incredible. So, what's been going on? Tell me."

Someplace warm, like in a cab on the way to my event I thought, but I didn't say it. Happy as I was to see him I hoped we got to the part where we changed locations soon.

"I told you that you had opened my eyes. And you did. Because I started to get that I wasn't getting into anything with anyone, and I started to find out why."

Doug looked at me with gratitude. He looked a lot less cocky, and a lot more real. Happier, more accessible. Real things. Good ones.

"I'm kind of thrilled to hear this," I said. "And…well, what did you find out?" I asked, already knowing he found he'd let a great one go when he let me off his line and now he was back, hoping to reel me in.

"Well, a lot of it is very personal, of course. My own…how shall we say…stuff!"

"We all have it." We both looked down and laughed as if our stuff was right there, on the ground, just waiting for us to pick up and throw away.

"But I also learned that I had to get in there and take a chance. If I met someone I liked. If I met a woman I thought was pretty and bright. Funny, sexy…I had to find out. And that's why I'm here," he said, extending his arm out to the left in a big gesture that showed me just where he was.

"How wonderful," I said.

I didn't know what I felt first. I had stopped thinking about Doug because I never thought he could become anyone to me. But now, here he was! I made a decision. I would take the very next step and let it lead to the step after that and the step after that and—

"I'm proud of you, Doug. I'm glad you came here. I really am, I—"

"Well, I felt I had to thank you, in person," he said, taking his left arm that was extended and wrapping it around a petite honey-blond *shiksa* dressed in an antiqued red velvet coat, who had suddenly walked out the front door of the theater and into Doug's arm! "Meet Ashley," he continued without missing a beat.

"Hi, Karrie," said Ashley, extending her left hand because her right wrapped around Doug and got tucked into his coat pocket. "Doug told me all about you. I feel I have a lot to thank you for. He said none of this would be going on, now, with us if it wasn't for you."

They took a moment to look at each other. I think they wanted to rub noses and do an Eskimo kiss, but for fear of leaving me out, they held off.

"Ashley. Hello. What a... Pleasure. To, uh, meet. You." I forced myself to smile. I breathed out, dispelling some of the hot hair. "A genuine surprise!"

"We met at Grand Central, just before Thanksgiving. Both waiting for a train. Ashley lives in Greenwich, and I had decided it would be fun to have a drink at the Campbell Apartments and she was at the bar, and well it's been, how long is it now, Ash?"

"Just three months," said Ashley, having just seen my show she looked at me in girl-agreement knowing I understood exactly what that meant.

"Coming here tonight with Ashley seemed like a perfect Valentine's Day date."

"Yeah, Karrie, it really was great," she chimed in.

"So thanks. You changed my life," said Doug. "Oh." He stopped and turned back around. "Happy Valentine's Day!" Then they walked away.

I stood in the cold feeling numb. I almost started to cry, not because I was so hurt as much as I was so over it. So over these things never working out! That thought did make me cry and the teardrop froze, but not before I knew it had done its damage to smear my makeup. I looked at my watch. Two minutes past ten. Did I show up at ERRATICA with two black eyes, or did I go inside and fix it before heading up?

Vanity prevailed. I walked back, pushing on the lobby door almost falling forward when, from the inside, my stage manager pulled it open.

"Thank God I don't have to run out in this cold and go

chasing you!" he said, dressed in nothing but a hooded sweatshirt.

"Donny, what's the matter? What's up?"

"I'm glad I caught you. A guy in the audience left you this and made me promise, promise I'd give it to you to-night," he said, letting me inside the warm lobby as he tucked a note into my hand. "In fact, I thought he was right—" He gave a quick look behind him before turning back to me. "Whatever. Oh dear! I hope you made the other guy look worse!" he said, pointing at what I now knew for sure were two noticeably black eyes.

"I'll save it for tomorrow," I said. "I know you want to get out of here. Just give me a minute to clean myself up." I shoved the note into my coat pocket, glad the handsome guy was gone and there was no one around to see me.

I wish I'd snuck past Doug and never seen him. What did I need that for? Did it make me feel good that I had re-formed a frog to become someone else's prince? And on Valentine's Day, no less?

I looked at myself in my makeup mirror. I was the same happy woman I was earlier when I put on the dress for to-night's event. My ego had been roughed up. That was all. Nothing else had changed. I had to pull myself together and go.

I exited the theater. The wind from the river was ripping up Forty-second Street while I searched for an available cab. There was nothing to be found. It was getting very late. So he just wasn't that into me after all. Who cares, I thought, getting very anxious as I could not find a cab. Half an hour ago I never expected to ever see the guy again, and I was fine. I was better than fine. I was on time!

I tried hailing one down but didn't realize it was taken until I had chased it across Ninth Avenue. If I didn't get lucky on this block I'd have to duck into the subway. It made no difference to me if Doug Fox was alone or with Miss Connecticut, I thought when I spotted another cab with its light on. He had his life and it had nothing to do with mine. He could just go frog himself.

"*Ta-xi!*" I screamed, in my best Queens school-yard yelp. I chased the cab, running up the street like I was running a maze, jumping over and around the slush and the ice left from the prior week's snowstorm. The cab stopped at a red light as it approached Eighth Avenue. Just as I went to open the back door, the driver turned the light off. I looked in the window and saw he had a fare.

"Damn it!" I shouted. I was falling apart at the seams.

"Get in!"

???

I wanted to be off the cold street and in the cab so badly that now I was hearing things?

"Get in." The man in the cab leaned over and opened the door for me. "You caught up to me," he said.

I was overheated from being overdressed, disappointed, out of breath, emotionally bruised and to top it all off now I was hallucinating. Oh yes, I was going to be a model of inspiration at tonight's singles event. Provided I ever got there.

"You got my note," the handsome face said as his beautiful brown eyes looked up at my distraught blue ones. "I didn't see you leave, and then I saw you talking to a couple outside. So I went to the bathroom and when I came out you were gone. But you read my note, right?"

I recognized the face as the handsome man standing by the bar when I first left the theater over half an hour ago. He had been waiting, but not for a date. That date in the bathroom was Doug's! But this guy left a note. Well…whatever he was couldn't be worse than what had just gone on. I got in the cab.

"Forty-two West Sixty-ninth," I told the driver. "I'm late

for an event I'm doing so would it be okay to drop me first?"
I asked the guy as an afterthought.

"Okay." He smiled at me. Almost like a wink. Like we
had some inside joke.

Relieved to finally be on my way, I took a breath and
composed myself before asking the guy what he… Boy, he
was cute. He was still smiling. Or grinning. Yeah, he had a
nice big grin. He was so well dressed, too, wearing a but-
tery thigh-length brown leather jacket, a checked cashmere
scarf and plush dark green corduroy pants.

"Okay now. You were that guy standing at the bar, right?"
He nodded.

"And you wrote me this note?" I dug my hand into my
coat pocket and pulled it out.

He nodded again. Then he grinned. Ooooo! I liked it.
His lips turned up into an inviting smile. His eyes peered
into me. Even in the dark taxi his olive skin glowed…and
his mouth. It had been a long time since I'd seen a mouth
like that. His lips. Soft lips, lush. The top lip curled slightly
over the bottom. It affected me in ways I…

We were driving up Eighth Avenue when I unfolded the
note to read. I could feel him breathing next to me. My heart
was racing; my eyes darted about the page so I could barely
make out the words. I tried to focus but could only scan the
note, heading straight to the signature down at the bottom
where he had signed his name.

Gary Waks

Oh. My.
God!

"Hi," the now sort of familiar voice said next to me. "You
didn't know it was me."

I looked up at him, taking in the features that had improved with age like a quality wine. He had acquired a ca-

sual confidence that was electric and sexy. If I ever had a "type" this was it.

"I didn't know it was you. How in the world did you get here?"

The cab swirled left around Columbus Circle. I looked over at Gary, as the stark glass and lights of the Time Warner Center twinkled through the window behind him. He took off his right glove to reach inside his jacket pocket and produce the clipping.

"I picked up the *Post*. This morning. Doing a project—"

"Engineer?" I asked, remembering M.I.T.

He nodded.

"I like to check up on the Knicks."

I remembered he was a great basketball player.

"And then I saw this." He showed me the article from today's paper. "You went from Karen Klein to Karrie Kline?" he asked.

"Stage name."

"It was the picture that made me put it together," said Gary. "You really haven't changed in thirty years."

"Well, that's nice to hear. But some things have changed," I said, looking down at his left hand to see if his status had, but it was covered with a leather glove.

"Oh yeah?" He was doing the smile/wink/grin thing again. "Let's see. You wanted to be an actress."

"I wanted to be an actress."

"I didn't know you wanted to write."

"*I* didn't know I wanted to write!"

"You never married."

I shook my head.

"You never married?" I asked, hopeful he hadn't.

"We'll talk."

Would we? We had just driven past Lincoln Center and were upon my destination.

"I have lost my virginity."

"That's probably good."

The cab stopped in front of CLUB ERRATICA. I opened my purse to get my wallet to pay.

"I got it." Gary's hand pushed mine away.

"Do you—" "Could I?"

We both talked at the same time.

"Sure!" "Great."

He opened the cab door and offered his hand to help me out. I pressed down on it for balance as I stepped on to the curb over the piled high slush. He was strong. I looked up and grinned. I felt good standing next to him, suddenly enamored with his physique and height, which was probably about five foot ten. We walked up the stairs to enter the club. The owner was waiting for me at the door.

"Sorry I'm a little late," I told Bobby. I glanced at my watch. It was coming up on ten-thirty.

"Can you start in about five?" he asked. A nervous leather-pants, blond Bobby looked over to Gary. "You have a ticket?"

"Oh. He's with me," I said, taking off my coat, scarf, hat, sweaters and gloves and handing it all over to the coat check.

"Whoa!" said Gary. "Look at you! What is this dress?"

My eyes locked with his and my head flew back when I laughed. Elated.

"Take a seat in the back," Bobby instructed Gary as he took me by my arm to bring me to the stage. I mouthed the words "see ya after" over my shoulder, as Bobby led me away.

Inside me I could feel it was all systems go. Ready. For this event, my work, my life and my love. For everything *bashert* for me. And everyone.

Gary's situation was unclear. It would remain to be seen. *We'll talk,* he had said. We would. Yes. After. But now. Now I felt filled up with the fluidity of life.

I was a teenaged girl. I was taking a walk. A boy jumped

off his bike. He kissed me. I felt something new. Anything was possible.

I was a grown woman. I was rushing to an event. A man left me a note. He held my hand out of the cab. I felt something renew. Anything was possible.

It's not just where you start, and it's not where you finish. It's where it keeps going. And how.

Every person and every event counted. Every success and every failure was important. The feelings of youth did not fade away. They continued to revisit, in packages that may be new and improved. We were where we're supposed to be, while we strived to get where we wanted to go. It's never too late.

I stepped out on to the small stage, pulling the microphone off its stand as I looked out to an expectant audience.

"Happy Valentine's Day!" I shouted.

"Boo! Yuck! Growl! Hiss!" cried the happy, hapless crowd.

"Oh come on!" I said over the mike. "It's not *so* bad, is it? At least we're still able to swim in this crazy pond of dates."

I clapped. Everyone followed. Soon everyone was up on their feet clapping. Cheering and swimming, upstream and down. I saw Gary stand up in the back, his hands clapping overhead as he cheered the pond on. Gary Waks. Who'd have thunk it? I wondered what that story would be. I hoped it could have a happy ending. After all, that's what kept people in the dating pond.